These thr
hard-edged an
everything
they m

These men w
exactly what they want, because
they are…

*Three fabulous, absolute stars of
romance, Helen Bianchin, Miranda Lee
and Emma Darcy, bring you this
exceptional collection of
bestselling novels.*

DID YOU PURCHASE THIS BOOK WITHOUT A COVER?
If you did, you should be aware it is stolen property as it was
reported unsold and destroyed by a retailer. Neither the author
nor the publisher has received any payment for this book.

RUTHLESS

Helen
BIANCHIN

Miranda
LEE

Emma
DARCY

DID YOU PURCHASE THIS BOOK WITHOUT A COVER?
If you did, you should be aware it is **stolen property** as it was reported *unsold and destroyed* by a retailer. Neither the author nor the publisher has received any payment for this book.

All the characters in this book have no existence outside the imagination of the author, and have no relation whatsoever to anyone bearing the same name or names. They are not even distantly inspired by any individual known or unknown to the author, and all the incidents are pure invention.

All Rights Reserved including the right of reproduction in whole or in part in any form. This edition is published by arrangement with Harlequin Enterprises II B.V./S.à.r.l. The text of this publication or any part thereof may not be reproduced or transmitted in any form or by any means, electronic or mechanical, including photocopying, recording, storage in an information retrieval system, or otherwise, without the written permission of the publisher.

This book is sold subject to the condition that it shall not, by way of trade or otherwise, be lent, resold, hired out or otherwise circulated without the prior consent of the publisher in any form of binding or cover other than that in which it is published and without a similar condition including this condition being imposed on the subsequent purchaser.

*M&B™ and M&B™ with the Rose Device
are trademarks of the publisher.
Harlequin Mills & Boon Limited, Eton House,
18-24 Paradise Road, Richmond, Surrey TW9 1SR*

RUTHLESS © by Harlequin Enterprises II B.V./S.à.r.l. 2009

The High-Society Wife, The Billionaire Boss's Forbidden Mistress
and *The Secret Baby Revenge* were first published in Great Britain
in separate, single volumes.

The High-Society Wife © Helen Bianchin 2005
The Billionaire Boss's Forbidden Mistress © Miranda Lee 2006
The Secret Baby Revenge © Emma Darcy 2006

ISBN: 978 0 263 87529 4

009-0409

*Printed and bound in Spain
by Litografía Rosés S.A., Barcelona*

THE
HIGH-SOCIETY
WIFE

Helen
BIANCHIN

Helen Bianchin was born in New Zealand and travelled to Australia before marrying her Italian-born husband. After three years they moved, returned to New Zealand with their daughter, had two sons, then resettled in Australia. Encouraged by friends to recount anecdotes of her years as a tobacco sharefarmer's wife living in an Italian community, Helen began setting words on paper, and her first novel was published in 1975. An animal lover, she says her terrier and Persian cat regard her study as as much theirs as hers.

Don't miss Helen Bianchin's new novel coming to you in October 2009 from Mills & Boon® Modern™.

To Danilo, Lucia, Angelo and Peter for their
love and support through the years

CHAPTER ONE

'SOMETHING bothers you?'

The male voice held a faintly inflected drawl, and Gianna met her husband's dark gaze across the master bedroom with equanimity.

It was a spacious room with two walk-in wardrobes with adjoining dressing-rooms, and two *en suite* bathrooms. Beautifully carved antique furniture complemented plush furnishings in muted colours of cream and pale green.

'What makes you think that?' There was no point in relaying she'd had the day from hell, and right now she'd sell her soul for a soothing session in the Jacuzzi followed by an early night.

Instead, she'd battled peak-hour traffic, arrived home late and raced upstairs to shed her tailored business suit and take a quick shower.

The thought of attending a fundraiser held in a city hotel ballroom, where she'd graciously participate in conversation, attempt to make her way through a three-course dinner, limit herself to one glass of champagne and play the *pretend* game held little appeal.

His eyes sharpened, and for a moment she thought he'd read her mind.

'Take something for that headache before we leave.'

Oh, my. 'You know this...*because*?' Her voice sounded vaguely truculent even to her own ears.

He stood tall, with the build of a warrior, well-honed muscle and sinew flexing beneath smooth olive skin, his lithe body unadorned except for black silk hipster briefs covering his tight butt.

His dark hair was damp from a recent shower, his strong facial features all angles and planes, the dark shadow beard clean-shaven.

Dark eyes held her own. 'You want to argue?'

She waited a beat. 'Not particularly.'

One eyebrow lifted in silent cynicism before he returned to the task at hand.

Franco Giancarlo was something else, Gianna reflected as she entered her *en suite* bathroom and began applying make-up.

A ruggedly attractive man in his late thirties, who commanded respect among his peers and wreaked havoc with many a feminine heart.

Something she knew only too well. He'd captured *hers* at an impossibly young age—an adoration for a teenager ten years her senior that had shifted to hero-worship with the growing years before taking the leap to love.

An entity that had made it easy for her to accept his proposal.

For the sake of the Giancarlo-Castelli conglomerate, founded by their respective grandparents during the last century. An extremely successful business temporarily put under pressure little more than three years ago by a fatal plane crash which had claimed both Franco's parents and Gianna's widowed father.

Losses on the share market had been regained when Franco assumed directorial control. Restoring shareholders' faith had taken three consecutive successful financial quarters. Yet future stability had remained in question, given Franco Giancarlo's bachelor status and Gianna Castelli's seeming lack of interest in choosing a husband.

The two widowed grandparents, matriarchal-Anamaria Castelli and patriarchal Santo Giancarlo, had presented what they had considered to be the perfect solution.

What better way to take Giancarlo-Castelli into the fourth generation than with children issued from a marriage between Franco Giancarlo and Gianna Castelli?

The fact Franco and Gianna had complied, for reasons of their own, had been cause for matriarchal and patriarchal delight.

The marriage had been accorded the wedding of the year, with a list of guests who figured high on Australia's social register. Distant relatives and far-flung friends had flown in from Italy, France and America. The event had garnered television coverage and had featured in several prominent magazines.

A year down the track they remained the golden

couple, their presence at various functions duly recorded and reported by the media.

In public she could play the part of adoring wife. Yet she was conscious of an invisible barrier.

Crazy, she silently chastised. She wore his ring, shared his bed, and played the role of social hostess with the ease of long practice. *His* in every way. Except she didn't have his heart. Or his soul.

She told herself it was *enough*. And knew she lied.

Dammit, what was the matter with her? Introspection wouldn't achieve a thing, and right now she needed to fix her hair, then dress.

Twenty minutes later she re-entered the bedroom to find Franco waiting with indolent ease, looking every inch the wealthy sophisticate in a black dinner suit, his black bow tie perfectly aligned.

Her heart leapt to a quickened beat as sensation surged through her veins. Breathe, she commanded silently, inwardly cursing the way her body reacted to his presence.

Did he know? In bed, without doubt. But out of it?

She didn't want to fall prey to such acute vulnerability. It wasn't fair.

'Beautiful,' Franco complimented her lightly, skimming her slight curves sheathed in red silk chiffon. Undoubtedly the gown was the work of a master seamstress, with its fitted bodice and spaghetti straps. The bill for which Gianna would have insisted on paying herself.

A slight intransigence which irked him. Independence was fine, up to a point. It appeased his sensibility she'd chosen to wear the diamond drop earrings he'd gifted her on their wedding anniversary.

A matching wrap completed the outfit, and she'd swept the length of her hair high into a smooth twist held fastened with a jewelled clip. A diamond pendant rested against the curved valley of her breasts.

Stiletto heels added four inches to her height, and he crossed the room, caught the subtle Hermes perfume, and offered a warm smile.

'*Grazie.*'

'For looking the part?'

The edges of his mouth lifted a little. 'That, too.'

He offered her a glass half filled with water, and two pills.

'Playing nurse?'

'Tell me you've already taken care of it and I'll discard the role.'

Gianna merely shook her head, popped the pills and swallowed them down. 'Are we ready to leave?'

Southern hemisphere summer daylight saving meant they joined the flow of city-bound traffic while the sun sank slowly towards the horizon.

'Want to talk about it?' He hadn't missed the slight edge of tension apparent, or the faint darkness clouding her expressive features.

Gianna cast him a wry glance. 'Where would you have me begin?'

'That bad?'

Her PA had called in sick, the replacement had proved hopeless, paperwork despatched via courier had been unavoidably detained, and lunch had been a half-eaten sandwich she'd discarded following a constant stream of phone calls.

'Nothing I couldn't handle.' Wasn't that what she'd been educated, trained and groomed for?

One goal... to take her rightful place in the Giancarlo-Castelli conglomerate. Yet, like Franco, she'd begun on the lower rung of the corporate ladder, learning firsthand how the business *worked* from the ground up, winning each subsequent promotion by her own merit.

Nepotism wasn't an option in either family, and no one with any *nous* could accuse her of riding on her father or grandmother's coat-tails.

Giancarlo-Castelli were generous supporters of several worthy charities, and tonight's event held prominence among Melbourne's social echelon. Children were very dear to Gianna's heart, and the terminally ill deserved maximum effort in raising funds. She would make her own sizable donation privately.

'Show-time,' she murmured as Franco brought the powerful top-of-the-range Mercedes to a halt outside the hotel's main entrance.

The spacious foyer adjacent to the grand ballroom held a large number of invited guests, mingling as they sipped champagne. Designer gowns from home and abroad, together with a king's ransom in jewellery, graced the female contingent, while the men appeared almost clones of each other in black dinner suits, white pin-pleated dress-shirts and black bow ties.

Wealthy scions of the corporate and professional world—although none, Gianna conceded, emanated quite the degree of power as the man at her side.

Beneath the sophisticated exterior lurked a latent primitive sensuality that held the promise of unleashed passion...and delivered, Gianna accorded silently, all too aware of the intimacy they shared, when it was possible for her to lose herself so completely in him that nothing, *nothing* else mattered.

Not the longed-for gift of his love, nor the unplanned delay in conceiving his child.

'Darlings! How *are* you both?'

The breathy feminine voice was familiar, and Gianna turned with a smile, exchanged the customary air-kiss, then gave a soft laugh as the stunning blonde touched light fingers to Franco's cheek.

'Shannay.'

'Ah.' Shannay's sigh held a wistful quality as Franco carried her fingers to his lips, and she offered Gianna a conspiratorial smile. 'He does that so well.'

'Doesn't he?'

The girls' friendship went back to boarding-school days and had continued through university. They shared a similar brand of humour, had been bridesmaid honours at each other's wedding, and remained in close touch.

'Tom?'

'About to join us,' Franco drawled as Shannay's husband came into view.

'My apologies. A phone call.' Tall, lean and bespectacled, Tom Fitzgibbon was a lauded heart surgeon, and one of those rare men who understood women. A widower with two young children, he'd allowed Shannay to do all the running in their relationship, only to take the wind out of her sails at the eleventh hour.

Gianna saw Shannay's eyes soften. 'A problem?'

Tom offered his wife a musing smile. 'Hopefully not.'

Together they began to circulate, greeting mutual friends, separating as they became caught up in conversation.

The society doyennes were in their element as they worked the guests, issuing verbal reminders for upcoming events and exchanging the latest gossip.

Gianna took another sip of champagne and allowed her gaze to skim the foyer. Soon staff would open the ballroom doors and begin ushering the assembled guests to their designated seats.

Franco stood at her side as he conversed with an associate, and this close she was supremely conscious of the faint muskiness of his exclusive cologne. It teased her senses and sent warmth coursing through her veins.

Acute sensitivity heightened by sensual anticipation as to how the night would end. And just how much she wanted to savour his touch, match it and become so caught up in electrifying passion that nothing else existed.

He had the skill to take her places her wildest imagination could never cover. An emotional nirvana that was wholly primitive and disruptively sensual when she begged for the release only he could give.

Had other women reacted with him as she did? Oh God no, don't answer that!

Franco had made her *his* by virtue of marriage. Albeit an arranged union cemented by mutual business issues. But what they shared in bed was special…wasn't it?

'Hungry?'

A trick question if ever there was one! A light musing smile lifted the corners of her mouth as she met his gaze.

'For food?'

His eyes assumed a humorous gleam. 'Naturally. Shall we go in?'

It was then she became aware numerous guests were moving towards the now open doors leading into ballroom.

Their designated table was well positioned, and the guests sharing it with them needed no introduction, which made for relaxed familiarity and ease of conversation.

Muted background music provided a pleasing ambience as wine stewards moved with swift precision among the tables, taking orders for wine and champagne, while waitresses followed in their wake bearing napkin-lined baskets of bread rolls.

It was the usual *modus operandi* for large charity events, where service, fine wines and good food formed part of the ticket price.

'You're very quiet. How is the headache?'

They were in the public eye, and as Franco's wife and a representative of Giancarlo-Castelli she was expected to *shine*.

For they numbered as one of the golden couples who were seen to have everything.

She could play the part. It was one of her talents.

Gianna let the edges of her mouth curve into a warm smile. 'Almost gone.'

He lifted a hand and brushed gentle fingers down her cheek. 'Good.'

She held his gaze, and attempted to control the way her nerve-ends began to shred at his touch. It wasn't fair to feel so emotionally naked.

With a steady hand she reached for the evening's programme and skimmed its contents.

'It looks an interesting mix,' she relayed lightly. 'A singer follows the customary speeches. There's an orchestrated fashion show. A surprise mystery guest.'

At that moment the music faded and the Master of Ceremonies took the podium, welcomed the guests, gave a brief *divertissement*, then introduced the charity's chairperson. A tireless matron who devoted her life to raising money to benefit numerous terminally ill children.

There was film coverage on the large drop-down screen of the charity's achievements, with the camera panning to children undergoing treatments in hospital, at supervised play. What really caught at the heartstrings was their expressive features. The solemn stoicism, the smiles, the childish laughter.

Life went on...other people's lives.

The chairperson made an impassioned plea for guests to provide generous donations.

Waitresses delivered the starters, and Gianna sipped her champagne, then offered a requested opinion as to the 'in' vacation spot of the moment.

'I thought the Caribbean, but Paul favours trekking through Vietnam. Can you imagine?'

'Alaska?' Gianna ventured. 'For its scenic beauty and the northern lights?'

'Darling,' the woman wailed. 'I want *shopping*.'

Why? she wanted to ask, when one upstairs wing of the woman's home was devoted entirely to storing clothes, with a room designated for each of the year's four seasons. Yet another room held a collection of shoes and matching bags. A veritable treasure trove of designer gear.

The singer gave a credible performance before the main course was served, and when the plates were cleared the MC announced the fashion parade.

Beautiful models, gorgeous clothes, all shown with professional panache.

One gown in particular took Gianna's interest, and she made a mental note to visit the designer's boutique.

'You'd look fabulous in the black. Franco must buy it for you. I know just the shoes to go with it. Manolo's, of course.'

Of course. Gianna gave herself a mental slap on the wrist for her facetiousness.

As waitresses delivered dessert, the MC took the podium to introduce the mystery guest.

'A young woman who has achieved international success as an actress.'

No...it couldn't be. Yet Gianna found it impossible to dispel a growing premonition.

'She has made the very generous offer to fund an all-expenses-paid holiday for three children and their families to Disneyland.'

The announcement brought a collective murmur of appreciation from the guests.

'We have had the medical team select the names of those children fit enough to travel.' He turned towards the charity's chairperson, who had stepped onto the stage with a top hat. 'I'd like one of our esteemed guests to select three names from this hat.' He paused for effect. 'Franco Giancarlo. Would you please come forward?'

A sickening feeling settled in Gianna's stomach as

Franco rose to his feet, and she watched as he crossed the floor and gained the stage.

'I'd like you all to welcome our mystery guest.' The MC paused for effect. 'Famke.'

Gianna didn't know if she could continue breathing. Tension constricted her throat and momentarily left her speechless.

Famke.

There she was, making an appearance from backstage, tall, blonde, in her late twenties, and far more beautiful than any woman had a right to be.

An actress who had initially achieved success in foreign-produced films before finding fame and fortune in America.

No one recalled her surname, for it had long been discarded in the rise to stardom.

A stunningly beautiful young woman who took pleasure in seducing wealthy men, and was known to be skilfully adept at gaining extravagant gifts of jewellery from former lovers.

Five years ago Franco had been one of them, during his sojourn in New York, before his parents' accidental death had brought him back to Melbourne.

Rumour at the time had whispered Famke wanted marriage, and the relationship soured when Franco wasn't prepared to commit. Whereupon in a fit of pique Famke had seduced an LA billionaire, married him in a blaze of media coverage and produced a child.

Gianna kept her eyes riveted on Franco, desperate

to gauge his reaction while a hundred questions hammered at her brain.

What was Famke doing here? Not only Melbourne, but *here*, tonight? And why go to such elaborate lengths to ensure a public face-to-face encounter with Franco?

'She's gorgeous, isn't she?' Gianna's dinner companion observed. 'I heard she's recently divorced.'

And *hunting*.

Not *any* wealthy man, Gianna concluded with sickening certainty.

Franco Giancarlo.

CHAPTER TWO

IT WAS difficult to produce a smile as Franco rose to his feet. Yet Gianna managed it with seemingly effortless ease, and joined the guests in applauding his progress to the podium.

No one could possibly guess at the pain knifing her mid-section, or the effort it took to regulate her breathing as she caught the sexual voltage Famke exuded as Franco joined her on stage.

The actress's effusive greeting was no doubt seen by most as an orchestrated act...the brush of Famke's lips to Franco's left cheek, then the other, as a familiar European gesture.

Famke's sultry laugh, the lingering trail of scarlet-lacquered nails, were like sharp daggers piercing Gianna's vulnerable heart.

Get over it, she bade herself silently. Famke is a witch, and Franco isn't playing into her game.

Not in the public arena, a devilish voice pursued. *But privately?*

The possibility tore at her composure and reduced it to shreds.

It said much for her social *élan* that she managed to smile, applaud, even *laugh* at the on-stage production...for the benefit of the guests, the excitement generated in favour of the three children whose names were chosen, and the television cameras.

How long did it take? With on-screen cameos of each child, the family, with commentary? Fifteen minutes…twenty?

To Gianna it felt like a lifetime as she endured witnessing Famke's touchy-feely antics on stage, the actress's sultry smile and provocative laugh as she endeavored to display a picture of remembered intimacy with the man who numbered among her previous lovers.

Was it physically possible to *burn* with resentment whilst presenting a calm and *cool* persona?

Body language was an art form, and one she'd studied to her advantage in the business and social sector. Consequently there was no visible evidence, no betraying signals that could be noted by those who might choose to observe the effect Famke's *play* might have on Franco Giancarlo's wife.

Gianna smiled with fellow guests as Franco left the podium and returned to his table. A smile she forced to reach her eyes as he resumed his seat.

'Well done, darling,' she complimented lightly, and was totally unprepared for the brush of his lips against her own, the slow sweep of his tongue.

Reassurance? A public declaration of espousal unity?

The latter, she decided as he lifted his head away from her own.

His eyes, so dark and faintly brooding…did he glimpse what she didn't want him to see? Sense it?

Doubtful. They didn't share that degree of empathy...did they?

Almost as if he guessed at her train of thought, he threaded his fingers through her own and brought them to his lips.

He was verging on overkill, and she took it to the brink by touching gentle fingers to his cheek...resisting the urge to press the tips of her pale-pink-lacquered nails *hard* against the smooth olive skin.

To any onlookers it presented a loving gesture, but the brief flaring of those dark eyes revealed he recognised her intent, caught her restraint...and the silent promise she was far from done.

She kept the smile in place and refrained from saying a word as coffee and tea were served.

There wasn't a question if Famke might circulate among the guests, but *when*...and if the actress would make a beeline for their table and Franco, or be a little more circumspect.

A tiny humourless laugh bubbled up in her throat. *Circumspection* didn't form part of Famke's *modus operandi*.

Something which became glaringly apparent within minutes as Gianna, together with the attending guests, saw the glamorous actress appear from backstage in the glare of a spotlight.

A brilliant smile, a light laugh, followed by a seemingly touching air-kiss to the crowd at the sound of more applause...and Famke stepped down onto the ballroom floor.

Admittedly her passage was interrupted. Not so her direction. However long it took...two minutes or ten...the actress's destination was never in doubt.

Act, Gianna bade herself silently. You're good at it.

All her life she'd conformed, aware how much it meant to her father to be an exemplary daughter. To excel in school, gain honours, *show* the Giancarlo-Castelli corporation she possessed the skill to climb the corporate ladder...in a manner that proved nepotism didn't enter the equation.

A gap year spent in France had provided an opportunity to tilt at windmills...something she'd refrained from—unless riding a motorcycle behind a male student at speed or visiting a few questionable nightclubs in his company counted. Besides, there had always been a shadow bodyguard in the background, ensuring she came to no harm.

'Franco.'

The feline purr made much of his name, while the sultry heat evident in the actress's gaze set Gianna's teeth on edge.

'I just wanted to thank you, darling, for joining me on stage.'

Darling. Oh, my.

Franco's smile didn't reach his eyes. 'A public request made it difficult for me to refuse.'

Was there the suggestion of a pout forming on Famke's beautifully shaped mouth?

'Fitting, don't you think?' The actress queried with

a hint of teasing censure. 'Considering your known generosity to the charity?'

With a deliberate gesture Franco caught hold of Gianna's hand and threaded his fingers through her own. 'Allow me to introduce Gianna...my wife.'

Impossible Famke was unaware of his marriage. It had received international media coverage at the time.

Blue eyes chilled to resemble an arctic ice floe for a fleeting second before the actress masked their expression.

'Such an...*interesting* alliance.'

'Famke.' She kept her tone light, and only those who knew her well would have detected the slight hint of steel beneath the surface.

'We must get together.'

'For old times' sake?' Gianna queried with pseudo-politeness, aware the invitation was aimed at Franco...solo.

A faint laugh emerged from the actress's lips. 'We *do* have a history.'

'The emphasis being *history*.'

Famke arched one eyebrow. 'I so dislike territorial women.'

'Really? Surely it adds to the challenge?'

'Afraid, sweetie?'

Gianna didn't pretend to misunderstand. Lines were being drawn, and the game was about to begin. She felt Franco's fingers tighten on her own, and ignored the silent warning. 'Perhaps Franco can answer that.'

'Why? When you're doing so well on your own.' His drawled comment caused Famke's gaze to narrow.

Unity was everything. She could do *polite*. She'd had years of practice. 'The evening is winding down, and we're about to leave.'

'Can't stand the pace?'

Gianna was sorely tempted to reveal she was taking her husband home for some hot sex. Instead, she merely smiled and rose to her feet as Franco stood and bade their immediate guests 'goodnight'.

'I'm sure we'll run into each other again before long,' Famke offered silkily.

Not if she could help it, Gianna vowed silently, barely controlling the itch to slap the actress's face.

Talk about eating a man alive!

There were friends and business associates who caught their attention as they began threading their way through the ballroom, reminders of invitations exchanged and news of upcoming social events.

She was conscious of Franco's arm along the back of her waist, the light stroke of his fingers...an attempt to soothe her ruffled composure?

Was he aware how his touch affected her? In bed, without doubt. The thought of their shared intimacy caused her pulse to leap into an accelerated beat. His mouth, hands...dear heaven. Heat flowed through her veins as sensation unfurled deep inside.

She needed the physicality of their loving, to lose herself in him and believe, for a while, that he cared. More than mere affection, and their marriage, although forging an alliance between two families, sur-passed *duty*.

He'd never *said* anything. Not once, even in the throes of their lovemaking, had he mentioned the *L* word. And he never lost control. Something which irked her unbearably.

'We'll look forward to seeing you Wednesday evening.'

Get with it, a tiny voice prompted, providing a memory jog…dinner party at the home of Brad and Nikki Wilson-Smythe. 'Of course,' she managed with a smile.

It was a relief to eventually gain the hotel lobby, even more so to slip into the car and lean back against the cushioned headrest as Franco eased into the flow of traffic departing the city.

Any attempt at small-talk was out, and she didn't offer so much as a word during the relatively short drive home.

Instead, she idly noted the passing scene through the windscreen. The bright neon lights, various ve-hicles, the dark indigo night sky, the sturdy leafed trees lining the main thoroughfare, an electric tram…the light sprinkling shower of rain that wet the bitumen and set the windscreen wipers in action. The changing cityscape as they reached the estab-lished suburb of Toorak, with its stately homes par-tially hidden behind high walls and security gates.

An almost inaudible sigh whispered from her lips as Franco eased the Mercedes into their driveway.

Strategically placed lights outlined the gentle

curve lined with topiary that led to the elegant two-storeyed home Franco had purchased on his return from the States.

He'd employed contractors to preserve the main Georgian-style structure, whilst completely renewing the interior to resemble the original. Refurbishment, beautiful antique furniture, original art gracing the walls, had made it one of the most admired homes in the district, receiving media attention when he'd acquired the adjoining property, razed the existing home and added a swimming pool and tennis court.

Franco brought the Mercedes to a halt inside the multi-vehicle garage, above which resided a two-bedroom apartment occupied their trusted staff, by Rosa and Enrico, connected to the house by an enclosed walkway shrouded from the front by shrubbery. A functional gym and studio had been cleverly constructed to fit behind the walkway between the house and garages.

Together they entered the large tiled lobby, whose focal point was an exquisite crystal chandelier and a curved double staircase leading to the upper floor.

She adored the large spacious rooms, with a splendid mix of formal and informal areas occupying the ground level, the exquisite marble tiling and huge luxurious oriental rugs, and the main and guest suites situated upstairs, superbly carpeted in aubusson and furnished with genuine antiques.

'Nothing to say?'

Gianna paused and turned towards him, aware of

his ability to read her so well. Too well for her peace of mind.

'An argument in the car might have proved too much of a distraction,' she managed evenly, meeting his gaze and holding it.

One eyebrow rose in silent query, and she went for the direct approach.

'Do you intend seeing her?'

His expression didn't change, although she had the distinct impression his body stilled, and for an instant there was something unreadable in those dark eyes.

'Why would I do that?'

His soft drawl sent shivers feathering down her spine, and her chin tilted a little in defence. 'Because it's what Famke wants.'

'Your trust in me is so tenuous?'

Gianna took a moment to compose the right words. 'I won't become a figure of public ridicule.'

'You want a promise of my fidelity?'

'Only if you mean it.' She turned towards the staircase. 'Promises can be broken.' It was as good an exit line as she could come up with.

Respect, affection, friendship and sexual compatibility formed the base of their marriage. *Love* wasn't supposed to enter the equation.

Yet it had, and she was willing to go on oath that a one-sided love was hell on earth.

Gianna sensed rather than heard Franco join her as she reached the upper level, and she directed him a steady glance.

'You evaded the question.'

Together they crossed the spacious central area separating each wing and made their way towards the main suite.

Gianna entered the room ahead of him and slipped off her evening sandals…a mistake, given it merely accentuated her diminutive height.

'It shouldn't require an answer.'

Her chin lifted a fraction, and her eyes were remarkably clear. She held up one hand and began ticking off each finger. 'We're joined together in marriage, legally bound in business.' Her gaze didn't waver. 'I deserve your honesty in our private life.'

Something moved in the dark depths of his eyes. 'Have I ever been dishonest with you?'

She didn't have to weigh her answer. 'No.'

'Accept that isn't going to change.'

Reassurance? Possibly. He was no fool, and she indicated as much.

He moved close and saw the way the pulse at the base of her throat jumped to a faster beat. 'A compliment, *cara*?'

That was the thing…she wasn't his *darling*. Merely a convenient partner when she longed for more…so much more.

There were those among the social clique who imagined she had it all. The trappings of extreme wealth, a perfect job, the ultimate man… Yet she'd willingly give it up in exchange for his love.

So…*dream on*, a tiny voice taunted. It isn't going to happen.

Franco took hold of her wrists, then shaped her

arms to settle on each shoulder. He lowered his head and sought her lips with his own, nibbling a little, teasing until he sensed her breath catch.

She nipped at his lower lip with her teeth, held on for a few seconds, then eased back. 'What do you think you're doing?'

Stupid question. She knew exactly what he was doing!

His mouth captured hers, seeking, exploring, and wreaking havoc with her emotions as heat coursed through her veins, bringing her alive as only *he* could.

Gianna felt the familiar swirling sensation begin deep inside, and she was scarcely aware of his fingers easing the spaghetti straps of her gown aside, or the zip fastening easing open...until the red chiffon slithered to a silken heap at her feet.

Lacy red bikini briefs were all that separated her from total nudity, and her body shook a little as he traced the lace, following its pattern with a deliberate finger before easing in to stroke the soft hair curling at the apex of her thighs.

Acute sensuality arrowed through her body, and she sought the buttons on his shirt, wanting, *needing* the sensation of skin to skin, to feel and savour his warmth and essence.

'You're wearing too many clothes.' Was that husky voice her own?

He trailed a path down to her breasts and savoured one dusky peak until she groaned out loud.

'Remove them.'

How had she not noticed he'd already shrugged out of his jacket, torn off his bow tie and toed off his shoes?

Because she lost all her senses when he kissed her…except one. *Sensuality* to a heightened degree… invasive and all-encompassing.

Franco had the power to make her forget who she was, her surroundings. Everything.

There was only him, his warm musky male scent, the magic of his touch…the heat, the passion, and the wild erotic sorcery he was able to weave with her emotions.

She barely registered her fingers slipping free the buttons on his shirt, nor did she make a teasing play to draw out the moment, or seek to provoke.

Need guided the speed with which she dispensed with his shirt, freed him of the fine tailored trousers…and sought the source of her pleasure.

His indrawn breath as she enclosed him brought a soft sensual smile to her lips, and her fingers slid slowly down to cup him, only to return to create a slow, tantalising pattern that had him grasping her bottom and lifting her high against him.

Gianna cried out as his mouth closed over her breast and suckled, teasing the tender peak with the edge of his teeth before exploring its soft curve.

It was almost more than she could bear as his fingers sought and found the aroused clitoris, caressing it until she went wild, swept high by mesmeric primitive sensation.

Just as she began to ease down, he sent her up

again, closing his mouth over her own in an invasive kiss that mirrored the sexual act itself.

It wasn't *enough*, and she wrenched her mouth free and told him so, demanding more...so much more.

Franco shifted, reached for the bedcovers and tossed them aside before drawing her down onto the bed.

What followed was a feast of the senses, a long leisurely tasting that drove them both to fever pitch, and it was she who lost control as her body sang to a tune only their shared sexual chemistry could evoke.

Passion...mesmeric, electric, tempestuous. A hungry slaking of the senses driven by shameless need and primeval desire.

The feel of him entering her, the long slow thrust as he slid in deep, sent every nerve and muscle into convulsing life, and she arched up to meet him when he began to move, exulting in the wonder of two people in perfect sexual accord.

Gianna became lost, so caught up in him she was unaware of the guttural cries emerging from her throat, or the soft feline purr of satisfaction so much later as Franco gathered her in against him on the verge of sleep.

Sated, she tucked a hand against his chest and burrowed in, a soft smile curving her generous mouth as he gently traced a soothing trail down her back.

Within minutes her breathing slowed into a regular pattern and she didn't feel the light touch of his lips against her temple. Nor was she aware he lay awake for some time.

CHAPTER THREE

GIANNA drifted awake to the realisation she was alone in the large bed.

Which was probably just as well, she decided as she arched her body in a preliminary stretch...and felt the faint pull of muscles, the awareness of sensitivity deep inside.

Even *thinking* about what she'd shared with Franco through the night brought renewed heat flooding her body, and she uttered a self-deprecatory groan, checked the time, saw it was early and aimed a frustrated punch at her pillow.

It was *Saturday*, for heaven's sake, with no rush to rise and begin the day.

Yet any further sleep wasn't going to happen, and she threw back the bedcovers and made for the shower.

Breakfast comprised yoghurt and fresh fruit, which she took out on the terrace.

Early-morning sun fingered the air with warmth, tempered by a wispy breeze, and lent promise to an early summer's day.

Rosa joined her with fresh coffee, and together they conferred over the coming week's schedule. Dinner at home, with the exception of Wednesday, and Gianna gave Rosa *carte blanche* with the evening meals.

A superb cook, whose culinary talents were unfailingly lauded by Gianna and Franco's guests, Rosa ran the house like clockwork, engaging outside help whenever the need arose.

It was almost nine when Gianna ran lightly upstairs to change, choosing dress jeans and a knit singlet-top. Make-up was minimal, and she swept her hair into a loose knot, secured it with a tortoiseshell clasp, then she slid her feet into stiletto-heeled boots, collected her shoulder-bag and descended the staircase.

Franco glanced up from his laptop as she entered his study, and she watched as he hit a key, then sank back in his chair.

Black jeans and black tee-shirt lent a casual air, making it impossible to ignore the way the cotton highlighted impressive muscle and sinew.

'On your way out?'

The deep drawl curled round her nerve-ends and tugged a little.

'Retail therapy,' she responded lightly.

Leading a social existence commanded serious attention to one's wardrobe. Men could wear a dinner suit several times over. If a woman wore the same gown twice to a gala event, it was assumed she couldn't afford the price of a new one. Appearance was everything, providing a benchmark for her husband's status in the business arena.

Dress designers of high repute were very much in

demand, earning veritable fortunes providing original couture, with consultations and fittings afforded only by appointment.

'Have fun.' Franco's eyes gleamed with latent humour, and she offered a wry smile.

'Pray Estella is in a good mood.' The Spanish-born seamstress possessed magic fingers when it came to fabric and thread. She was also vocal, volatile, lethal on occasion when adjusting pins...and known to dismiss clientele on the slightest whim.

'Want to eat in tonight, or dine out?'

It was no contest. 'Home. Will you tell Rosa?'

'I'll cook.'

The fact he could, and well, had long since ceased to surprise her. 'OK.'

He joined her as she reached the door, and silently she tilted her head askance.

'You forgot something.' His hands cupped her face as he laid his lips against her own, then went in deep, and she held on as he bestowed an evocative tasting that blew her mind.

How long did it last? Mere seconds?

She was incapable of saying a word when he released her, and it took effort to control the slight tremble threatening her mouth as he pressed a light thumb against her lower lip.

Damn. She didn't want to appear vulnerable. Yet he had only to touch her and she became limbless.

'Go enjoy your day.' He waited a beat. 'There's just one thing. You might want to repair your lipstick.'

Repair didn't quite cover it. She'd have to start over.

'Bite me.'

His soft chuckle stayed with her as she reversed her BMW from the garage and slid in a CD, turning up the volume as she eased through the gates and gained the street.

Estella worked out of an old-style home whose rooms had been converted into a fashionista's salon. Parking rarely presented a problem, and Gianna greeted the receptionist as she entered the front lounge.

Within minutes a middle-aged flamboyantly dressed matron appeared at the door, hair covered in a deep crimson headpiece that defied description, with make-up pronounced to the point of absurdity.

'You are late.'

'I'm on time,' Gianna declared politely, and incurred a haughty look.

'You would dare argue with me?'

'Perhaps we can compromise by agreeing our watches are not in sync?'

A raven eyebrow arched in disdain. 'My timepiece is correct. Follow me.' Estella swept down the hallway into the fitting room.

'Remove your outer clothes,' the seamstress demanded. 'No talking. I do not have the inclination for chit-chat.'

Beige, taupe, cream and ivory. Who would have thought?

Gianna watched as Estella folded the glorious silk

chiffon, pinned, tucked...all the while muttering beneath her breath.

'No one has this. The fabric, the style.' The woman swept an expressive hand high. 'Your hair. Wear it up. It will give balance.' She stood back a pace. 'Jewellery minimal. Focus the gown. Shoes taupe. Fine heels. I give you fabric sample for matching. Next fitting you bring shoes. Now change and go. Next week, same time.'

Coffee, Gianna decided as she slid her sunglasses in place and slipped in behind the wheel of her car. Hot, strong, black and sweet in one of the boutique cafés, then she'd look for shoes before heading to the hairdresser.

It was after one when she consigned several brightly emblazoned packages into the boot of her car. There were still a few things she needed to do, and it made sense to take a break for lunch.

Toorak Road hosted several upmarket café's, and she chose one, ordered a long cool drink and an open salad sandwich, leafed through one of a few complimentary newspapers while she ate...and managed not to choke as Famke's image leapt off a page.

Correction. Famke and Franco, on-stage, captured on film in a momentary embrace.

Gianna forced herself to read the small print beneath the caption...then she pushed aside her plate.

It was bad enough more than a thousand guests had witnessed Famke's deliberate act. Now the incident was accessible to the entire state. Australia-wide, if other newspapers had decided to run it.

She muttered an unladylike oath beneath her breath. The doubts, ever present beneath the surface, began to emerge, insidiously invading her emotions.

Dammit. *Love* wasn't supposed to be such a *pain*.

Spending money, *serious* money, was a woman's prerogative in times of stress. And there were those stiletto heels she'd looked at, liked, and passed over.

She could afford them. Several pairs. The whole darn shop if she felt so inclined!

With that thought in mind she picked up her bag, slung the strap over her shoulder, paid her bill, emerged out onto the pavement...and came face-to-face with Famke.

The day, which had already taken a downward turn, suddenly nosedived.

'Gianna!' The actress gave a credible act of being surprised. 'This is unexpected.'

Really? Upmarket Toorak, Saturday, shopping and personal maintenance high on any career woman's list... It wouldn't be hard to do the maths.

Which meant Famke had a purpose.

Gianna gave herself a metaphorical slap on the wrist for being cynical.

'Famke.' She could do polite civility...for now.

'Let's share coffee.'

Do you honestly think I'll fall for that? 'Thanks, but we have nothing to discuss.'

'Not even the fabricated excuse of a pressing appointment?' A perfectly shaped eyebrow formed a deliberate arch. 'Afraid to hear what I might say, darling?'

Confrontation, or a silent exit? *Verbal*, definitely!

'Enjoy the hunt, Famke.'

'Straight to the point?' There was a marked pause. 'Don't bother drawing battle lines.'

'Waste of time.'

The smile didn't reach Famke's eyes. 'I'm glad you agree, darling.'

Leave, *now*. She took a step forward, only to come to an abrupt halt as the actress placed a hand on her arm.

'Don't discount the lure of sexual chemistry.'

Gianna tried for the last word. 'Yours...or mine?'

Grrr. She badly wanted to *hit* something, except it wasn't the thing to do in public.

Instead, she made for the shoe boutique, followed the purchase with a manicure, pedicure and a facial.

Consequently it was after five when she garaged her car and gathered all her purchases together.

She made the foyer and was about to ascend the stairs when Franco appeared.

'Want some help with those?'

His musing drawl put her on the defensive. So did his close proximity. He'd shaved, showered and donned black trousers and a light chambray shirt, the sleeves folded back almost to each elbow.

'I'm fine.'

Gianna missed the faint narrowing of his eyes as he examined her expressive features. 'Come toss the salad when you're done.'

'OK.'

He watched her progress up the stairs, the slight

sway of her denim-clad rear, the tightly held shoulders that owed nothing to the weight of the emblazoned carry-bags in each hand.

She was a piece of work. There was strength of character, integrity, pride…and vulnerability. A combination he found intriguing.

A glass of chilled white wine rested on the kitchen servery when Gianna entered the kitchen. She'd taken time to unpack and stow her purchases, shower, and don tailored trousers and a fashionable top before slipping her feet into heeled sandals. Her hair was caught in a loose knot atop her head, and her one concession to make-up was pink lipgloss.

Franco picked up the glass and handed it to her. 'For you.'

'Because you think I need it?'

He collected his own glass and touched its rim to her own. *'Salute.'*

She wanted to slip into the light camaraderie they shared, to enjoy the anticipation of how the night would end. To *know* she could lose herself in him and emerge whole.

Except she had to deal with the spectre of Famke intruding between them. If what he'd shared with the actress came close to what he shared with *her*.

The thought of his tightly muscled body locked with Famke in the throes of lovemaking almost destroyed her.

A vivid imagination was fast becoming her own worst enemy. Something she must fight to control, or she'd be lost.

Pretend, a silent voice bade. You're good at it.

A redolent aroma wafted from a small pot simmering on the cook-top, and she wrinkled her nose in appreciation. 'Marinara sauce?'

'Uh-huh. Want to choose the pasta?'

Gianna didn't hesitate. 'Fettuccine.'

With easy co-ordinated movements he extracted a packet from the pantry and forked the contents into a large pot of boiling water, adjusted the heat, then turned towards her.

'How was your day?'

You really don't want to know. Yet he saw too much and read her too well. 'Fun, until Famke appeared on the scene.'

His eyes narrowed. 'Would you care to elaborate?'

She took a sip of wine, savoured the light golden liquid, then let it slide down her throat. 'Facts, or my summation?'

'Both.'

She looked at him carefully, and gained nothing from his expression. 'I bumped into her outside a café.'

'Indeed?'

'Let's go with coincidence.' Gianna lifted a hand and tucked back a lock of hair. 'I really don't want to contemplate *design.*'

She crossed to the sink, caught up the washed salad greens and began breaking the leaves into a bowl. Only to have a hand cup her chin and lift it.

'We did this last night.' His voice was pure silk.

So they had. Except it hadn't resolved a thing.

'She's on a mission.' Wasn't that the truth? 'And determined to succeed.'

'Don't let her bother you.'

'I can handle her.' *Sure* she could…verbally. Emotionally, she didn't stand a snowflake's chance in hell.

His eyes were inscrutable as he traced her mouth with his thumb, and for a few seconds she felt as if she couldn't breathe.

Then he released her and crossed to the cook-top, leaving her to finish fixing the salad.

When it was done, she set the kitchen table, checked the garlic bread heating in the oven, grated parmesan cheese and saw Franco drain the pasta.

'This is seriously *good*.' Gianna lifted her wine glass in appreciation as she sampled the food. Simple fare eaten in a homely atmosphere provided a pleasant change from their hectic social life.

'*Grazie.*'

His lazy drawl made her lips twitch. '*Prego.*'

'Italian conversation to match the meal?'

'Practice,' she responded lightly. 'Or have you forgotten we're entertaining Anamaria and Santo tomorrow night?'

'The grandparents,' Franco mused. 'What do you have you in mind for Rosa to serve?'

She took a sip of wine, then twirled pasta onto her fork. 'I intend to cook.'

He caught her speculative look, and bit back his amusement. 'You're planning something ambitious?'

'Uh-huh.'

'With or without Rosa's help?'

Gianna offered a brilliant smile. 'Solo. I'll devote the day to it.'

'Which will make for an interesting evening.'

Her eyes assumed a mischievous sparkle. 'Ah, you get the drift.'

She'd taken a course during a sojourn in Rome and had learnt from the best. In another life she could have been a chef. Except the sole surviving Castelli had no future in a restaurant kitchen.

Annamaria Castelli prided herself on her culinary expertise, and had personally trained her housekeeper to serve her favourite dishes. She had an acute knowledge of taste and smell, and could, she liked to boast, sample a dish and divulge not only every ingredient, but the precise measure in any recipe.

Santo Giancarlo, on the other hand, loved to eat. If it tasted fine and didn't upset his digestion, he had no inclination to examine and dissect the ingredients.

Two grandparents who were as chalk to cheese in personalities, yet with more in common than they were prepared to admit.

Gianna forked the last of her fettuccine, followed it with a morsel of garlic bread, then finished off her wine.

'You cooked; I'll take care of the dishes,' she declared, and gathered up their plates. Leaving them for Rosa didn't enter her head.

'Coffee?'

Franco rose to his feet. 'I'll make, and take mine in the study.'

'Likewise.' She needed to check e-mails, send out a few, peruse the week's business and social diary, and decide what to prepare for Sunday evening's dinner.

With deft movements she soon restored the kitchen surfaces to their former state of gleaming cleanliness, settled for tea instead of coffee, and took it into the room she used as a study.

It was late when she closed down her laptop and went to bed.

Gianna was on the verge of sleep when she sensed Franco's presence, and she went willingly into his arms as he gathered her close.

Warm skin, hard musculature, he was intensely male, and in the darkness she could pretend *want* and *need* were one and the same as his lips nuzzled the hollow at the base of her neck.

Skilled fingers trailed her slender curves, teased and tantalised until the breath hitched in her throat.

Now…dear heaven, *now*.

His mouth covered hers in a kiss that tore her apart, and she used her teeth to nip his tongue as she wound her legs around his waist.

'Greedy, hmm?'

She didn't answer, *couldn't*, as he slid inside, filling her, and she became lost, aware only of the man, the acute sensation spiralling through her body, and deep unrestrained passion…hers.

Afterwards he rolled onto his side and drew her in against him.

CHAPTER FOUR

GIANNA rose early, showered, then dressed in cargo pants and a singlet top before joining Franco on the terrace for a leisurely breakfast.

When she was done she left him reading the Sunday newspapers while she examined the well-stocked pantry.

Anamaria vowed the culinary skills of *her* house-keeper outweighed those of Santo's housekeeper, with the honour in culinary expertise being held by Anamaria herself.

Two opposing grandparents, Gianna mused, who delighted in an ongoing game of verbal one-upmanship simply for the sheer mischief it provided each of them.

After considerable thought to a menu, Gianna settled for *bruschetta*, *risotto*, with roast chicken and salad as a main. A glazed fruit flan would suffice for dessert.

She made a list, checked the chilled wine, collected her shoulder-bag, went in search of Franco and found him in his study.

He glanced up from his laptop. 'Shopping?'

'Just a few items. What are your plans for the day?'

He sank back in his chair and indicated the laptop. 'Catching up. Want any help this afternoon?'

A faint smile teased her lips. 'You can set the table.'

'Formal, of course?'

A mischievous gleam lit her eyes. 'Oh, let's do the whole bit.' Fine linen, Baccarat crystal, Christofle flatware, floral centrepiece…she made a mental note to add flowers to her list.

'Think it'll work?'

She took in his strong features, the breadth of his shoulders beneath the casual polo shirt, and felt her stomach flip at a sudden wayward thought. What would he do if she crossed round the desk, sank onto his lap and angled her mouth to his?

Reciprocate? Be amused? Indulge her?

The heat, she knew, would be all *hers*.

She had his affection. But *love* wasn't part of the deal.

Oh, for heaven's sake…*get a grip*. 'I aim to try.'

The edges of Franco's mouth lifted a little. 'Candles?'

Anamaria would wonder at the romantic setting, surmise the reason, and ask the inevitable question. 'Overkill, definitely.'

Her failure to fall pregnant after a year wasn't an issue…*yet*, Gianna qualified as she slid into her BMW and fired the engine.

A child, she contemplated as she gained the road and headed towards the main thoroughfare. Hers, but undoubtedly *his*. Something both grandparents hoped for…and assuredly one of the main reasons for the marriage between the sole surviving grandson of Santo Giancarlo and the granddaughter of AnaMaria Castelli.

What if it didn't happen?

Oh, for heaven's sake! She was young, healthy, and there was no immediate need to rush into parenthood.

Focus on the day, she bade herself silently as she made for the closest supermarket and parked.

Fresh produce was high on her list, together with a freshly baked French baguette from a nearby patisserie.

Almost an hour later she retrieved her purchases from the car, carried them into the kitchen and diligently set to work.

Gianna bypassed lunch and nibbled on the end pieces of the baguette, some cheese and fruit in between tending to dinner preparations.

'Everything under control?'

Gianna glanced up from stirring the sauce for the *risotto*, caught Franco's amused smile and wrinkled her nose at him. 'You want to sample?' She took a spoon, scooped up a small portion, held it to his lips…and waited for his verdict.

'Perfect.' He lifted a hand and tucked a stray lock of hair behind her ear. 'I'll tend to the table.'

He'd already changed into black tailored trousers and a white chambray shirt. A quick glance at her watch revealed she should go exchange casual gear for something more respectable.

The grandparents would arrive separately around four-thirty. They'd share a glass of wine, sample a little *biscotti*, and chat. Dinner at six-thirty, coffee at nine, after which Anamaria and Santo would depart at ten.

The pattern rarely changed, Gianna conceded as she donned black evening trousers and a white silk shirt, applied make-up, added a dab of subtle perfume, slid her feet into stilettos, and retraced her steps to the kitchen.

The dining-room, she determined minutes later, resembled perfection, and she made ready a variety of serving dishes, ran a last-minute check everything could be put on hold, then cast a glance at her watch.

Security at the front gates beeped right on time, and she entered the foyer as Franco initiated the electronic release.

Would it be Anamaria or Santo heading the arrival?

Each grandparent adhered to a strict punctuality schedule, but there was the inherent need to have an edge…

Franco indicated the video screen. 'Want to check?'

'And spoil the surprise?'

Santo, by mere seconds, purring up the driveway in his red Ferrari, Gianna determined as Franco swept the imposing double entrance doors wide. With Anamaria following a car's length behind in her conventional Bentley.

Santo laughed at Anamaria's baleful glare as they

each emerged from their vehicles, then graciously indicated she should precede him indoors.

'Bah,' came out as a condemnation. 'You should be ashamed of yourself, driving that ridiculous vehicle at your age.'

'Why? When it appeals to my inner child?'

'*Child* is the operative word.'

'One day I'll persuade you to take a ride with me and change your mind.'

'The whole of Venice will need to flood before I get into that contraption.'

Gianna rolled her eyes expressively as she leant in to greet her grandmother with the customary kiss to each cheek. A similar gesture from Santo followed.

'You both look well.'

A familiar compliment which she graciously accepted as she sailed…there was no other word for it…into the formal lounge.

'Tea, Nonna?'

'*Grazie.*'

'Espresso, Santo?' He'd vetoed Nonno from the onset, relaying it made him feel old.

'Too much caffeine,' Anamaria admonished. 'You won't sleep.'

'*Vecchia*, I sleep just fine.'

'You like to be called *vecchio*?'

Old woman, old man… Five minutes in, and they were already indulging in verbal warfare.

'You want I should serve pistols instead of tea and coffee?' Dammit, she was slipping into their vernacular!

Anamaria offered a sweet smile. '*Cara*, go bring the *vecchio* his coffee. He obviously needs it.'

'Don't forget to add a splash of *grappa*.' Santo's conspiratorial grin held a devilish quality.

Anamaria didn't disappoint. 'Before dinner?'

'*Vecchia*, I begin each day with it.'

A fact Anamaria knew very well. Gianna waited for the expected pithy response, but her grandmother settled for an expressive, 'Hurumph!'

'You might do well to follow my example.'

Anamaria chose to ignore him, and turned her attention towards her granddaughter.

'Is there anything you need to tell me?'

Now, there was a loaded question if ever there was one, Gianna decided with a degree of musing cynicism. 'Franco can fill you in while I go tend to the tea and coffee.'

Passing the buck? She caught the silent query and a humorous gleam in Franco's dark eyes as she sought her escape.

Tea, coffee and conversation...talk that was partly business oriented, social, and amazingly free from the grandparents' usual argumentative banter.

Had Franco issued a warning dictum? Possibly. A superb strategist, he was immune to even the most persuasive ploy.

'Gianna will show me the gardens.' Anamaria rose to her feet, indicating Gianna should do likewise. 'When we return we'll share a little wine before dinner.'

'Some fresh air will sharpen the appetite.' Franco

followed her actions and sent his grandfather a musing glance. 'Santo?'

'Why disturb him?'

Santo offered Anamaria a rakish gleam. 'My dear, it will be a pleasure to walk in the garden with you.'

Anamaria's response was a castigating, 'Fool.'

'Ah, yes. But think of the fun it provides me.'

Anamaria murmured something inaudible, and at a guess it was hardly complimentary.

The early-evening air held a cool edge, and there was a premature dullness in the slowly sinking sun which surely spelled a precursor to impending rain.

Impeccably kept garden borders displayed perennials in glorious colour, clipped shrubbery planted with immaculate precision, splendid topiary and beautiful green lawn which was a testament to Enrico and the services of a regular gardening assistant.

'The roses will make a lovely display,' Anamaria ventured. 'So, too, the gladioli.'

Gianna agreed. Plants ranked high on her grandmother's list of favourite things. It was maintaining the earth, nurturing it with food and water so the seeds could stretch and grow to perfection. The right insecticides, preferably natural products.

Anamaria's garden was something to behold, with a conservatory housing indoor plants and a greenhouse filled with exotic blooms.

While Giancarlo-Castelli represented her life's work, her garden and plants assumed a secondary interest.

Now that a marriage between Gianna and Franco

had been achieved, she was impatient for the birth of a great-grandchild.

Together they examined the grounds, two women with a span of almost fifty years separating them, while grandfather and the son of his son followed at a leisurely pace.

Gianna sensed the heritage, the strong bond linking each of them together, appreciating on one level the need to preserve it.

Surely a child deserved two loving parents?

Yet who would dare to suggest a child conceived from such a marriage wouldn't be loved and adored?

As a mother, her love would be unconditional...and Franco? She had a vision of him carrying a laughing child braced high atop broad shoulders, indulging the pleasure of fatherhood.

Was it asking too much for it to be the real deal? To know *she* was the love of his life, the *only* one?

Sure, Gianna discounted. That was as likely as snow falling in summertime.

And what of Famke? The glamorous actress wasn't going to fade into the woodwork any time soon.

So get your head out of the clouds and face reality, a tiny imp chastised.

'Tell Enrico a little more mulch will work wonders.'

Gianna recovered quickly. 'I'm sure he'll be delighted with your advice.'

'It's getting cool.' Franco drew level and slid an

arm along the back of her waist. 'Shall we return indoors?'

They were in the presence of the grandparents... the instigators of this marriage and all too aware it wasn't a love match. Consequently there was no need to maintain any pretence.

She gave him a measured look, and gleaned nothing from his expression.

Then the moment was lost as a fat plop of rain fell on her cheek, followed by another, and they made it inside as a vivid fork of lightning rent the skies, followed almost immediately by an ominous roll of thunder.

Dinner proved a success, the serving of each course achieved with smooth expertise.

'Rosa has outdone herself.'

Anamaria's compliment was genuine, and Santo lifted his wine goblet in a silent salute and kissed his fingers in eloquent approval. 'Everything was superb.'

Gianna watched as Franco leaned back in his seat, and she fielded his musing glance with equanimity. 'I'll fetch dessert.'

The delicious glazed fruit flan added a pleasant finishing touch to the meal, and earned appreciative praise from Santo, whose penchant for anything sweet was well known.

'Go make yourselves comfortable in the lounge while I make coffee.' The suggestion followed Santo's second serving of dessert.

'Rosa has retired for the evening?'

Gianna didn't miss a beat. 'There was no need for her to stay.'

'In that case, I'll help clear the table.' Anamaria began stacking crockery while Gianna collected the serving dishes.

'You're a guest,' she admonished with a smile, and was immediately put in her place.

'Family.' Anamaria's tone didn't brook argument.

'Leave the girl alone. She doesn't want you in her kitchen.'

Santo received a withering glare in response.

'You know nothing of the kitchen.'

'I live alone. How do you imagine meals appear on my table?'

Anamaria gave a memorable snort. 'You have a housekeeper.'

'So, too,' Santo declared, 'do you.'

Franco glanced from one to the other, and positioned himself between them. 'Let's adjourn to the lounge, shall we?'

Gianna set up the coffee-maker while she dispensed china and flatware into the dishwasher, then she set up a tray, added the carafe of aromatic coffee and walked through to the lounge in time to hear Anamaria query Franco.

'You will, of course, use whatever persuasive measures are necessary?'

She placed the tray down onto the coffee table, filled each cup and handed them out. 'Are you going to enlighten me?'

'Your pregnancy,' Anamaria said without pre-amble.

Gianna picked up her own cup with a steady hand, and took a sip before fixing her grandmother with a level look. 'Be assured you'll be one of the first to know when it happens.'

'I'm not getting any younger, child.'

She took a deep breath, then expelled it slowly. 'You orchestrated the marriage, and I complied, aware of the necessity for a Giancarlo-Castelli heir.' Tact and diplomacy were admirable qualities, and she possessed both.

'The conception of which is our decision,' Franco intercepted silkily.

Anamaria's expression was priceless for the few seconds it took her to recover.

'Leave it alone, *vecchia*.' Santo, damn him, sounded distinctly amused. 'You obsess too much.'

'I don't require your advice.'

'Doesn't stop me from giving it.'

Anamaria replaced her cup onto its saucer and stood to her feet. Spine straight, shoulders squared, she resembled the matriarchal epitome as she gathered up her purse. 'I must thank you for your hospitality.' Good manners won out, although her voice was singularly lacking in warmth. 'My compliments to Rosa for an excellent meal.'

Gianna joined Franco as he escorted her grandmother to her car.

'Drive carefully.' The gentle edict brought a softening in Anamaria's eyes, and she laid a gentle palm to Gianna's cheek before slipping in behind the wheel.

Santo joined them as Anamaria's car disappeared through the gates. 'Women.'

The succinct disparagement brought forth a smile. 'All women?' Gianna posed with a touch of humour. 'Or one woman in particular?'

'Anamaria Castelli needs taking down a peg or three.'

She tucked a hand beneath his elbow. 'Something you've made your mission in life, huh?'

His answering chuckle said it all.

'You're wicked.' She leaned up and brushed his cheek. 'Promise me you won't speed.'

'I'll be the model of propriety.' He crossed to the red Ferrari and maneuvered himself into the bucket seat, fired the engine, then roared down the driveway, only to ease back to a discreet purr as he gained the avenue.

Gianna momentarily closed her eyes as Franco trailed his hand between her shoulders and soothed the knot of tension there.

'Interesting evening.'

'You think?'

They gained the foyer, and his hand slid to her waist as he set the security alarm.

'Sarcasm doesn't suit you.' His drawl held a tinge of amusement, and she met his level gaze with equanimity.

'I guess I should thank you.'

'For what, specifically?'

'Rescuing me.'

His dark eyes assumed a disruptive gleam. 'What do you have in mind as a reward?'

'Absolving you from helping me restore the kitchen to Rosa's preferred state of perfection?'

His soft chuckle slid along her nerves and shredded them. 'Doesn't come close.'

'You'll probably be asleep by the time I finish up.'

He pulled her in close and laid his mouth over hers. 'Doubtful.' He let her go, and moved in the direction of his study.

Yet the bedroom was empty when she entered it, and she removed make-up, discarded her clothes in favour of an over-size cotton tee-shirt and slid between the sheets.

She must have fallen asleep, for she stirred at the touch of a hand sliding over one hip in a seeking trail to her breast, and warm lips nuzzling the vulnerable curve at the base of her neck.

It was so easy to turn in to him, to savour his warmth, the hard muscled male frame, his strength. To believe, in the darkness, the intimacy they were about to share meant more than just the slaking of desire. *His*.

In his arms she became a witching wanton, eager for his touch, the sensual nirvana he unleashed, and the shattering incandescence of primitive, almost pagan sex.

Every nerve in her body vibrated with it, and afterwards she lay spent, totally lost to him. Complete, in a way she'd never dreamed possible.

CHAPTER FIVE

TRAFFIC flow was unusually heavy and therefore slow as Gianna drove into the city, with such a build-up of vehicles it took two and sometimes three changes of lights to clear each computer-controlled intersection.

Why *Monday*, for heaven's sake?

Franco had left the house an hour earlier, preferring an early start to the working day, and would have missed the congestion.

She drummed her fingers against the steering wheel and fought against reactive thought.

Famke. How long would it take for the Dutch-born model to make her next move?

Any day *soon*. Had to be. After all, why would the long-legged blonde waste time before homing in for the figurative kill?

Gianna saw the cars in front begin to move, and sent a silent prayer to the Deity she'd clear the intersection before having to battle the next. Except no one was listening.

The morning didn't get any better, with her PA calling in sick again, and just as she thought she had a handle on the workload Franco entered her office...something he so rarely did she had the feeling the day was about to get worse.

Attired in Armani tailoring, hand-stitched Italian shoes, expensive cotton shirt and silk tie, he looked every inch the directorial executive. But it was the man himself who drew attention, for he exuded an aura of power envied and coveted by many.

Gianna examined his features, and could gain little from his expression.

'I take it this isn't a social visit?'

He withdrew a folded page of newsprint and handed it to her. 'This appeared in today's edition.'

Not an extract from the city's leading newspaper, she noted, but definitely one with a wide circulation.

She skimmed the social gossip page, honed in on the photograph of Franco and Famke, read the caption, and endeavoured to control the painful knot twisting her stomach.

Famke hadn't wasted any time.

Gianna sank back in her chair and forced herself to hold his dark gaze. 'And you thought to minimise my reaction? Spare me subsequent embarrassment?' She was on a roll. 'Offer an explanation?'

'Yes.' His voice held a dangerous silkiness she chose to ignore.

'How...' The pause was deliberate. 'Considerate of you.'

'Gianna.'

Her name emerged as a husky growl, and she had the unbidden thought he wanted to wring her slender neck.

'I don't need your protection,' she managed coolly, and felt her gaze begin to waver beneath the barely leashed anger she sensed lay beneath the surface of his control.

A muscle bunched at the edge of his jaw. 'How magnanimous of you.'

'Merely your discretion.'

She could no longer look at him, didn't *dare*, for fear he'd glimpse the emotion she fought so hard to hide. Dammit, she hadn't thought anything could hurt so much. And this was only the beginning...

Franco moved round the desk, caught hold of her chin between thumb and forefinger, and tilted it.

'For the record,' he revealed with deadly softness. 'the photograph was taken five years ago. The caption is sheer conjecture, and the article itself ignores journalistic licence and lurches close to slander.'

Control yourself, she bade silently. Don't lose it.

'You're telling me this...*because*?'

He remained silent for what seemed an age, then he brushed his thumb-pad along her lower lip and released her.

'I've already fielded a few enquiries from the media. I imagine you're next on their list.'

'And you want our stories to match? Confirm our marriage is rock-solid?' She couldn't seem to stop. 'State Famke doesn't pose a threat?' She waited a beat. 'In other words...*lie*?'

His eyes hardened. 'Are you done?'

'You have my loyalty,' she said quietly. 'Do I have yours?'

A muscle bunched at the edge of his jaw. 'You have no reason to doubt me.'

It took effort to keep her voice even. 'Thank you for bringing the article to my attention.'

The air between them was electric. Something dark moved in the depths of his eyes, then it was gone.

At that moment her cellphone beeped with an incoming text message, and she heard his husky oath as she indicated the need to read it.

She was shutting him out. Had to, otherwise she'd crumble before his eyes. And she couldn't, *wouldn't* allow that to happen.

Practice allowed her to act a required part, and she arched an eyebrow in silent query.

His eyes flared, and his features hardened as he turned towards the door.

Gianna waited a few seconds before activating the SMS, and read the text with a sense of disbelief.

Like the photo? Watch this space.

There was no name, nothing to indicate the sender's identity.

Famke? Who else would text such a cryptic message?

It bothered her for what remained of the afternoon, niggled during the drive home, and by the time she entered the grounds she was ready to do battle.

Franco's top-of-the-range Mercedes sat in its customary bay, and she drew to a halt alongside, then entered the house.

The kitchen was first, and she found the comfortably proportioned housekeeper intent on fixing dinner.

'Hi, Rosa. Everything OK?'

The housekeeper offered a warm smile. 'Sure. Special delivery package came for you. I put it on your desk.'

'Thanks.' She hadn't ordered anything. Franco? She breathed in the redolent aroma. 'Mmm. Pasta *alfredo*?'

Rosa inclined her head. 'With garlic bread and salad.'

Gianna pressed fingers to her lips in a gesture of silent gratitude, then made for the stairs.

All afternoon she'd seethed in silence, cogitating how Famke could have accessed her cellphone number. And if the actress had *hers*, then it was a given she also had Franco's number.

She took a deep steadying breath as she reached the master suite, then swung open the door...only to discover an empty room, and the sound of water running in the adjoining *en suite* bathroom.

She didn't pause, just marched straight through and pulled open the shower door.

Franco, *sans* clothes, was something else. Masculinity in its most potent form, his tall muscular body sculpted to male perfection. Powerful, virile, and infinitely dangerous.

All it took was a look, and...she closed her eyes, then opened them again to meet his musing appraisal.

Damn him, he didn't appear in the least surprised, and it irked her unbearably.

'If you want to join me,' Franco drawled, 'I suggest you get rid of the clothes.'

'As if that's going to happen any time soon.'

The heat and steam proved an isolating factor as the water spray hit the marble-tiled shower base. The fact it cascaded over his tall frame did much to diminish her composure.

Get a grip. Ignore the man, focus on why you're here.

Famke...remember?

Oh, hell, maybe this wasn't such a great idea! How could she rail at him when he stood naked, water-drenched, and far too close for comfort?

'You're getting wet.'

His indolent tone prompted her into action, and she picked up the first thing that came to hand...a plastic bottle of shampoo...and threw it at him.

Two things registered simultaneously...the warning flare in his dark eyes as he fielded it with one hand and his reaching out with the other hand to haul her into the spacious shower cubicle.

'What do you think you're doing?' The words emerged as a scandalised scream as the shock of water streamed over her head, soaking her hair, her clothes...and oh, Lord, her shoes!

'If you want to fight, we should be on equal terms, don't you think?'

She offered something unladylike and aimed a fist at his chest. 'I could *kill* you!' She spared a glance at her suit and groaned out loud. 'Look what you've done.'

'Provide provocation, and I won't answer for the consequences.'

He was *enjoying* this. There was amusement apparent, and she lashed out at him, only to have her wrist caught in a steel-like grip.

'No, little cat.' His husky growl touched her nerve-ends and sensation skidded through her body.

'Don't.'

It was a helpless plea he ignored as he divested her of her clothes…not easily, as she fought him every inch of the way.

Naked, she stood before him in open defiance. 'I hate you.'

'Uh-huh.' He caught up the shampoo and began lathering it into her hair, rinsed it off, and massaged conditioner with such soothing effect it was difficult not to sigh her thanks and sink in against him.

She was mad at him…wasn't she? So why in hell was she just standing there?

Because it felt so darned *good*. Was that so wrong?

Next he picked up the soap and ran it over her body, then turned her away from him and eased the kinks from her neck, her shoulders, then angled the shower spray to remove the suds.

When he was done, he placed the soap in her hand. 'Your turn.'

Return his ministrations in kind? Was he kidding? How far would she get before *soaping* him became something else?

Without hesitation she handed the soap back. 'I don't think so.'

'Afraid, *cara*?'

She tilted her chin and met the devilish gleam in those dark eyes. 'Sex in the shower doesn't interest me.'

He didn't need to say he could easily prove her wrong. All it would take was the touch of his mouth on hers, the intimate brush of his body as he drew her in…and she'd be lost.

His husky chuckle almost undid her, and Gianna stepped out from the shower cubicle, caught up a towel, wrapped it sarong-wise round her slender curves, then curled another into a turban over her damp hair.

She emerged into the bedroom ahead of him, and she chose a tailored skirt and cotton top, twisted her hair into a knot atop her head, and was in the process of applying moisturiser and lipgloss when Franco joined her.

Without a word she retrieved hangers and returned to the bathroom to allow her suit to dry, then she gathered up everything else and popped them down the laundry chute. As to the shoes…hopefully, if they were dried carefully and polished, they'd remain wearable.

'Replace them.'

Franco's drawled dictum held a touch of cynicism, and she turned to face him.

'If I do, I'll hand you the bill.'

'Naturally.'

He'd pulled on jeans and a polo shirt, and he didn't look any less dangerous. There was a speculative, vaguely brooding gleam in those dark eyes, making it difficult to gauge his mood.

'There's something you wanted to discuss?'

'You mean, before you became *macho-man* and hauled me into the shower?'

The element of surprise had temporarily defused the situation. Temporary being the operative word.

'You want to take it up before or after we eat?'

'Before.'

'Famke,' he divined accurately.

Cynicism lent a dark tone to her voice. 'How did you guess?'

'She is bent on making a nuisance of herself.'

'Tell me something I don't know.'

'It's not something I can control, unless she steps over the line.'

And you think she won't?

There was nothing like the direct approach. 'Does she have your cellphone number?'

His eyes hardened fractionally. 'I didn't give it to her.'

Her stomach curled into a tight ball. 'That doesn't answer the question.'

'Yes.'

The pain intensified. 'She's contacted you?'

'Personally and via SMS.' He waited a few seconds. 'I haven't responded.'

'Do you intend to?'

'No.'

Could she trust his word? Did she have a choice?

'Is there anything else?'

Suspicion wasn't proof.

'Not right at this moment.'

Franco cupped her face between his hands. 'That's it?'

She wanted to say *Don't do this to me.* Instead, she conceded steadily, 'For now.'

'Then let's go eat, hmm?'

And make pleasant conversation, while pretending Famke didn't loom like a dark spectre between them?

She'd give it her best shot.

The pasta was superb, so too was the excellent red wine they shared with the meal.

Gianna cleared the table, set up the coffee-maker and took care of the dishes while the coffee brewed.

'I'll take this in my study,' Franco indicated as he joined her, and she did likewise.

There were personal e-mails, some business data... stuff she needed to take care of, plus running a check of her social diary.

The first thing she saw when she opened her study door was the delivery package sitting on her desk, and she placed the coffee down and examined the wrapping. The destination and date stamp were partially obliterated, and, turning it over, she discovered no sender's address.

Intrigued, she undid the taping, removed the wrapping...and discovered a slightly smaller box.

A frown creased her forehead. Was this a joke?

Two more layers followed, each time revealing a smaller box. So small it could only contain jewellery...ear-studs? A ring?

Not from Franco. It wasn't his style.

Gianna removed tissue and discovered a silk-covered box. Inside was a delicate velvet pouch, which at first sight didn't appear to hold anything.

No, wait… She extracted a small piece of paper, a picture of a wedding ring. With a diagonal line through it.

The meaning was unmistakable.

She took a deep breath, then slowly released it.

Her initial instinct was to dump it on Franco's desk and demand an explanation. Except that was presumably what Famke anticipated.

The actress's goal, after all, was to cause trouble… and what better way to achieve it than to keep the barbs constant.

OK, so she'd deal with it.

Action brought reaction…but what if she didn't react as expected?

Cool, calm and collected. She could do that.

With no hesitation she scooped the packaging together and binned it.

CHAPTER SIX

TUESDAY came and went without *mishap*…if mishap related solely to contact from the stunning actress via one form or another.

Waiting for the next strike to fall made for a fraught day, and by evening's end Gianna dismissed relief as premature.

It was a game, with Famke as the master player.

Wednesday moved the tension up a notch, and although she set her cellphone for all calls to go direct to the message bank, none of them were from the actress.

'Relax.'

Gianna spared Franco a level glance as he drew the Mercedes to a smooth halt in the semi-circular driveway outside Brad and Nikki Wilson-Smythe's elegant mansion.

'I'm perfectly relaxed.'

A contradiction, but one Franco chose not to pursue as they were greeted at the door by their hostess and led in to the lounge.

'You look gorgeous,' Nikki complimented. 'Love the necklace. A recent gift?'

OK, you can do this, Gianna determined. You're good at the social thing. Educated, groomed and prepared for it. 'Thanks.' Her smile was genuine.

She'd dressed with care, choosing a classic black dress with a scooped neckline and lace overlay, and added black stilettos. Skilfully applied make-up, her hair swept into a smooth twist, and her mirrored image revealed a sophisticated young woman. Confident, assured...

How looks could be deceiving!

With practised ease she moved at Franco's side, greeting fellow guests, offering conversation, sipped the excellent Chardonnay served by her host's hired staff, and when directed she took her designated seat at the magnificent long table set with china, crystal and gold flatware.

Nikki was too well-versed in the social mores to think of seating her guests while waiting for a late arrival.

Some of Gianna's tension began to ease.

'I see you've been the recipient of a little...' there was a delicate pause '...media exposure.'

There was inevitably one person who put common sense aside in a quest to make titillating conversation.

How would Franco handle it?

As if she needed to ask!

'Interesting.' His drawled voice held deceptive indolence. 'How the press seize a past event, attach innuendo and drag it into the present.'

'Distressing, I imagine?'

'For my wife. Yes.'

Gianna placed a hand on his and a warm smile curved her mouth. 'Darling, it's of no consequence.'

She even managed to keep the smile in place as he lifted her hand to his lips and brushed a light kiss to her palm.

The tactile gesture sent the blood fizzing through her veins, heating her body at the implied intimacy. For a few timeless seconds the guests, the room, faded as she became caught up in something she couldn't afford to analyse.

Then the moment was broken by light laughter and the buzz of conversation.

Had his action been a deliberate ploy to defuse the situation? Or a genuine attempt to ease her tension?

It would be nice to think it was the latter.

Nikki had selected a number of small-portion courses to tantalise her guests' palates. Dinner parties hosted in her home involved a celebration of the senses, with the evening's theme chosen with extreme care.

Tonight the theme was Thai, and the delicacies won praise for artistic presentation and taste.

Fine food and scintillating conversation spread over several hours and, capped by superb coffee, a pleasant evening drew to a close just before midnight.

The witching hour, Gianna perceived as the Mercedes purred through the darkened streets.

'You're very quiet.'

She turned her head and took in his profile in shadow, the strong planes, the classic outline. 'I'm all talked out.'

'Tired?'

'Yes.' He could take that any way he chose!

Yet it was she who lay awake, conversely wanting his touch long after he'd fallen asleep.

What would he do if she reached out and initiated a seduction? The thought he might still her hand, her lips, was enough to prevent any move in his direction.

So much for thinking Famke might be considering a reprieve, Gianna decided as she checked her cellphone while waiting for the traffic lights to change.

Enjoy him while you can

Just what she needed to start the day. The temptation to key in a blistering response was overwhelming, except she refused to give the actress the satisfaction.

She checked the time, and saw it had been sent the previous evening.

A further SMS followed later that afternoon, equally as telling, and Gianna muttered something unladylike beneath her breath.

Last-minute data download meant she took work home and spent the evening hours cloistered with her laptop, aware Franco was similarly occupied with international conference calls.

'Ensure you leave the office on time tonight, and have Rosa serve dinner at six.' Franco drained the last of his coffee, then shrugged into his suit jacket and collected his briefcase.

Gianna looked askance, and met his studied gaze.

'Minoche,' he enlightened succinctly.

How could she have forgotten?

For the past few days they'd been like ships that passed in the night...or it seemed that way! The constraints of work, each leaving and arriving home at different times, with bed the only time they connected.

Thank heavens it was almost the weekend.

Galerie Minoche numbered high among Gianna's list of favourite art galleries, situated in a rambling old two-storeyed home whose ground level interior had been cleverly converted and beautifully crafted to retain its originality.

Privately owned by one of the city's *grande dames*, whose flamboyant persona was legend, attendance was by invitation only, with a percentage of every sale donated to a charity devoted to assisting disadvantaged children.

The ticket price was exorbitant, given it served as an obligatory donation to the same charity, with a guest list comprising the cream of Melbourne's highest social echelon.

Elegance and style were apt descriptions for what could only be termed an *event*, Gianna mused as the validity of their invitation was checked by a security guard at the main entrance, ensuring only genuine invitees were granted admission. One of several guards employed to safeguard the premises, the artwork—and the guests…guests who were given a time-frame in which to arrive, after which the gallery went into lock-down, and at evening's end an identical time-frame was provided for the guests to leave.

Dinner suits and black bow tie were *de rigueur* for the men, while the women dressed in their finest and wore jewellery whose collective worth could feed an entire Third World country.

It was strictly *smile time*, Gianna perceived as she entered the spacious reception room, for there was Minoche, hostess supreme, poised to greet them.

A tall imposing figure, attired in one of her outrageously garish kaftans, and wearing so many gold bracelets it was a wonder her arms didn't ache from the weight of them, Minoche had so long discarded any first name it was doubtful she'd ever been gifted one.

Married one year and divorced the next, she'd become a female Croesus who appeared to live only to please herself.

Little was known about her early life, and various stories abounded as to how she'd acquired her wealth.

'Gianna. Franco.' Her well-modulated voice held a trace of an accent from her French ancestry, and was at odds with her appearance.

Something, Gianna suspected, deliberately orchestrated to foster intrigue.

'So kind of you to accept my invitation.'

As if any guest would refuse! To do so without

just cause would be akin to committing social suicide.

'Please, go join the guests...and enjoy!'

The finest champagne served in crystal flutes was in abundance, and the catered canapés were to die for.

Uniformed staff proffered both at every discreet turn, and it was a known fact hired staff stood in line for the opportunity to serve at Minoche's soirées.

Familiar faces, from High Court judges to scions of the medical profession, captains of business and industry, those representing old money and new, each incredibly wealthy in their own right.

These men bought with a trained eye for capital gain, should the artist ascend from relatively unknown to legendary fame, and to indulge their wives and/or mistresses.

Professional photographers were forbidden, and no cameras were permitted.

Women dressed to impress, and racked up a small fortune in body maintenance. Social gossip included a guessing game as to who had recently undergone the latest procedure. Names of good cosmetic surgeons were exchanged...preferably those residing overseas to mask the real reason for a trip.

For Gianna, it was the art which drew her interest.

Displayed in rooms and annexes, assembled by category, the canvases encompassed the avant-garde, the exotic, even the bizarre, and varying attempts to compare with the Impressionists and the Great Masters.

Vivid slashes of colour in some, muted brush-strokes in others, they represented the mood and expression of the individual artist.

Furniture and furnishings lent an ambience which heightened the works' appeal, and owed much to Minoche, whose keen interest in art lay reflected in each room, each annexe.

No expense had been spared, and Gianna had little doubt the *objets d'art*, exquisite porcelain, jade, were priceless originals, and not merely very good copies.

'See anything you like?'

She turned at the sound of Franco's voice and viewed him carefully. 'Maybe one,' she qualified on reflection. 'The artist employs a similar brushstroke technique to that favoured by Claude Monet.' The colours, however, were a little too delicate to do the garden scene justice.

'Franco. Gianna.'

The soft feminine voice was familiar...far too familiar for Gianna's peace of mind, and one she'd never thought to hear at Galerie Minoche, given the strict invitation protocol.

'Famke.' She could do polite...for now.

The actress looked even more strikingly beautiful in a black barely-there gown that alternately clung and revealed with designer perfection.

And there, at her side, stood the reason why the stunning blonde had gained entry. Gervaise Champeliere, the son of one of Minoche's closest friends, whose family wealth went through the strato-sphere.

Gianna mentally gritted her teeth.

With Gervaise at her side, Famke was guaranteed entry to any soirée in the city. Oh, why not go for broke and include the entire nation, Europe, America and the United Kingdom?

'Gervaise,' Gianna acknowledged, and allowed him to kiss her hand.

Given Gervaise and Franco were friends as well as business associates, it seemed inevitable they'd spend part of the evening together.

Something Famke had deliberately orchestrated, Gianna decided, and it provided concern for just how far the actress would go in her 'Get Franco' campaign.

Nervous anxiety was hell and damnation. It kept her awake nights and clouded her thought processes.

He was *hers*, dammit.

On reflection, Franco had always been part of her picture. Older, taller, more *physical* than any male she knew. At first she'd imagined the sensual aware-ness she'd experienced was simply a female/male thing, perhaps even verging close to a healthy dose of hero-worship. Then he'd disappeared out of her orbit...New York, London, Milan, returning at inter-vals, often with a different woman in tow.

Until the accident which had altered the structure of Giancarlo-Castelli and provided the power to change their lives.

Now he was hers, and she intended to fight to keep him. Whatever it took.

'Shall we examine the exhibits?'

Franco's smooth drawl drew the actress's swift response, together with a seductive smile that hinted at a thousand delights.

Forget *hint*, Gianna accorded wryly, and go with *promise*. Damn, the woman was good! What man wouldn't rise to the occasion…literally!

She closed her eyes, then quickly opened them again. *Get a grip.*

Watching Famke work both men was a fascinating experience. Gervaise, however, was no one's fool, and Gianna doubted he was unaware of the actress's guile.

Could she attribute to Franco the same *nous*? Or was his memory enhanced by having slept with the inimical Famke?

Although *sleep* wouldn't have been on the agenda!

Dammit. If she could, she'd walk out and take a cab home. Except good manners and social etiquette forbade such an action.

It was relatively easy to slip into social mode, to smile, make conversation and give every appearance she was enjoying herself.

If Franco noticed she was overly vivacious, he gave no sign. In public, and especially in Famke's presence, she had no recourse but to accept the touch of his hand to her waist, the occasional soothing brush of his fingers down her spine, his smile, with its latent gleam of amusement, almost as if he could read her mind, her mood, and was mildly entertained by her thought processes.

After one flute of champagne she switched to mineral water, thereby ignoring the temptation to suffer Famke's presence beneath a mind-numbing influence of alcohol.

An hour in the actress's presence was too much, and she sought temporary escape in the ladies' powder room.

It didn't last long, for just as she was about to emerge Famke walked through the door.

What now?

Verbal pistols at five paces?

Gianna stifled the bubble of hysterical laughter that rose in her throat. Unless she was mistaken, the actress was on a mission, for her features lacked polite civility.

'When will you get the message?'

Oh, my, no pretence, just shoot straight for the heart, why don't you? OK, she could play this game. Hell, she even managed to dredge up a smile. 'Step aside and let you have Franco?'

Famke's eyes took on an unnatural brilliance. 'He was always going to be mine.'

'Really?' Giana inclined her head. 'Somehow that doesn't compute, given you married someone else…and so did he.'

'You poor starry-eyed fool. You think he married you for *love*?'

Forget the verbal pistols and go with up-front personal combat!

'Of course not. It's a business deal.' She waited a beat. 'The fact he's an animal in bed is a wonderful bonus.'

The actress's mouth curved into a dangerous smile. 'I doubt you indulge in any wild fantasies.'

Gianna matched the smile. 'Depends on your definition of *wild*.'

As a parting shot it didn't work, as Famke came back with a silky threat guaranteed to send shivers down the most hardened spine.

'Watch your back, darling.'

It wasn't so much the words, but the deliberate intent that accompanied them.

A fellow guest entered the vestibule, and Gianna took the opportunity to exit with a degree of dignity.

Franco appeared deep in conversation with a colleague as she re-entered the main room. Almost as if he sensed her presence he glanced in her direction and subjected her to a searching appraisal.

Looking for battle scars?

'I see no visible signs of distress,' a male voice drawled, and she turned to find Gervaise at her side.

'An interesting observation,' she offered, and glimpsed concern in his dark gaze.

'You think?' The warmth of his smile could melt a thousand feminine hearts. 'Walk with me. Let us admire the works of art, and you shall choose one for me to buy.' He glimpsed her momentary indecision. 'Famke will zero in on Franco, who in turn will choose to rescue you from my clutches.'

'Really?'

'An action which won't please Famke at all.' Amusement lit his eyes. 'Score one for Gianna.'

'Maybe.'

'If I'm wrong, you can penalise me by insisting I double my donation to Minoche's worthy charity.'

She couldn't help the soft laughter as she tucked her hand beneath his elbow. 'You're irrepressible.'

'Ah, that's what all the women say.'

Together they moved from one annexe to another, noting comparisons, studying, and were intent in discussion when Famke's voice announced, 'There you are.'

Her feline purr set the hairs standing up on the back of Gianna's neck.

'We've been looking for you.'

Sure…and little pink pigs can fly.

Gervaise indicated the pale Monet look-alike. 'Gianna has persuaded me to purchase this painting.'

'It's adorable.' The actress lifted a hand in an expressive gesture. 'The colours, the scene. And the frame is perfect.'

Adorable applied to a baby, a kitten, a puppy. A painting might live and breathe in the eye of the artist, but the end result was an inanimate entity.

'It would make the perfect gift.'

She was good. Make that very good, Gianna accorded. The question being whether Gervaise would accept the bait.

'My mother will love it.'

Madame Champeliere owned not one but two original works by the famed Claude Monet. She wouldn't give a look-alike wall-space. So what was Gervaise's purpose, other than gifting Minoche's favourite charity a sizable donation?

Dared she assume he wasn't going to play Famke's game?

'The canvas is one Gianna admired,' Franco drawled, and Gervaise offered him a startlingly direct glance.

'Your wife has excellent taste.'

'Yes, she does.' He placed a casual arm across her shoulders. 'You'll excuse us? It's almost time to leave.'

Famke touched a hand to the lapel of Franco's jacket, then traced the seam with her finger. 'So soon?'

Minoche, the ever-vigilant timekeeper, activated an electronic buzzer on cue, then called upon her guests to settle their purchases and donations.

Millions of dollars changed hands, receipts were generated, delivery instructions given, and the guards began politely shepherding guests towards the front entrance.

Very few lingered over-long, and Gianna reached the Mercedes as Franco deactivated the car alarm.

A faint weariness settled over her shoulders as she slid into the passenger seat. Thank heavens the weekend lay ahead, with no reason to wake early and begin a workday.

It was bliss to lean back against the headrest, and she closed her eyes for the few seconds it took Franco to slip in behind the wheel.

A light sprinkling shower dotted the windscreen and rapidly intensified as Franco negotiated traffic.

'Tired?'

'Headache.' Not entirely untrue. Famke's presence tended to have that effect on her.

'You want to dissect Famke's unexpected appearance now, or later?'

His musing drawl irked her. 'You're driving, and I might want to hit you.'

She caught his gleaming gaze and barely resisted the temptation carry out her threat. Instead she opted for silence, and didn't break it when he eased the car into the garage and cut the engine.

Indoors, she made for the stairs and entered their bedroom, aware he followed close behind her.

'Don't sulk.'

Gianna whirled to face him. 'I do not *sulk*. Ever,' she added for good measure.

Did she have any idea how magnificent she looked with the fire of temper lighting her eyes? He wanted to pull her into his arms and tame that splendid rage...as only he could.

Yet she bore a fragility that made him pause, and he shucked off his jacket, undid his tie, and began loosening the buttons on his dress-shirt.

His eyes didn't leave hers, and one eyebrow slanted as she made no move to take off her clothes.

In one fluid movement he pulled his shirt free and tugged it off, then reached for the fastening on his trousers.

'Waiting for me to undress you?'

'No.'

'Pity.'

'I don't want you to touch me tonight.' Had those words been uttered impulsively by her mouth?

He toed off his shoes, stripped his socks, and followed them with his trousers. 'Your choice.'

Gianna turned away from the sight of him. Not that it did any good at all, for his image remained indelibly imprinted in her mind.

The perfectly proportioned male body, sculpted musculature, olive skin…lethal to any female's libido, especially hers.

More than anything she needed the security he offered, the warmth of his embrace…and oh, dear God, the touch of his mouth on hers. The sex, intimacy…

Fool that she was, she'd just denied herself all that with a few words issued in a moment of stupidity.

With jerky movements she discarded her evening purse, dispensed with her stilettos and removed each ear-stud, her bracelet, then reached for the clasp on her pendant.

Her fingers shook slightly and she cursed beneath her breath as the clasp failed to release. Oh, for heaven's sake, what was wrong with the darned thing?

'Let me take care of it.'

He did, easily, then he reached for the zip fastening on her gown, dealt with it, and let the silk chiffon slip to the floor.

All she wore was a thong, and he slid his fingers beneath the silk and gently slipped it free.

'Franco…' The plea whispered from her lips as his hands curved over each shoulder.

'Hush.' Franco buried his mouth in the curve of her neck, then pulled her in, savouring the taste of her, the sweetness beneath the lingering perfume, and sought her mouth with his own in a kiss that melted her bones.

With one easy movement he swept an arm beneath her knees, slid into bed and doused the lamp.

It felt so good to be held like this, with her cheek pillowed against his chest. His heartbeat rhythm was strong beneath her ear, and she stretched an arm across his midriff, then sank in as he brushed a soothing path along her spine.

'Sleep, hmm?'

He didn't see the shimmer of tears before she stilled their fall.

She would have given anything to possess the courage to arouse him with her hands, her mouth. Pleasure him as he pleasured her and gift him anything he chose to ask.

Would he reciprocate?

The insecurity of not being able to anticipate his reaction, together with the possibility of his rejection, stayed with her long after he fell asleep.

CHAPTER SEVEN

GIANNA left the house mid-morning for a final dress fitting with Estella. The stilettos she intended to wear reposed in their shoebox, and she'd collect material swatches to ensure the right choice of lipstick.

The charity fundraiser ball wasn't scheduled for another fortnight, but there was nothing like being prepared.

'Ah, *yes*.' Estella applauded. 'The shoes are magnificent.' Her features became stern. 'You will remember my suggestion for jewellery. And you will wear your hair up...yes?'

'Of course.'

'You intend shopping? You leave the gown here and collect on your way home. No one must see it in your car.'

Payment was made, swatches provided, and she gave the gifted seamstress an impulsive hug as she left. 'Thank you.'

'Go,' Estella bade gruffly.

The manicurist was next on Gianna's list, followed by lunch, then she spent time with a beautician, matching lipstick and eyeshadow until it was agreed the perfect blend had been achieved.

It was almost five when she arrived home, and as soon as she stowed her packages she hit the shower, pulled on jeans and a tee-shirt, then joined Franco for dinner.

'I take it you had a successful day?'

'Shopping,' Gianna enlightened him succinctly. 'It's one of women's finest sins.'

His soft laughter curled round her heart and squeezed a little.

'Should I even suggest you define other sins?'

She pretended to consider a mental list as she forked the last morsel of food from her plate. 'What else is there?'

'I can name a few.'

'Well, there's gourmet food. Belgian chocolate. Cristal champagne. Then there's pleasures of the flesh…a fabulous massage, facial, pampering time at an upmarket luxury spa.' She paused imperceptibly. 'I guess good sex deserves a place.'

Best not to tell him she placed the latter very high on her personal list of fine things. He took good sex and made it into a sensual banquet…truly a feast of the senses. A lover who ensured his woman derived the ultimate pleasure before joining her to take his own.

Gianna checked her watch. 'Time to go change.'

She cleared the table and stacked china and flatware in the dishwasher, then ran lightly upstairs.

Choosing what to wear didn't pose a problem, and Gianna selected black silk evening trousers, a matching silk camisole, and added a black velvet jacket beautifully decorated with delicately patterned gold thread. Black stilettos, exquisite gold jewellery, subtly applied make-up, and she was ready.

Franco shrugged into his suit jacket and adjusted his tie as she collected her evening purse.

His presence dominated the room, his aura of power disruptive, and he exuded a compelling sensuality that never failed to catch her breath.

Attired in Armani, shod by Magli, he was something else. No one man deserved to look the way he did.

Excellent genes. Had to be, Gianna decided as she slid into the passenger seat.

Was it any wonder he drew the eye of every woman between seventeen and seventy?

Tickets for the Cirque du Soleil held at the city's casino had sold out within days, with a review for the current show according it sensational.

Glitz and glamour ruled as they entered the large foyer, and Franco curved an arm round her waist as they made their way towards the auditorium.

Due care? An outward sign of ownership? Projecting a public image?

Oh, for heaven's sake, Gianna chided beneath her breath. Stop analysing his every action!

What was the matter with her? Since when had she become so super-sensitive?

The answer was simple. Ever since a certain tall long-legged blonde actress had burst onto the scene.

'You're very quiet.'

His indolent drawl curled round her nerve-ends and tugged a little.

'What would you like me to say?' Gianna sent him a stunning smile. 'It's a beautiful night? The show promises to be great?' *Are you spending time with Famke?*

'Can I get you a drink?'

Now, there's a thought. A flute or two of champagne and she'd float through the next few hours. 'No, thanks.'

'Something bothers you?'

Someone, she amended silently. 'What makes you think that?'

He read her too well. The too-bright smile, a tenseness that made her pulse beat a little faster.

'Shall we take our seats?'

Within minutes the lights dimmed, the curtains slid aside, and the show began.

At that moment two latecomers passed by, to occupy the two adjoining seats.

'Gianna.'

She didn't believe it. 'Shannay?'

'Franco's idea,' Shannay revealed quietly.

The evening had just become better, and she settled down to enjoy the stage presentation.

Such colour, balance and symmetry. Beauty in fluid movement and spectacle. The highly trained performers deserved all the plaudits afforded them. The audience were enthusiastic and generous with their applause, and Gianna experienced regret when the show came to an end.

'Let's go find somewhere quiet and share a drink.' Shannay tucked a hand beneath Gianna's elbow.

'Tom's mother is staying over, so we don't need to rush back to relieve a babysitter, and—'

'My wife wants to party.'

Tom's slightly rueful expression brought a bubble of laughter as Gianna joined in the game. 'Well, then, what are we waiting for?'

'An hour.' Shannay reached up and planted a kiss on her husband's mouth. 'I promise.'

'I've booked a suite here overnight.'

Shannay turned towards Gianna. 'Let me rework that suggestion.' She gave a mischievous grin. 'Ten minutes, one drink.' Then she swung back to embrace her husband. 'I adore you.'

'Same goes.'

Sweet pain pierced Gianna's heart at the look they exchanged. It was the stuff of wishes…the highly emotive kind, and unconditional love. Beyond price.

For a moment it made her ache for the impossible, then she banked it down, and kept a smile pinned in place.

They found a bar, Franco ordered champagne, and Gianna had barely taken a few sips when Shannay warned quietly, 'Isn't that—?'

'Franco! Who would have thought to see you here?'

'Famke,' Shannay concluded.

Gianna killed the uncharitable thought the actress seemed bent on discovering their every move. Coincidence wasn't a believable option.

'I'm with friends.' Famke outlined the lapel of

Franco's jacket with a scarlet-lacquered nail. 'We'll join you.'

Not if she could help it! 'Thanks, but—'

'No thanks?' The actress offered Franco a seductive smile. 'Another time, *caro*. Hmm?' She didn't wait for an acknowledgment as she walked away.

Swayed was a more apt description, and in a perfectly timed manoeuvre, Famke paused at ten paces and took a few seconds to shoot Franco a provocative glance over one shoulder.

'Should we applaud?'

Gianna caught Shannay's quiet cynicism and rolled her eyes. 'Overkill, definitely.'

'She's a witch.'

'Dangerous.'

'And then some. We need a strategy,' Shannay declared with determination, and Gianna lifted an eyebrow.

'*We* do?'

'Uh-huh.' She leaned in close. 'I'll call you.' With that she tucked a hand through her husband's arm. 'You mentioned a suite?'

Gianna bit down a wistful smile as she watched them leave.

'Want to try your luck in the casino?'

Why not? 'OK.'

Bright lights, a heavy crowd, and noise. Fun for a while, Gianna decided as she changed cash for chips and chose the spinning wheel, won and lost, and gave up on it. Franco, on the other hand, won. Naturally.

'Had enough?'

A whoop of excitement sounded from a nearby table, and she saw the croupier push a pile of chips towards the winner.

A roll of the dice looked interesting, but first the powder room. 'Five minutes,' she indicated. 'I'll be back.'

There was an opportunity to freshen her make-up, and she'd no sooner smoothed her hair and capped her lipstick when Famke joined her at the mirrored wall above the long bench of washbasins.

The thought the actress might be on a stalking mission was slightly freaky. Ditto the startlingly blue gaze via the mirrored reflection, for the smile was absent and there was no pretence at civility apparent.

Great. Verbal sabres at midnight! Just what she needed. What was it about attack being the best form of defence?

'You have something you want to say?' Nothing like diving headfirst into deep waters.

'Franco's mine.'

Gianna arched an eyebrow. 'And I'm history?'

'Got it in one, darling.'

'If you think I'll meekly step aside…forget it.'

Famke directed a pitying look. 'Sweetheart, I can do things for him you've never even heard of.'

Oh, my. This was getting down and dirty. 'You think?'

The actress ran the tip of her tongue over the edge of her teeth. 'Without doubt.'

Time for the punchline. 'Sexual tricks, Famke? How sad you need to resort to them.'

She almost made it to the door.

'Jealous, darling?'

Gianna didn't qualify the taunt with an answer.

'Want to leave?' Franco drawled when she rejoined him.

Now, there's a leading question! Cut and run...or stay. 'Soon.' She offered him a brilliant smile. 'After I roll the dice.' And ensure Famke doesn't see me slink away like a wounded warrior.

Luck had apparently taken a holiday, for the dice didn't roll in her favour, and she stood back, choosing to watch rather than participate.

It was almost midnight when Franco eased the Mercedes onto the main road and headed towards suburban Toorak. The night was clear, with an indigo sky sprinkled with stars indicating the promise of a fine day.

The Cirque du Soleil had been fantastic, and she said so as he garaged the car, adding, 'It was kind of you to invite Tom and Shannay.'

'My pleasure.'

They ascended the stairs together, and entered the bedroom.

The stilettos were the first to go, followed by her tights. The jacket, the camisole...the make-up, then the pins from her hair.

He followed her action in discarding his clothes, watching idly as the sophisticated image gradually diminished as she loosened her hair and shook it free.

Petite, and possessed of a false air of fragility that was at odds with her inner strength. A pocket dynamo, Franco mused, who, given her private wealth, could easily have become a social butterfly intent on working the social scene. Instead, she'd chosen 'the firm', unhesitating in her determination to succeed. Driven, as he was, to preserve and foster their heritage.

Women he'd slept with in the past had delighted in wearing figure-hugging nightwear in silk and lace...or posed naked for his pleasure.

Yet this woman defied the norm and chose an oversized cotton tee-shirt, which, dammit, made her look infinitely more sexy than any silk or lace concoction ever could.

'Leave it.'

Gianna's fingers stilled from gathering her hair together prior to twisting it into a braid. 'It gets tangled if I leave it undone.'

Franco crossed to stand behind her and removed her hands, then gently thread his fingers through its silky length.

Liquid fire pooled deep within and slowly rippled through her body as it brought her *alive* in a way only he could achieve.

He used his fingers to work a subtle circular massage, probing, soothing, until she almost sighed from pleasure.

It felt so *good*, and a soft sound purred from her throat as he eased forward to her temples, then worked his way down to her neck, her shoulders.

He bunched her hair away from her nape, then pressed his lips to a sensitive curve, sought the hollow at the edge of her neck, then pulled the tee-shirt free and curved an arm beneath her breasts.

The desire to tease and torment him was uppermost as she turned in his arms and began a tantalising exploration that had the breath hissing through his teeth.

Feather-light touches along highly sensitised skin, and she glimpsed the clench of muscle, the ripple of sinew as she tested his control.

Primitive pleasure, intensely tactile, incredibly intimate.

Not content, she brushed her lips in a delicate pattern over his chest, seeking a male nipple and savouring it, nibbling a little, then catching the sensitive nub with the edge of her teeth.

A husky groan sounded deep in his throat as she transferred her attention to its twin and rendered a similar pleasure before trailing to his navel, exploring it with the tip of her tongue, then brushing a path over his taut stomach to the dark silky hair couching his fully aroused penis.

Size and strength, its rigidity fascinated her, and her inner muscles clenched in anticipation of Franco's possession. The long slow slide, the withdrawal, the deep thrust as he began a pagan rhythm that carried her with him to the edge, held her there, then tipped her over to join him in raw primal sensation so intense she cried out with it.

'Enough.' His voice was a barely audible groan as he hauled her high against him and possessed her mouth with his own.

In one easy move she wrapped her legs round his waist and held on, exulting in the power and the passion as he took her on an evocative ride, utilising all the primitive sexual energy of good sex.

Very good sex, she conceded much later as she lay spent in his arms.

Santo Giancarlo adored company, and he was a generous and gregarious host. Whereas Anamaria Castelli was a stickler for order and everything in its place, Santo seemed content to live with ordered clutter…ordered by virtue of his housekeeper's diligent efforts to maintain a semblance of tidiness.

His home, he assured everyone, was *his*, and all he required was comfort, cleanliness and good food. The grounds and gardens, however, were something else.

It was hardly surprising the grandparents clashed on every level, Gianna determined as she walked around the garden at Santo's side. The one exception was their love of gardening.

Yet the comparison between grandfather and grandson was evident.

Icons in the corporate industry, driven to succeed. To look at both men, it was easy to see the connection…the same tall frame, chiselled features, the direct gaze that saw much, and beneath the surface the hard ruthless edge that set them apart from their peers.

Thirty years from now would Franco assume his

grandfather's persona, and take *life* in both hands and shake it a little?

Would she be around to know? Or would she have passed her use-by date and joined the first wives' club? Superceded by the latest young thing in eye candy?

'You're *thinking*.'

Gianna met Santo's musing gaze. 'That's a no-no?'

'Depends on the importance of the thought.'

Well, it was pretty difficult *not* to accord importance to the woman threatening to tear her heart apart!

Worse, she couldn't discuss any of her fears and insecurities about the survival of their marriage with Franco. What if he hesitated in providing reassurance or brushed off her concerns as unreasonable?

'You can bank on Franco's loyalty.'

Where had that cryptic statement come from? Was she so transparent?

'I know.' *Did she?* What a joke! She had serious doubts about her ability to know anything any more.

'We've exhausted the garden,' Santo said gently. 'And you haven't confided what's worrying you.'

Was it that obvious? She'd have to smile a lot, and try harder playing the 'pretend I'm absolutely fine' game. 'Why do you imagine anything is?'

'Put it down to a lot of practice reading between the lines of the female mind.'

It was on the tip of her tongue to ask what he

thought he saw in hers…except the answer might not be what she wanted to hear.

Franco was on his cellphone when they entered the lounge, and he cut the call…the third in succession since his grandfather had led Gianna outdoors on a tour of the garden.

He took in the faint edginess apparent, the too-bright smile, and his eyes narrowed slightly. The likelihood Santo might have said something to upset her didn't exist. So what…?

'Tell me about the Cirque du Soleil,' Santo encouraged as they did justice to the excellent *pasta al forno* his housekeeper had prepared.

'It was incredible,' Gianna enthused, and described the high points…*sans* Famke's intervention.

They shared coffee in the lounge, and around nine Franco indicated the need to leave.

'I have a report to prepare.' One that would involve at least an hour of his time. And he was due to catch an early flight to Sydney in the morning, with meetings scheduled all day, followed by negotiations Tuesday, and hopefully a satisfactory resolution. Something he'd fight tooth and nail for…and walk away from if he had to.

Gianna brushed a kiss to Santo's cheek as Franco fired the ignition.

'Will you wrap everything up tomorrow?'

He spared her a glance as he cleared the avenue and swung on to the main road. 'No. Is that a problem?'

'Of course not.'

Did Famke know he was going to be out of town? Hot on the tail of that question came another... Was the actress planning on meeting him in Sydney?

The mere thought it could be a possibility nearly destroyed her.

Gianna didn't offer a further word during the short drive home, and she merely inclined her head as he reiterated his intention to complete the report.

She'd take a book to bed and read for a while in the hope she'd become immersed in the story, the fictional characters...to the extent Famke's image couldn't intrude.

Fat chance, when her head was already filled with the unwanted vision of Famke and Franco wrapped in each other's arms!

It was almost midnight when Franco entered the bedroom, and he undressed, then slid in beside her and gathered her close.

She didn't stir, and he resisted the temptation to tease her into wakefulness.

There was an advantage in being kept busy, Gianna determined as she handled one call after another, participated in a conference call and attended a meeting.

As the day progressed it was impossible not to spare a thought to how Franco intended to spend the evening. A business dinner...or dinner *à deux* in his hotel suite with Famke?

Oh, for heaven's sake! Talk about paranoia! There was every chance Famke knew nothing of Franco's business schedule.

Yet within a week the actress had managed to inveigle a spot as guest at a charity dinner, expose photographs in the social column of the city's newspaper, appear at Saturday evening's show…and let's not forget the few verbal warnings.

Famke's intention was crystal-clear.

Franco's reaction, however, was not.

Gianna's cellphone rang, and she picked up to discover Shannay on the line.

'Feel like taking in dinner and a movie tonight?'

'Tom—?'

'Said Franco's out of town, and you might feel like a girls' night out.'

Good friends were wonderful! 'You're on,' she agreed at once. 'Give me a time and place, and I'll meet you there.'

Shannay reeled off both with alacrity, and as soon as Gianna cut the call she immediately made another to Rosa.

The day suddenly took a brighter turn, and she took time to go home to shower and change before meeting Shannay at Southbank.

'A glass of wine with dinner. We both have to drive,' Shannay determined as they perused the menu, made a selection, then gave their order.

'OK…now, *give*,' Shannay demanded as soon as the waiter had moved away from their table.

Gianna raised both eyebrows. 'Be specific.'

'Famke.'

'Ah.'

'What are you doing about her?'

'Aside from wanting to tell her go jump?'

Shannay leaned back in her chair. 'Thank God. For a moment I had serious doubts.'

'She and Franco—'

'I know. But that was ages ago, and it was over before it even got started.'

She had a vivid memory of *weeks* rather than days. Anguish, heartache, *pain*. Imagination was a terrible thing!

'But now she's divorced and—'

'Has Franco in her sights.' Shannay took a sip of wine, and became contemplative. 'Not that she stands a chance.'

'You think?'

'Why?' Shannay argued. 'When he has *you*?'

'Shannay, I adore you. But let's not forget my marriage isn't exactly a love match.'

'Isn't it?'

'Maybe on my part, but not on his.'

'Oh…*fiddlesticks*.'

'You've arrived at this conclusion *because*?'

The waiter delivered their starter, and Shannay paused until he'd moved out of earshot.

'I've seen the way he looks at you.'

Gianna surveyed her friend over the rim of her glass. 'Lust.'

'There are those who are not blind, but cannot see.'

'Uh-huh. And there are those who only see what they want to see.'

Shannay lifted both hands, palms out. 'OK, let's

break for a while.' Her features became serious. 'But if you think I'm done, forget it.'

The fact Shannay didn't bring up the subject again until after they'd finished the main course said much for her restraint.

'You can't allow Famke to see her strategy is getting to you.'

'I'm working on it.'

'Don't underestimate her,' Shannay warned. 'She's a bitch.'

'Already got that one.'

The waiter appeared, cleared their plates, and queried dessert preferences.

'Fresh fruit, and coffee—black.'

Shannay checked her watch. 'We should move soon if we want to make the movie on time.'

They made it into the cinema just as the lights began to dim. Light and funny, with good acting, believable characters and wonderful dialogue, the movie provided plenty of laughs.

'Coffee?' Shannay suggested as they emerged into the main foyer. 'You're in no hurry to get home, and Tom indicated pumpkin time.'

Gianna looked askance.

'Cinderella…midnight?'

She should have got it. The fact she hadn't said much for her state of mind!

Coffee—decaf otherwise she wouldn't sleep—sounded like a good idea, and she entered a trendy café at Shannay's side.

'Looks as though everyone has the same idea.'

It was crowded, and they managed to find a table more by luck than anything else, and ordered two decaf lattes.

'What you need to do,' Shannay began, 'is be friendly with the enemy. In public.'

'Don't give up, do you?'

'Hey, we shared kindergarten, boarding school, and we did the bridesmaid thing at each other's wedding. I'm first in line to kick butt.'

'Loyalty is a wonderful thing, and I thank you for it,' Gianna said with a tinge of amusement.

'But it's your butt to kick?'

'Yes.'

'Shannay. Gianna. Two of my favourite women.'

The faintly accented voice was familiar, and they turned in unison to see Gervaise Champeliere and his brother, Emile. Gervaise indicated the two empty chairs.

'There don't appear to be any empty tables. May we join you?'

'Of course.'

'No women in tow tonight?' Shannay teased after they'd placed an order for coffee.

'A business dinner.' Gervaise effected a light shrug. 'A walk in the night air seemed a good idea, and maybe a coffee...'

Two powerful businessmen, friends and associates of both Tom and Franco. What could be more pleasant than to share coffee and conversation for a while?

The only down moment was provided by a photographer, who reeled off several shots as they were about to leave. One of the social paparazzi on the night prowl, hoping for a scoop.

A telling caption would turn innocence into compromise, for the name of the game was to sell copy.

Gervaise murmured something vicious beneath his breath.

'Well, that was fun.'

Emile tossed a note onto the table to cover the bill. 'Where are you parked?'

They reached Gianna's BMW first, and the girls hugged, murmured mutual thanks, and within minutes Gianna entered the main stream of traffic.

It was almost midnight when she entered the house, and she checked the answering machine, discovered two messages, neither of which was from Franco. Her cellphone wasn't registering any SMS texts, and the doubts she'd held at bay over the past few hours rose to the surface, invading her mind and eventually her dreams.

CHAPTER EIGHT

WHAT price fame? Gianna wondered cynically as she opened the morning newspaper and flipped to the social page. For there, featured in a prominent position, was a photograph taken inside the café the night before.

Four people, happy, with an implied intimacy that didn't exist. The caption endorsed the image, employing subtle speculation that caused Gianna to close the newspaper in disgust. The social grapevine would have a field-day as gossip became embellished and blown out of all proportion.

She was all too familiar with the process.

Syndication posed the question whether the photograph might also appear in one of the Sydney newspapers. Next, if Franco might see it before she had the opportunity to explain.

Which meant she should make a phone call and alert him.

Her cellphone pealed and she checked the caller ID, recognised Shannay's number, and picked up.

'It's in.' Her voice was brisk. 'Tom suggests damage control. He'll run it by Franco. You OK?'

'About to walk out the door. I'll call you later.'

She had Franco's cellphone number on speed-dial,

and she hit it, only to have the call go straight to the message bank.

Damn. He could be in the shower, having breakfast, or…indulging in a bedroom romp with Famke?

Don't go there, an inner voice screamed.

It took effort to bank down the image and mentally discard it.

Focus on what you have to do, she bade herself firmly. Right now, that involves going in to the office to work.

She almost made it…almost. Would have, if she hadn't opened an incoming text message as she sat in traffic waiting for a set of lights to change.

Loved photo. Sydney wonderful. Famke.

Gianna tossed the cellphone onto the passenger seat with an audible growl of anger. What had taken her so long?

Until Franco had left the hotel suite and taken a cab to wherever he was due for the day? After Famke had ensured he'd sighted the appropriate page in the morning newspaper?

Dammit, she had no problem visualising *that* scenario in vivid detail.

To say it ruined her day was an understatement. She didn't know whether to weep, rage…or throw the worst hissy fit in known history!

Instead, she buried herself in work, made the necessary calls…except to Franco. *Him* she'd deal with in person!

Anamaria phoned, with an invitation to morning tea on Saturday.

Lunch was a salad sandwich eaten at her desk, and she was so *businesslike* during a mid-afternoon marketing meeting it was almost a joke. Except the façade was the only thing that permitted her to hold everything together.

The cracks began to appear as she battled peak-hour traffic, and she hammered her car horn twice, muttered something ugly beneath her breath...when normally she would have contained herself.

Franco's Mercedes wasn't in the garage, and she didn't know whether to be disappointed or pleased at gaining extra time ahead of initiating a confrontation.

Yet he could drive up any time soon, and with this in mind she went through to the kitchen. It was better Rosa wasn't within earshot when she launched into combat mode!

Food was the last thing on her mind, but she gave Rosa the necessary assurances regarding dinner before going upstairs to change into sweats and a pair of trainers, then she caught her hair back in a ponytail and descended the stairs to the gym.

A workout might serve to channel some of her anger, and she did time on the treadmill, utilised hand-weights, used the rowing machine, the Exercycle, then she donned boxing gloves and worked up a sweat pounding the punching bag.

Gianna was almost done when Franco entered the gym, and she didn't break until he moved into her line of vision.

Seconds were all it took to register he'd abandoned

the trappings of formal business apparel for sweats and trainers.

'You have reason to go so hard with this?'

'It's a substitute for *you*.'

He reached out and stilled her flailing arms with galling ease. 'How so?'

She glared at him. 'As if you don't know!'

Franco caught the pent-up anger, the darkness evident in her eyes, and tightened his grasp. 'Gervaise has been in touch and filled me in with—'

'This isn't about Gervaise.'

His features hardened. 'Then what the hell is it about?'

'Let go of my hands.'

He did…only to visibly wince when she lashed out with an unexpected punch, and he fielded another before it could connect.

'You want to fight with me?'

Gianna ignored the silky threat evident. '*Yes*, damn you!'

The top of her head barely reached his shoulder, and he had to be twice her weight. 'Pick something at which you might have half a chance.'

Kick-boxing wouldn't cut it. He had the expertise, longer and more powerful legs, and he'd never give her an opening to get in close enough to connect.

Her growl of frustration was very real, and her eyes gleamed with anger as he pulled off her gloves.

If looks could kill, he'd be dead already.

'You're trying my patience.'

She'd tortured herself with painful images all day.

A strenuous workout had done nothing to diminish the anguish, and she desperately wanted him to *pay*.

'So…bite me.'

'Now, there's a provocative thought.'

Gianna slapped his face. Hard. And nearly died at the cold anger evident.

'You have two minutes to explain yourself.'

Two angry people facing off. How much worse could it get?

'One minute fifty seconds.'

Belligerent temper wasn't her thing. Never had been. So why resort to it now?

Because she couldn't bear the thought of losing him…yet was terribly afraid she might.

'Gianna.' His voice held a silky warning that prompted her into speech.

'Famke sent me an SMS informing me that she spent the night with you in Sydney.'

Dear heaven. Did he have any idea how *tortured* she felt by it?

'You believed her?'

She'd tried so hard not to! Even given the actress's propensity for diabolical behaviour, the SMS had provided that one grain of doubt. By the end of the day, that was all it had taken to set her mind into overdrive.

'She's an ex-lover, she wants you, and she's made it clear she's prepared to do anything to get you.' Without a care if she destroys me emotionally in the process.

'Therefore making it a *fait accompli*?' His eyes

were dark, and tinged with latent anger. 'Aren't you forgetting something?'

Gianna looked at him in silence.

'Famke might have a picture in mind...but I don't choose to be in it.'

'You might care to tell her that!'

'I already have.'

Could she believe him? *Should* she?

'Whatever happened to trust?'

If I was secure in your love, trust wouldn't be an issue. Words she couldn't bring herself to utter without revealing the depth of her feelings. And she didn't want to give him that power.

'You think I'd break my vow of fidelity?'

I don't know.

'If Famke flew in to Sydney, I was unaware of it.' His voice reminded her of silk-sheathed steel. 'You have my word. It should be enough.'

He crossed to the rowing machine, and she refused to observe, even for a few seconds, his impressive muscles flex as he began to work the machine.

Instead, she went upstairs, stripped off her sweats and took a leisurely shower, then she donned casual jeans, added a top, and sequestered herself in her study.

The thought of food made her feel almost physically ill, and she opened her laptop and set to work.

Shannay phoned around eight-thirty, and began without preamble, 'You were supposed to return my call.'

How could she have forgotten? 'I'm sorry. It's

been quite a day.' A gross understatement if ever there was one.

'Tom has made a reservation for the four of us to dine together tomorrow night. Franco has the details.'

She tried for enthusiasm, and made it...just. 'Great.'

'Did you receive any flak re the newspaper photo?'

'A call from my grandmother, suggesting morning tea Saturday. I'm expecting words of wisdom together with a reminder to observe circumspection at all times.' She paused. 'You?'

'Mother, ditto. No breath of scandal...etc.'

Shannay ended the call, and Gianna put in a further two hours' work, then shut down the laptop and retired for the night.

Alone. Of Franco there was no sign, and she slid into bed and snapped off the lamp.

There was a note written in Franco's script propped on the table when Gianna went down to breakfast next morning.

Meeting Tom and Shannay, six-thirty, city

Damage control. Two couples, projecting happiness and togetherness, ensuring they gained the necessary exposure to warrant a photograph in the social page of tomorrow's newspaper. Thus contradicting media innuendo regarding the state of each marriage.

It sounded like a plan.

Had Franco alerted Rosa they would be dining out?

Gianna wrote a note and attached it with a magnet to the kitchen fridge.

The restaurant numbered high as one of the city's finest, and was deliberately chosen because it was a known haunt of the rich and famous.

'You think this is going to work?'

Shannay lifted her crystal flute and tipped it in silent salute. 'Who cares?' She offered an elfin smile. 'We get to enjoy each other's company, eat fine food and drink champagne.'

Gianna touched the rim of her flute to Shannay's in agreement. 'What more could anyone ask?'

Her friend's mouth assumed a mischievous tilt. 'Gervaise, Emile, and call it a party?'

'That might be taking things a bit far.'

'You think?'

'Behave,' Tom admonished.

'It's been a difficult day,' Shannay confided. 'My stepdaughter demoted me to the stepmother-from-hell because I failed to agree purple is the hair colour of choice with the *in* crowd. This was at breakfast, which is not my best time of the day. A brief respite during school hours, after which my stepson decided to test me by assuring an ear-stud *is* a permissible accessory to his school uniform.'

Gianna endeavoured to hide a smile. 'Oh, dear.'

'Yesterday,' Shannay continued, making the most of her moment, 'one of his friends said I was cute, and earned himself a bloodied nose. This, of course, did not go down well and gained a detention.'

'Totally your fault you were under the right table when *cute* was being handed out.'

Shannay fixed her with a telling look. '*You* are supposed to be my very best friend. Shall I go on?'

'Must you?' Gianna teased.

'There's more. The ultimate sin for a stepmother is to wear a size smaller than her stepdaughter.'

'Tears and tantrums duly evolved,' Tom elaborated. 'And yet she wants babies.'

'Ours will be different.'

'Darling, they too will grow to be teenagers.'

'What a sobering thought.'

Tom engaged Franco in stock market graphs, and Gianna considered the dessert menu, then opted for tea.

As the waiter moved away she caught sight of a camera flash, and she alerted quietly, 'Paparazzi.'

The photographer was quick...he probably had to be in order to cover several hot spots in an evening.

'Mission accomplished,' Shannay declared as he disappeared out through the door.

They lingered a while, enjoying the camaraderie of established friendship.

'We must do this again.' Franco caught hold of Gianna's hand and threaded his fingers through her own as Shannay bestowed a hug.

'Lunch, some time soon?'

'Call me.'

They strolled in different directions to where their

cars were parked. The city streets would soon come alive as diners emerged from various restaurants. But for now it was relatively quiet, and Gianna leaned back against the headrest and closed her eyes.

She had a busy few days ahead of her. So too did Franco. He worked long hours, rising early to do a daily workout in the gym, and he travelled frequently. Interstate, overseas. Wheeling and dealing, maintaining that essential edge to keep Giancarlo-Castelli ahead of the rest.

Summoned to report, Gianna mused as she slid her BMW to a halt beneath the portico attached to Anamaria's imposing home with little doubt as to the reason behind the invitation to share morning tea.

Ten minutes, possibly fifteen, she calculated, before her grandmother launched into chastising mode.

Less…which meant this must be more serious than she'd first thought. Worse, a folded newspaper lay within hand's reach.

'Gianna,' Anamaria began without preamble as she indicated the pertinent photograph, 'what were you *thinking*?'

Her explanation wasn't going to fly…sometimes the most simple truth never did. However, she could only try.

'I met Shannay for dinner and a movie. We went for coffee later. Two friends were among fellow customers, and they joined us.'

'Two *male* friends.' Anamaria barely gave pause. 'With whom you were photographed.'

Why did she feel like a recalcitrant pupil being called to account by a headmistress? 'It was spontaneous, and completely innocent.'

'Of course.'

Well, thank heavens for small mercies! And a degree of familial loyalty!

'However, that isn't how it appears. The caption gives cause for speculation.' Her grandmother drew in an imperious breath and slowly released it. 'And merely adds fuel to that foolish actress's *contretemps* with the media.'

A discreet knock at the door heralded the housekeeper's arrival with a loaded tea tray, from which Anamaria indicated she herself would serve...and immediately did so.

'It would be advantageous if an announcement could be made.'

The morning just got worse.

'Prior to conception?' It was impossible to keep the edge of cynicism from her voice, and her grandmother's eyes narrowed.

'The inability to conceive bothers you?'

There was never going to be a better time. 'It bothers me that you continually stress the issue.'

Anamaria appeared to straighten her shoulders and draw in breath...with no visible sign of movement. An optical illusion?

'You do...sleep together?'

'You mean...have sex?' It was difficult not to burst into laughter, except it might veer towards the hysterical. 'With active frequency.' Oh, why not go the full distance? 'And, no, we don't use protection.'

Was that a tinge of colour beneath the delicate rouge on her grandmother's cheeks?

'Can we agree for you to leave the subject alone?' Gianna said gently. 'It's become tiresome.'

'Very well. I apologise.'

She couldn't recall a time when Anamaria had offered an apology to anyone. Certainly not within her presence. 'Thank you.'

CHAPTER NINE

IT WAS almost midday when Gianna left, and she visited a few exclusive boutiques along Toorak Road, then took time to eat something healthy for lunch before heading for an antiques auction.

One of several such auctions held throughout the year, today's event featured select hand-crafted pieces and formed part of a collection.

A number of cars lined the suburban avenue, and she joined many potential bidders intent on viewing the various items on display in the old, beautifully kept home.

A deceased estate, with family choosing to sell.

Gianna was almost moved to tears at the thought of several exquisite rosewood pieces being separated and taken to different houses, when they so obviously belonged together.

Fool. They're inanimate pieces of wood, they have no soul... But the craftsmanship was superb, carved with loving hands and an empathy with the tool.

Then she saw it...a small desk, with a delicate inlayed top and beautifully carved legs. Perfection.

Gianna traced gentle fingers along its surface, felt the smoothness of the wood, and fell in love with it.

'Pretty, isn't it?'

I don't believe it. Famke? *Here?*

Without doubt, the actress's appearance at every turn went way past the possibility of coincidence.

'Why don't I give you a copy of our social calendar?' she ventured silkily. 'Then you won't have to knock yourself out discovering my every move?'

Famke gave her a withering look. 'Darling, who cares about *you*?'

'Of course. I'm merely the appendage inconveniently attached to Franco.'

'Yes.'

Succinct, and delivered with a poisonous sting. So what else was new?

It was way past time she did a little stinging of her own! 'How is your daughter?'

Blue eyes assumed the iciness of an arctic floe. 'My daughter has nothing to do with this.'

Gianna arched an eyebrow. 'No?' Her pause was deliberate. 'I assume you've left her in very good care while you're absent on the other side of the world?'

'She has a nanny.'

'Poor child. Deprived of a mother who pursues what she wants...professionally and personally.'

'I share custody with her father.'

Gianna pretended to examine her nails. 'Aren't you afraid you might have your custody reduced, or even lose it completely?'

'Are you *threatening* me?'

'Not at all. Just making conversation.'

'I'm entitled to a life of my own.'

'Yes, you are. But not with my husband.'

'But then, he's never really been *yours*...has he?'

She was never going to have the last word. So she made it easy, and simply turned and walked away.

Not so easy to dispel her irritation. So far the day was turning out just peachy...

The auction began promptly at two-thirty, with spirited bidding and high closing figures as one by one the items were sold.

The beautiful desk Gianna coveted attracted several bids, soon diminishing to four, then three, and finally two serious bidders...

It became a game, and all about winning, as she topped every bid Famke made, going ridiculously high in a room strangely quiet apart from the auctioneer's voice.

Those present caught there was something more going on, and soon there were whispers, conjecture Gianna chose to block out.

A male voice joined the bidding, a voice she recognised only too well, and she spared Franco a quick glance, then looked away.

That *he* might want the desk for himself was ludicrous. So why was he bidding? The more pertinent question had to be for *whom* the desk was intended?

Gianna registered the excessively high bid and made her final call. It had gone way past sensible bidding and become a pathetic game between two women determined to outdo each other.

Well, she was done. Over it.

Franco made an astronomical bid that drew a collective gasp from those gathered in the room...

followed by an ensuing silence signifying his success, and the bidding was closed.

'Franco!'

Famke's exuberance was overwhelming, including
as it did the wrapping of her arms round his shoulders. However, the overt kissy thing to each cheek
went way over the top.

Although, to do him justice, he immediately ex-
tricated himself and caught hold of Gianna's hand in
a bone-crushing grip.

The temptation to wrench free was difficult to resist, and she dug her nails in *hard* as a silent protest.
An action which resulted in Franco threading his fingers through her own.

Famke, who should have registered their public
solidarity and melted into the crowd, merely tucked
her hand beneath his arm and hung on.

Flanked by two woman...one of whom was his
wife, the other his former lover. It resulted in a photographic moment which irked Gianna no end.

Orchestrated by Famke?

Or was she becoming delusional? Surely that was
Famke's field?

When in doubt...*smile*. She could do that.
Anything less would send the gossip grapevine into
overdrive.

Even Franco's deliberate action in removing
Famke's hand did little to ease the anger simmering
beneath the surface.

She wanted to leave and escape the veiled conjecture, except she was too well-schooled in the need

for public unity. In private, however, she intended to nail him to the wall!

If he thought brushing a soothing thumb-pad across the veins at her wrist would diminish her frayed temper, he was sorely mistaken.

The auction continued, with Franco successfully bidding for an exquisite leg sofa table.

Famke, not to be outdone, took an active part in the bidding, choosing to defer to Franco on occasion via an expressive lift of an eyebrow, a smile in a deliberate attempt to claim his attention.

It hardly mattered he didn't respond. The implication was there, and that was enough.

'I'll go organise the relevant details,' Franco indicated when the auction came to an end, and Gianna proffered a sweet smile.

'I'll go on ahead.'

'This won't take long. Wait for me.'

Life a dutiful wife? Stay here and watch Famke take every opportunity to play-act the coquette? Not if she could help it!

She kept the smile in place, and waited only until he was engaged in paperwork before slipping quietly out through the door.

The BMW purred to life, and she headed towards the city and Southbank, where she could wander the boardwalk, choose a café along the river-front and sip a latte. Anything to delay going home for a while.

The insistent peal of her cellphone provided a momentary distraction she chose to ignore as she slid into a parking space and cut the engine.

Franco, she determined as she checked Caller ID.

She should probably send him a courtesy text message…no, dammit, he could suffer a little!

Another call came through as she sat sipping coffee at an outdoor umbrella-covered table overlooking the river, and she let the call go to the message bank.

Ten minutes later her cellphone beeped with an incoming text message.

State your location. F

Really! As if she would meekly comply any time soon!

Gianna studied the cityscape, then idly observed the traffic flow before turning her attention to the people strolling the boardwalk.

Young couples, groups… It was Saturday evening—what better than to wander a little, eat a meal, then take in a movie, a play, or go bar-hopping before transferring to a party?

A waiter hovered, checking if she was ready to order food, and she studied the menu, chose something light and requested bottled water.

Famke's image remained a tangible entity as Gianna did a mental rerun of the afternoon.

Surely Franco saw through the actress's guile?

In the business arena he'd earned a reputation as a merciless strategist. But when it came to a conniving woman? Especially one he'd bedded in the past?

The waiter delivered the bottled water, uncapped and poured the chilled liquid. Her hand shook a little as she reached for the glass, and she swore beneath her breath.

Gianna became conscious of the sounds around her, the background music and snatches of conversation as people passed by. The excited shriek of a child, the distant traffic, an occasional horn-blast.

The early-evening air turned cool as a brisk breeze rolled over the riverfront. Waiters began lighting numerous heated standard lamps, and within minutes she was served with her meal.

Artistically presented, it looked delectable, and she savoured the aroma before forking a portion to taste.

After a few mouthfuls she pushed the plate to one side. An action which soon caught the waiter's attention.

'There is something wrong with your meal?'

'It's fine,' she assured him. 'I'm not very hungry.'

'Would you like me to remove the plate? Perhaps you would like coffee?'

Maybe a different hot drink? 'Tea?' She quickly added her preference.

Her cellphone pealed with an incoming call, and it went straight to the message bank. Minutes later it signified a text message. Franco.

Please respond.

It was the *please* that did it, and within seconds she keyed back.

Home later. G.

Within seconds back came:

Want company?

No.

She wasn't ready to face him yet.

There was no point wandering aimlessly, and on the spur of the moment she opted to take in a movie. Preferably something light and funny.

Walking alone in the city after dark wasn't a good idea, and she retraced her steps to her car, then drove to a cinema-plex, chose a movie, and tried to lose herself in the plot, the characters, the comedy.

Without much success. And it was almost eleven when she reached Toorak and garaged the car.

The slim hope Franco might have gone to bed and, please Lord, be asleep, was ill-founded, for when she entered the foyer he was there waiting for her, his hands thrust into trouser pockets.

Looking, Gianna determined, a little less than his usual well-groomed self. Unless she was mistaken he hadn't changed clothes, though his tie was gone, his shirt buttons were loosened, the cuffs rolled back, and his hair looked ruffled.

Concern? For *her*? Or was it merely contained anger he would unleash any minute soon?

'Perhaps you'd care to offer an explanation?'

His drawled query sounded like silk being razed by steel, and she unconsciously stiffened beneath the dark intensity of his gaze.

There was nothing like facing the issue head-on.

'I had a meal at Southbank, then went to the movies.'
Her eyes speared his. 'I needed some time alone.'

'You could have answered your cellphone.'

'I did. Eventually.' She stepped past him and
headed towards the stairs. 'Goodnight.'

'Don't ever do that again.'

Gianna turned and shot him an indignant glare.
'Or...*what*?'

'Don't push it.' His silky warning slithered the
length of her spine.

'Same goes.'

The silence was almost audible as she challenged
him with fearless disregard.

She was a piece of work, a conflicting mix of
strength and fragility, and she tore at his emotions in
a way no woman had been able to achieve.

Her eyes raked his tall frame, settled briefly on the
sensuous curve of his mouth and killed the thought
of how it felt on her own. She tilted her head in a
defiant gesture.

'Right now I don't feel inclined to do verbal battle.'

His ensuing silence had more effect than anything
he could have said.

For a moment she felt the surge of victory, only
for it to deflate as she undressed and made ready for
bed.

A warm shower did nothing to ease the tension,
and she emerged into the bedroom unsure whether

to feel relieved or peeved Franco was nowhere in sight.

She slid between the sheets, switched off the bedside lamp and lay staring at the darkened ceiling until sleep finally claimed her.

CHAPTER TEN

MONDAY became one of those days when whatever could go wrong, did. The planet Mercury in retrograde? The Irish gremlin, Murphy, causing mischief and mayhem?

Maybe both, Gianna decided grimly as her hairdrier refused to heat, she laddered one pair of tights and put a fingernail through a second pair. Breakfast didn't happen, and she filched a banana and tub of yoghurt from the fridge to eat at her desk, then fought bumper-to-bumper traffic into the city.

Appointments, fine-tuned to dovetail during the morning, consequently backed up and overlapped, causing her PA to issue one apology after another, which Gianna reiterated in person.

Lunch was something her PA sent out for and Gianna nibbled at between client appointments and phone calls. But mid-afternoon she'd caught up, and she began inputting data into the laptop. God willing, she'd be done around five.

Franco's text-message— *Business meeting. Don't wait dinner*—just she walked out through the door barely raised an eyebrow, although a call on her cellphone as she sat stationary at a set of traffic lights on Toorak Road did.

'Don't wait up, darling,' a familiar feminine voice

informed her with a light laugh. 'I plan to keep him out very late.'

Famke.

It didn't take much to do the maths...but was the answer the right one, or merely another attempt by the actress to cause trouble?

Gianna's first instinct was to ring Franco and demand the truth, except the opportunity was lost as the traffic began to move, forcing her to wait until she reached home.

When she did make the call, it went straight to his message bank, and for a second she hesitated...leave a message, or just cut the connection?

Cut, she decided, and endeavoured to ignore the pain in the region of her heart.

The possibility Franco might be dining with Famke almost destroyed her. To imagine them sharing wine, food...and intimate looks across the table, the anticipation, the promise. It almost tore her apart.

However, there were practicalities to deal with, and she entered the kitchen, greeted Rosa and relayed Franco was joining a colleague for dinner.

It was truth by omission. 'Please, take the food and share it with Enrico.'

'But what about you?' the housekeeper responded with concern. 'You need to eat.'

The mere thought of food made her feel ill. 'I had a substantial lunch.' Another untruth, but she didn't want to offer an explanation. 'I'll fix something light later on.' A smile came easily. 'Go.'

Rosa looked doubtful. 'Are you sure?'

'Positive.'

What she needed, she decided after Rosa left, was something constructive to *do*. Shower first, she decided, then she'd change into jeans and tee-shirt, maybe turn on the television and channel-hop for a while.

It didn't work, for she still felt as restless as a caged animal, beset with a tension that ate at her nerves as she clock-watched and endeavoured not to let her imagination run riot.

She wanted to call someone...but *who*? Shannay? Except Shannay was attending a medical dinner with Tom.

Damn. She was dying here.

OK, so she'd retreat to her studio and paint.

Tucked between the garages and the house, the room was large, airy, and held everything she needed to indulge her artistic bent. It was a hobby, something that stirred her soul and lent an ability to express her emotions with paint on canvas.

It didn't take long to change into old jeans and top, and slip her feet into worn trainers, then she caught up her cellphone, some bottled water, and entered the studio.

There were a stack of CDs—mood music to help create the ambience she wanted. Soft, dreamy wind music, opera sung by Pavarotti, Bocelli...and, at the opposite end of the spectrum, hard rock.

Tonight she needed something with spirit, and preferably loud. Tempestuous.

Gianna set up a fresh canvas, selected paints...and

began. Red, black, splashes of orange slowly took on an abstract form.

Expressive, explosive, it screamed something a psychologist would undoubtedly have a field-day with in analytical interpretation.

Quite frankly, she didn't give a fig. The method of applying paint to canvas served as a mild catharsis, and she lost track of time.

It was there Franco found her, and she was unaware of his presence as he stood watching her body language, the sure brushstrokes. He caught her intense concentration, and the edge of temper transferred onto the canvas in something vivid and in stark contrast to anything she'd previously painted.

Music swelled to a crescendo, the tenor's voice unwavering as he reached and held the high note.

Fitting, Franco determined as he crossed to the CD player and lowered the sound.

It was then she paused, holding the brush away from the canvas as she turned to look at him.

He'd removed his jacket and held it hooked over one shoulder. He'd also loosened his tie and undone the top few buttons of his shirt.

Or had Famke loosened them for him?

Although he didn't, she had to admit, look like a man who'd very recently been well satisfied by a woman.

A faint laugh rose and died in her throat. Could you really *tell*?

'That looks interesting.'

She ignored his silky drawl for a few seconds, then offered, 'You think?'

He crossed to stand next to the canvas. 'I imagine there has to be a reason why you're closeted down here at eleven o'clock at night?'

Gianna shot him a wide-eyed look. 'You mean, instead of waiting in bed eagerly anticipating your return?'

His eyes narrowed. 'The meeting ran late.'

'Uh-huh.'

'You have a problem with that?'

'This...*meeting*,' she began with masked cynicism, 'took place in a restaurant?'

'You want me to go into detail with the menu?'

She closed her eyes, then opened them again. 'I'm sure Famke will delight in filling me in.'

'Famke told you she was with me?'

His query held a deadly softness she chose to ignore.

'Affirmative.' The glare she threw in his direction would have withered a lesser man.

Franco turned slightly and tossed his jacket over a nearby chair. 'Again you chose to take her word over mine?'

There was steel beneath the silky voice, and she drew herself up to her full height...which nowhere matched his. A fact which didn't deter her in the slightest.

'Dammit, her call came through a short time after your text message.'

'So you put two and two together, and came up with ten?'

'I tried to call you.'

'I had the phone on message bank, as it usually is during delicate negotiations.'

Delicate proved the catalyst, and she threw her brush at him, then followed it with a small pot of bright blue paint.

It hit his chest, cascaded paint over his shirt, then clattered down onto the tiled floor to roll in a drunken semi-circle before tilting to a stop.

He swore briefly, with emphasis, then he undid the remaining buttons, shrugged out of the shirt, bunched it up and binned it.

Without a further word he caught her up over one shoulder and strode from the studio.

'Put me down!' Gianna beat her hands against his back, with little effect. 'What do you think you're doing?'

'Taking you to bed.'

'The hell you are!'

'It's the one place where we're perfectly in accord.'

He entered the foyer, then made for the stairs, carrying her with an ease that was galling.

'Damn you!' She tried kicking him without success. 'If you don't put me down *now*, I'll—'

'What? Hit me again?'

'Worse.' A few possibilities flashed through her mind, and she fixed on at least one of them.

They reached the bedroom, and he crossed to the

en suite bathroom, caught both her hands together, then stripped off his clothes and reached for the hem of her tee-shirt.

'Don't you dare!'

One tug, and the tee-shirt came off and hit the floor. She hadn't bothered with a bra, and she threw him a fulminating glare as he reached for the snap on her jeans.

'This is pathetic machoism!' Anger had crossed the line into fury, and her eyes blazed with it.

'Is that a new word?'

He skimmed her briefs free, and she bent her head and bit him, uncaring *where*, as long as she connected.

A vicious oath hissed between his teeth as he hauled her close and fastened his mouth over hers in angry possession.

One hand cupped her nape to hold fast her head, while the other slid to the base of her spine.

He gave no quarter as he plundered deep, wreaking a flagrant devastation of her senses until she beat her hands against his shoulders in an attempt to get him to desist.

Dear heaven. Nothing, *ever*, had come close to this.

She could hardly breathe, couldn't think, and a heartfelt groan rose in her throat, only to subside into a helpless whimper.

It seemed an age before he lifted his head, and he momentarily closed his eyes against the sight of her ravaged mouth.

'*Madre di Dio,*' he breathed in husky self-admonition.

His eyes were dark, almost black, and she swallowed nervously as he slid his hands to cup her face.

Her jaw hurt from the force of his invasion, and she stood perfectly still, mesmerised by the stark remorse evident in his expression.

You wanted to challenge him, a tiny voice intruded. Slip beneath the surface of his control and test his emotions. Unleash the tiger…

Well, now you have.

Gianna drew a deep shuddering breath, then released it. 'Please. Just…let me go.'

He brushed a gentle thumb over each cheek. 'Not in this lifetime.'

There wasn't an adequate word she could think to utter, and her lips trembled as he pressed his lips to her forehead, lingered there, then slipped down to cover her mouth with such incredible gentleness she wanted to weep.

Franco lifted his head a little and his eyes were dark, almost still as they met her own. 'If you want to check, ring the *à la carte* restaurant at the Langham Hotel and ask for the *maître d'*. He'll confirm I arrived with a male business associate at six-thirty and left three and a half hours later.'

Famke…spinning lies and creating bedlam?

Gianna became conscious of her nakedness, *his*, and she pushed free of him, then gathered up her clothes, shrugged into a robe, and walked to the door. 'I'm going to sleep in another room.'

'No.'

'You can't stop me.'

He could easily.

'But you won't,' she said quietly, reading his mind, and resisted the temptation to slam the door behind her.

It was doubtful any of the beds were made up, so she collected linen, a blanket, and crossed to the opposite wing in the house.

What price *principle*? she chastised beneath her breath as she plumped the pillow for the umpteenth time.

Sleep had never seemed more distant, yet she must have slipped into that somnolent state, for when she woke it was morning, and she was alone in the large bed she shared with Franco.

How on earth…?

Hot on the heels of wondering how she'd got there came the question as to whether they'd had sex.

She'd know. And she didn't feel…

Last night, painting, the scene in the studio, the bedroom…it all came back in vivid recall. So, too, did a degree of disquiet.

Had Franco told the truth?

Dammit, she needed to *know*.

Oh, Lord, she groaned minutes later. The time… what was the *time*? Another groan left her throat as she checked, and she hit the floor running, showered and dressed, then grabbed some fruit from the kitchen and made for the garage.

Most of the morning was spent making and taking

calls, and she enjoyed a leisurely lunch at a nearby café before returning to the office to check out targets for a forthcoming marketing campaign.

Instant visual, Gianna determined, as she considered advertising mock-ups. Simple, striking, with words that got the message across.

Hmm, now, if they took the background from one, the words from another...maybe they'd have something.

She went to work, scanning images into her laptop, adjusting, merging, until she had it almost right.

Her cellphone pealed, and she picked it up automatically, without bothering to check Caller ID.

'It's Famke, darling.'

Wouldn't you just know it!

Civility was out. A stark, 'Yes?' sufficed in acknowledgment.

'Franco appears to be incommunicado.'

She didn't comment, and after a moment's silence the actress continued, 'Convey my gratitude for the desk. It's utterly gorgeous.'

Famke cut the call, and Gianna barely resisted the temptation to hurl the cellphone against the nearest wall.

Instead, she checked the number for the Langham Hotel, and eventually connected with the right person, who confirmed without hesitation Franco Giancarlo had indeed dined there the previous evening, in the company of a male colleague, and, yes, on checking the date and time imprint on the restaurant's copy receipt, the account had been paid at ten twenty-five pm.

Famke's lies were beginning to stack up.

Could the supposed gift of the desk be another?

It was almost six when Gianna slid her BMW to a halt in the garage. Franco's Mercedes wasn't there, which meant he was taking the late flight from Brisbane.

She went through to the kitchen, breathed in the delicious aroma of roast chicken, and felt the pangs of hunger. 'Hi, Rosa. Franco is going to be late.' She checked the time. 'Half an hour, OK? I'll go shower and change.'

The housekeeper offered a cheerful smile. 'There was a delivery for you. I had it put in your study.'

'Thanks.' A delivery? From whom? And why her study?

Tension coiled in her stomach as she ascended the stairs. Not another one of Famke's nasty surprises?

Gianna reached her study and opened the door, unsure quite what she'd find.

Ohmigod… She opened her mouth, then soundlessly closed it again.

There, perfectly positioned, was the antique desk on which Franco had bid a small fortune.

She didn't know whether to smile or cry…or both. For a moment she simply stood and drank it in, then she crossed the room and ran light fingers over the wood, lingered over the inlay, checked the beautifully fitted small drawers, the keys with their tassels.

A gift purchased by a man who knew how much

it meant to her to own it. Not for its monetary value, but for its exquisite craftsmanship.

Pleasure unfurled deep inside and encompassed her body, crept into her heart and touched her soul.

Maybe she could begin to believe Famke was out of the picture. Was it possible the actress had never been *in* the picture?

Delusion, or deliberate meddling? An attempt to destroy…simply because Famke thought she could? For kicks? Revenge for Franco ending their relationship several years ago?

Gianna crossed to the phone and keyed in Franco's cellphone number, heard the muted burr, then he picked up.

'Gianna?'

The sound of his voice sent heat surging through her veins, and she was willing to swear her pulse accelerated to a faster beat. 'Thank you.'

'For what, specifically?'

'The desk.'

'It has arrived?'

There was no time like the present, and her fingers tightened on the phone. 'I owe you an apology.' Did he have any idea how much it cost her to say that?

'You called the Langham Hotel.'

She didn't pretend to misunderstand. 'Yes.'

'I'm about to board my flight.'

'OK.'

She heard his faint chuckle. 'Wait up for me, *cara*.'

He cut the connection before she had a chance to respond.

Her world suddenly became a brighter place, and she found herself humming beneath the shower. Attired in jeans and a cropped top, she returned downstairs, collected the delectable meal Rosa had prepared and took it out onto the terrace.

The sky was pale, almost opalescent in the pre-dusk light. Soon the sun would sink below the horizon and the colours gradually fade to a muted shade, then assume various shades of grey as the shadows fell.

Street lamps would provide pinpricks of light, and the tall city buildings would glow with varied coloured neon.

At this hour there was a stillness in the air, almost as if the remains of the day drew an imperceptible sigh before handing over to the darkness of night.

For it was then a different scene emerged, Gianna perceived. Some of it bright and vivacious as people dined, partied and entertained. While in the deep underbelly of the city there were those who arose with ill intent in mind, inhabiting areas where no sensible person would dare intrude.

It was pleasant to simply sit and absorb the evening tranquillity, Gianna mused. Right now Franco would be in mid-air, on a flight path to Melbourne. Two hours from now he'd be home.

There was a sense of anticipation, a spiral of sensation that began in her belly and gradually encompassed her entire body.

Could there be a chance he cared for her? *Really* cared?

She felt as if she was standing at the edge of a precipice...yet hesitant to take the final step in case she'd got it horribly wrong and Franco wasn't there to catch her.

Conflicting emotions didn't come close!

The light began to dim a little, and Gianna retreated indoors, secured the lock, carried her plate through to the kitchen, then went upstairs

She had yet to download e-mails, and she could work on the marketing strategy.

Franco found her there, deeply engrossed with data on the laptop screen, and he wandered into the room, crossed to her side and ran a light hand over her shoulder.

'Hi.' He leaned down and brushed his lips to her temple. 'Busy?'

She glanced up, met those dark eyes, and couldn't look away. 'Just...waiting for you.'

His smile melted her bones. 'Hold that thought while I go shower, hmm?'

He touched a light finger to the tip of her nose, then he turned and left the room before she should think of anything sensible to say.

The cursor blinked on the screen, and she made a few keystrokes, then closed the system down.

It was then she caught sight of the antique desk, and she closed her eyes in remorse at not having thanked him in person when it had been the first thing she'd intended to say.

Gianna entered the bedroom just as he emerged from the bathroom, a towel hitched low on his hips, his hair glistening damp from his shower.

Primitive male and intensely sexual, she accorded as he lifted his head and looked at her.

For a second the air seemed trapped in her lungs, and she couldn't move.

Ridiculous, she silently derided. She'd slept with him, shared every intimacy. Why so hesitant and shy now?

Did he sense it? See it?

Heavens, she fervently hoped not.

'The desk is beautiful. Thank you.'

'Come here.'

His voice held a gentleness that destroyed the fragile tenure of her control, and she couldn't move.

For a moment he simply looked at her, then he closed the distance between them and lifted a hand to trace the outline of her mouth...lips which trembled slightly beneath his touch.

'Famke has a lot to answer for.'

Ain't that the truth!

'She called you today.' It was a statement, not a query. 'Let me guess...she implied I bought the desk as a gift to her?'

'Yes.'

Franco's eyes hardened. 'She's a dangerous woman.'

Tell me something I don't know!

He cupped her face between his hands. 'I swear

on my mother's grave...there's nothing between us except in Famke's mind.'

There was too much evidence against the actress, too many proven discrepancies for Gianna not to believe him.

'If she calls you again, refer her to me.'

Somehow she thought it a matter of *when*, not if, as she doubted the actress was anywhere near done.

'I can handle her.'

He pressed his lips to her forehead and lingered there. 'I have no doubt you can.' He trailed a light path down the slope of her nose, then fastened over her mouth in a gentle evocative kiss that stirred her emotions and sent them soaring high.

'Hmm,' she accorded lightly, minutes later. 'This is nice.'

He swept an arm beneath her knees and carried her to bed. 'It's about to get better.'

He'd kept his word, she aknowledged on the edge of sleep. And then some. With a long, slow loving that had touched her heart and reached right down to her soul.

CHAPTER ELEVEN

DINNER held in the ballroom of a city hotel, an entertaining speech by a prominent international author, followed by the launch of his latest book, promised to provide an interesting evening.

Doubly so, given a percentage of the ticket price comprised a donation to the author's favoured charity.

Gianna dressed with care, choosing an elegant evening gown in floral silk chiffon. Make-up was understated, with emphasis on her eyes, and she swept her hair into a casual twist and secured it with a jewelled comb. A diamond pendant, matching ear-studs and bracelet completed the outfit, and she slid her feet into stilettos, caught up an evening purse and descended the stairs at Franco's side.

'Anamaria and Santo will be joining us. We'll collect Anamaria first, then Santo.'

Surprising, considering the grandparents had handed over nearly all evening social obligations more than a year ago.

'Tonight's guest of honour numbers high on a list of Anamaria's favourite authors.'

Anamaria *and* Santo…together? Oh, my, the evening had just gone from entertaining to *interesting*.

'Maybe we should seat them apart?' Gianna sug-

145

gested as Franco sent the Mercedes down the driveway, and he shot her a musing look.

'You think it'll make any difference?'

It didn't, of course. Anamaria was at her imposing best, while Santo seemed determined to tease.

Gathered in the lobby adjacent the hotel ballroom it was barely noticeable, given the number of mingling guests. However, seated at their designated table it was something else.

'Wine, my dear?'

Anamaria threw her nemesis a haughty look. 'The wine steward will take care of it.'

'Can't see one in sight.'

'Don't be impatient.'

'You are bent on telling me how to behave, *vecchia*?'

'I don't know *why* you had to be here,' Anamaria offered grimly, and pursed her lips at his slightly wicked smile.

'To keep you on your toes.'

Gianna barely avoided rolling her eyes. It was going to be a doozy of a night!

She nudged Franco's thigh, and pleaded quietly, 'Do something.'

'What would you suggest?'

'A slap on each wrist?'

'Figuratively?' he said with mocking humour.

'Of course.'

'They'll quiet down soon.'

Now she did roll her eyes. 'Don't bet on it.'

There was a lull as Anamaria pointedly conducted

what appeared to be a pleasant conversation with a neighbouring guest, and Santo, not to be outdone, turned to the guest seated next to him and did the same.

The wine steward tended to the wine, while the MC provided background information on the author, cited the nominated charity, then announced the first course would be served.

'About time,' Santo declared as a waiter delivered starters to their table.

'Incorrigible man,' Anamaria accused, *sotto voce*, and accompanied it with a look set to kill.

Santo merely smiled.

The main course duly followed, and they managed to get through it without further mishap.

'He's quite a character, isn't he?' a fellow guest murmured as a waiter began collecting china and flat-ware.

'Quite,' Gianna agreed, aware in private he was a very warm-hearted man. It was only in the company of Anamaria Castelli he became a teasing fiend who delighted in ruffling the older woman's feathers.

She cast an idle glance over the large ballroom, stilled suddenly as she caught sight of a familiar head, and wondered why she should be surprised to see Famke the centre of attention at a distant table, with yet another high-profile male as her partner.

To prove she could get anyone she wanted?

The MC appeared at the podium and began the lead-up to the guest author's appearance by listing his credits on the *New York Times* and international bestseller lists; then he gave the introduction.

Enthusiastic applause greeted the dapper middle-aged man who took the microphone with professional ease. Practised in the art of crowd-pleasing, he proceeded to do just that, with an amusing tale of his path to publication, fame and fortune.

Dessert was served, followed by coffee, and afterwards the book-signing was announced, whereupon guests began to form a queue in order to buy the book and have the author script a personal message.

Anamaria leaned forward. 'Shall we join them?'

The queue had become incredibly long. 'Why don't you stay here?' Gianna suggested. 'I'll organise a copy for you.'

'Thank you.'

She began threading her way through the many tables, and reached the end of the queue mere seconds ahead of Famke.

Coincidence, or a staged confrontation?

The latter, she cynically alluded beneath her breath. Had to be. And just what she needed to cap the evening!

'Famke,' Gianna acknowledged with marked civility.

'When are you going to get the message?' the actress demanded without preamble.

Why play pretend? 'Maybe you should ask yourself that question.'

The queue moved forward a few paces.

'There's a law against harassment and stalking,'

Gianna continued quietly. 'Persist, and you'll find yourself in an invidious position.'

For a moment she thought Famke would strike her, and she mentally reeled at the degree of hate mirrored in the actress's eyes.

'Don't gamble on keeping Franco,' came the cool rejoinder. 'You'll lose.'

She was way past playing *polite*. 'With you continuing to lie?' She waited a beat. 'Did you think I wouldn't check?'

Gianna caught sight of Franco walking towards her, and she sent him a warning look. This was her fight, and she'd do it alone.

'We speak on the phone every day.'

'You send text messages...which Franco chooses to ignore.'

Famke gave a vicious smile. 'You can't be sure of that.'

'Yes,' she said carefully, 'I can.'

'I'm not done with you.'

'Give it up, Famke,' she advised quietly. 'Leave with your credibility and your reputation intact.'

'Go to hell.'

Gianna effected a slight shrug. 'Your choice.'

The actress gave her a withering look, then turned and walked back to her table.

Oh, my, that was fun.

Franco closed the distance between them, and she looked at him wordlessly.

'I take it Famke changed her mind about waiting

in line?' Franco drawled as he threaded his fingers through her own, then brought them to his lips.

Warmth seeped into her body at his touch, and for a few timeless seconds her eyes locked with his.

Something was happening here, an intrinsic magic that had everything to do with the senses. And more. So much more. Almost as if their souls merged and became one.

Crazy.

Everything faded, and she became oblivious to the venue, the people, noise.

There was only the man.

Had she been so intent on examining her own feelings she hadn't seen what she'd perceived as the impossible?

Because she'd prepared herself so well to accept a convenient marriage, to accept affection in place of love…that she'd dismissed the possibility it might change?

Franco hadn't uttered the *love* word…but then neither had she.

Oh, Lord, was it fanciful thinking on her part, and she was seeing something that didn't exist?

The answer was simple…she could ask him.

Sure, a tiny voice derided. Just come right out with *Do you love me?*. That would go down well.

Even a one-second hesitation on his part, and she'd die.

A slight movement, the touch of his hand against the back of her waist, and she became aware of her surroundings.

'Not long now,' Franco indicated, and she realised they must have moved forward, for there were only about a dozen people standing in front of them.

Minutes later they bought the book, the author signed it, and they returned to their table.

'Thank you.' Anamaria opened the cover, read the inscription, and smiled. 'I shall treasure it.'

'That actress give you any trouble?'

Santo's questioning demand resulted in a faint smile.

'Nothing I couldn't handle,' Gianna assured quietly.

'Can't abide stupid women.' Santo turned towards Franco. 'Take care of it.'

'Already done.'

The drawled pitch in his voice feathered her spine.

Somehow she couldn't see Famke walking away without one last attempt at creating trouble. Delusion didn't factor in logic or reason, and unless she was mistaken the actress would push until she reached the limit.

Where and when that might occur would be difficult to predict.

'Are you ready to leave?'

The guest of honour stood encircled by a group of avid fans, and several people were drifting towards the exits.

Anamaria stood to her feet. 'If you don't mind?' She shot Santo a dark glance as he prepared to take her elbow. 'I'm not exactly decrepit.'

'Last time I heard, you complained of a sore ankle.'

She had? Gianna couldn't recall her grandmother mentioning any such injury.

'You're imagining things,' the older woman dismissed.

It was late when they finally reached home. It had been quite an evening, and Gianna ascended the stairs while he locked up and set the security alarm.

She felt unusually tired, and she slipped out of her stilettos when she reached the main bedroom and discarded her clothes.

Bed had never looked so good, or felt so comfortable, she decided minutes later as she slid in between the cool sheets.

When Franco entered the room she was already asleep, and he stood looking at her pale features in peaceful repose…the soft texture of her skin, the gentle fan her eyelashes formed as they lay closed over her eyes. The delicate curve of her mouth.

Her inviting kissable mouth, which he doubted he'd get to kiss any time soon.

She was something else, he mused as he shucked his clothes. Woman, witch, and the light of his life.

How could he so much as *look* at another woman when he had her?

Soon, very soon, they needed to talk.

But not tonight, he determined as he slid into bed.

He snapped off the bedside lamp, then settled close and gathered her in.

CHAPTER TWELVE

THIS ball numbered high as one of the major charity events of the year, with funds raised donated to aid a Leukaemia foundation.

Held in the ballroom of a major city hotel, the many guests included the wealthy, the society matrons and those who liked to appear to be *seen* attending every event on the city's social calendar.

An eclectic mix, Gianna observed as she entered the spacious lobby at Franco's side.

The men looked resplendent in black dinner suits, and there were designer gowns in abundance. Jewellery sparkled beneath the lights, and there was the buzz of conversation as guests caught up with friends, associates, while sipping champagne.

Judging by the attendance the night's goal for funds raised would be met. With several guests contributing large donations, the equipment needed would soon be in place.

Would Famke put in an appearance tonight?

A bubble of cynical laughter rose and died in her throat. *What are you thinking?* The chances of the actress missing an opportunity to put herself within Franco's radius were nil.

Yet, although it irked her, even brought her to anger, the deep-seated fear she'd harboured from the moment Famke appeared on the scene had begun to diminish.

There were too many inaccuracies in the actress's barbs. Franco could dispel them with unquestionable proof.

Mayhem didn't cover what Famke intended to cause. It went deeper than that as she systematically and very cleverly launched one attack after another.

Delusional psychosis?

The actress's behaviour was a worry, and verged close to requiring legal intervention.

Would Franco take that step?

'I doubt Famke will be here.'

Gianna glanced up at his powerful features, glimpsed the warmth apparent in those dark eyes, and felt a piercing sweetness flow through her body.

For a moment she could almost believe he cared...really cared. And she slipped a hand into his, felt the answering pressure, and watched his mouth curve into a generous smile.

'Want to bet?'

There were friends they needed to catch up with, polite exchanges with several acquaintances as the lobby became crowded with fellow guests.

'Love your gown.'

Gianna turned to find Nikki Wilson-Smythe within touching distance, and she returned the compliment. Nikki looked stunning...with the perfection it took most of the day to achieve.

'Estella has excelled herself.' It was true, for the colours emphasised Gianna's skin colouring, enhanced by make-up and the subtle shadings of eyes-hadow and lipstick.

She'd adhered to Estella's advice and swept her hair into an elegant smooth twist, and worn the jewellery pieces suggested.

'The ballroom doors have just opened,' Franco advised. 'Perhaps we should take our seats?'

Their reserved table was well positioned, and within minutes the remaining eight seats were filled.

Gianna breathed an inward sigh of relief. If the actress did show this evening, she hadn't been able to manipulate the seating arrangements.

The MC gave an amusing introduction to the charity's president, who in turn lauded the tireless work of committee members, achievements, goals, and projections. Images shown via slide projection and video camera touched the hearts of many. Children, some very young, with large solemn eyes, a smile at simple pleasure, and laughter in spite of adversity.

There was entertainment carefully slotted in between each course, and the food was superb.

It was during the main course that Gianna experienced a vague prickling between her shoulderblades, and she moved her shoulders slightly in an attempt to ease it.

'Something wrong?'

She incurred Franco's swift gaze with equanimity. 'I'm fine.'

Except the feeling persisted, and she glanced around the room, witnessed nothing untoward and continued with her meal.

There was a break as waiters moved swiftly to clear the many tables, and it gave her the opportunity to turn slightly in her seat.

It was then she saw Famke, seated two tables away, and for a few heart-stopping seconds the breath caught in her throat at the stark venom evident.

'You've seen her.'

How did he guess? 'You have eyes in the back of your head?'

Did she know her pulse had picked up its beat and visibly thudded at the base of her throat? Or that her breathing changed when she became mildly agitated?

He knew everything about her, *aware* and attuned to her in a way he'd never experienced with another woman.

'Yes. Don't visit the powder room alone.'

'You plan on causing a riot by coming with me?'

His fingers tightened over her own. 'Accompanying and waiting for you.'

'My own personal bodyguard,' Gianna alluded with a touch of musing cynicism.

'Minimising any opportunity Famke might seek to upset you.'

Well, there you go. 'Protection, huh?'

'That bothers you?'

'Not in the least.'

The MC took the podium and announced another round of entertainment, after which dessert and coffee were served.

It was then Gianna excused herself and rose to her

feet. 'There's no need—' She left the rest of the sentence hanging as Franco followed her actions.

Was Famke watching?

Without a doubt.

It sickened her to think the actress was willing to go to extraordinary lengths to cause trouble.

When would she give up?

The line in the powder room was quite long, and it was a while before she emerged to join Franco and resume their seats.

She didn't spare a glance in the direction of Famke's table, and now the meal was concluded, so too the evening's entertainment, it was pleasant to converse with the guests sharing their table.

'Bart wants to spend the rest of his days on board ship,' his wife confided. 'Can you imagine?'

'Restrictive, perhaps?' Gianna suggested, aware Franco appeared deep in conversation with the woman's husband.

'Sweetie, no. We'd live permanently on board and travel the world. With the option to stay anywhere we chose, then fly to rejoin the ship.'

Ah, *that* ship. Touted to be the world's largest floating hotel, with luxury suites resembling small apartments.

The society doyenne would have a ball…literally.

'I'm sure you'll love it,' she endorsed warmly. 'Think of the fun, the shopping. And the social life must be incredible.'

'Hmm, perhaps you have a point. We *do* have family scattered all around the globe.'

'Dinner with the Captain, the senior staff. The people you'll meet.' She was getting carried away here. 'The privileges. The food.' Maybe she was in the wrong business! 'Entertaining.'

'Keep talking.'

'Permanent duty-free shopping?'

'Uh-huh.'

'No cooking or cleaning? No need to fight traffic or find parking?'

'I'll tell Bart to pull out all those brochures again. This could be a very good thing.' She patted Gianna's hand. 'Thank you, my dear.'

'You should be in marketing,' a male voice suggested with quiet amusement, and she turned to the attractive young man seated opposite.

An irrepressible smile curved her lips. 'I am.'

'Perhaps I should head-hunt you.'

'With an offer I can't refuse?'

It was light-hearted fun, for he knew exactly who she was, and to whom she was married.

He named a figure that was so far over the top it was ridiculous, and wrought an appropriate response.

'You're a comedian.' Laughter emerged as a sultry chuckle. 'Your CEO would throw an apoplectic fit.'

'Ah, but then I am the CEO.'

'Really?' She wasn't quite sure she should believe him.

'Really.'

'Well, now there's the thing. Franco has no option but to afford me a higher salary package.'

'Failing which, you *will* join my company?'

He couldn't be serious, surely?

'No,' Franco intruded smoothly, 'she won't.'

'Pity. She's quite something.'

'Yes, she is.'

Mine. The word remained unspoken, but the implication was crystal clear.

Wow. She felt quite…bemused. Franco acting the proprietorial husband was an unaccustomed role.

The waiters circulated the tables, offering more tea and coffee, which Gianna refused.

The MC took the opportunity to thank the guests, the hotel venue, and then proceeded to announce the amount raised by the evening function.

Several of the older guests began to drift towards the exits, while staff efficiently reorganised sufficient floor space to enable those choosing to dance.

The band assembled, the music began, and couples gradually took to the floor.

It seemed natural to take Franco's hand and join them.

She'd danced with him countless times, and being held in his arms wasn't a new experience. Except there was some ephemeral magic heightening the existent sensuality and taking it to a place where it was all too easy to imagine they were one being. Twin halves of a soul.

It made her want to wind her arms around his neck and pull his mouth down to hers. To take and possess. Without reservation or inhibition.

This close, she was aware of the strong substance of his arousal, could feel the beat of his heart and sense the slight muskiness of his skin beneath the civil sheathing of clothes.

Humans in an animal kingdom...or vice versa? Each prey to the emotional and physical needs of the flesh.

'Home?'

There was a slight huskiness in his voice, and she shifted a little, easing out of his arms as he led her back to their table.

It took only minutes to bid goodnight to those remaining seated, and considerably longer to clear the ballroom and arrange for the concierge to have the Mercedes brought to the hotel entrance.

It had been a pleasant evening, and she said so, enjoying the silence as the car whispered through the broad streets.

'It's not over yet.'

She turned towards him. 'Promises, huh?'

Lovely. Every minute of it. From the time they ascended the stairs and entered the bedroom.

Franco removing the jewelled clip from her hair, letting its length fall free.

The sensuously slow peeling off of each layer of clothes, followed by a leisurely loving that lasted long through the night and continued into the early dawn hours.

Perfect.

CHAPTER THIRTEEN

THE third morning in succession, Gianna pondered when she felt...*different*.

It wasn't anything she could pin down, just a subtle change. A slight increase in appetite, a mild aversion to some of her favourite foods, and her breasts seemed more...sensitive.

Maybe something she'd eaten? And she'd developed a tendency towards tiredness after dinner, was ready for bed earlier than usual, and falling asleep almost as soon as her head hit the pillow.

Then realisation began to dawn...

No, it couldn't be.

She did the maths, counting back...and sank into a nearby chair as she absorbed the possibility.

A whole gamut of emotions swirled through her body...excitement, anticipation, joy. And a smidgen of concern.

A baby?

The need to *know* brought her to her feet, and she collected her shoulder-bag, caught up her keys and headed the BMW towards the nearest pharmacy.

There was a tendency to purchase the pregnancy test and rush home. Except she forced herself to wait, and spent time visiting one of the city's Sunday markets, browsing the stalls, checking out crafts and pottery, needlework.

She bought a few things, one of which would serve as a gift for Rosa, paused long enough to sip a cool drink, then retraced her steps to the car and drove home.

Franco appeared for dinner, then disappeared into his study to check his notes. Meetings on the Gold Coast were scheduled for the next day, and there was a need to plan his strategy.

Gianna delayed going upstairs on the pretext of selecting a book, one of several she'd been recommended to read.

Do the test.

OK, so she'd read the instructions and think long and hard about it.

Idiot.

Oh, for heaven's sake. *Just do it.*

It came up positive.

A pleasurable glow suffused her body, and she hugged her arms together over her midriff. Well, isn't that something?

First up in the morning, she'd make an appointment and have her doctor complete an official test.

Meantime, she'd keep the news to herself.

It was easier than she thought, for she didn't stir when Franco came to bed, and when she woke in the morning he'd already left for the airport.

Gianna managed to snare an appointment at three that afternoon, and the day seemed inordinately long as she dealt with phone calls, made several, and participated in a three-way conference call with executives in Brisbane and Sydney.

There was a half-hour delay at the medical centre, but she emerged with the knowledge she was seven weeks pregnant.

It seemed incredibly *real*, this tiny foetus, and she was sure her feet didn't touch the ground during her walk to the car.

A baby.

Gianna's mouth curved into a winsome smile as she took the elevator up to the high floor housing the offices of Giancarlo-Castelli.

She wanted to call Franco, but he was tied up in meetings and wouldn't be home until late, and she needed to share it in person, not over the phone.

It was almost six when she finally made it home.

There were a few messages, and she showered, changed, then fixed herself a mushroom omelette, added salad, and followed it with fresh fruit.

She was keying notes into the laptop when her cellphone buzzed with an incoming message, and she read the text with a sense of mounting anger.

Famke, bent on creating mischief and mayhem.

Don't wait up. We're on late flight.

Gianna's eyebrows rose. *We?*

Dammit! The chances of Famke being with Franco were slim. Discovering his movements wouldn't be difficult, given the blonde's resourcefulness combined with a total lack of scruples.

Logic provided realistic answers. Yet it was the *illogical* Gianna had a problem with!

Oh, get over it!

She knew where he was at any given time…didn't she? He made sure she was aware of his schedule. He rang in if he was going to be late. It was a courtesy they each observed.

Except there were gaps. Slices of time he could easily manoeuvre to his advantage…if he chose to.

Don't go there. You have no need to.

It was useless to wish Famke to another planet. Another country would be ideal! Hell, she'd even settle for another city!

Yet the actress was determined to create mischief and mayhem in Melbourne.

Worse, she was adept in covering her tracks.

Franco didn't appear to buy into it. In fact, Gianna was almost willing to swear he found Famke's persistence just as tiresome as she did.

At that moment her cellphone rang, and she activated it automatically.

'Dinner took longer than expected,' Franco offered. 'I'm taking a later flight.'

Gianna's fingers tightened on the slim flip-top 'So don't wait up?' Her voice was cool, cooler than she'd intended.

'The delay is unavoidable.' His voice was a silken drawl.

'Of course.'

'I'm about to take a cab to the airport. I'll see you when I get in.'

'I'll be asleep.'

'In that case, I'll wake you.'

He disconnected the call before she could answer, and she issued a heap of pent-up ire on his unsuspecting head, only to retract most of it minutes later.

She attempted to continue working, only to give it up after half an hour. For a while she surfed the television channels, then she closed it down, collected a book and settled herself in bed.

When she discovered she was re-reading pages and skipping others entirely she consigned the book to the bedside pedestal and turned off the lamp.

Sleep came easily, with the hormonal weariness of early pregnancy. At some stage she sensed Franco's presence, felt his body warmth as he gathered her in, and luxuriated in the brush of his lips to her temple, her cheek, before her mouth.

The inclination to murmur a token protest became lost as his hands skimmed beneath her oversize tee-shirt and sought delicate curves, exploring sensitive hollows with a touch that brought her *alive* and aching.

Oh, dear heaven… She wanted, needed to hold on and never let go.

'Shh,' Franco murmured as he removed the tee-shirt and buried his lips into the curve at the base of her neck. 'Let me do all the work, hmm?'

He did, with a gentle thoroughness that brought forth a shimmer of tears. The acute sensual awareness he aroused was almost too much, and the breath hitched in her throat as he savoured each pleasure pulse until she begged for his possession, exulting in the magic they shared.

Passion, at its zenith, with the power to liquefy her bones.

Together they reached the heights, held on, and lost themselves in mesmeric sensation so exquisite she wanted to capture it and never let it go.

Good sex, she acknowledged on the edge of sleep. Better than *good*, and was aware it was more, so much *more*.

They should talk. And they would. Tomorrow.

Except she woke late, discovered she was alone in the bed, and a glance at the time sent her racing for the shower.

Franco was shrugging into his suit jacket when she entered the kitchen, and she crossed to his side, cupped his face and brought it down to her own.

'What's your schedule for today?'

He deepened the kiss, and took it to a place where she had to catch her breath.

'Are you suggesting we play truant?'

His drawled query brought forth a rueful smile. As if!

'Lunch,' Gianna capitulated.

Did she imagine his brief speculative appraisal? 'One o'clock?' He named an upmarket restaurant within a short walking distance from their city office building. 'I'll book a table.' He reached the door. 'I have a late morning appointment across town. I'll meet you there.'

'OK.'

She had muesli and fruit for breakfast, followed it with hot sweet tea, then drove into the city.

The morning proved uneventful, for there were no panic calls, no dramas requiring her immediate attention, and at ten to one she freshened her make-up, caught up her shoulder-bag and took the elevator down to street level.

It was a lovely day, the sun high in a cloudless sky, and she stepped onto the pavement with a light heart.

Lunch with her husband. A secret smile curved her lips. A child. Theirs. Boy or girl? She had no preference, only that it was born healthy. Names? Was it too soon to give names a thought?

A nursery? A bedroom close to their own. For a minute or two she thought colour schemes, a nursery mural... It was like discovering a new world. She entered the restaurant, spoke to the *maître d'*, then followed in his wake.

She saw Franco, and was about to lift a hand in greeting when she glimpsed a familiar blonde being seated by a uniformed waiter.

'Ah,' the *maître d'* relayed, 'your friend has arrived.'

Friend? You have to be kidding!

The temptation to turn and walk right out again occurred as a momentary thought. Except as a solution it sucked.

Franco, to give him credit, appeared to be dealing with a mixture of surprise, dismay...and as she drew level his facial features assembled into a hard mask.

Famke, on the other hand, acted the shocked mistress caught out to perfection. *'Gianna.'*

Oh, my, she was good.

'We didn't expect to see you.'

How could the actress have known *which* restaurant, the time...unless she was bent on deliberately checking every restaurant booking within a walking radius of Giancarlo-Castelli?

Gianna suppressed a faint shiver, and speared Famke's guileless blue gaze.

'Really?' She injected cynicism into her voice. 'I find that strange, given Franco and I made arrangements to meet here.'

She shifted her attention to Franco, and her eyes hardened in silent warning as he appeared to speak.

This was her game. She was the one in control.

'What will it take for you to butt out?'

Famke gave a tinkling laugh. 'Perhaps you should ask yourself that question.'

'I already know the answer.' Hell, she hoped she did! 'I'll make it easy for you.'

This had to stop, and stop *now*. If it involved a public display...then so be it.

'I'm going to walk out of here. Franco can follow or stay.' She waited a beat. 'His decision.'

She was oblivious to the silence, the veiled interest of fellow patrons. What was more, she didn't really care!

Nor did she spare him so much as a glance as she turned and threaded her way towards the entrance. The *maître d'*, the waiters, suddenly became galvanised into action, and there was the clatter of flatware on china, the chink of goblets as patrons returned their attention to the meal.

She wouldn't look back. Instead, she inclined her head to the *maître d'* as she passed the front desk, and kept on walking.

Gianna reached the pavement and automatically turned and began retracing her steps to the office. On a subliminal level she registered how her mind seemed separate from her body…she was walking, weaving her way through the lunchtime men and women crowding the pavement, but she didn't *see* any of them.

'You were quite something back there.'

Her heart seemed to stop, then kick-start into a faster beat at the sound of Franco's voice.

'Go away.'

'Not in this lifetime.'

Her stomach executed a crazy somersault. 'I'm not in the mood for small-talk.'

'Small-talk isn't what I have in mind.' He took out his cellphone and keyed in a number on speed-dial. 'Reschedule all my afternoon appointments for next week.' He paused fractionally. 'Notify my wife's PA with an identical instruction.'

Gianna looked at him in consternation. 'You can't do that.'

Franco slanted an eyebrow, then keyed in another digit on speed-dial.

It was the first of several…arranging for Enrico to

collect Gianna's car...notifying Rosa they'd be away for a few days.

They reached the entrance to their office building, summoned the elevator and took it down to the underground car park.

Seconds later the doors slid open.

Disbelief was etched on her features. 'You can't just walk out.'

He fastened his mouth on hers for a brief moment, then released her. 'Watch me.'

He led her towards his Mercedes and unlocked the passenger door. 'Get in.'

Stunned, she complied without argument. Home in the middle of a week-day afternoon didn't sit well, and she was about to say so when she noticed they weren't heading towards Toorak.

'Where are we going?'

'To a hotel.'

'Excuse me?'

Franco spared her a brief musing glance. 'You heard.'

'Why?' The query sounded impossibly childish even to her own ears, and his husky chuckle was almost her undoing.

Minutes later he swept the Mercedes into the entrance of one of Melbourne's most luxurious hotels, handed the keys to the concierge, and dealt with check-in.

'What do you mean, we're staying here a few days?' Gianna demanded as they took the elevator to a high floor.

'No interruptions, no intrusions.'

'But we don't have so much as a change of clothes!'

The elevator slid to a halt and they exited the cubicle. 'So we purchase whatever we need.' He checked the numerical directions and led her to their designated suite.

The carded access provided entry, and she uttered a startled gasp as he swept an arm beneath her knees and carried her inside.

'Are you mad? Put me down.'

He did, but he didn't let her go, and Gianna looked at him wordlessly as he slid his hands up to cup her face.

'Franco—'

'Shut up,' he bade gently as he lowered his head down to hers.

His mouth was incredibly gentle, and he sensed the faint trembling of her lips as he brushed them softly with his own.

She was so petite, yet so strong. Vivacious in a way that lit up his world.

'Do you have any idea what you do to me?'

She wasn't sure she could even *think* as he teased open her mouth and deepened the kiss into something that made her lose all sense of time and place.

'You're wearing too many clothes.'

His soft laugh feathered down her spine. 'Let's take this slow, *cara*. Hungry?'

'Are you talking food or sex?'

'Both.'

'I get to choose which comes first?'

He was here, with her, which had to mean something. His belief in the sanctity of marriage? A deep-seated sense of duty?

Oh, dear heaven...something more than affection? She hardly dared hope it could be *love*.

'We're going to talk,' Franco voiced gently. 'Make love. And eat.' He traced the curve of her mouth, lingered a little, then drew her in, so close she couldn't help but be aware of his arousal. 'Not necessarily in that order.'

Sensation spiralled through her body, meshing with heat and need.

She'd come this far, weathered much...and she wanted for it to be right.

An impish smile curved her lips and lent a sparkle to her eyes. 'Food.'

He wanted to laugh, and almost did. 'Witch.'

Gianna crossed to the courtesy table, selected the Room Service menu, picked up the phone and placed an order.

Franco extracted his cellphone, set it to the message bank, and suggested she do the same.

'Incommunicado?'

'Is that such a sin?'

For a man who was so business-oriented, accessible at any time of the day or night either by cellphone or e-mail, it was quite a departure.

She looked at him carefully, noting the well-defined facial bone structure, the slight groove slashing each cheek and the fine lines fanning from his eyes.

She bore his name. She was pregnant with his child.

He had her heart, her love, unequivocally and without question.

'No,' she managed calmly. 'Just...unusual.'

'Impossible I might choose to make you the sole focus of my attention?'

A sharp rap on the door announced the waiter's arrival, and minutes later Gianna began doing justice to a delicious Caesar salad.

Franco's prawn risotto looked tempting, and she had no hesitation in sampling a proffered offering.

There were questions she wanted to ask, but they seemed difficult to voice, and she felt as if she were teetering on the edge of a precipice...unsure whether she'd maintain her balance or fall off the edge.

A panoramic view of the Yarra River and tall city buildings of steel, concrete and glass in varying architectural design stood against the skyline. Trees, their wide-spreading branches heavy with green foliage. Traffic building up at intersections.

'Are you done?'

Gianna viewed the small amount of salad remaining in the bowl, aware she couldn't eat another mouthful. 'Thanks.'

Franco stacked the tray and deposited it outside their suite.

If there'd been luggage she could have unpacked...except that wasn't an option. She rose to her feet and endeavoured to conjure up something to do.

'Don't.'

She shot him a startled glance and lifted an involuntary hand, only to let it fall as he crossed to her side.

'Look at me.' He caught hold of her chin and tilted it, then cupped her face between his hands and brushed a thumb-pad along her lower lip before fastening his mouth on hers in a kiss so incredibly gentle it brought the sheen of unshed tears to her eyes.

'What does that feel like?'

Someone who cares. 'Good,' she acknowledged, and glimpsed his faint smile.

'And this?' His mouth took possession of hers, and it became more, so much *more*.

She lifted her hands and linked them at his nape, drew him close and held him there as she savoured the intimacy, the heat, the passion…and, unable to help herself, she answered it with her own.

A tiny seed of hope took root and began to grow as he lifted his head and slanted an eyebrow in silent query.

Gianna offered a witching smile. 'One of your better efforts.'

'With room for improvement?'

A teasing verbal dance…she could do that. 'On a scale of one to five, I'll award a score of three.'

Liar. He achieved top score every time.

His soft laughter curled round her nerve-ends and pulled a little. 'Minx,' he accorded lightly.

There was never going to be a better time, and her amusement faded. 'Famke.'

Franco didn't pretend to misunderstand. 'Taking the first available flight to London.'

The blonde actress had finally got the message? 'Really?'

His eyes momentarily hardened. 'The threat of a stalking charge proved a convincing factor.' His hands slid beneath her breasts and lingered there, soothing the full curves, each sensitive peak.

'I see,' Gianna managed quietly.

'Do you?'

Did he have any idea how emotionally fragile she felt?

'You decided not to upset the status quo.'

He wanted to shake her, and almost did. 'Fool.'

Franco searched her expression, caught the latent tremulousness beneath the surface of her control, and sought to demolish it.

'A long time ago Famke occupied a few months of my life,' he stressed gently. 'She wanted a commitment I wasn't prepared to give.' He paused fractionally. 'Not then. Not ever.'

His eyes seared her own, and she couldn't look away.

'You were determined to see what she wanted you to see.'

'She was very convincing.'

A muscle bunched at the edge of his jaw. 'Indeed.' He lifted a hand and brushed gentle fingers across her cheek, then let them rest at the edge of her mouth. 'She's not *you*,' he said quietly.

The *hope* plant grew an inch. She couldn't say a word, dared not, and his smile assumed a warmth that came close to melting her bones.

'Do you seriously think I put a ring on your finger out of *duty*?'

'I was given that impression.'

'Not by me.'

Her eyes widened. 'Anamaria—'

He pressed a finger over her mouth. 'Conspired with Santo. And succeeded. Only because *love* was part of the equation.' He caught the sheen of unshed tears, and pressed his lips to each eyelid in turn.

'Fool,' he reiterated gently. 'How could you not know?'

'You never mentioned love.' If he had, she'd have gifted him her soul, along with her heart.

'I thought I did…with my body as I worshipped yours. Each kiss, every touch.'

She wanted to weep, and struggled to keep her emotions intact. 'You do the sex thing very well.'

The edge of his mouth lifted in humour. 'Is that so?' His lips touched hers, nibbled a little, then rendered a punishing nip.

Gianna responded in kind, sensed his indrawn breath, and couldn't resist teasing him. 'Maybe we can work on it a little.'

'I plan to. Soon.' He held her at arm's length, and the look in those dark eyes made her catch her breath. 'But first…the words, hmm?'

The air seemed trapped in her lungs, making it difficult to breathe.

'You're the light of my life. My love...everything,' he vowed quietly. 'For as long as I live.'

Somewhere in her mind the *hope* plant burst through into the sunlight and embraced new life.

'Same goes.' The breath hitched in her throat. 'No one comes close.'

She needed to show him just how much he meant to her, and she lifted a hand to cup his cheek, felt the press of his lips as he caressed her palm, and felt her bones liqueify.

Gianna reached for the buttons on his shirt and dealt with them, suppressing the desire to rush. They had time...all the time in the world...and she wanted to share something infinitely slow. A mutual supplication of the senses. *Lovemaking*.

Almost as if he *knew*, he began dispensing with each layer of clothes until none remained, and Gianna stood still as he took in her slender curves.

'You're beautiful,' Franco accorded gently.

A lump rose in her throat, and she swallowed it down.

'In your heart, your soul,' he added. 'Where it counts.'

'I think you'd better stop with the words right now.' Her voice choked. 'Or I'm going to cry.'

'*Cara—*' He glimpsed the evidence of tears. 'Don't.'

With one hand he dispensed with the bedcovers, and drew her down with him onto the fresh bedlinen.

His hands skimmed her silken skin, soothing, arousing as he created havoc with each and every sensual hollow, then followed the path with his mouth.

She became lost, swept into a sea of passion where there was only the two of them. Skin on skin as they rose together, scaled the heights, urging each other on until they merged body and soul.

It was a while before they rose from the bed and showered. Towelling guest robes hung in the wardrobe, and they pulled them on, then stood together at the window, watching the lights spring on over the cityscape as dusk descended, together with multicolored flashing neon signs.

The Yarra River became a wide dark grey ribbon, and the traffic from this height resembled cars in miniature.

Franco's arms curved her in close against him. 'Do you want to eat in, or go out?'

'In,' Gianna said without hesitation, and felt the slight pressure of his chin as he rested it on top of her head.

They conferred over the menu, ordered, and when the food was delivered they fed each other morsels, then settled back replete.

It didn't seem fair to keep the news to herself any longer.

'How do you feel about parenthood?'

Franco leaned back in his chair and his eyes acquired a quizzical gleam. 'In general, or in particular?'

For a moment she didn't answer, and she saw his eyes sharpen.

'Are you trying to tell me something?'

'I'm pregnant.' So much for setting the stage! Just blurt it out, why don't you?

He sat forward in one fluid movement, and she rushed on before he had a chance to say a word. 'Seven weeks. It was confirmed yesterday.'

His features were a study of concern and joy.

Gianna focused on the joy. 'I planned to tell you over lunch.'

A man so in control of his emotions, she doubted anyone had seen him so vulnerable.

It made her feel…empowered, as only a woman could be. Sure of her love, the man in her life, and sharing the special gift of the child—God willing—she'd bring into the world around seven months from now.

Franco crossed round the table and hunkered down at her side. 'Are you OK with it?'

She touched a hand to his cheek, and felt her heart turn over when he covered it with his own. 'Are you?'

'You need to ask?'

A smile curved her generous mouth. 'I take it that's a *yes*?'

'Without question.'

A light laugh bubbled from her throat. 'The grandparents are going to have a field day.' She rolled her eyes expressively at the thought. 'Can we keep the news to ourselves for a while?'

'Anamaria is sharp as a tack. You think she won't pick up on you declining wine with a meal?'

'Probably not.'

He leaned in and kissed her...long and slow, with incredible gentleness. 'Let's celebrate.'

'I thought we'd decided to stay in?'

Franco rose to his feet and lifted her into his arms. 'We are.' He crossed to the bed, propped up the pillows with one hand, then settled down with her on his lap.

'I need to hold you. Be with you.'

'Oh. That kind of celebration,' she teased.

'Love you. All the days of my life.'

'Not the nights?'

'Those, too.'

Gianna reached up and traced the outline of his jaw. 'You're going to be a very busy man.'

He caught hold of her hand and pressed it to his lips. 'Count on it.'

EPILOGUE

GIANNA GIANCARLO gave birth to twins via Caesarean section seven months later. A boy and a girl, possessed of their mother's eyes and dark hair.

Named Samuel and Ann-Marie, they were the light of their parents' lives.

The christening proved to be a joyous event, with family and close friends present to witness the blessing of two infinitely precious children, after which a celebratory lunch was held at Franco and Gianna's home.

Shannay cradled Ann-Marie, who cooed and smiled, and kicked her little legs in delight at all the attention.

'She's beautiful. And so content.'

Franco curved an arm around his wife's shoulders. 'Like her mother.'

Gianna looked up with a smile that touched his heart. 'While Samuel is very much his father's son.'

Right on cue Samuel cried, and Anamaria scooped him from Santo's arms with a glare in silent accusation.

'They need to be fed and put to sleep.'

'The child told you that?'

'What would you know?'

'They're at it again.' Gianna felt the brush of

Franco's lips against her temple. 'I'll go rescue the infants and tend to them.' She offered Shannay a smile. 'Want to come with me?'

'Thought you'd never ask.'

Gianna took Samuel, and together they ascended the stairs to the nursery.

Murals in pastel colours decorated the walls, attractive mobiles hang suspended high above each cot, and stuffed toys of varying size sat bunched on every surface.

'Wow, I'm impressed.'

Gianna settled in a comfortable rocking chair and began nursing her son.

'I hope I manage as well when I have mine.'

She shot Shannay a piercing look. 'Is that a general comment, or…?'

'Three months.' Shannay's smile lit up her features. 'Apart from family, you're the first to know.'

'Hey,' she said gently. 'That's wonderful.'

'Tom thinks so, too.'

'And Tom's children?'

'There's the thing…they're delighted—dreaming up names, suggesting which room will be best for the nursery. And Tom's mother is over the moon at the thought of another grandchild. So it's all good.'

Shannay hadn't had an easy transition as stepmother.

'I'm glad.' She disengaged Samuel and held him out to Shannay. 'Want to try your hand at getting him to burp while I feed Ann-Marie?'

It was later, when both babes had been changed

and were settling sleepily in each cot, that Gianna had a chance to give Shannay a congratulatory hug.

'Who'd have thought a year ago we'd each be embracing motherhood?'

'It's lovely to see you so happy.'

'Thanks.' It's lovely to *be* happy. No need to pretend, or adopt a façade. No insecurities or doubts.

'Famke created a maelstrom.'

'Oh, yeah, and then some.'

Gianna adjusted the baby monitor, then caught hold of Shannay's hand. 'Let's go join the party, shall we?'

Franco crossed to Gianna's side as she re-entered the lounge. 'They've settled OK?'

'You've had the entire house wired so their slightest sound can be heard in every room,' she teased. 'If they cry, we'll know about it.'

There was much laughter and convivial pleasure as gifts were exchanged, gorgeous outfits in pink and blue added to an already extensive collection of baby clothes.

Anamaria presented each child with documentation for a sizable trust fund, which Santo generously matched.

It was late afternoon when the last guest departed, with the exception of the grandparents, who were invited to stay on for dinner.

A meal that survived without opposing banter from Anamaria or Santo. Something which surprised their grandchildren and drew speculative interest as the evening progressed.

Anamaria, who never added alcohol to her coffee, suggested a nip of brandy would do very well— which, given the champagne toasts, and wine with dinner, put her over the limit to drive.

'Perhaps you should consider staying in one of the guest rooms?' Gianna suggested.

'Rubbish,' Santo refuted. 'I'll drive her home.'

Anamaria lifted an eyebrow in imperious query. 'In the Ferrari?'

'You have a problem with that?'

Gianna glimpsed the silent challenge, and wondered at it.

'Grazie.'

You're joking…aren't you?

'Well, what do you know?' Gianna said quietly, as Santo saw Anamaria seated, then climbed behind the wheel and sent the gleaming red Ferrari purring down the driveway. 'My grandmother hates that car.'

'Does she?'

Gianna gave him a perceptive look. 'You think…?'

'They have a thing going?' Franco closed the door and set the security alarm. 'Do you?'

Did she? Maybe. 'I'm trying to get a handle on the possibility.'

A plaintive cry sounded as they crossed the lobby, and was followed by another when they ascended the stairs.

'Right on time.'

They entered the nursery together, and Franco

lifted his daughter and deftly effected a diaper change while Gianna tended to her son.

She glanced at the man cradling their daughter, and her eyes misted at the sight of them. The babe so infinitely precious, the man equally so.

'Thank you,' Franco said gently. 'For being the love of my life. The gift of our children. The world as I know it.'

'Right back at you.' She felt tears gather, and blinked them away.

Her son finished feeding, and she nursed Ann-Marie while Franco took care of burping Samuel.

Both babes settled with barely a murmur, and Gianna checked the monitor, dimmed the lights down low, then quietly followed Franco from the room.

In one fluid movement he swept Gianna off her feet and carried her to their bedroom.

'My turn, I think.'

She'd seen the need in those dark eyes, and the love.

It overwhelmed her, as it always did, to know she alone possessed the power to enchant and delight him.

'I love you so much,' Gianna said quietly as he drew her in and began to show her, as only he could, just how much she meant to him.

Love beyond doubt. Unconditional and everlasting.

Two kilometres distant, Santo Giancarlo assisted Anamaria Castelli to her front door, unlocked it and watched her step inside. Then she turned towards him, head held high, and solemnly thanked him for the ride.

'There's just one thing.' She paused. 'Next time you take me out in that car, perhaps you can open it up a bit? I understand it's built for speed.'

'It's Italian,' he said solemnly.

'So,' came the dignified reply, 'am I.' And she closed the door on him.

Who'd have thought?

Santo almost laughed out loud as he swung in behind the wheel, and there was no one to see the teasing smile curving his mouth.

Life, he decided, was about to become even more interesting.

THE BILLIONAIRE BOSS'S FORBIDDEN MISTRESS

Miranda
LEE

Miranda Lee is Australian, living near Sydney. Born and raised in the bush, she was boarding-school educated and briefly pursued a career in classical music, before moving to Sydney and embracing the world of computers. Happily married, with three daughters, she began writing when family commitments kept her at home. She likes to create stories that are believable, modern, fast-paced and sexy. Her interests include meaty sagas, doing word puzzles, gambling and going to the movies.

**Don't miss Miranda Lee's new novel,
The Billionaire's Bride of Convenience, out in
June 2009 from Mills & Boon® Modern™.**

CHAPTER ONE

LEAH DIDN'T STOP swimming till a full twenty laps were behind her.

Satisfied with her workout, she stroked over to the side of the pool and grabbed the silver handles on the ladder. As she hauled herself upwards out of the water, her gaze connected with her left thigh and the rough ridges of white skin that criss-crossed it.

Leah didn't look away, as she usually did. Instead, she forced herself to study the scars in the early morning sunshine.

They had faded quite a bit over the past two years. But they were never going to go away, she accepted as she climbed out on to the tiled pool surround and reached for her towel.

Leah sighed. She wished her disfigurement didn't bother her so much. It seemed pathetic to be upset about a few wretched scars when the car accident that had produced them had taken the life of her mother.

Nothing compared with that tragedy, not even Carl

leaving her a few months after the accident. Though she'd been shattered at the time.

Leah clutched the towel tightly in her hands, rubbing at her scars less than gently as she recalled the expression on Carl's face when he'd taken his first good look at her scarred leg. He'd been utterly revolted. And repulsed.

He'd made excuses not to make love to her for weeks after she came home from hospital, till finally he'd announced that he wanted a divorce, saying it was because she had changed.

Leah agreed that she had. During the long, painful weeks she'd been in hospital, she'd found a different person inside herself. A better person, she liked to think. A person with more character, and insight, and compassion.

Carl claimed she'd become far too serious and was no fun any more. Leah's desperate argument that she'd just lost her mother and was naturally feeling sad made no impression on him at all.

His leaving her had nothing to do with her personality having changed, she thought bitterly. It was all to do with her scars. And her limp.

Well, the limp had long gone but the scars would never go. Not the scars on her legs. Or the scars on her heart.

Still, she'd finally come to terms with Carl's calling it quits on her. After all, what woman would actually want to stay married to a man who could not tolerate a wife who was no longer physically perfect?

Which, before the accident, she had been. Or so she'd been told all her life.

Leah had been the image of her mother, a natural blonde with lovely green eyes, perfect teeth and skin, and a very pretty face and figure. Leah had grown up taking her good genes for granted. Taking her privileged lifestyle for granted as well.

As the only child of one of Sydney's most successful stockbrokers, she'd never wanted for a thing. She'd been spoiled rotten all her life, her pampered upbringing producing a precious little society princess who thought the world was her oyster. Working for a living had never been on Leah Bloom's agenda. She had a monthly allowance, plus a credit card. Why work nine to five in some dreary job?

When people had asked what she did for a living, she had told them she was an aspiring writer, a minor ambition that had come to her during her last year at school when her English teacher complimented her on one of her creative writing assignments. She'd even attended a fiction-writing course at one stage, bought herself a computer and started a chick-lit novel, which was little more than a diary of what she did every week.

Which meant extremely silly and shallow, Leah decided in hindsight.

How could it be anything else when her life *was* silly and shallow, every day filled with shopping and charity luncheons and idle hours spent in beauty salons getting ready for the evening's outing. By the time

Leah was twenty-one, she'd been to more parties and premieres and black-tie dos than she could count.

Falling in love and marrying Carl had been the icing on her seemingly never-ending cake. He'd been attractive and charming and rich. *Very* rich. Leah's family didn't mix with any other kind.

Carl had been thirty when they married, the heir to an absolute fortune made in diamonds. She'd been twenty-three.

They'd only been married for six months when the accident happened. Way too short a time for Carl to fall out of love with her. Leah had long come to the conclusion that she'd just been a trophy wife, a decoration on his arm to show off, a possession that he'd only valued when she'd been glitteringly perfect.

Once she'd become flawed, he hadn't wanted her any more.

'Mrs B. said to tell you breakfast will be ready in ten minutes,' a male voice called out.

Leah glanced up to see her father leaning over the balcony that adjoined the master bedroom.

Dressed in his favourite navy silk dressing-gown and with a tan that a summer of swimming and yachting had produced, her father looked much younger than his sixty-two years. Of course, he did keep himself very fit in his home gym. A thick headful of expertly dyed brown hair didn't hurt, either.

'That's the only reason I come home every weekend, you know,' she replied. 'For Mrs B.'s cooking.'

This was a lie, of course. She came home every

weekend to spend time with her father, to feel his parental affection, up close and personal.

But Leah didn't want to live at home twenty-four seven. Joachim Bloom was far too dominating a personality for that. Leah knew she would find herself giving in to him if she was always around, like her mother had. As happy as her parents had been in their marriage, Leah had always been well aware who was the boss in their relationship.

'Rubbish!' her father retorted. 'You're skinny as a rake.'

'You can never be too thin,' she quipped.

'Or too rich,' he finished for her. 'Which reminds me, daughter, there's something important I have to discuss with you over breakfast, so shake a leg.'

'The good one?' Leah shot back at him. 'Or the gimpy one?'

Pretending to her father not to care about her scars had become a habit. She didn't want him to know that they bothered her as much as they still did. Or that they were the reason she never went to the beach any more, or swam anywhere else but here, at home, when there was no one around but her father and Mrs B. to see them.

'Very funny,' he said with a roll of his eyes, and disappeared back inside.

Leah threw the towel over her shoulder and headed for her bedroom, one of six in the two-storeyed, waterside mansion that she'd been brought up in and which was probably worth many millions on the current market.

Vaucluse was *the* place to live in Sydney's eastern suburbs.

For a while after his mother's death, her father had thought of selling the house and buying elsewhere, but Leah had talked him out of it. And she was so glad she had. It was a comfort at times, to be around her mother's things. To feel her presence in the rooms.

Such beautiful rooms. Such a beautiful house, Leah thought wistfully as she climbed the curving staircase that led up to the bedrooms.

The thought didn't come to Leah till she was in the shower that her father might have changed his mind about the house. He might still want to sell. Maybe that was what he wanted to discuss with her.

I won't let him, she resolved as she snapped off the water. I'll fight him to the death!

A couple of minutes later, she was running downstairs, dressed in cut-off blue jeans and a pink singlet top, her long damp hair up in a ponytail.

Joachim's heart lurched as his daughter raced into the morning room. How like her mother she was! It was like looking at Isabel in her twenties.

'If you think you're going to sell this house, Daddy,' Leah tossed at him with a feisty look as she sat down at the breakfast table, 'then you can think again.'

Joachim sighed. Like her mother in looks, but not in personality. Isabel had been a soft sweet woman, always deferring to him. Never making waves.

Leah *looked* soft and sweet. When she'd been younger, she'd even *been* soft and sweet. But over the past eighteen months, she'd become much more assertive, and very independent. Not hard, exactly. But quite formidable and forthright.

But who could blame her for turning tough, came a more sympathetic train of thought. Carl had a lot to answer for. Fancy leaving Leah when she needed him the most. The man was a weasel and a coward. Joachim wouldn't spit on him if he was on fire.

His daughter had had two alternatives during that awful time in her life. Go to pieces, or develop a thicker skin.

For a while it had been touch and go. Joachim was very proud that Leah had eventually pulled herself together and moved on.

'No, Leah,' he told her with a reassuring smile. 'I'm not selling the house. I know how much you love it.'

Leah's relief was only temporary. Then what *did* Daddy want to talk to her about?

'What's up, then?' she asked as she reached for a slice of toast from the silver toast rack. 'You're not going to make a fuss about my working, are you? I thought you were proud of my getting a job.'

Perhaps *surprised* would have been a better description of her father's reaction. When Leah had first mentioned a year ago that she was going to find a job, her stunned father had asked her what on earth she thought she could do.

'Even waitresses have to have experience these days!' he'd told her.

Leah understood his scepticism after she went to have her resumé done. Because there was nothing much she could put on it, except a very average pass in her Higher School certificate—studying had not been high on Leah's society princess agenda—plus that very brief creative writing course. She had absolutely no qualifications for employment other than her social skills and her looks and a limited ability to use a computer.

Which was why the only job she'd been able to find after attending endless interviews was as a receptionist. Not at some flashy establishment in the city, either. She currently worked for a company that manufactured beauty products, and had their factory and head office at Ermington, a mainly industrial suburb in western Sydney.

'I *am* proud of your getting that job,' her father insisted. 'Extremely.'

Mrs B., coming in with a plate piled high with scrambled eggs, hash browns, fried tomato and bacon, interrupted their conversation for a moment.

'This looks delicious, Mrs B.,' Leah complimented her father's housekeeper as she placed the plate in front of her.

Leah was privately thankful that she only had to eat Mrs B.'s breakfast one day a week, or she'd have a backside as big as a bus.

'Just make sure you eat it all,' Mrs B. said with a

sharp glance at Leah. 'You're getting way too thin, missie.'

'You won't catch yourself another husband with that waif look, you know,' her father agreed.

Leah could have pointed out that she turned down several offers of dates every week. Instead, she smiled sweetly and tucked into the food till Mrs B. left the room. Then she put down her knife and fork and looked straight at her father.

'I have no intention of getting married again, Daddy.'

'What? Why not?'

'You know why not.'

'Not every man is as weak as Carl,' he grumbled. 'You're a beautiful young woman, Leah. You should have a husband. And babies.'

'I don't want to argue about this, Daddy. I just want you to know my feelings on the matter so that I don't have to put up with that kind of comment any more.'

'You'll change your mind,' he said. 'One day, you'll meet the right man and fall in love and that will be that. Nature will have her way with you. You mark my words.'

Leah suppressed a sigh. She'd been marking her father's words all her life. She loved him to death, but over the past two years she'd come to realise he was an incredible bossy-boots who thought he knew what was best for everyone.

'Can we move on, please?' she said, picking up a piece of crispy bacon with her fingers, and munching into it. 'You wanted to discuss something with me?' she asked between swallows. 'I presume it didn't have anything to do with my remarrying. It sounded like it was about money. Which reminds me. Don't start telling me what I can and cannot do with the income from my trust fund, either. It is my money to do with as I please. Mum made no conditions on her legacy in her will. If I want to give it all away, I can. Not that I am. *Yet.* At the moment, I have to keep some back each month to make ends meet.'

'I don't wonder,' her father said. 'From what I recall, you only earn a pittance.'

'The women in the factory earn even less,' Leah pointed out. 'Yet some of them bring up a family on their salary. My aim is to support myself on my salary alone. It will do my character good to see how the other half lives. It's just taking a while for my champagne taste to catch up with my beer income. Now, what did you want to talk to me about?' she asked, and munched into the bacon again.

'Eat your breakfast first. I see you're enjoying it. We'll talk over coffee afterwards.'

Leah's curiosity was intense by the time she cleared her plate and picked up her coffee cup. 'Well?' she said after a couple of sips. 'Out with it.'

'What do you know about the takeover of Beville Holdings?'

'What? You mean it's a done deal?' Leah asked with alarm in her voice. So far there had only been rumours at work of a possible takeover. But lots of Leah's fellow employees were genuinely worried.

Leah had heard from more than one source that when companies were taken over, they were invariably subjected to 'restructuring'. Leah had been chatting to one of their newest reps on Friday, a really nice man with a wife and young family. He told Leah that new management always pruned staff and usually adopted a policy of last-in-first-out, regardless of ability. Apparently, Peter had lost his previous job that way and was worried sick about the same thing happening again.

'Yes, it's a done deal,' her father confirmed. 'There's an article about it in the business section of the Sunday paper here. Plus a photo of your new boss, Jason Pollack.'

'Jason Pollack,' Leah repeated, the name not ringing a bell. 'Never heard of him.' Leah might not have joined the work force till late in her life, but she'd been brought up on dinner table discussions about the wheeler dealers of this world whose faces and names often graced the dailies.

'Not all that many people have,' her father informed her. 'He keeps a very low media profile.'

'Show me,' she said, and her father passed across the relevant pages.

'Goodness!' Leah exclaimed, having expected to see a photo of a man who was at least middle aged. And a good deal fatter.

Takeover tycoons were rarely this young. Or this slim.

Or this handsome.

Something inside Leah tightened when her eyes met those of Jason Pollack's. Dark brown, they were. And deeply set, hooded by eyebrows that were as straight and uncompromising as his mouth. His hair was black. And wavy. Brushed neatly back from his high forehead with no part. His nose was straight, with widely flared nostrils, his jawline squared off, with a small dimple in its centre.

'Is this an old photo?' she asked brusquely.

'Nope,' her father said. 'If you read the article, you'll see he's only thirty-six. He's very good looking, isn't he?'

'I suppose so,' Leah said. 'If you like the type.' Which she obviously did. She couldn't take her eyes off him.

Yet he was nothing like Carl, who'd been big and blond, a Nordic giant of a man with a raw-boned handsomeness.

Jason Pollack's face had a model-like quality, probably because of the perfect symmetry of his finely sculptured features.

Yet no one would mistake him for a male model. There was an air about him that was unmistakably magnate material. A maturity in his eyes—and an intelligence—that Leah found both attractive and irritating.

Irritating because she didn't want to find the new boss of Beville Holdings in any way attractive. She didn't want to find *any* man attractive for a long, long time.

'How on earth did he get to be so rich and successful so young?' she queried sharply. 'I know he's not old
money. I would have met him before, if he was.'

'Nope. He was an immigrant from Poland, brought
over here by his father after his mother died in child-
birth. He grew up in the Western suburbs and never
even went to university. Started in sales straight out of
school.'

'Must have been a *very* good salesman to acquire so
much in such a short time,' Leah said.

'Seems so. But he also married into money when he
was in his late twenties. His wife was his first em-
ployer's widow. Her husband owned the WhizzBiz
Electronics chain of shops. Jason Pollack sold himself
to his new lady boss within a year of her husband's de-
mise. She herself died of cancer a couple of years later,
leaving her adored young husband everything.
Admittedly, by then, he had reversed WhizzBiz's dwin-
dling sales. After his wife's death, he sold the whole
chain for an enormous price. That's become Pollack's
trademark. He buys ailing companies, fixes them up,
then sells them.

'But only if he thinks fixing is feasible,' her father
continued whilst Leah kept staring at Jason Pollack's
photo. 'He reveals in that article that on one occasion,
after he gained access to the company's records and
employees, he judged that a salvage operation simply
wasn't on. So he cut his losses and dismantled the company altogether, selling off whatever assets were involved.'

'Regardless of the poor employees,' she scorned.

'I gather he gave each of them more than their entitlements.'

'Which he could well afford,' she snapped, dragging her eyes away from Jason Pollack to scan the rest of the article. The man had to be worth squillions, his current residence being the top floor of a skyscraper in the middle of Sydney's city and business district.

'Maybe, but he didn't have to, Leah. The man has a good reputation for being more than fair. Look, Beville Holdings has not made a profit for two years now. That's what I wanted to talk to you about. Whether Beville Holdings is salvageable, or not?'

Leah frowned. 'Why do you want to know?'

'I happen to own a nice little parcel of Beville Holdings shares. Bought them two years ago when they were rock bottom. Are they going to increase in value?'

'According to this article they've already gone up a lot.'

'Yes, but they'll go up a lot more in the end if Pollack can work his usual miracle. So tell me, daughter, can your company be turned around, or do you think your new boss will sell it off in pieces?'

'How on earth would *I* know?' Leah replied, tossing the paper back over to her father to stop herself from staring at the infernal man any more.

'Come now, Leah, don't be coy. You're one of those girls everyone tells everything to. People like to confide in you. I've seen it for myself many times. You've been at that company for over eight months now. I'll bet you know exactly what's going on there. Just because you didn't put your mind to your studies at school doesn't mean you didn't inherit my brains. You're smart as a whip, when you want to be.'

'I wasn't too smart when I married Carl.'

'That's different. Love can make a fool of even the smartest person. Now give me an honest opinion. Is my investment going to grow?'

Leah thought about all the information she had gleaned at work over the past few months.

Her father was right. People did like to confide in her. More so now than ever. Since the accident, she'd developed a genuinely compassionate ear, whereas before, her being a good listener had just been a social skill, learned from her mother.

Leah knew exactly what was wrong with Beville Holdings. The problems were fixable. *If* the new boss knew where to look, and whose advice to take.

'Beville Holdings has excellent products,' came her carefully worded reply. 'But poor management. I think your shares will increase in value.'

Joachim smiled. Smart girl, his daughter. Smart and beautiful and not cut out to spend her life being a receptionist out in the boondocks. Or for living alone, for that matter.

Joachim could understand that her husband's defection had hurt her terribly. But life went on.

Leah was only twenty-six. Time for her to start dating again. But he couldn't force the issue. He'd have to be subtle. Maybe he'd surprise her with a dinner party for next Saturday night, invite a few old friends, people he knew she liked. But he'd also slip in someone new, some handsome, highly eligible young man who might impress her.

But who?

Joachim couldn't think of anyone. With a sigh he picked up the paper again and found himself staring down at the photograph of Jason Pollack. Suddenly, a voice whispered to him that he should invite *him*. Jason Pollack.

Joachim's first reaction was hell, no. Not some ambitious bastard who'd married for money. But the voice insisted. If he hadn't known better, he would have thought it was Isabel, whispering to him. Isabel, who hadn't liked Carl one bit and who'd said Leah needed to marry a different type of man. A stronger, self-made man.

Isabel had been right about Carl.

Jason Pollack was a strong man, Joachim told himself. And a self-made man. A man who could probably do with a new wife. A younger one this time who could give him children.

Joachim still had his doubts, but that soft voice was very persistent.

All right, he whispered back in his head.

Don't tell Leah, the voice added.

Joachim flicked a quick glance across the table at his daughter.

'What?' she said.

'Nothing. Nothing.'

But the die was set. He would invite Pollack to dinner, and he would not tell Leah. Which left him with the problem of getting her to attend. Not an easy task. But he would persuade her. Somehow.

CHAPTER TWO

LEAH TURNED INTO the driveway of Beville Holdings, stopping at the security gate and smiling over at Ted, the man who manned the gate on the morning shift. Usually, he just smiled back and pressed the button that lifted the barrier, allowing her to drive through.

Today, Ted slid back the window and waved for Leah to wind her window down. Which she did.

'He's here,' he called to her in a conspiratorial voice. 'The new boss.'

'What?' Leah's stomach twisted into an instant knot. She'd expected Jason Pollock to show up at work sooner or later, but not this soon.

'Didn't you read about the takeover in yesterday's paper?' Ted asked her.

'Er...no, I didn't,' Leah replied, not wanting to seem too on the ball. She didn't exactly play a blonde bimbo role at work, but at the same time, she didn't drop any clues over who she really was. She liked it that she was treated as a simple working-class girl from Gladesville.

No one at Beville Holdings had ever been to her waterview apartment or connected her surname—Johannsen—with the diamond dynasty.

'Well, his name is Mr Pollack and he arrived over an hour ago to check out the factory. He'll be heading over to your section soon, I'll bet, so just as well you're not late.'

'What's he like?' Leah asked, her curiosity getting the better of her.

'Not too bad. I think my job's safe. When he drove up to the gate just after seven and announced who he was, I still asked him for ID, and he seemed to like that.'

'Good for you. What's he driving? A flash car, I'll bet.'

'A dark blue sporty one.'

Leah's top lip curled. Typical. Her father had declared yesterday that Jason Pollack *wasn't* some kind of playboy—despite his living in a penthouse.

But men like that always ran true to form. Give a man money and he didn't choose to putter around in anything small, or sedate. Rich people picked cars that supposedly reflected their personality, and power.

Leah had once zipped around Sydney in a red, top-of-the-range roadster, a present from her father on her twenty-first birthday. She'd traded it in for a white, second-hand hatchback when she got this job, not wanting anyone at work to think of her as a rich bitch. She wanted to be liked for herself, not her money.

'Thanks for the warning, Ted,' Leah said, and drove

on, turning into the staff car park, which was surprisingly full. All the managers' cars were there, an unusual occurrence for this hour on a Monday morning. They must have heard about the takeover, too, and decided to put their best feet forward.

The only empty car space in the row nearest the main office building was right next to a dark blue sports car.

Leah hesitated, then slid her vehicle in next to it, determined not to surrender to these silly nerves, which were currently turning her insides into a washing machine.

He was just a man, for pity's sake. She'd met men just as attractive. And just as rich. Heck, she'd been married to one!

Okay, so she'd found Jason Pollack's photo extremely attractive. So what?

Once she actually met the man, his undoubtedly up-himself personality would soon stop these ridiculous stomach flutters.

Admittedly, a dark blue sports car suggested that Jason Pollack wasn't a total show pony, like her ex. Carl would have rocked up in something flashy and gold, or silver. That was exactly what she'd seen Carl sitting in the last time their paths crossed. Something flashy and silver.

Leah climbed out from behind the wheel and walked round to her passenger side, opening the door there to retrieve her handbag and peeping into the blue sports car at the same time.

Not a thing on the leather seats, or on the floor. Nothing to give her a glimpse of Jason Pollack's character. Except that it looked like he was neat freak. There wasn't a single piece of rubbish anywhere. Or a spot of dirt. The car gleamed in the morning sun, both inside and outside.

People like that were usually very critical, and controlling.

'Better get a move on then, girlie,' she muttered to herself as she zapped the lock on her key and hurried up the path that led to the head office, a rectangular brick building built in the early sixties, but which had been totally renovated late last year.

You couldn't tell by looking at the place that Beville Holdings hadn't made a profit lately. You'd think everything was coming up roses.

Pushing through the front door, Leah headed across the deserted reception area straight for the nearby powder room. Her wrist watch said twenty-three minutes past eight. She only had five minutes to check her appearance before she was due to be sitting behind the semi-circular reception desk, looking cool, calm and collected.

Despite her self-lecturing, Leah felt anything but.

Jason said goodbye to the factory foreman, thanking him for his help, but brushing aside the man's offer to accompany him over to the head office.

Jason wanted to think. And he thought better when he was by himself.

He walked slowly along the well-signed path, wondering what he was doing, buying a company that made shower gels, shampoos, sunscreens and moisturisers. What in hell did he know about such products?

Nothing at all.

Still, he supposed retail was retail. Get the advertising right and good sales usually followed.

Judging by their performance over the last two years, Beville Holdings had not got their advertising right. Either that, or they were charging too much for their products. Or their management was less than efficient.

Jason wished he'd done some more market research before plunging in last Friday and buying a controlling share.

Never in his life before had he bought a company because of a dream. A *dream*, for pity's sake!

It had happened last Saturday night, the night he'd broken up with Hilary. He'd been upset because she'd been upset, and the last thing he'd ever wanted to do was to hurt Hilary.

They'd met just over six months ago, at a dinner party that Jason had been persuaded to attend, and which had been cripplingly boring till Hilary winked at him from across the table. Later, he'd discovered that their hostess had been doing some match-making, Hilary having not long been divorced. She was his age, slim, dark, and very attractive, as well as intelligent and confident. Jason had ended up in bed with her that night, his first woman since Karen's death four years earlier. His libido had finally bypassed his grief and come to life again, and, having come to life, wasn't going to stay silent any more.

In hindsight, Jason was amazed that he'd stayed celibate for so long. Sex had always been very important to him.

He'd first discovered the pleasures of the flesh when he'd been sixteen, his partner an older girl of nineteen who knew a thing or two. She'd lived two doors down from him, and she'd spent many a Saturday afternoon during one long hot summer, showing Jason exactly how to please her, and vice versa. When her family moved, Jason had been devastated for a while. At sixteen, it had been impossible to separate lust and love.

Eventually, he'd recovered from his broken heart, and, after that, never been without a girlfriend. Though he'd never fallen in love again.

Till he met Karen.

Jason smiled softly to himself as he thought of his wife.

Another older woman, but this time fifteen years older. Forty-two to his twenty-seven. Yet they'd been perfect together. And so ecstatically happy.

Of course, everyone else thought he'd married his boss's widow out of cold-blooded ambition. Hilary probably hadn't believed him when he had said he'd loved his wife.

Jason supposed it was only reasonable that, after sleeping with Hilary every weekend for six months, she might expect him to propose.

In his defence, he'd made it clear right from the start of their relationship that he wasn't interest in remarrying.

But last Saturday night, Hilary had started pressing for him to marry her and he knew he couldn't. Because, as attractive as Hilary was, he just wasn't in love with her, and once you'd been in love—really, deeply in love—you couldn't settle for less.

After Hilary flounced out, saying she never wanted to see him again, he hadn't been able to sleep. So he'd popped one of the sleeping pills that the doctor had prescribed for him after Karen died and which were hopelessly out of date. But at the time, he hadn't cared. He just wanted oblivion.

But his sleep had been full of dreams, mostly of Karen, telling him—as she often had during that final awful week—that he wasn't to grieve, that, one day, he'd meet someone else, someone more right for him than she'd been, someone who'd give him babies and a wonderful life.

Silly dreams, because Jason knew that wouldn't happen.

And then, seemingly only seconds before he woke, had come this other odd, startlingly vivid dream.

He was driving out in the country and suddenly, in the middle of a mown paddock, he saw this massive bill-board with a blonde on it. She'd been photographed from the back from her hips up, and was naked. The effect was incredibly sexual. She had a slender but curvy shape, porcelain-like skin and dead straight, glisteningly golden hair streaming halfway down her bare back. Her arms were stretched up in front of her, tossing a bottle of shampoo up into a bright blue sky, golden rays coming out from it as if it were the sun. Across the bottom of the billboard were the words: START EVERY DAY WITH SUNSHINE.

Jason had driven right off the road in the dream as he stared at the blonde, the accident jolting him awake. He'd been relieved to find it was only a dream, but the image on that bill-board had stayed in his mind all day, tantalising him. Haunting him.

He knew he'd never seen such an ad before. He *had* heard of a brand name called Sunshine. Vaguely. But he thought it was attached to cleaning stuff, not shampoo.

That evening, he'd rung Harry Wilde—Harry ran an advertising agency he used occasionally—and asked him if he knew of Sunshine shampoo, or of such an ad.

He hadn't.

Jason had then gone to an all-hours supermarket and found that there was indeed a range of products with the Sunshine label, all made by a company called Beville Holdings. Further investigation via his broker revealed Beville Holdings was a small but well-established manufacturing company, owned by a parent company in England. Their shares were quite low, due to their not making a profit and not declaring a decent dividend for the past two years.

'And a week later, here I am,' Jason muttered to himself. 'The owner of said profitless company.'

Jason found himself standing outside the main door of the head office building, shaking his head wryly up the Beville Holdings sign. He didn't really believe in fate, or karma. In the main, he was a practical man.

But he could not deny that he'd been less than practical this past week. That crazy dream had robbed him of his savvy approach to business. As soon as he'd found out there was a real company that made Sunshine products, he'd felt compelled to buy the place, without doing any solid market research, a process that normally took many weeks.

Bob had thought he'd lost his marbles.

Still, if he listened to Bob all the time, he'd never buy anything. Bob was a great PA, but not the most decisive of men. Not a risk taker in any way, shape or form.

Businessmen had to take risks, occasionally. In the main, however, they were informed risks. Jason had to admit that, this time, he'd gone out on a limb.

Still, it could be an interesting project, he told himself, turning Beville Holdings around. A real challenge. He'd been getting into a rut lately.

Success would depend on what he discovered in here, Jason decided as he pushed through the half-glass door. If serious problems lay in the sales and marketing departments, things could get tricky.

Golden handshakes were the only answer for getting rid of bad management, and that was very costly.

So was this décor, Jason realised as he set foot on the plush jade carpet that covered the spacious recep-

tion area. His eyebrows lifted as he glanced at the
cream leather seating and the expensively framed wa-
tercolours that graced the cream walls, his thoughtful
gaze finally resting on the very modern, but very un-
manned reception desk.

He was glancing at the time on his watch—it was
eight twenty-seven—when a movement caught the corner of his eye. Jason turned in time to see a young
woman emerge from the ladies' room across the way.

Jason's heart skipped a beat.

She was blonde, and beautiful, wearing a pale green
dress that clung to her perfect breasts and swished
around her perfect legs. She seemed startled when she
saw him, stopping in mid-stride. But then, with a toss
of her lovely head, she headed in his direction, her
hips swaying provocatively.

'Good morning, Mr Pollack,' she said crisply as she
stretched out her hand towards him. 'I'm sorry I wasn't
here to greet you when you came in, but I'm not due
to start till eight thirty.'

So she knew who he was, did she? Probably saw his
photo in the paper yesterday, Jason realised as he took
her hand, holding it within both of his as he absorbed
more of her incredible beauty at closer quarters.

'That's perfectly all right, Miss…er…'

'Johannsen,' she supplied. 'Leah Johannsen. I…I'm
the receptionist here at Beville Holdings.'

Jason knew lots of companies hired lookers to man
their front desk, but this girl was totally wasted here.
She could have been a model, she was so striking.

Those eyes. That mouth. That stunning hair. So shiny and silky looking, with just the hint of a wave as it rippled down over her slender shoulders.

It made you want to touch it. Kiss it. Wrap it around your...

Jason gave himself a severe mental shake, hoping his face did not reflect his thoughts. Indulging in that type of sexual fantasy was not Jason's usual bent.

But once the image filled his mind, it was joined by others. To his annoyance, his flesh soon followed and he found himself glancing down at her left hand to see if she was wearing any rings.

The shot of adrenalin that came when he saw that her fingers were bare startled Jason. It wasn't like him to lose it over a pretty girl.

But of course this girl wasn't just pretty. She was perfection.

And suddenly, he wanted her. Wanted her more than he'd ever wanted Hilary.

But then he hadn't ever really wanted Hilary as such, had he? He'd just wanted regular sex. Any attractive woman would have done.

But you really want *this* girl, came a voice from inside that Jason didn't recognise. It was dark and driven and utterly ruthless. You want her and you're going to have her, come hell or high water!

CHAPTER THREE

IT FELT LIKE an eternity to Leah before Jason Pollack let her hand go.

But maybe that was just her imagination. Time seemed to have slowed down since she came out of the ladies' room and found her new boss standing just inside the main door, looking over at her.

His photo hadn't done him justice. But then, how could a two-dimensional head-and-shoulders shot capture the essence of such a man?

Yesterday, Leah had thought his dark, deeply set eyes had exuded magnate material. In the flesh, they exuded something else, a powerful magnetism that had pulled at her from across the room.

She'd been unable to breathe for a moment. Unable to move. But then her pride—and a measure of pique—had come to her rescue, snapping her out of her fatuous state and propelling her towards him with cool eyes and creditable composure. She even managed to observe—and ruefully admire—his taste in clothes.

His black, single-breasted business suit was sleek and expensive, tailored to compliment his tall, elegantly lean body. He'd matched it with a deep blue shirt that highlighted his olive skin. His silvery grey tie was classy, and nicely understated. So was his watch, also silver, with a black leather band.

By the time she reached him, Leah imagined—mistakenly, as it turned out—that she could shake his hand and come away unscathed.

But the moment his hands—*both* of them—enclosed hers, she'd been totally rattled, reduced to stammering when he asked her name.

Yet she never stammered. Or felt swamped by the kind of feelings that had overtaken her.

Within moments, she'd wanted to forget where she was and who he was. When he'd stared deep into her eyes, she'd dissolved inside. When he'd glanced down at her left hand—rather pointedly, she'd thought—she'd wanted to blurt out that, yes, she was free, free to do whatever he wanted, wherever he wanted, whenever he wanted it.

The wanton submissiveness that overwhelmed her had been mind-blowing. And totally shocking. Leah had never experienced anything like it. Not even with Carl, whom she'd loved.

But this had nothing to do with love, Leah realised shakily after he released her hand.

His no longer touching her helped Leah gather herself a little. Now, if only he would stop looking at her the way he was looking at her, she might be able to pull herself totally together. But he continued to gobble her up with his eyes.

Leah knew men found her attractive. What was on show, that is. Jason Pollack might not be so interested if she revealed her left thigh to him.

Thinking about her scars did what it always did to Leah. Brought her sharply back to the real world, reminding her also that Jason Pollack had once married an older woman for money, a crime on a par with marrying a girl for her physical perfection alone. The last man on earth Leah would want to become involved with was another cold-blooded, conscienceless devil who had a computer chip for a heart.

Even if he was the sexiest man she'd ever met!

'I must get to my desk, Mr Pollack,' she said, her manner and tone suitably frosty. 'It's gone eight thirty.' And, turning her back on him, she walked with stiffly held shoulders to her work station, not looking back at him as she settled herself at her desk.

But she could feel his eyes still on her, burning right through her clothes.

Jim Matheson charging down the hallway into the reception area was a godsend.

'Mr Pollack! So there you are! They just rang from the factory to say you left some time ago. Leah, why didn't you let us know Mr Pollack was here?' Jim snapped at her.

'I've only just walked in,' came the new boss's smooth reply before she could defend herself. 'And, please, make it Jason. I don't stand on ceremony. And you'd be?'

'Jim. Jim Matheson. I'm the national sales manager here at Beville Holdings.'

And the biggest creep in the place, thought Leah. Matheson had made a pass at her on her very first day, but she'd soon put him in his place. Still, he hadn't forgotten and was never nice to her.

'Jim,' the new boss said warmly, coming forward to shake his hand. 'Nice to meet you. And you too, Leah,' he added, throwing her a look and a small smile that carried several subtle messages which Leah understood only too well.

One—I'm interested.

Two—You don't fool me for a minute with that cold-shoulder act.

And three—I'll get back to you later.

A shiver ran down Leah's spine as she watched the two men walk together down the corridor that led to the sales and marketing divisions. He was going to ask her out. She could feel it. He was going to ask her out and she wasn't going to have the willpower to say no.

But by lunchtime that day, events hadn't developed quite as Leah had expected. For one thing, she hadn't set eyes on Jason Pollack again that morning. He'd stayed down in Jim's office, having meetings with the various section managers. She'd been informed of this by the general office girl who relieved Leah at the reception desk at eleven every day so she could have her morning tea break.

Mandy hadn't met the great man herself, but she'd

already heard on the grapevine that he was a hunk of the first order. All good-looking men were hunks to Mandy, who was eighteen, a slightly plump, rosy-faced girl with an infectious smile and a happy manner.

Leah had spent her morning tea break in the canteen, listening to the gossip from the factory girls who were there, having their lunch break, as their hours were from seven till three. Leah got sick and tired of hearing how drop-dead gorgeous the new boss was.

Leah had returned to her desk, resenting Jason Pollack all the more because she knew he was being gushed over, mainly because for his looks. She'd learned to hate that kind of superficial attraction, yet there she was, suffering from it herself.

Trays of coffee and food had appeared from the canteen around twelve thirty, delivered to Jim's office by two of the female kitchen hands who'd been literally swooning as they hurried back past reception.

'He's so hot!' Leah heard one of them say. 'And he smiled at me.'

'He smiled at me too, honey,' the older woman said. A bit more drily. 'He's a charmer all right. But don't get your hopes up. Men like that don't take out waitresses,' she added as they both swept out the door.

Or receptionists, Leah realised with a perverse rush of disappointment.

What a fool she'd been, getting herself all het up over nothing. He hadn't been coming on to her earlier. He was just being his so-called charming self. Hadn't her father said Jason Pollack had originally been a top salesmen?

Since working here, Leah had met quite a few sales-men and most of them had the gift of the gab. Most of them were good-looking men, too. And outrageous flirts. There wasn't a sales rep at Beville Holdings who hadn't asked her out. And that included the married ones.

Except for Peter. The one with the sick wife. *He'd* never asked her out. That was why Leah liked him so much. He was a really decent guy. Honest and hard working, unlike some of the others around here. If Jason Pollack even thought about making Peter redun-dant, she would have something to say about it.

No, she would have *a lot* to say about it. After all, what was the worst that could happen to her? Okay, so she could lose her job. Not a total disaster, since she didn't rely on her salary to survive. Unlike poor Peter.

But she wouldn't go quietly. She'd take Prince Charming to the unfair dismissal board if he dared do that. She'd take him to the unfair dismissal board if he sacked Peter as well! She'd make him wish he'd never bought Beville Holdings before she was finished. That's what she'd do!

'Would you come and have lunch with me, Leah?'

Leah's head snapped up to find Trish standing there, looking anxious. Trish was Jim's secretary, an attractive redhead in her late twenties who deserved better, in Leah's opinion, than to be sleeping with her married boss.

Of all the women who worked at Beville Holdings, Leah liked Trish the most. They often had lunch together out on the lawns, and Leah usually sat with Trish when they all trundled down to the local pub for drinks after work every Friday night.

Trish claimed she wanted a husband and children of her own, but wouldn't listen to Leah's advice to break it off with Jim and find herself someone who was free. The last time they'd had a woman-to-woman chat over lunch, Trish had confided to Leah that Jim promised to leave his wife when his kids were older.

Famous last words!

Leah didn't really want to hear more of the same today, but Trish was Jim's secretary, with whom Jason Pollack had been installed all morning. Much as Leah despised her own ongoing curiosity and breathless interest, she jumped at the chance of finding out more about the man.

'Be right with you,' she returned. 'Just let me turn on the answering machine. I have to stop at the loo on the way as well.'

'Me, too,' Trish said.

Five minutes later, they were sitting at one of the wooden tables under the clump of willow trees behind their building, a lovely shady spot for eating outdoors on a summer's day. The humidity of January had finally gone—as had the summer storms—February so far having the kind of beautiful weather that brought tourists to Sydney in droves.

Trish had her lunch with her—sandwiches and juice brought from home. Leah hadn't quite got into that kind of budgeting as yet, and had a standard order with the canteen for a no-butter salad sandwich, low-fat muffin and black coffee, which she collected every day right on one.

'The new boss keeping you busy?' she said as soon as they sat down.

'I'll say,' Trish told her as she unwrapped her ham and tomato sandwiches. 'Under those disarming smiles of his, he's a regular power house, and very clued-up. He's had Jim answering some sticky questions, I can tell you. I think Jim's a bit worried.'

'And so he should be,' Leah said wryly.

'What do you mean?'

'You know what I mean, Trish. There's been a lot of money wasted around here. That very expensive Christmas party last year, for instance. Not to mention the sales conference at one of the most expensive resorts in Australia. Then there was the total refurbishing of the offices. To top it off, the whole sales fleet of company cars have just been replaced after only being on the road one year, with all the managers getting more expensive models.'

'When you put it like that, things could look bad.'

Leah could have also added that the new field sales manager hadn't gotten her job because of her experience in the position. The only position Shelley had experience in were those in the *Kama Sutra*.

Trish wasn't the only little dolly bird Jim had on the side. How Trish didn't know about Shelley constantly amazed her. All the reps knew. Heck, just about everyone here knew. Except Trish.

Leah didn't have the heart to tell the girl herself. She'd find out what a rat Jim was soon enough.

'A man like Jason Pollack is going to put it all together like *that* in no time flat,' Leah said, snapping her fingers.

Trish looked worried. 'Jim might get the sack.'

Now *there* was a satisfying thought. Leah believed in bastards getting their comeuppances.

The trouble was, they rarely did. From what she'd heard, Carl was as happy as Larry with a new fiancée, some stunning, up-and-coming actress who no doubt didn't have a single physical flaw.

As for Jim... He was a clever and consummate liar. He'd probably worm his way out of things. Or end up with a golden handshake, plus another top sales job somewhere else. Jim was only in his early forties, a good-looking man who could be very impressive when he wanted to be.

His silly wife *adored* him.

No, bastards didn't always get their comeuppances in life, came Leah's cynical thought. Take the new boss himself. He'd have to be a right bastard, marrying a much older woman for her money like that. And what happens? She conveniently died after no time at all, leaving him scads of money, plus the freedom to do exactly what he liked for the rest of his life.

How convenient!

'It's all very worrying,' Trish said, having not yet touched a bite of her lunch.

A wave of sympathy pushed aside Leah's sarcastic thoughts.

'*You* don't have to worry,' Leah said, reaching across to touch Trish gently on her arm. 'You haven't done anything wrong.'

'Haven't I?' Trish's eyes suddenly filled. 'I've been sleeping with a married man, Leah. Trying to take him away from his wife and family. That's not right. I know she loves him. And so do his kids. My mother would be utterly ashamed of me, if she knew…'

Leah handed over the paper napkin that came with her lunch, shaking her head as Trish made a right mess of her makeup with her tears.

'Break it off with him, Trish,' she advised. 'Give yourself a chance to find someone else.'

'It's all very well for you to say that, Leah,' Trish said with a flash of envious eyes as she mopped up her tears. 'You could get any man you want. Just look at you. You're utterly gorgeous, and you're not even wearing much makeup.'

'Skin-deep beauty is not all it's cracked up to be, Trish. Or a recipe for success with men. My first husband dumped me.'

Trish blinked her surprise. '*What?* I didn't even know you'd been married!'

Leah had carefully avoided mentioning Carl. When she'd filled in her application form she'd put single as her status. And when she chatted with the girls at work, she always carefully steered the conversations round to their lives, not hers.

When they occasionally asked her about her love life, she always said she was between boyfriends.

When any of her co-workers asked her on a Monday morning what she'd done that weekend, she say she'd gone home to visit her widowed father. She had admitted she'd lost her mother in a car accident not long back, but had never mentioned her marriage. Or her hated scars.

'How long were you married for?' Trish asked.

'Six months.'

'He left you after six months!'

Leah smiled a dry smile at Trish's bug-eyed surprise. 'Why do you think I'm a bit cynical at times?'

'I don't think you're cynical. I think you're very nice.'

Leah laughed. 'Scratch the surface and you'll find a bitter divorcée.'

'Really? Well, at least that explains why you don't have a boyfriend. I was beginning to think you were having an affair with a married man too, and didn't want to admit it. But I can see now that that's not your style.'

'Certainly not,' Leah said. 'And, Trish, please don't mention my marriage to anyone.'

'Why not? People wonder about you, you know.'

'What? *Why?*'

'Because you're clearly too good for this job, Leah. It's not just the way you look, but the way you talk, and walk. You went to one of those schools, didn't you? The kind that does deportment and stuff. I'll bet you were an aspiring model at one stage. Or an actress.'

'I...er...yes, I did do a modelling course once,' she

admitted. Her grandmother had given it to her for her sixteenth birthday.

Dear Gran. She was gone now, too. Along with her mother.

'Eat up,' Leah advised, not wanting to think about sad things any more. 'And give that Jim the flick.'

'I'll try,' Trish said, but didn't look too sure.

Leah returned to work in a depressed mood. Talking about relationships was a real downer, especially ones which had no chance of working out.

Jason Pollack remained incognito, having moved on the human resources division for the afternoon, according to Mandy when she stopped for a chat of her way to post the day's mail. By four, Leah was living in nervous anticipation of his walking by on his way out. But he didn't, even though she lingered a few minutes after her normal knock-off time of four thirty.

'I can get any man I want, can I?' she muttered irritably to herself as she finally made her way to the almost empty car park.

Only a couple of the managers' cars remained, plus the dark blue sports car.

Not that she really wanted Jason Pollack, she told herself. She'd have to be crazy to want a man like him, except perhaps on a purely physical basis. He might be all right for a wild fling. If she was the kind of girl who had wild flings. Which she wasn't.

Never had been, really. There again, sex had never been a driving need with Leah.

She'd had awful trouble with her early boyfriends, fighting them off and finding all sorts of excuses not to sleep with them. Some of them had called her frigid. Others had tolerated her saying no to their advances, perhaps because they had their eye more on her money than her body.

And then Carl had come along.

Leah had fallen madly in love for the first time and been more than happy to go to bed with Carl.

He'd been intrigued by her virginity—to begin with.

In hindsight, Leah wondered if her lack of sexual experience had been a contributing factor in his eventually leaving her. She had to confess that she wasn't the most adventurous person in bed.

As she opened her car door and just stood there, letting the heat out for a minute, Leah found herself thinking that Trish probably stayed with Jim because they had great sex together. Every single time.

She hadn't thought of that.

But was that kind of sexual pleasure and satisfaction so damned wonderful that it made you lose your head, that it made you let yourself be used, even though you knew the relationship was going nowhere?

'Are you waiting for me?'

The heat escaping from the car was nothing to the heat that filled Leah's face as she whirled to face Jason Pollack.

He looked just as good as he had that morning. Maybe even better.

'Of course not!' she denied even as her eyes drank him in. 'I was waiting till the car cooled down.'

His eyes narrowed on hers, as though he was trying to gauge the truth of her statement. 'Pity.'

What could she possibly say to that?

He closed her passenger door, which was blocking his entrance into his car, gazing at her over the rather low roof of her hatchback.

'So I'd be wasting my time if I asked you out to dinner tonight?' he said, his eyes remaining locked with her.

She stared back at him, willing herself to say no.

'Just dinner, Mr Pollack?' she managed to throw at him in a wonderfully haughty fashion.

'But of course, Ms Johanssen,' came his suave reply, those dark, sexy eyes of his telling her an entirely different story. If she agreed to dinner with him, she was definitely on the menu for afters.

'If that's all *you* want,' he added.

That did it! That tipped the scales back in favour of reason.

'What I want, Mr Pollack,' she said sharply, 'is for you to leave me alone. Please do not ask me to go out with you again, or I will report you for sexual harassment. Do I make myself clear?'

She didn't wait for him to answer. She climbed in behind the wheel, slammed the car door and gunned her engine.

Thank goodness the car park was nearly empty, because she probably would have crashed into something, so recklessly did she reverse out of her spot and accelerate away. The last she saw of Jason Pollack, he was standing by his car, staring after her with an annoyingly unfathomable look on his face.

During her longer than usual drive home—the traffic along Victoria Road was extra heavy, due to an overturned truck—Leah was besieged by mixed emotions.

Regret that she'd now never know what it would be like to be made love to by Jason Pollack, hunk extraordinaire. But relief also that she would never have to face the dilemma of taking off her clothes for him and exposing her scars.

Leah could not bear the thought that he might look at her the way Carl had looked at her that last humiliating time.

But her most overriding emotion was resentment over the man's utter arrogance.

He'd just assumed—because he was the new boss and a billionaire and good looking—that the blonde bimbo receptionist at Beville Holdings would go out with him if he asked. He hadn't even enquired if she had a boyfriend. He probably didn't even care!

Of course, by the time Leah arrived home, worry had set in. Would he find some excuse to sack her? Going to work the next morning suddenly held all kinds of hazards.

'He'll be sorry if he tries to fire me,' she muttered as she went straight to the fridge and grabbed the bottle of Verdelho, which was chilling in the door. A soothing drink was definitely called for tonight. 'He has no idea who he's dealing with here,' she muttered as she reached for the bottle opener. 'No idea at all!'

CHAPTER FOUR

'MR POLLACK WANTS to see you in the function room.'

Leah stiffened in her grey leather office chair.

The moment she had been dreading all day had finally arrived.

He'd said a polite hello to her when he'd arrived this morning with his male PA in tow, a dark-haired, solid fellow in his early thirties. But she hadn't set eyes on either man since. According to Trish at lunchtime, both men had spent all morning going over the sales figures for the past two years, and were planning on spending the afternoon talking to the managers in the marketing division.

By four o'clock, Leah had thought she'd escaped a confrontation over what she'd said in the car park. But it seemed she was wrong.

'Why on earth would he want to see me?' she queried Mandy as she rose reluctantly to her feet.

Mandy shrugged. 'Don't ask me. I'm just the messenger. Maybe he wants to ask you out,' she added with a mischievous twinkle in her eye.

'Very funny.'

The temptation to dash off to the ladies' room to check her appearance was intense. But Leah refused to indulge her vanity, or that secret part of herself that still found Jason Pollack cripplingly attractive. She hadn't stared at him when he arrived this morning, looking suave and smooth in a navy pinstriped suit, crisp white shirt and wine-coloured tie, along with matching kerchief in his breast pocket.

She'd looked at him, as he had looked at her. And said a polite hello, as he had to her. But that was all.

Taking a deep, gathering breath, Leah squared her shoulders and set off down the corridor that ran off the reception area to her right, at the end of which lay a large room that the company used for meetings and functions.

The door was ominously shut, which only increased her nerves. Hopefully, he wouldn't be alone.

Her tap tap on the door sounded firm, despite her hand shaking.

'Come in,' ordered a rich male voice through the door.

His, of course.

Another deep breath as she turned the silver door handle, then pushed open the door.

He was alone, sitting at the boardroom table whose polished length stretched along in front of the tall windows that overlooked the back lawns. That wall faced west and, at this hour, the rays of the low-set sun slanted through the uncurtained sheets of glass, casting his handsome face into shadows, but lighting up his jet-black hair.

Leah hated the way her stomach was churning. Hated *him* for making her feel like this. So vulnerable, and so very foolish.

Jason had steeled himself against her beauty.

What a futile exercise!

She took his breath away again as she entered, her walk as bewitching as the rest of her. She must have once taken ballet lessons, he decided. Or been a model. Her posture was superb. So was the rest of her.

She was wearing pale pink today, a softly feminine dress that wrapped around her slender yet curvy body, covering everything, hiding nothing. Her hair was up, but loosely, a style he'd always liked. As she came closer he could smell her perfume, a tantalising scent that reminded of him faintly of vanilla.

His flesh leapt to attention, making him glad he was sitting at a table.

'You wanted to see me, Mr Pollack?' she said, her green eyes still flashing a frosty dislike at him.

Jason wished he hadn't sent for her now. He was wasting his time here. Torturing himself for nothing. Clearly, he'd misread her yesterday morning. He'd thought he'd seen a spark of mutual attraction in her eyes at the time; thought she'd just been playing a hard-to-get game when she'd walked away and ignored him.

Even after the incident in the car park, his male ego

had managed to momentarily convince himself that her spirited attack was another ploy of the same hard-to-get game. Jason had been the target of many beautiful but ambitious female employees over the last few years, and had become somewhat familiar with their tactics. Some were quite brazen, others more subtle, feigning an initial uninterest, despite their body language telling him otherwise.

During his drive home, Jason had desperately clung to the hope that Ms Johanssen had been one of the latter kind. But as he'd brooded over dinner last night, he had finally come to the more logical conclusion that the girl probably had a steady boyfriend, and was sick to death of being hit on by men. Given how stunning she was, that must happen all the time.

Unfortunately, the thought that Leah Johanssen had a boyfriend, that she might even be living with someone, had not sat well with Jason. The image of her wrapped in some other man's arms that very night had kept him tossing and turning into the wee small hours.

By morning, a bleary-eyed Jason decided not to make a fool of himself with her a second time. He would ignore her from now on, as she had ignored him.

He might have succeeded in this strategy if Bob hadn't told him over afternoon tea that office gossip had the beautiful blonde receptionist of Beville Holdings *without* a current boyfriend.

Which was why Jason had sent for her.

Bad move, as it turned out. All that had been

achieved was a more acute reminder of how devastatingly desirable he found this girl.

As confident as Jason was in his own attractiveness to the opposite sex, there seemed little hope that Leah Johanssen secretly fancied him. Women who secretly fancied men didn't look at them the way she was looking at him at this present moment—like he was a snake that had crawled into her bedroom.

'Please, sit down,' he said to her in curt tones, and indicated the chair opposite him.

'It's ten past four,' she shot back without moving an inch. 'I go home at four thirty.'

Brother, she really had it in for him for whatever reason. He supposed he had come on a bit strong yesterday. Not one of his most subtle invitations.

But someone might like to tell *her* that threatening her new boss with sexual harassment charges wasn't exactly a good career move.

'This won't take long,' he said a bit sharply.

'Very well,' she said, and with a toss of her lovely head, pulled out the chair and sat down, her back ramrod straight, her knees primly together.

Jason gritted his teeth. 'I wanted to apologise to you for what happened in the car park yesterday.'

An apology! It was the last thing Leah was expecting.

'It was arrogant and presumptuous of me to ask you out like that,' he added, using the exact words she'd called him in her mind. 'I'm sorry, Leah. I realise how annoying it must be to be on the end of unwanted attentions and invitations. A girl as beautiful as yourself is probably always getting hit on by men. It must be doubling annoying when it's your new boss at work. Trust me when I say it won't happen again.'

Leah just sat there, totally dumb-struck. Her fear all day had been over his asking her to leave. An apology had not been expected.

Men like him rarely apologised for anything!

'That's all, Leah,' he went on abruptly. 'Thank you for coming.'

As Leah levered herself up out of the chair, she found that her hands were clenched tightly together and her heart was racing like mad. Suddenly, she wanted to say something to him, to soften that hard, tight-lipped expression on his face. But what?

I'm sorry too. I overreacted. I really would have loved to go out to dinner with you last night. But I was afraid you'd make me want to go to bed with you and then I'd have to take off my clothes and you'd see my scars and...

A small shudder rippled down Leah's spine as she realised her thoughts seemed to be spinning out of control.

'I will be calling you in for a proper interview later in the week,' he added matter of factly. 'Only about work matters,' he hastily reassured. 'I hope to interview *all* the employees of Beville Holdings. I trust you won't find that a problem?'

'Not at all, Mr Pollack.' Thank heavens she *sounded* normal!

'Jason, please,' he insisted. 'I always do business on a first-name basis.'

'Jason,' she repeated, the name feeling right for him. A strong name for a strong man. Leah was already beginning to forget why it was she hadn't liked him.

Oh, yes. He'd married an older woman for her money, hadn't he? And now he was single again, a bachelor playboy with a penthouse and a sports car and eyes that kept telling her he wanted to add her to his list of successful takeovers.

His mouth might have apologised, but those burning black eyes kept betraying his true agenda.

Leah hadn't come down in the last shower. Jason Pollack was still interested in her. Men like him didn't back away gracefully. They went after what they wanted with every means at their disposal.

And he had lots of means at his disposal. Money. Position. Power. And more sex appeal than any man had a right to.

Their eyes met and locked, hers struggling to hold on to the coolly haughty expression that she'd adopted since entering the room. She could feel herself melting, surrendering to the heat that radiated from his gaze. Not just her eyes. But her mind. And her whole insides. Melting to mush.

What would it be like, she wondered, to be his girlfriend? To eat with him, and sleep with him. To just *be* with him.

Images filled her mind. Erotic images. Corrupting images.

Just in time she snapped out of it and spun away from him, her hands making fists by her side as she marched towards the door.

'Have a pleasant evening, Leah,' he called after her. 'I'll see you in the morning.'

Jason was still sitting there, mulling over Leah's contradictory body language when Bob came in, holding a couple of plastic folders.

'Well?' Bob said, sitting down in the chair that Leah had just vacated. 'How did it go with the delectable Ms Johanssen?'

'So-so,' Jason replied. Better, actually, than he'd expected. He'd finally seen that spark in her eyes again, the one he'd glimpsed when they'd first met. Though this time, for a few seconds, it had been more than a spark. More of a sizzle.

'Did you ask her out?'

'Not yet.' Despite her momentary lapse, when she'd shown him that she *was* attracted to him, Jason knew he was going to have to be patient.

Not that he felt like being patient. He was still wildly erect under the table, a most unusual state of affairs. The prospect of more nights of tossing and turning was not a pleasant one.

'You have that look in your eye,' Bob said ruefully. 'The one you have when there's some company you're really keen on acquiring. Haven't seen it directed towards a girl before, though.'

'There's a first time for everything,' Jason said,

thinking that he hadn't met a girl quite like this one
before.

Karen would have liked Leah, came the sudden and
highly unexpected thought.

Karen had always hated women who fell at his feet.
Which they had. Most of his life.

Karen had been the first member of the opposite sex
who'd initially spurned his advances. And meant it.

It had taken Jason three months of persistence and
lots of persuasion before she consented to go out on a
date with him. Their age difference had really worried
her. Plus what other people thought, especially once
she promoted him to CEO of WhizzBiz Electronics.

Jason wondered what it was that worried Leah about
him. Something did. He could sense it. His training as
a salesman had made him very sensitive to body language.

Maybe she had a hard and fast rule not to mix business with pleasure. Or maybe she'd been burned, like
Bob had been last year, and was wary about dating
again.

He needed to know more about her. Knowledge
was, indeed, power.

'Did you get what I wanted?' he asked Bob.

Bob placed the orange plastic folder on his own lap,
then slid the blue one across the table, right into Jason's
waiting hands.

Jason's conscience bothered him only slightly as
he opened the file and began flicking through the print-
out of Leah Johanssen's employment record.

I'm the boss, he told himself. It's my right to know the background and qualifications of my employees.

Yeah, especially ones you fancy, his dark side pointed out mockingly.

'I…er…printed out Trish's file as well,' Bob suddenly confessed. 'You know—Jim Matheson's secretary.'

Jason's head snapped up to stare at his PA. 'What on earth for?' He sure as hell didn't fancy *her*.

'I think she's nice. I like her.'

'You do realise she's having an affair with Matheson, don't you?'

'Yeah,' Bob said. 'I sort of gathered that. But Matheson's married, and I'm not. You and I both know he's not going to leave his wife for his secretary. Men like Matheson are serial adulterers. You can bet that Trish isn't the only piece of skirt he's had around here.'

Bob's observation sent the most awful thought into Jason's head. Possibly because he was looking at Leah's resumé at the time.

His stomach contracted fiercely as he saw that she had had no qualifications for her present position when she'd been hired last year. No qualifications for any job, really.

Which meant…what?

Jason had spent a dreadful night last night, imagining her in the arms of some nameless boyfriend. Thinking of her being taken by Jim Matheson on his oversized desk—or on the leather chesterfield in his office—made him feel physically ill!

Logic came to his rescue just in time. Would a girl who'd knocked *him* back so forcefully sleep with a creep like Matheson for some second-rate receptionist job?

Absolutely not. If she'd been that type, she'd have accepted *his* invitation to dinner yesterday.

No, Leah Johanssen was deeper than that. And far more complex. A real mystery woman. Not only did she not have many employment qualifications, she had no past employment record. What had she been doing with her life before starting work here?

'Look, let's get back to business,' he said suddenly, and shoved the pages back into the folder. He'd look at them later, when he had to time to think about nothing but her. 'Give me your first impressions of Beville Holdings as a company.'

Bob leant back in his chair, hooking his right foot over his left knee. 'Well, the problem clearly lies with management, both in sales *and* marketing,' he said. 'But the sales division is by far the worst. Jim Matheson is one slick but rather shifty customer. He'll definitely have to go. And I have no ulterior motive for saying that,' he added swiftly.

'Good. Because no way will I be firing Jim Matheson just yet. Not till *after* I find out what damage he's done. By the way, did you manage to hire someone yesterday to do some speedy market research on all their products?'

'Yep. Should have a report by the end of the week.'

'Great. You'll be coming with me here again tomorrow, by the way. And every day this week.'

'Thank you. And I don't have an ulterior motive for saying that, either. I simply hate staying in the office all by myself, doing nothing but take phone calls. Yesterday was such a bore.'

Jason gave Bob a droll look. Their office was located within Jason's penthouse, with every possible mod con and a heated lap pool a few metres away in which both men swam every day. When he sold WhizzBiz Electronics and became a corporate pirate, Jason decided that renting office space was a waste of time and money. So he'd sold the large home he'd shared with Karen, and bought the top floor of a new skyscraper smack dab in the middle of Sydney.

It had cost him fifteen million dollars, but was probably worth double that now.

'Poor Bob,' he said, with not a trace of sympathy in his voice. 'Any important calls yesterday, by the way?'

'Let's see now. The usual canvassing crap and invitations to stuff you hate. There was *one* rather interesting invite, though. From Joachim Bloom, asking you to a dinner party at his home next Saturday night. I told him I'd get back to him.'

'Joachim Bloom,' Jason repeated thoughtfully. 'Name sounds familiar. Remind me. What does he do?' This was Bob's greatest asset as Jason's PA. He knew everything about everyone who mattered—money-wise—in Australia. Read all the business magazines from cover to cover every month, as well as the business section in every newspaper, every day.

'He's a stockbroker. Old money, but he's managed

to increase his fortune somewhat. Always makes it on to the top two hundred richest in Australia list. A great contact if you want to start taking over strange little companies you know nothing about. He'd probably be able to tell you more about Beville Holdings in one night than we'll be able to find out this entire week.'

'A bit late for that, don't you think?' Jason remarked, toying with the idea of actually saying yes. He wasn't partial to dinner parties, but he'd spent every Saturday night for the past six months with Hilary and suspected he might not want to spend this Saturday night alone. He might be tempted to ring Hilary out of sheer sexual frustration and that would not do. Because it wasn't dark hair he wanted to wake to on the pillow next to him, but blonde.

'Where does Mr Bloom live?' he asked, still thinking of long blonde hair spread out on his pillow.

'Vaucluse.'

'Is there any other address for old money? Okay. Ring him back and accept.'

'Will do,' Bob said as he fished out his phone. 'I have his number and address in here.'

Whilst Bob rang Mr Bloom and accepted the dinner invitation on his behalf, Jason gathered up his papers into his briefcase, including the folder with the file on Leah.

He'd bring her in for that chat soon. But not too soon.

Friday, he decided. By then, he might know how best to handle her.

By then, you're going to be in a bad way, whispered a frustrated voice inside his head.

Just keep busy, he told himself.

'All done,' Bob said. 'You're expected at seven thirty. Saturday night. Black tie.'

'Black tie! Good God, who's coming? The Queen?'

'The best of Sydney society, I suppose.'

'Then why's he asking *me*? I've never been part of that crowd.'

'You want me to ring and cancel?'

'No, no. I'll go. At least the food will be good. And the wine.'

'By the way, he enquired if you had a partner and I said no. Hilary *is* history, isn't she?'

'Absolutely.'

'Good.'

Jason frowned. 'You didn't like Hilary?' As much as Jason didn't make a habit of discussing his personal life with Bob, it was impossible to hide it. Hilary had often dropped in at the penthouse during the day when Bob had been there.

'She was after you for your money,' Bob pronounced, startling Jason.

'But she had money of her own.' Hilary's first husband had been well off, her divorce settlement considerable. She'd owned a very nice house at Harboard Beach, where Jason had spent many weekends with her.

'Some women can never be too rich.'

Jason thought about Hilary's fury when he wouldn't

marry her. She'd claimed to be madly in love with him. But maybe it had never been a matter of love. Jason respected Bob's judgement of character, plus his intuition about people.

'You could be right,' he said. 'Come on. Let's get going. It's been a long day.'

The reception desk was deserted by the time they walked past. Leah's car wasn't in the car park, either. She was gone.

Jason wondered for a moment where she lived. But then he realised he had that detail in his briefcase. He had lots of details about her, not just her address.

Suddenly, he couldn't wait to get home to discover every single one of them.

CHAPTER FIVE

LEAH'S PHONE WAS ringing as she let herself into her apartment. Throwing her bag on to the marble hall stand, she hurried into the living room and swept up the receiver.

'Yes?'

'Hi, there. You sound breathless.'

It was her father.

'I've just walked in the door. Can you hang on till I pour myself a glass of wine?'

'Sure.'

Leah went into the kitchen and poured herself a glass from the bottle of Verdelho that she'd opened the night before, taking it with her and settling into her favourite armchair, which was positioned right next to the phone.

'I'm back,' she said down the line after a couple of refreshing sips.

'Stressful day?'

'No,' she lied. 'I'm just a bit hot and bothered from contending with peak-hour traffic.

'I'm ringing to warn you early in the week that I'm having a dinner party on Saturday night. Nothing too large. Just a dozen or so people.'

'That's all right,' she said. 'I'll stay in my room and read.'

'No, no, I want you to be there, by my side. That's why I'm calling.'

'Oh, Daddy, you know I'm not into that kind of thing any more.'

'Yes, I do know that, more's the pity. You are so very good at making people feel comfortable. Just like your mother was.'

'Mum was marvellous at dinner parties, wasn't she?' Leah said with fond remembrance and a tinge of sadness.

'Yes,' her father agreed. 'And you take after her. The thing is, darling, there's this one gentleman in particular that I've invited. I'd like to sit you next to him at the table. Please come, as a favor to me.'

'Who is he? Not some lecherous old billionaire, Daddy. I have no intention of spending an entire evening, slapping his hands away under the table.'

Her father laughed. 'Would I do that to you?'

'You can be quite ruthless where money is concerned. So who is this mystery dinner guest, exactly?'

'Someone who has everything, except me as his broker.'

'If you won't tell me his name, my guess is he *is* old and lecherous.'

'Not at all!' her father denied.

Leah rolled her eyes. Most of her father's male clients were over sixty, multi-millionaires who still thought they were God's gift to women, despite their balding heads and pot bellies.

'Promise me he's not too revolting.'

'He's not at all revolting. Honestly.'

'I suppose you'll want me to doll myself up.'

'You could never look anything but beautiful, Leah. But, yes, it's black tie.'

Leah sighed. She'd once loved black tie parties. Loved dressing up to the nines. Loved wearing designer dresses and diamonds.

Somehow, such dos seemed pretentious now, filled with pompous, privileged people who had no idea how the other half lived.

But she loved her father and it would be churlish of her to refuse. He rarely asked anything of her.

So come next Saturday night, she'd doll herself up and sit next to this rich old codger and do her best to charm him.

'Okay,' she agreed.

'Darling, that's wonderful. I do appreciate it. And you'll enjoy yourself, I'm sure. I'm having the food done by that catering company your mother always hired. More than a dozen people is a bit much to expect Mrs B. to cook for. And I'm going to open some of my best wines.'

'Heavens!' This potential client must be very rich indeed.

'The invitations are for seven thirty, but I presume you'll already be here long before then.'

Leah spent most Saturdays at Westmead Hospital, visiting the children's wards and doing what she could to bring a little joy into the lives of the poor kids there, especially the ones in the cancer ward. During her own long rehabilitation in that same hospital, she'd taken to wandering the corridors, discovering that there were plenty of people worse off than herself. It had been the children, however, who had affected her most deeply. Poor little mites.

Yet so brave. Sometimes she felt quite ashamed of herself when she visited them. They rarely complained, even when all their hair had fallen out. She knew she'd be devastated if all her hair fell out. Yet she was ashamed of a few miserable scars that didn't even show.

She usually left around four—the children were getting tired by then, anyway—and drove straight to Vaucluse, arriving at her father's around five.

'I'll try to make it home by four,' she told him. 'It's so long since I've dolled myself up to this degree, it might take a while. Do you want me to help with the flowers? Or the table setting?'

'No. I don't want you to do a thing. Just look beautiful.'

Leah winced. That was what Carl always said to her when they had a party. She had liked it at the time but had since read an awful shallowness into the comment, as though she had nothing more to offer than her physical beauty.

Which, as it turned out, had been correct where Carl

was concerned. He hadn't valued her intelligence. Or her joy of life. Or her soul. His love for her had been as skin deep as her supposed beauty.

Leah sighed. And what if I were ugly, Daddy? she felt like asking. What if I had no hair? Would you still want me to co-host your dinner party? Was her father's love for her tainted by her looks as well?

'I have to go cook myself something, Daddy,' she said abruptly. 'All this talk of food has made me hungry.'

'You do that, daughter. See you Saturday. Love you.'

And he hung up.

Leah gripped the phone for a few seconds before dropping it back into its cradle. He *did* love her. She knew he did.

But then, he was her father.

No other man had ever really loved her, she accepted painfully. Not any of her silly boyfriends. And Carl, least of all.

True love encompassed more than sexual attraction. It was deeply caring, and strongly committed, and totally unconditional. True love didn't abandon you when things got tough. True love was like a rock.

And true love, Leah realised ruefully, was not be found in a pair of dark eyes that sizzled and smouldered whenever they looked at her. She knew exactly what Jason Pollack wanted from her, and it wasn't commitment and caring. He didn't want to be her true love, just her lover.

The man had to be resisted.

Not an easy task, she conceded as she recalled what had happened to her this afternoon.

How long, she wondered, before he made his next move? And he would. She was sure of it.

Maybe it was time for her to move on. To resign and find herself another job. She shouldn't have the same trouble as she had the first time. She had experience now.

Yes, Leah decided. That was what she had to do. Resign.

She'd type out the letter at work tomorrow. And when Jason Pollack brought her in for that interview, she'd give it to him.

CHAPTER SIX

BY FOUR O'CLOCK Friday, Leah had worked herself up into a state. Jason hadn't called her in for that interview, though everyone else seemed to have trundled down to the function room over the past three days. Today, all the reps had been brought in off the road, going in for their interviews one by one, then stopping by her desk afterwards to tell her how absolutely fantastic the new boss was, and that their jobs were safe.

Peter, of course, was very relieved, though he confided to Leah that he hoped someone eventually told Mr Pollack—or his offsider—how hopeless their field sales manager was. Shelley had totally botched up their territories, he'd complained. As well as their country runs.

By four twenty-five, Leah had given up hope that she was going to have the opportunity this week to hand in her resignation personally.

Part of her was relieved. She hadn't been looking forward to another confrontation with Jason Pollack, which is what it would have become.

On another level, she wished it was over. Now, she would think about that infernal man all weekend.

Leah started tidying up her desk, ready to leave at four thirty, when Trish showed up, looking flushed and excited.

'I'm not going down to the pub for drinks tonight,' she announced. 'Sorry.'

'That's all right,' Leah returned. 'I'm going straight home tonight, anyway.'

She'd been afraid the new and much-lauded boss might show up at the pub, since he didn't stand on ceremony. The last thing Leah wanted was to be with him in a semi-social situation. It had been bad enough, greeting him politely every morning and afternoon this week, as well as during the day when he walked past on the way to the factory, or the canteen, or wherever he'd been going. He always smiled at her, and it was impossible not to smile back. Her mouth simply didn't obey her when he was around. Neither did her eyes. She hadn't ogled him, exactly. But it had been a close call.

'Where are you off to instead?' she asked Trish.

'You'll never guess. Bob's asked me out.'

'Bob who? Oh, you mean Bob, the right-hand man.'

'Yes.' Trish beamed.

'That's great, Trish,' Leah said with a warm smile. 'Bob seems nice.'

'He is. *Very.* Jim's most put out, but I'd already told him it was over between us. He's gone off home in a huff.'

Leah frowned. 'I didn't see him leave.'

'He went out the side door.'

'Has Mr Pollack left the same way?' she asked hopefully.

'No. He's still in the function room with Bob. And you'd better start calling him Jason. He hates being called Mr Pollack.'

Leah sighed. 'I won't have to worry about that for much longer, Trish. I've decided to resign.'

'What? But *why*?' Trish looked upset.

'I think it's time I tried something a little more challenging.'

'Oh, dear, I'm going to miss you terribly. Couldn't you possibly find something more challenging here? Bob told me Jason is planning a brand new advertising campaign to get sales moving. You might be able to help with that.'

'I don't think so, Trish,' Leah said, switching on the answering machine, then bending down to get her handbag from where it was sitting on the floor under the desk.

'You haven't resigned yet, have you?'

'What's this about resigning?'

Leah's head snapped up to find Jason striding towards them, his handsome face not smiling at her *this* time. Bob was a few steps behind, *his* face full of smiles as he looked at Trish.

'Leah. She says she needs something more challenging,' Trish said before Leah could assemble her thoughts, and her defences. 'You could find her something in marketing, Jason, couldn't you?'

The boss's darkly frustrated eyes went to Leah's. 'I would not dream of forcing Ms Johannsen into doing anything she didn't want to do,' he replied, the use of her last name showing he was not pleased by her decision. 'But if she wishes, yes, I'm sure something could be arranged. I would hate to lose such a valued employee.'

'See?' Trish said happily.

'I hear you and Bob are going out to dinner tonight,' Jason directed toward Trish. 'Why don't you two run along and leave me to have a private word with Leah? I was meaning to speak to her today, but time simply ran out on me.'

Leah hated the feeling of people talking around her. Hated the feeling of losing control of her own life.

She didn't want to have a private word with this man. She didn't want to have a private *anything* with him.

But Bob was swift to obey his boss's command, and soon they were alone together. Though thankfully, not for long. The office staff kept going by on their way out, saying a polite cheerio to Jason, then calling out to Leah that they'd see her later down at the pub.

Finally, however, the trail of people ceased and Leah was forced to face her nemesis, alone.

'You go somewhere for drinks on a Friday night?' he asked from where he was still standing on the other side of the desk. Thank goodness.

'Usually. But not tonight.' She stood up, her handbag at the ready to make a quick exit.

'Why not?'

'Trish won't be there. I usually sit with her and I don't like to go alone.'

'I could take you,' came his immediate offer.

'Absolutely not!'

'Why not?'

'I don't like to be the object of office gossip.'

'But you're resigning. Or so you say,' he added, a slightly cynical edge creeping into his voice.

Leah bristled. 'I always mean what I say. I am resigning, and there's nothing you can say or do to stop me.'

He stared at her, his head cocking slightly on one side. 'Why are you afraid of me?'

Leah stiffened. 'I am not afraid of you.'

'Oh, yes, you are. Yet you shouldn't be. I don't mean you any harm, Leah. I like you. No, that's a rather colossal understatement. I'm extremely attracted to you. I'd love to take you out.'

'You'd love to take me to bed,' she snapped, the words tripping off her tongue with a flash of venom.

His smile was her undoing. Because it was so damned honest.

'That, too,' he admitted. 'But is that such a crime? Look at it from my angle, Leah,' he went on persuasively. 'I'm a single man. You're a single woman. Without a current boyfriend, I'm told. Yes, I also admit to asking around the office about you. That's what men do when they're interested in a woman. And I am very interested in you.'

'Why?' she threw at him.

He looked rattled for a moment.

'Why not?'

'Do *you* have a current girlfriend?' she quizzed him.

'No.'

'Now why do I find that hard to believe?' she scoffed.

'I did have a girlfriend till recently. We split up a couple of weeks ago.'

How typical, she thought. Out with the old and in with the new. Men like him were never long without a woman on their arm, and in their bed. Good-looking women. Never plain ones.

'Come out with me tonight, Leah. Get to know me. I'm not what you think.'

But you *are*, Jason's conscience jeered. You're not interested in a real relationship with this girl. You don't want to marry her, or have children with her. She's dead right about you. You just want her in your bed, at your beck and call.

A measure of guilt flooded in with this admission. But it wasn't as strong as his desire, a desire that had become almost obsessive this past week. He'd had extreme difficulty putting his mind to the takeover of this company, his thoughts constantly distracted by her physical nearness. He kept making excuses to walk by reception, just to see her, and to reassure himself that the chemistry between them was mutual.

It was. He *knew* it was.

He'd delayed interviewing her, in the hope of calming her concerns about him. But that hadn't worked. She was going to resign.

Exasperation joined his desperation. 'If you're not afraid of me and you're going to resign, then there's nothing to stop you coming out with me tonight. *Is* there?' he ground out.

'Maybe I just don't like you,' she snapped back. 'Or hasn't that occurred to your highness?'

Jason's teeth clenched hard in his jaw. Damn, but if that desk wasn't between them, he'd sweep her into his arms and kiss that saucy mouth of hers into total silence.

As it was, all he could do was glower at her.

She glowered right back.

If only he knew *why* she was fighting the chemistry between them. Her employment file hadn't helped him all that much. She was still one big mystery.

The arrival of the cleaners gave Jason the opportunity he was looking for.

'We need to talk,' he pronounced firmly. 'In private. Come with me.'

Leah threw a frantic glance at the two cleaners who steadfastly ignored her. Other than making a scene, she had no option but to do what he asked.

Grabbing her handbag, she followed him down to the function room, thinking to herself that it would be ages before the cleaners got down there. She would be alone with him for far too long without any hope of interruption.

'This is all nonsense,' he declared after he banged the door shut behind her. 'Your resigning is nonsense. *That* is nonsense,' he said, waving an impatient hand in her direction.

'I have no idea what you're talking about,' she retorted, though she suspected he was referring to the way she was clutching her handbag in front of her, like a shield.

He began to pace about the room, raking his hands through his hair and muttering to himself. When he reached the far side of the boardroom table, he ground to a halt, his eyes stabbing across the room at her.

'What in hell's wrong with you?' he demanded to know. 'You say one thing, but your eyes keep telling me a different story. Are you or are you not attracted to me?'

Leah swallowed. A direct interrogation was the last approach she'd expected. She'd been worried he might do something more physical.

'Don't give me some bulldust answer, Leah. Tell me the truth.'

She drew herself up as tall as she could, doing her best to maintain her dignity, whilst all the while thinking he was devastatingly attractive when he was angry. The passion in his eyes and his face was extremely flattering, and incredibly seductive. Because it was all for *her*.

'You are a very handsome man,' she said, shaken by the dizzying waves of desire which started washing through her.

'Handsome is as handsome does,' he returned sharply. 'What I want to know is do you want me as I want you, damn it?'

'I…I…' She could not go on. Could not say another word. Not yes. Or no. Nothing.

Her mouth had gone bone dry. Her mind went blank.

Her inability to answer thrilled Jason. Then aroused him. He had to touch her. Had to kiss her.

When he strode around the table towards her, her eyes blinked wide, her lips falling slightly apart.

But she didn't turn and run.

Jason didn't know why she'd been afraid of him. Or if she still was. But he was beyond caring. All that mattered at that moment was what her eyes kept telling him.

She was standing there, waiting for him, wanting him as he wanted her.

Disposing of that silly handbag took less than a second. Pulling her into his arms even less.

He groaned as his mouth took possession of hers, his arms folding her close, then closer still. Technique seemed unimportant in the face of the emotion that threatened to overwhelm him. Triumph mingled with the most intoxicating pleasure. The kiss went on, and on, and on. Not foreplay, but an experience in itself, satisfying him with the way her body melted against his, her soft moans music to his ears.

Jason knew, long before his head lifted, that she was his. He didn't need to rush things now. A quickie in this office was not what he'd been thinking about and craving all week. He wanted her in his bed. Tonight. All night.

And that was only for starters.

'You are so beautiful,' he whispered against her hair, his arms holding her close, close enough to feel the instant stiffening of her muscles.

What had he done wrong now?

She wrenched out of his arms, her face flushed, her eyes tormented as she stumbled back from him.

'I'm sorry,' she choked out. 'But I can't do this. No, don't touch me again!' she threw at him when he took a step toward her. 'If you do, I'll scream.'

He froze, his body as frustrated at his mind. What on earth was the matter with this girl?

'You're crazy, do you know that?'

'Yes,' she replied with a funny little laugh. 'Yes. I think I must be.' And she bent to scoop up her bag from where he'd dropped it on the floor.

Panic filled his heart that she would go and he would never see her again. Without thinking of the consequences, he reached out and grabbed her on the arm.

'You can't just leave without explaining yourself.'

The emotional distress in her eyes was instantly replaced with a defiant fury. 'I don't have to explain myself to you,' she spat as she shook his hand away. 'I'm going home now and I strongly suggest you don't try to stop me.'

His mouth opened to demand she tell him if she would be here on Monday. But she was already out the door, fleeing from him like he was the devil himself.

Jason had never felt so helpless before. Or more frustrated. Logic told him to just let her go. Clearly, the girl had some serious problem where men were concerned.

But then he remembered how she'd felt in his arms and he knew that he could not follow his own advice.

This wasn't over yet. Not by a long shot.

CHAPTER SEVEN

As JASON NEARED the address he'd found in Leah's employment file, he tried telling himself once again that this was not a good idea.

But it was no use. Common sense was not directing his actions, the same way it hadn't when he'd bought Beville Holdings.

On that occasion, he'd felt compelled by a silly dream. This time, his dark side seemed to have taken complete control, driving him on to pursue Leah Johanssen tonight, regardless of her earlier rejection.

No, not rejection. More of a defection. When he'd been kissing her, she'd very definitely been kissing him back. But something had happened to make her freeze up, and flee. Some thought had come into her head. Some fear. Underneath her panic, she had still wanted him. He was sure of it.

Or so he'd like to convince himself.

The clock on the dash said it was nearing eight as he turned the corner into her street. The battle between his conscience and his desires had already taken a couple of angst-filled hours, but, in the end, his desires had won, hands down.

And here he was in Gladesville, every pore in his body aching with the need to have her in his arms once more. The effects of the cold shower he'd had when he'd first arrived home that evening had long dissipated. Wanting her had become a need almost as essential as breathing.

He would not rest until that need was satisfied. He would use every means at his disposal to win her. Every method of persuasion. Every tactic. Every weapon.

A measure of surprise hit Jason as he slid his car into the curb outside the number that housed his prey.

This was not what he expected.

He'd known Gladesville had gradually moved from strictly working class to a more trendy suburb over the past decade or so. But most of the apartment blocks in the area were still plain brick buildings, built half a century ago, unlike the cream, cement-rendered, very modern building he was currently staring at.

On top of that, this building sat directly opposite Sydney's inner harbour.

Waterfront addresses of any kind in Sydney were prized, and added heaps to the price of any apartment. Jason could also see a smartly dressed security man seated in the large, well-lit foyer, which indicated an exclusiveness associated with top-line addresses.

No way could Leah afford to rent such a place on her own. Not on the salary Beville Holdings paid her, anyway. Maybe she shared with a couple of other working girls.

Jason hadn't thought of Leah as having flatmates, let alone a security man barring his way in.

Suddenly, his showing up here like this seemed a very bad idea. And doomed to failure.

Yet going home with his tail between his legs didn't appeal, either.

Damn, but he wished he knew more about this girl. Asking around about her at Beville Holdings hadn't revealed anything worthwhile, other than her apparent lack of a boyfriend. Her employment file hadn't provided much help, either.

Her past history was chock full of holes. He would love to know what she'd done with her life from the time she'd left school till she started work at Beville Holdings last year at the age of twenty-five. According to her resumé, not a thing, other than a brief creative writing course.

Maybe she'd lived at home whilst she'd tried to make it as a novelist, wherever home was. The section on her job application form where she was supposed to list her next of kin had been left suspiciously blank.

Maybe she was an orphan, or a runaway. Maybe she'd been a very bad girl at one stage in her life, doing things you didn't include on your resumé.

No...no, a bad girl would not have bolted when her wealthy boss came on to her. A bad girl would have done anything he wanted.

He didn't really want her to be a bad girl, anyway,

did he? Not down deep. He'd felt nauseous at the thought of her having sex with Jim Matheson. He liked her not having fallen at his feet. He liked her character and spirit. What he didn't like was not knowing what had made her run from the obvious chemistry between them. It didn't make sense. It was crazy, like he'd said.

What to do, Jason? Go home, or take a chance and ring her? He had her phone number, just as he had her address.

His cell phone was in his hands in no time flat. Because there really wasn't any contest, was there? He could not go home without at least trying to find out the truth.

Leah tied the sash on her silk bathrobe before carrying the glass of Chablis back into her kitchen and pouring the lukewarm contents down the sink.

Now what? she wondered.

When Leah had first arrived home from work, she hadn't been able to settle to anything. Eating was out of the question. She was too churned up to eat. She'd paced her apartment for ages, calling herself all sorts of names, from a fool to a coward. She'd taken herself out on to her balcony and stared at the water for ages, but it hadn't soothed her, as it usually did.

In the end, she'd run herself a hot bath, poured herself a glass of wine and lain there in the perfumed bubbles for ages, clasping the undrunk Chablis till it went warm and the water was stone cold, all the while trying desperately not to think of how it had felt when Jason kissed her.

Futile exercise.

It was all she could think about.

The sensations of his mouth on hers had been amazing. She'd never felt anything like it. She'd been in heaven. Even so, her silly fears had finally overridden her pleasure, forcing her to cut and run.

Jason had called her crazy and she'd agreed with him. It seemed crazy to turn her back on something so pleasurable, and which promised even more pleasure in the future.

It felt even crazier now that the heat of the moment had subsided and she could think about the situation more rationally.

How long was she going to let her fear of humiliation and rejection spoil everything? Did she honestly plan never to have sex ever again in her entire life?

Leah sighed. She'd made a right mess of things with Jason this afternoon. Now she really would have to resign first thing on Monday morning. There was no other way out. She could not possibly work with the man after this.

'I shouldn't have let him kiss me,' she muttered as she walked into the kitchen to get herself a fresh glass of wine. But, oh, it had felt so good.

The phone ringing brought a burst of frustration.

'Botheration!' she exclaimed. She didn't want to talk to anyone. Especially her father. And she couldn't think who else it might be at this hour on a Friday night.

Hopefully, it was a carpet-cleaning company, trying to get some business with some cold calls.

Not that they would have any success. Her carpets didn't need cleaning.

Leah hurried into the living room, put down her glass of wine then swept up her mobile phone.

'Yes?' she said rather impatiently.

'Leah?'

Leah's heart stopped. It was him. Her soon-to-be ex-boss. Jason Pollack. Driving her crazy some more.

Her heart lurched back to life, thudding noisily behind her ribs whilst her head whirled with conflicting emotions. Anger fired her blood. But there was excitement, too.

He wasn't going to take no for an answer. What a perversely thrilling thought!

'How did you get my phone number?' she demanded, her voice literally shaking.

'I looked it up in your employment file.'

Leah sucked in sharply. How utterly conscienceless he was. Like Carl.

'I know I shouldn't have,' he went on immediately in urgent tones. 'I know you could really charge me with sexual harassment this time. But I just couldn't sleep tonight without finding out what I did wrong earlier.'

Leah could not help but be impressed by his seemingly sincere tone. Maybe he wasn't as conscienceless as she imagined.

'You didn't do anything wrong,' she conceded tautly. Except perhaps be a far-too-good kisser.

'Then what happened? One moment you were right there with me. The next you were out the door. Were you worried I might push things further right then and there?'

Leah shuddered with the image of his lifting her up on to that boardroom table, then pushing her skirt up to expose her scarred thigh. 'In a way…'

'But I wouldn't have. Not with those cleaners wandering about. I wouldn't have done that, Leah.'

Wouldn't he? She wasn't so sure, either of him or of herself. The sexual heat they generated together was extremely powerful.

She'd wanted him. She still wanted him, despite knowing what kind of man he was. Maybe not totally conscienceless. But arrogant and ruthless. A taker.

'Tell me what the problem is, Leah,' he insisted down the line, his tone bewitchingly gentle and understanding. 'I get the feeling it's not me personally. It's something else, isn't it?'

Leah wanted to tell him. She really did. Yet still she hesitated. Because if Jason didn't react the way Carl had, then she would be left with no defences against him at all.

She wouldn't be able to resist the man if he still wanted her, despite her scars. She would be his for the taking.

Leah hated the thought of becoming some rich man's sexual puppet. She'd battled over the past two years to throw off the legacy of her pampered past and find purpose in her life. To take control of her own destiny. To become a true adult.

She would not throw away her new sense of independence and self-worth because her body wanted this man to make love to it.

If she was going to have an affair with Jason—and she really wanted to—it would be on her terms, not his. And only if she truly believed her scars didn't bother him.

Leah decided then and there not to tell Jason about the accident over the phone. She would not give him the chance to become used to the idea of her being scarred. She would *show* him. Without warning. And she would watch his eyes.

His eyes would tell her all she needed to know.

'I think we need to talk,' she said abruptly. 'Could you come over to my place?'

Jason did a double take at his end of the line. But he pulled himself together quickly. He'd never been a man to look a gift horse in the mouth.

'When?' he asked.

'How about now—tonight?'

His heart leapt. So did something else.

'I'll be right up.'

'*What?* You mean…' Leah ran across her living room, through the open glass doors and out on to her balcony, almost dropping the phone when she leant over the railing.

Directly below sat his blue sports car, the driver's door swinging open as she peered down.

He climbed out, his phone still clamped to his ear.

He was casually dressed, the charcoal business suit

he'd been wearing at work now replaced by bone chinos and a dark open-necked shirt that shimmered faintly purple under the street light. His dark hair shone as well, indicating a recent shower.

Even from that distance Leah experienced a squishy feeling in her stomach as she stared down at him.

'I got your address from your employment file as well,' he confessed drily as he banged the car door shut, then glanced up the three floors towards her balcony. When their eyes connected, Leah swallowed.

'You're a wicked man,' she choked out.

'You're a very beautiful woman,' he replied smoothly.

Leah's chest tightened. So they were back to that again. Her so-called beauty. This time, however, she wasn't going to run away. She was going to see what Jason was made of.

'I'll tell Keith to let you come up,' she said abruptly, and swung away from the railing. 'I'm in apartment 3a.'

Unnecessary information, she realised after she let the doorman know the name of her imminent visitor. Jason already knew her address. And her phone number. And whatever else was in her resumé.

Though that wasn't much. She'd protected her true identity and her past from prying eyes at work.

Jason knew nothing of her marriage to Carl, or that she was an heiress in her own right.

How much should I tell him? she wondered, and then worried. A man who had once married for money should possibly be kept in the dark about her wealth.

But how could she explain this apartment?

She would have to tell him something.

Her doorbell ringing sent Leah into a spin. She should not have just stood there, dithering. She should have gone and put some clothes on. To answer her door with nothing on but her bathrobe was brazen in the extreme.

Yet she wasn't brazen. Not at all!

She was, however, determined to be master of her own destiny. Given that, there was little point in dressing now, Leah decided.

Tightening the sash around her waist, she scooped in a deep breath, then walked with a renewed sense of composure towards the door.

CHAPTER EIGHT

JASON COULD NOT believe how nervous he felt as he waited for Leah to answer her doorbell. Like a schoolboy on his first real date.

Once she'd invited him up, he hadn't had the patience to take the lift. Instead, he'd charged up the three flights of stairs, taking several steps at a time, arriving at her floor with his blood hot and his heart galloping like a racehorse in the final furlong of the Melbourne Cup.

The door finally opened, and his pounding heart skidded to a halt.

During his swinging single years—before he'd met and married Karen—Jason had had apartment doors opened to him by sexily dressed women. And scantily clad women. Once, he'd even been met at the door by a stark naked woman.

But none had affected him as powerfully as the sight of Leah Johannsen, encased in a Japanese-style robe that was almost as exquisite as she was.

The fact that she was braless beneath the red silk kimono was swiftly all too evident. So was the fact that she was either as excited as he was…or very cold.

Given it was summer, he didn't think the latter was an option. Not a calming thought.

Jason suddenly didn't know where to look. Certainly not at her rock-like nipples. Or into her seductive green eyes. Or that softly luscious mouth whose lipstick he could still taste on his own lips.

He found himself staring over her shoulder into the main living area of her apartment, noting its spaciousness, and style. Nothing bargain basement in there. Or shared. Jason knew, without being told, that Leah didn't have any flatmates. She lived here alone. The only unknown was how she could afford it.

A dark suspicion invaded his mind. Maybe she didn't always live here alone. Maybe someone else paid the rent, then paid her the occasional visit. Maybe that was where the problem lay with her. She already had a rich lover and wasn't free to take another.

'Come in,' she said throatily, taking a step back and waving him inside.

As he moved past her, Jason glanced down at her bare but beautiful feet with their scarlet painted toes, thinking to himself that he would have those feet wound around him before this night was out, regardless.

His heart jolted back into life, thudding with wicked purpose.

'This is a pretty swanky place,' he heard himself

saying as he moved across the plush, sable-coloured carpet towards the elegant seating arrangement in the centre of the room. 'How on earth can you afford it on your salary?'

He turned to find her regarding him with an expression that made him feel ashamed of his suspicion.

'I can't,' she replied coldly. 'I own this apartment. I bought it with some money that was left to me a couple of years ago.'

Jason's eyebrows lifted. Had to have been a reasonably sizeable inheritance. 'I see,' he said.

'I doubt it,' she snapped, and walked over to pick up a glass of wine, which was sitting on one of the two side tables flanking the rich cream sofa.

'Forgive me if I don't offer you a drink just yet,' she said, and gulped down the wine. 'I need a little Dutch courage here,' she added as she placed the glass back where it came from.

Before he could open his mouth to ask her what was going on, her hands went to the sash around her waist.

Shock had him swallowing. As much as he wanted this girl, he didn't want her to strip off in front of him like…like some cheap slut. He wanted to take her in his arms and kiss as he had before. He wanted to hear her moan, feel her melt against him. He wanted to make love to her, damn it!

But she didn't undo the ties. Instead, she gripped them tightly in one hand whilst her other hand moved down to splay across her stomach, like she was holding it in. Suddenly, she shoved her right leg forward, the action parting the robe right up to mid-thigh, but no further. All Jason could see was her leg. A very beautifully shaped leg with a nice calf muscle and slender ankle.

But just a leg.

Leah watched his eyes like a hawk watches its prey. Watched them and waited.

But the only emotion she could find in his startled gaze was surprise, followed by a weird kind of relief.

Was the man blind? Surely he could see the scars. Surely!

But he didn't seem to notice them.

When she looked down, Leah saw that the worst of the scars were still hidden by the robe. In her efforts to maintain her dignity, she'd kept the darned thing shut too far.

'*Now* can you see them?' she said, thrusting her leg out a bit further, at the same time pointing her toe and unbending her knee.

He just blinked. Nothing more. Just a blink, followed by a small frown of bewilderment.

'Yes,' he eventually replied. 'I can see them.'

'*And?*' she ground out, totally thrown by his reaction. He had to be pretending. Had to be. No one could look at those ugly white ridges and not feel some repulsion. *She* was repulsed, and she'd lived with them for two years.

'Is this what the problem is?' he questioned her quietly, his gaze no longer on her leg, but on her face. 'Those little marks on your thigh?'

'Little marks?' she practically screamed at him as she pulled her leg back in and wrapped the robe back defensively around it. 'They're not little marks. They're *scars*. Horrible, hideous, huge scars. Stop pretending they aren't.'

He seemed taken aback. 'Show them to me again,' he said. 'Maybe I didn't see them correctly.'

Jason saw the horror in her face at his suggestion, sympathy filling his heart as he remembered how Karen had felt about her mastectomy scars. He'd had a lot of trouble convincing his wife that he still found her a desirable woman without her breasts. She would cover her scarred chest all the time.

His heart sank as the reality of this situation sank in. This girl was far too vulnerable for him to use as he'd been going to use her. No point in his pussy-footing around with his own less-than-honourable intentions. He had to be straight with himself. His plan had been a rather callous seduction tonight, followed by a strictly sexual affair.

Some women could cope with that kind of thing. But Leah wasn't one of them.

'They're not so bad, Leah,' Jason said with a soft sigh. 'I didn't even notice them at first.'

'Yeah, right,' she said, her arms lifting to wrap around herself.

Jason just stood there, not sure what to say and do. 'So what happened?' he finally asked.

'Do you really want to know?' she threw at him.

'Yes,' he returned firmly.

'I was in a car accident. Two years ago.'

'And?'

'And I don't really want to talk about it. Look, you don't have to stay and make sympathetic noises. I can see by your body language that you'd rather just cut and run. I understand. Truly. I've been there, done that, with another man just like you. I mean…you only want physical perfection, don't you? Not damaged goods.'

Jason stared at her. She was right. And she was wrong. He didn't give a damn about the scars. He still found her incredibly beautiful and desirable.

But he did want to cut and run, before he was tempted to totally forget his conscience and exploit her vulnerabilities for all they were worth. Some man—some contemptible bastard—had done a right number on her at some stage. Probably told her she was ugly now, or some such stupid thing.

'Who was it, Leah?' he demanded to know.

Her green eyes flashed at him. 'Who was what?'

'The man who made you so self-conscious about your scars?'

'My husband, if you must know.'

'Husband!' So that was what she'd been doing all those years. She'd been married.

'Yes. I was married,' she confirmed sharply. 'Once. But never again, I assure you.'

Her bitter assurance was a temptation in itself. After all, he didn't want to get married again, either.

Not because he'd been betrayed. But because he'd loved too much.

That was what *this* girl needed. To be loved the way he'd loved Karen. Jason knew he didn't have that kind of love left in him any more. But maybe somewhere there was some man who did, some really decent guy who would show Leah that her life wasn't over because of one man's shallowness and cruelty.

If he left her alone, she might find that man. She'd just be wasting her time with him.

When he came towards her, alarm filled her face and her arms tightened around herself.

'What…what are you doing?' she said, stumbling back against the sofa when he reached out to cup her face.

'I'm going to kiss you goodbye,' he said, and planted a soft peck on her forehead. 'Not because of your scars, Leah. I won't let you believe that, because it isn't true. I still think you are the most beautiful, most desirable girl I have ever met. But because you deserve someone a lot better than me in your life.'

Her eyes swam with tears as she gazed up at him. 'You…you don't want me any more.'

His heart actually twisted. 'I want you now more than ever.'

'Then show me,' she begged him.

'God, but you're making it hard.'

'I don't want you to go,' she sobbed, and suddenly wrapped her arms around his back, pulling him tightly against her. 'Please. Please don't go. Stay with me to-night.'

He jerked back to stare down into her tear-stained face and pleading eyes.

'You don't mean that.'

'I do. I do.'

The desperation in her voice was an even more persuasive force than the feel of her body pressed up to his. And that was pretty persuasive.

How could he possibly leave her now? Her self-confidence would be shattered for ever if he did.

But even as his mouth began to descend, Jason vowed to himself that tonight was all there would be. One night, he would give her. And himself. He wasn't that much of a hypocrite that he didn't recognise he was going to get something out of this, too.

But by morning he would be gone. Gone from her bed and her life. Otherwise, he wouldn't be able to live with himself.

CHAPTER NINE

HE STILL WANTS me, Leah cried to herself as his mouth took passionate possession of hers.

No peck on the forehead this time. A real kiss, deep and hungry, flooding her with waves of desire, so hot and strong she thought she might faint with them. She could not get enough of his mouth, but especially his tongue. Each time it slipped past her teeth, she wanted to keep it there, a prisoner of her own passion.

'No, don't stop,' she cried aloud when his head finally lifted.

His wry laughter was reassuring.

'I don't think you have to worry about my stopping, beautiful,' he told her as he swept her up into his arms. 'I presume this is the way to your bedroom,' he added as he carried her down the only hallway in her apartment.

She didn't reply. She was too busy looking up at him with wildly adoring eyes. How handsome he was. Perfect in every way, from his dark, deeply set eyes to his incredibly sexy mouth.

When her right hand lifted to touch his full bottom lip, his step faltered, his eyes glittering as they dropped to hers.

'If you keep doing that,' he growled, 'and looking at me like that, I won't be able to control myself.'

'I don't want you to control yourself,' she confessed.

His four-letter word shocked her, but only because it excited her beyond her own control.

She almost told him yes, yes, that's what I want you to do to me. Nothing gentle. Nothing romantic. I want it rough and wild.

'Tell me you can't possibly get pregnant tonight,' came his gruff request.

'I can't possibly get pregnant tonight,' she replied obediently, whilst thinking to herself that it *was* unlikely. Her period had only just finished a couple of days ago.

But, in truth, she didn't care. She didn't care about anything but having him make mad passionate love to her.

'Thank goodness,' Jason muttered darkly as he carried her into her bedroom.

The room was exactly what he would have expected her bedroom to look like. Soft and pretty and feminine, with pale cream walls and a buttery cream carpet. The brass bed resting against the far wall looked like a genuine antique. High, but not that wide, with a cream lace valance, cream satin quilt and a mound of matching satin and lace pillows resting against the bedhead. The brass-based lamps sitting on the two antique bedside chests were exquisite, their cream shades edged with long drops of crystal. They were both switched on, casting soft circles of lights over the bed.

The realisation that he would soon be on that bed with Leah did little to help Jason's uncharacteristic lack of control. He'd never been like this with Hilary. Or even Karen, whom he'd loved. Truthfully, he hadn't *ever* been like this.

How on earth am I going to make this good for her? he worried as he carried Leah across the room. Already he was painfully erect, his blood charging through his veins at the rate of knots. He ached to throw her on to that virginal-looking quilt and just do it. Without foreplay. Without anything. Just straight into her. Pounding away.

'Do you have *anything* on under that robe?' he asked thickly as he lowered her to her feet beside the bed.

She shook her head and swayed against him, the silken tips of her breasts connecting with his stomach.

He sucked in sharply. 'Hell, Leah, I hope you meant it about wanting me to lose control. Because I'm losing it right now.'

'Good,' she said, her glittering green eyes not in any way shy, but suddenly surprisingly bold.

Jason needed no further encouragement.

He yanked the robe back off her shoulders, not bothering with the ties. But when he dragged it down her arms, the damned thing stopped at her waist, trapping her arms by her sides and leaving him staring at the most provocative and perfect breasts he had ever seen.

Lusciously full, they were. High-set, not heavy, with large aureoles and the pinkest, pointiest nipples.

He had to touch them. Tug at them. Taste them.

'Oh, Leah, Leah,' he groaned as he scooped her up and laid her down in the middle of her quilt, his eyes hot on her as he straightened to stand at the side of the bed.

'No, don't move,' he ordered her when her arms wriggled in the sleeves of the robe, clearly trying to extricate herself. 'Stay exactly as you are.'

He loved the look of her spread out on that sensuous satin quilt, her lower half covered, but her chest and upper arms totally exposed. The paleness of her naked skin against the red silk was incredibly erotic. So was the richness of the red against the pale cream of the bed.

Only one thing was wrong with the picture. Her hair. It should be down.

Her eyes widened when he bent forward to remove the clip that anchored her hair to the top of her head. He heard her breath quicken, watched her eyes follow him as he stroked her hair down over her shoulders, pulling several strands down over her breasts. But not over her nipples.

When he scraped the hair clip over one, her back arched off the bed, her lips falling apart on a startled gasp.

The sight of her stunningly erect nipples reminded him of his own arousal. But he was too intoxicated by her responses now to think about his own frustrations.

He scraped the clip over her other nipple, loving the way her suddenly expanded lungs thrust both her breasts up towards him.

'You like that,' he said throatily, then did it again, and again.

Her answer was a series of soft moans.

Finally, however, the torment became his own, and he threw the clip away, busying his hands on his own body, stripping off his clothes and tossing them aside.

He watched her watch him undress, her eyes telling him that his body met with her approval.

Jason had been blessed with a naturally masculine physique, his shape due more to Mother Nature than with working out. But he did swim every day, and did a hundred situps, both of which keep the flab away and his stomach muscles well toned.

Jason had always felt confident of his body, as well as his lovemaking technique. Usually, he took his time, spending ages on foreplay.

Unfortunately, Leah's eyes staring at him with need sent him right back to where he'd been before he'd started stripping her, desperate to be inside her, driven by a force that was as primal as it was urgent.

Within a flash of being naked, he was with her on the bed, his hands moving with rough caresses over her swollen breasts, his head dipping to take her mouth with a kiss as wild as he was. His lips crushed hers, then drove them apart, his tongue sliding deep, then deeper still.

But it wasn't enough. Not nearly enough. His hand

moved down to pull her robe apart, then her legs, and before his brain could catch up with his body he was between her thighs and pushing into her, groaning as her flesh encased his, its soft slickness enveloping his aching hardness.

Her arms might have been imprisoned by her side, but her legs were free to lift and wrap high around his back. Her bottom lifted with it, the angle of her body taking him in even deeper. It was all a bit much for a man who'd been thinking of nothing else all week but Leah Johannsen.

He slowed his rhythm, trying to last, trying desperately to wait for her. But when she started squeezing him with delicious little movements of her muscles, his body gave up the fight and he came with a raw cry, his body shuddering with the force of his release.

For a split second, his male ego threatened to spoil his ecstasy, but then he heard her cry out his name, and felt her flesh tighten around him like a vice.

His sense of triumph was both physical and emotional. Because he hadn't wanted to be totally selfish. Not tonight. He'd wanted to make it up to her for what that bastard of a husband had done to her. He'd wanted to reassure her that a few scars didn't mar her desirability as a woman.

And it didn't.

Peace came to Jason's body first, leaving him to stare down into her flushed face and watch what his lovemaking had done to her. Her eyes were closed, but her lips were open, panting softly. He felt the last ebbings of her climax. Finally, her legs slipped from around him on a long, voluptuous sigh, and her eyelids fluttered upwards.

He smiled down at her, and she smiled back, her eyes a little embarrassed now, as nice women often were after their first time with a man.

'I'm sorry I was so quick,' he said, bracing his arms on either side of her with his elbows whilst he pushed some strands of hair back from her lovely face.

'You weren't.'

'It's been a while since you've been with a man, hasn't it?'

'Two years.'

'Aah. I see.'

The thought occurred to him that it had only been two weeks since he'd been with Hilary.

Men were different creatures to women. No doubt about that.

He was still tempted to tell her that he'd been thinking of nothing else but her all week, that she was something special to him. But that smacked of an emotional involvement, and he wanted to keep this night strictly physical.

'I'll take longer next time,' he said, deliberately curving his mouth into a wicked smile. 'By the tenth time, you'll be begging me to stop.'

She blinked up at him. 'The *tenth*?'

'Didn't I tell you I was a braggart?'

She laughed. 'No.'

'A braggart and a bastard.'

'I don't believe you.'

'You will, beautiful. You will.'

'Leah…'

Leah surfaced slowly. Dreamily. Happily.

'Mmmm?'

'It's morning,' she heard Jason say through her fog of contentment. 'I have to go.'

Leah opened her eyes to find Jason sitting on the bed beside her, fully dressed in the clothes he'd been wearing when he'd arrived the night before.

'You're going?' she said, still a bit sleep-befuddled. 'But…do you have to rush off? Can't you stay for breakfast at least? It's Saturday, you know.'

'Yes, I know,' he said, his face somewhat grim.

It was then that it came to her what he was saying. He was *going* going.

'I told you last night I wasn't the man for you,' he went on. 'You begged me to stay. So I stayed.'

Leah blinked her surprise. How holier than thou he sounded, as though he'd been forced into staying and accommodating a desperate woman against his better judgement.

'You certainly did,' she agreed, her tone tart.

'I didn't do anything you didn't want me to do, Leah,' he reminded her.

She stared at him, thinking of how she'd given him a lot more than she'd ever given Carl.

There again, he'd given her a lot more than Carl had given her. He'd been incredibly tender and loving that second time. And after that. He certainly wasn't at all grossed out by her scars. He'd even kissed them on one occasion. And washed them in the shower.

The memory of their shower together sent shivers down her spine. She'd washed him too, during which she'd been absolutely shameless. This time together had been as wild as their first with her feet wrapped around his hips.

Then they went back in the bed, for long and languid lovemaking that had ended with her gradually tipping into sleep.

And now here she was, wide awake and being rejected once more.

'You said you had a girlfriend till recently,' she argued, trying to sound calm when inside, desperation was gnawing at her stomach. 'Why can't I be your new girlfriend?'

'You need a man who can love you, Leah. I'm not that man.'

Oh, how it hurt, his saying that he could never love her.

'It…it's not because of the scars, is it?' she heard herself saying in a pitiful voice.

'Don't be ridiculous! Leah, how many times do I have to tell you that your scars don't bother me a bit? Look, if you must know, it's because of my wife, the one you and everyone else thinks I married for her money.

'I didn't,' he growled. 'I loved Karen, more than I could have ever thought possible. Watching her die was terrible. No. *Unbearable.* I thought I would feel relief when she died. Instead, I wanted to die myself.'

'I'm s…sorry,' Leah said, stumbling over the words as she tried to cope with the emotions that his heart-felt confession had produced. Jealousy jabbed at her heart, followed by guilt that she'd judged him so harshly. Finally came the dismaying realisation that the feelings his incredible lovemaking had evoked in her last night would never come to fruition.

Leah knew she could easily fall in love with this man. But what was the point, if he could never love her back?

She was way past being a fool to love. Or she thought she was.

'I'm sorry, too,' he said, and reached out to touch her softly on the cheek.

Tears pricked at her eyes.

'Please don't cry, Leah. Last night was very special. But best we leave it at that.'

'Yes,' she agreed, bravely blinking back the tears.

For a good minute, they maintained an awkward silence, each with their own thoughts.

'Are you still going to resign on Monday?' he asked at last.

'Yes,' she said, nodding. 'Yes, I think that would be for the best.'

'You're right. Of course.'

Leah sighed. It was going to be difficult, living through the two weeks' notice she had to give.

'I'll give you a great reference,' Jason said.

She glared at him for a moment, but then she laughed. 'You'd better.'

He looked at her for a longer moment, and she could have sworn she glimpsed true regret in his eyes.

'I must go,' he said, and stood up abruptly.

She could hardly bear to look at him. Suddenly, she just wanted him to go. Quickly, before she made a right fool of herself.

His bending to kiss her on the forehead made her cringe. She didn't want that kind of kiss from him. She wanted the kind he'd given her last night, the hot hungry intimate kind which had made her squirm and moan. She wanted him to stay. Oh…she just wanted him.

'Just go, for pity's sake!' The words burst from her mouth, sounding bitter and angry.

Leah recalled what he'd said the night before about being a braggart and a bastard. How she wished that he was both! But he wasn't either of them.

She didn't watch him leave. But she heard him shut the front door. It was a horrible sound.

Leah rolled over into her pillows, and wept.

CHAPTER TEN

JOACHIM STRAIGHTENED HIS bow tie, then knocked on Leah's bedroom door.

'It's seven thirty,' he called out. 'The first guests will be arriving soon. I'll wait for you in the foyer.'

'I won't be long,' his daughter replied.

Joachim had barely set foot on the soft blue rug that warmed the cold marble floor of the spacious foyer when the voice of the security man on the gate came through on the intercom, announcing the arrival of a taxi.

'Hope it's not Pollack,' Joachim muttered.

He was just about to dash back up and collect Leah when she started coming down the stairs.

The sight of her literally took his breath away.

She was wearing black. Not a colour he'd ever seen Leah wear before. She always said she didn't like black. But against her fair hair, the black was particularly striking. So was the dress.

It was long, and slinky, and sexy. Yet in a very subtle way, with a deceptively modest top, which was loose fitting and gathered in to a high, round collar. There was a slit, however, which ran from neck to waist at the front, providing the occasional glimpse of cleavage as she moved. Her arms and shoulders were bare as well, Leah's pale skin the perfect foil against the black of the dress.

Her only jewellery was the shoulder-length diamond drop ear-rings, which Joachim had given her for her twenty-second birthday. They'd cost him a small fortune at the time.

'You look simply stunning tonight, Leah,' he complimented when she finally joined him on the rug.

'I'm glad I meet with your approval.'

Joachim heard the edge in her voice and wondered what it meant. Leah had been in an odd mood ever since she'd arrived at the house around three. She confessed she hadn't been to visit the children's wards at Westmead Hospital, as she usually did, claiming she'd woken with a migraine that morning.

Yet she hadn't looked unwell. If anything, she'd looked better than he'd seen her look in ages. If he hadn't known better, he might have thought she'd been lying to him.

But why would she lie? What had she been doing lately that she felt she couldn't admit to?

'Is that dress new?' he asked as he opened the door in anticipation of his first dinner guest—or guests— reaching it. Not Pollack, Joachim saw with relief, but the Hawkinses, long-time friends of the family. Nigel was an orthopaedic surgeon, Jessica his nice but slightly mousy wife. They'd alighted from the taxi, but were still at the bottom of the wide stone steps that led up to the front porch.

'No,' Leah replied. 'Carl bought it for me on our honeymoon. He thought it looked sexy on me.'

Joachim had to agree with his ex son-in-law. His daughter's dress might have worried a father if he was of the narrow-minded, or prudish, kind.

Joachim wasn't. He'd always believed beautiful women like Leah were born to be made love to. And to have children.

But not with any man.

Joachim wanted his next son-in-law to be a man of substance, and character.

He'd had some lingering doubts about Jason Pollack, despite Isabel's voice urging him on, so he'd made a few discreet enquiries on the Monday morning before issuing the dinner invitation, and now felt reassured that Jason Pollack wasn't a fortune hunter, despite the rumours about his first marriage.

His source of information—a journalist friend at a well-known newspaper—gave Pollack a glowing recommendation, both professionally and personally.

Still, if he didn't impress Leah tonight, Joachim resolved to scout around for some other likely candidates to bring into his daughter's life. He wasn't about to let his lovely daughter waste herself, just because her first husband had been less than a man.

'You've done something different with your hair,' he said, noticing when Leah turned away slightly to smooth the long tight skirt over her hips. It was brushed straight back from her face and had been blow-dried dead straight, a shining blonde curtain falling down her back. 'It looks sexy like that.'

She glanced up at him, her glittering green eyes reminding him of Isabel when she was excited about something. 'Do you mind my looking sexy?'

'Not at all. But I thought you didn't want my mystery guest making a pass at you.'

'Is he capable?' she quipped back.

'Any man is capable of a pass. Aah…here's Nigel and Jessie…'

Leah rolled her eyes, then put her mind to playing the role her father wanted her to play for tonight.

Her mother had taught her well how to be a gracious hostess. Leah automatically knew the right things to say to please, plus how to accept a compliment without blushing or stammering.

But she had a moment's worry when Nigel kept staring at her chest. Perhaps she shouldn't have given into the impulse to wear this dress tonight. And to leave off her bra.

But she'd wanted to feel her bare breasts against the silk lining of the dress. Wanted to remember what Jason had done to them last night.

Because that was all she was ever going to have of him.

Memories.

Several couples arrived in quick succession, one after the other, all of whom Leah had met before. Her father's stockbroking partners and their wives. His accountant and his wife. His solicitor and his current partner.

A local politician and his second much younger wife made their entrance a few minutes later, soon to be followed by a quite famous television actor with his current live-in lady, along with his agent, a woman Leah's father knew from way back.

Leah guided them all smoothly into the elegant sunken living room, which ran across the back of the house and where a white-coated waiter circled continuously with trays full of pre-dinner drinks. Some couples chose to sit together on the brocade-covered sofas that Leah's mother had been particularly proud of. Others wandered out on to the back terrace to stand by the pool and to admire the view of the harbour, which stretched out before them at the bottom of the garden.

A full moon shone high in the clear night sky, bathing everything in its bright light. The evening was quite warm, which was just as well, Leah thought, given her choice of clothes and lack of underwear.

By eight fifteen, everyone, it seemed, had made an appearance. Everyone except her father's mystery guest. Leah kept mingling as a good hostess should, sipping champagne as she made small talk with her father's friends and colleagues. She was actually enjoying herself more than she'd thought she would. She was even becoming a little curious over their missing guest. Who *was* he? she began to wonder.

Someone who thought himself important enough to be late.

'Maybe your man's stood you up?' Leah murmured somewhat mischievously to her father as she passed by him on her way to the kitchen to check if everything was ready for dinner. Her father might have blind faith in catering companies, but Leah's mother had always said an overseeing eye was necessary for a successful dinner party.

The doorbell rang before she could leave the room.

She turned to glance at her father who smiled, made his excuses and came over to her, taking her elbow and shepherding her back towards the front door.

'Must be our man now,' he said on their way. 'Everyone else is here.'

'He must be seriously rich to have you this eager. But not to worry. I'm ripe and ready for the old coot. Bring him on, I say!'

Her father laughed. 'I'm so glad to see you've finally recovered your sense of humour. But I think you're in for a surprise.'

'Nothing you do would ever surprise me, Daddy,' she replied, lifting her rather tight skirt a little as she mounted the two marble steps that connected the living room with the foyer. 'Mum turned a blind eye to your naughtinesses. And your controlling ways. But I always knew what kind of man you were.'

'Did you now?'

He slanted a smile at her and Leah smiled back. Her father was a bit of a rogue, but a charming and lovable one.

Leah was thinking how much she loved him—despite everything—when he opened the door and there, before her, was the last man she expected to see tonight.

Jason Pollack, dressed in a superb black dinner jacket and looking more devastatingly handsome than she'd ever seen him.

She fairly gaped.

But if she was shocked, so was he.

'Leah!' he blurted out. 'Good God.'

'Leah?' Joachim repeated, staring first at Jason Pollack, then at his daughter. 'You already *know* each other?' he asked her.

'We...er...we met at B...Beville Holdings this week.'

Joachim had never heard his daughter stammer in her life. Or blush the way she was blushing at this moment.

Joachim was no fool. He knew at once that more had gone on between this pair than a simple meeting at work. Intuition told him that Leah's new boss was the reason she had been acted strangely today.

'You never mentioned it,' Joachim said, playing devil's advocate.

'Didn't I?' came her evasive reply.

Joachim became aware that his guest was glowering at both him and her with dark suspicion in his eyes. It occurred to him suddenly that Pollack had no idea Leah was his daughter. Clearly, he'd jumped to the mistaken conclusion that she held a very different but still intimate role in Joachim's life.

That of mistress.

And he looked as jealous as sin.

Joachim felt pleased as punch at this development. But he thought it best to clarify things, post-haste.

'Leah is my daughter, Mr Pollack,' he pronounced proudly, sliding a possessive around her slender waist. 'My only child and the apple of my eye.'

Pollack's deeply set eyes betrayed definite relief, followed by puzzlement. He frowned at Leah, who was still blushing furiously.

'But you go by the name of Johannsen,' he said to Leah, almost accusingly. 'Not Bloom.'

'Her ex-husband's name,' Joachim informed him when Leah couldn't seem to find her tongue. A most unusual occurrence, lately. 'Rich as Croesus, but a cur of a man. Leah is well rid of him, aren't you, sweetheart? But let's not talk of unpleasant things tonight. Dinner will be served shortly. Just enough time for Leah to get you a pre-dinner drink.'

Joachim removed his hand from her waist and leant it lightly on her shoulder, giving her an indulgent smile at the same time. 'I'll leave Mr Pollack in your good hands, shall I, Leah, whilst I check things with the chef.'

Bloom walked off, leaving Jason feeling more rattled than he'd ever felt in his life.

He hadn't been going to come tonight. He hadn't felt like socialising, especially with people he didn't know. It had been Karen's voice in his head saying that it was best not to be alone when you were troubled over something that had driven him out of the house.

So at the last moment he'd thrown on his tux and ordered a taxi, telling himself—as he had earlier in the week—that at least the wine and food would be good.

Seeing Leah standing next to Bloom like that had given him a dreadful shock. For a few stomach-churning moments, he'd entertained appalling thoughts about their relationship. Thank heavens Bloom turned out to be her father, or he didn't know what he might have done.

Jason hadn't realised till that moment just how primal his feelings for Leah had become. One night spent together, and he already thought of her as his, and his alone.

As he stared at her, his mind began stripping her of that far too sexy black dress. He saw her as he'd seen her last night, without a stitch on, her beautiful body stretched out before him, to do with as he pleased.

He'd been trying not to think of her like that all day, telling himself he'd done the right thing to leave things at a one-night stand. But now here she was, tormenting him with her beauty once more.

Still, the pieces of the puzzle that made up Leah Johannsen were finally slotting into place. She was a rich man's daughter. She'd been married to a rich man. Now he understood why she'd had no work record till recently.

'I had no idea you were coming here tonight,' she said agitatedly. 'You have to believe me.'

'I do believe you,' he returned. If she'd expected him, she wouldn't have looked so embarrassed.

'This is all my father's doing,' she said, shaking her head, the action setting those incredible ear-rings swaying and sparkling.

'Yes, I can see that.'

Her eyes flashed with frustration. 'Daddy likes to think he knows what's best for me. He's obviously matchmaking, despite my having told him just last Sunday that I wasn't interested in getting married again. Or falling in love again, for that matter!'

'You're not?' Jason wished she'd told him that this morning.

'No,' she said quite firmly. 'I'm not. Look, the only reason I'm here tonight is because my father asked me to. He said he needed me to sit next to some billionaire he'd invited to dinner and wanted to impress. He refused to tell me your name, though he cleverly let me assume that you were some ageing tycoon whose investment account he wanted to secure. He knew, if I knew your real identity, I wouldn't have agreed to help him.'

'Why not?'

'Because I'm not into wealthy playboy types who think they're God's gift to women,' she threw at him, her delicately pointed chin lifting the way it had that first day in the car park.

Jason opened his mouth to deny he was a playboy. But then closed it again. He supposed he was, in a way. Hilary would certainly describe him as such.

'And please don't throw last night in my face,' she added angrily. 'You caught me at a weak moment. Trust me when I say it won't happen again.'

Jason looked deep into her defiant green eyes, then down at the outline of her stunningly erect nipples before deciding that the lady doth protest too much. Her body language spoke different words to those she was mouthing.

His own body responding to the still-smouldering desire he sensed in hers, Jason wondered how on earth he was going to get through this evening without misbehaving.

'I'm glad you've come over to my way of thinking,' he returned drily. He'd have no hope of containing his own desire if she indicated she'd be willing for a repeat performance. 'Now, how about that drink your father promised?'

CHAPTER ELEVEN

'WHAT A LOVELY room.'

Leah flashed Jason a resentful glance over the rim of her crystal flute. She didn't want to stand here next to him, sipping champagne and pretending that the whole evening was not going to be a total disaster. She didn't want to make small talk with him. She wanted to get out of here more than anything she'd ever wanted, except perhaps this man.

She looked at him hard again and wished he wasn't so attractive. And so decent. If decent was the right word. Maybe he'd just been protecting himself this morning from a girl he decided might become a neurotic cling-on in his life. Clearly, emotional complications weren't on Jason's agenda.

Sex was fine. But nothing more.

Leah wished she could have hidden that she wanted more.

'You can handle this, Leah,' Jason said softly, as if reading her mind. 'You can handle just about anything, from what I've seen. Don't let your father's manipulations bother you. They're irrelevant. I won't be pushed into doing anything I don't want to do. And neither will you. We have minds of our own.'

She stared at him, both impressed and flattered. She really was much weaker than he believed. Around him, anyway.

'And I genuinely like this room,' he added, smiling at her with a warm smile that made her want to weep.

Why couldn't she have married a man like this, instead of Carl? Why couldn't she have met Jason first, before his wife stole his heart and left him without the ability—or the desire—to love again?

'It was my mother's favourite room,' she replied, her heart lurching a little.

'Am I right in presuming that your mother has passed away?'

'She…she died in the same car accident that gave me the scars.'

'I'm so sorry,' he said with true sympathy in his voice and face. 'I never actually knew my mother. She died when I was born. But Dad and I were very close. He passed away when I was in my twenties, so I know what it feels like to lose a much-loved parent.'

'Not a day goes by that I don't miss Mum terribly.'

'I know what you mean,' he muttered. 'You just can't get used to the fact that they're not there any more.'

Leah looked at his bleak eyes and suspected he was now thinking about his wife. Thinking about her and missing her. Every day of his life.

Oh, God.

'Tell me about your mother.'

A wistful sigh whispered from Leah's lips. 'She was a lovely sweet woman, too sweet in some ways. A great wife and mother. She had a wonderfully calming effect in the house, and on Daddy. Everyone loved her. Unfortunately, she was a dreadful driver...'

'Do you look like her, or your father?'

'People say I'm the spitting image of Mum. But not in nature,' she added. 'I'm not quite as amenable as Mum was.'

Jason smiled. 'No kidding.'

Leah felt herself bristle. She opened her mouth to make some snappy reply when her father announced that dinner was ready.

Leah glared at her father as she and Jason walked past on their way into the dining room.

'I want a quiet word with you,' she bit out.

'It won't be during dinner,' came his smiling answer. 'The seating arrangement is not conducive.'

An understatement. The regimented place names put her father at one end of the huge mahogany dining table, and Leah at the other end, almost shouting distance away. Jason had been placed on Leah's immediate right, with Nigel's wife on her left, a shy woman who rarely said a word. No doubt a deliberate ploy on her father's part.

The first two courses were an absolute trial, not because she was forced to talk to Jason and Jason alone, but because he cleverly drew Jessica out of her usual shell till she was fairly sparkling with wit and previously untapped charm.

Jealousy consumed Leah as she watched *all* the women at the table—not just Jessica—flick admiring glances towards Jason. She wanted to scream at them that they couldn't have him. That he was *hers*.

But of course he wasn't.

The trouble was, the memory of his lovemaking was still pleasurably, painfully sharp. She could almost feel his hands on her breasts. Her stomach. Her bottom. Her body literally began to burn as her mind relived that torrid mating in the shower. She could hear her cries echoing against the tiled walls, feel his swollen sex buried deep inside hers.

'Your father's wines are superb.'

'What?' Her head jerked around at his voice, her face flushing when her eyes met his.

Jason was an expert at reading body language. When he'd first started out in sales, his take-home pay had depended on it. There was no doubt in his mind that Leah still wanted him, regardless of what she'd claimed earlier.

His resolve not to sleep with her again shattered under the force of his own immediate and intense desire.

Dessert arrived, a wicked-looking chocolate concoction that had most of the women at the table protesting—though only half-heartedly. Jason used their momentary distraction to lean across the corner of the table towards Leah.

'Come home with me tonight,' he invited softly before he could think better of it.

Her nostrils flared as she sucked in sharply, her eyes blinking wide in shock on him.

'Please,' he added, his own eyes fixed firmly on her stunned face.

Leah just stared at him.

Yes, was the obvious answer. It was what she was wanted more than anything. So why did she hesitate? Why did she feel the urge to punish him for rejecting her this morning?

In that moment, Leah began to understand why pride was one of the seven deadly sins, and not a virtue as some people imagined. It could be perverse, and very self-destructive.

'So what's happened to change your mind?' she snapped, without thinking who might hear.

Fortunately, everyone was busy chatting away to someone else. And also fortunately, Jason didn't take offence. He just smiled at her, as though he'd expected this reaction.

'*You* happened again, Leah,' he said quietly, his eyes gleaming with seductive force. 'Along with that dress. I'm just a man, you know, not a saint.'

'Oh.' His honesty was as irresistibly attractive as he was.

'Is that a yes?'

She nodded, suddenly unable to say a word. Her

mouth had gone as dry as the Sahara. She stared at him again, drowning in his dark, sexy eyes and dying for this dinner to be over so tonight could begin.

The impatience of her desire astounded Leah. Was it just his lovemaking she was craving? Or the man himself?

Impossible to separate them. The man *and* his lovemaking. They came together, as they had come together, last night, not once but several times.

This had to be why Trish had kept going back to Jim, even though she knew there was no future with him. Because the sex was great.

Leah couldn't imagine anything, however, being as perfect or as powerful as what she'd shared with Jason last night. How was she going to feel when he called it quits a second time?

And he would. If not tomorrow morning, then eventually.

Don't think about that, she told herself as she dropped her eyes to the dessert and picked up her spoon.

Leah was partial to chocolate of any kind. But her taste buds seemed to have gone on strike, her focus on nothing but what was going to happen later tonight after she went home with Jason.

Slowly, she lifted her head and gazed down the long table to where her father was enthusiastically attacking his dessert. Perhaps feeling her eyes on him, he stopped with his dessert fork mid-air and looked back across the expanse of mahogany.

The smile that curved her lips was full of irony. Whatever her father had planned for tonight, it certainly wasn't for his daughter to go home with his mystery guest.

Clearly, her father was on the lookout for a new son-in-law, not a new client.

Joachim Bloom believed in love and marriage and family. Even before Leah married the first time, he'd expressed the wish for a grandson, his one regret over his own marriage being that they hadn't been able to have more children.

Leah would have liked to give her father what he wanted. *This* time. Unfortunately, the man sitting beside her was never going to marry her, or fall in love with her. He certainly didn't want her having his child. He'd made his position quite clear, both this morning and tonight. His offer of another night together was a strictly sexual one.

Leah knew her only chance of having any kind of relationship with Jason, as opposed to just one more night, lay in her ability to convince him that this was all she wanted, too.

Could she do that? Would he believe her?

It was a plus that she'd already revealed tonight that she didn't want to get married again. All she had to do was slip in somewhere that she didn't want to fall in love again, either.

A shudder ran through Leah. She'd never been all that good a liar.

'You don't like chocolate?' Jason enquired.

Leah hardly dared look at him, lest he see the machinations going on in her mind. 'I seem to have lost my appetite.'

'Just as long as you're not dieting.'

'I'm not. When I'm upset or excited, I simply can't eat.'

'And are you upset over something?' he asked softly, the implication behind his clever question drawing her eyes to his.

'No.'

'When I'm upset or excited, I eat all the more,' he said, his dessert already gone.

'And are you upset over something?' she heard herself ask on a husky whisper.

'No,' he mouthed in reply.

Leah swallowed. How on earth was she going to bear the rest of the evening? But her father's dinner parties were never rushed affairs.

After dessert, coffee and cognac would be served back in the living room, along with large cheese and fruit platters. Finally, bottles of his prized port would come out. No one would be expected to leave till midnight, at least. No one ever left Joachim Bloom's dinner parties early. No one ever wanted to. Except when they were desperate to be dragged by their sexy new boss into bed and kept there.

By the time everyone rose from the dining table, Leah began thinking about places she could take Jason to where she could at least be alone with him, where they could talk naturally and not in hushed whispers or coded messages, where he might kiss her and touch her and maybe even…

'I'm taking Jason down to the boathouse to look at your cruiser, Daddy,' she said to her father as soon as the time came to leave the table. 'He's interested in buying a boat. You did say you wanted to sell it, didn't you?'

'But only if it's a bargain,' Jason piped up by her side, not batting an eyelid at this invention of Leah's. What a clever man he was. What a gorgeous, clever, co-operative man!

Leah's father gave a mock sigh. 'I see I'll have to teach my daughter the art of negotiation. Never show your hand, Leah. Make people think you don't want to give them what they want. That the way, isn't it, Jason?'

'Most of the time,' Jason replied with a brilliant poker face. 'There are occasions, however, when it is more…effective…to let a person know what you want. Don't you agree?'

'Indeed I do,' her father said, glancing from Jason to Leah and smiling a rather smug smile. 'Off you go then, Leah, and show this young man my boat. But leave the final negotiation of any sale to me.'

Jason took her hand the moment they were alone on the terrace, pulling her off to one side into the shadows and pressing her up against a side wall.

'This is what you want, isn't it?' he muttered just before his mouth collided with hers.

The kiss was long and wet and wild, leaving Leah's lips bruised and her heart thundering in her chest. Who knew what she would have allowed then and there if he hadn't taken her hand again and started pulling her past the pool towards the garden beyond.

She didn't say a word during their silent journey down the moonlit pathway that led to the boathouse. What was there to be said even if she was capable of saying it?

'Is it locked?' Jason threw at her when they neared the boathouse.

'Yes. But I know where the key is.'

'I'm sure you do.'

He sounded angry, she realised. Either that or just as impatient as she was.

'You're not angry with me, are you?' she asked when they reached the boathouse door.

He swung her round, then yanked her hard against him.

'Angry with myself, more like it,' he ground out, and kissed her again, this time for even longer. By the time his head lifted, she'd forgotten the thread of their conversation.

'The key,' he demanded. 'Where's the damned key?'

Her hands were shaking as she reached round behind a nearby downpipe and removing a small black magnetised box, sliding it open and retrieving the key.

Jason took it from her and jammed it into the lock. The hinges creaked a little as he pushed open the door.

'Is there a light in here somewhere?'

'Do we have it turn it on?'

'We do, if I'm to look at this boat.'

'You mean you actually do want to look at the boat?'

'Only the part where the bunks are.'

'Oh.'

She turned on the light.

The boathouse was just large enough to house her father's cruiser, a sleek white vessel, which did have sleeping quarters below deck. The sight of her mother's name painted on the side, however, had a dampening effect on Leah's passion. So did the musty smell inside the boathouse. When she heard something rodent-like scurrying beneath some empty cartons piled up in a corner, she squealed and grabbed Jason's arm.

'What's wrong?'

'I…I think I heard a mouse. Or maybe a rat.'

'A rat…'

'Yes. I hate rats,' she said, and shuddered.

Jason almost told her that she was mistaken. She liked rats. She'd married one, hadn't she? And she was about to have an affair with another one.

After all, nothing had changed since this morning. He still couldn't offer her anything more than his body.

Unfortunately, the state of Jason's body refused to totally let him change his mind about taking her again. But he could wait a little longer. He didn't have to do it here, in a wretched boathouse.

'Let's go,' he said, grabbing her hand and dragging her back outside into the moonlight.

'Go where?'

He locked the door and put the key back in its box.

'I'm taking you home to my nicely air-conditioned and rodent-free apartment.'

'Right now, you mean?'

'Yes.'

'But the dinner party isn't over.'

'It is for us.'

CHAPTER TWELVE

'HOW ON EARTH did you manage that?' Leah asked as the taxi sped from Vaucluse to the city.

Jason curved an arm around her shoulders and pulled her close. 'Manage what?'

'Manage to get me out of there in double-quick time with my father's approval.'

'Simple. While you were in the powder room, I told him the truth.'

'You *told* him I'd be spending the night with you?'

'Not in so many words. I said I was taking you on to a nightclub. Your father's an intelligent man. He doesn't have to have everything spelled out for him.'

'But you don't understand. I wasn't going back to my place after the dinner party. I was going to stay the night at home. I usually do every Saturday night. My father will expect to see me at breakfast.'

'You'll have to give him a call tomorrow morning then, won't you? Tell him you didn't come home and won't be down for breakfast.'

Leah groaned.

'Leah, darling.' Jason's voice was firm. 'You're a beautiful, twenty-six-year-old divorcée living in Sydney in the twenty-first century. Your father realises you have a sex life.'

'But I haven't,' she denied. 'I mean…last night was the first time since…since…'

'Yes. I know that. But that was only because you were self-conscious about your scars. You're over that nonsense now, aren't you?'

'*Am* I?'

'Absolutely.' And, as if to prove it, he slid his hand up under her dress and caressed the ridges which criss-crossed her left thigh.

Leah's first reaction was to stiffen, but, gradually, she melted under his gentle touch, her breath quickening when his fingers moved further up her thigh to press against the already damp satin of her black G-string.

The contact of his fingertips against electrified nerve-endings twisted her stomach into knots, her belly tightening as the tension began to build down there. If he kept doing what he was doing, she would come, right there, in the back of the taxi.

Her eyes darted to the back of the driver's head, then at the tall buildings flying past. She sucked in sharply and tried to think of other things.

'See?' he murmured into her right ear. 'You're cured. And we're here.'

The taxi lurching to a halt at the curb coincided with his hand abandoning her.

A low moan of frustration escaped her lips before she could stop it. She looked at him with desperate eyes, and he dropped a light kiss on her mouth.

'Not much longer to wait,' he murmured before climbing out of the taxi first. Once on the pavement, he turned to help her out on to her feet, then paid the driver through the front window.

Unfortunately, to do so, he had to let go of her hands.

How did she manage to stand up all by herself? Her bones had gone to water and her head was spinning out into the stratosphere.

By the time the taxi sped off, Leah was teetering on her high heels. Jason caught her against him as she swayed.

'You drank far too much wine over dinner,' he said, holding her tightly against him as he ushered her into the tower like building.

Had she? She couldn't remember. Dinner had become a bit of a blur.

The security guards behind the reception desk waved to Jason on his way past, but he just nodded to them, then steered her into one of the empty lifts in the far corner of the massive foyer and inserted his key card.

'You're not going to fall asleep on me, are you?' he asked a bit worriedly during the lift ride upwards.

'I certainly hope not.'

He smiled. 'That's my girl.'

She stared up at him and thought how much she'd like to be his girl.

'And what does that look mean?' he chided, tipping her chin up with his fingertips.

'Nothing. Please kiss me.'

'Yes, ma'am.'

Jason was happy to do just that, happy to take her mouth and let desire obliterate the qualms that kept surfacing whenever he was with this girl. Soon, he wasn't thinking of anything much except the need to have her in his arms once more.

The lift slid to a smooth halt on the top floor of the tower, the doors opening straight into his luxury penthouse apartment.

But neither of them had eyes for anything but each other. Jason couldn't wait any longer, swinging her around against the wall and pinning her there with his body. His hands clasped her head and his kisses turned savage.

The need for air finally forced him to wrench his mouth away. But there would be no slowing down. No waiting this time.

He didn't undress her, or himself. He just yanked open his zipper and lifted her dress. Her panties gave way with a ripping sound and then he was there, wedging himself between her legs and pushing up into her deliciously ready body.

Once safely anchored, he straightened, then let the dress fall, his hands lifting to cup her face.

'I don't want to hurt you,' he said thickly, aware that his rough penetration had stretched her up on to her toes.

'You're not.'

'But I might,' he said with a grimace. His passion for her had been uncontrollable from the start, appealing to his dark side, making him forget all common sense and decency.

'No, no.' She shook her head violently against his hands. 'I'm fine. Please. Just do it, Jason.'

Her urgency stirred his dark side ever further. As Jason began to pump up into her, he vowed to make her want him like this all the time. He would keep her here with him for the rest of the weekend, making love to her over and over till having him inside her was as natural to her as breathing. He'd make her crave sex as she had never craved it before. And with the craving would come complete surrender to his will.

By Monday morning, there would be no more talk of resigning. She would be totally at his beck and call, both at work and here, every single night. She'd be his, in every way. Unable to say no. Every man's fantasy come true.

'Mine,' he muttered against her mouth when she splintered apart. His own climax swiftly followed, Jason hoisting her up on to his hips whilst his flesh was still pulsing inside of hers.

Her forehead flopped against his shoulder, her arms winding up around his neck. A sigh of satisfaction whispered at the base of his throat.

'That was incredible,' she murmured as he carried down towards the master bedroom. 'You're incredible.'

Leah felt his arms stiffen around her. His step even

faltered for a moment. She knew she'd have to say something very quickly to redress the damage she'd just done. If not, tonight would become just another one-night stand.

'You're a much better lover than Carl, you know,' she went on hurriedly, lifting her head to throw what she hoped was a saucy smile up at him.

He laughed, which was good. 'So good sex matters to you?'

'I was one of those romantically foolish females who imagined true love did the trick for them. And then you came along and proved me wrong.'

His smile had an odd edge to it. 'We aim to please.'

'I wish I'd met someone like you sooner.'

Now he ground to a total halt. 'What do you mean by that?'

Her shrug was magnificently nonchalant. 'You know. Someone whose only priority is having a good time, and has the know-how to deliver it. We're perfect for each other, Jason. You don't want love and marriage, and neither do I. I've been there, done that, and I'm not in a hurry to go there again.'

Leah could not tell if he believed her, or not.

'Which reminds me,' she raced on. 'You're going to have to start using condoms soon. This weekend should be safe, but, in a day or two, we'll be entering danger territory.'

The horror on his face underlined how much Jason didn't want consequences. Or commitment. Or complications.

'I'd forgotten all about that! Damn, but you do make me lose it, Leah.'

Her smile carried some degree of satisfaction. 'Do I?'

'You know you do. I can't seem to get enough of you.'

'Mmm. Yes. I'm beginning to feel the evidence of that for myself,' she purred. 'So what do you want to do about it?'

'First things first. As much I like this dress on you, I prefer you without it. And those earrings will have to go. I might end up swallowing one and be charged with grand larceny. Then we're going to share a spa bath.'

'And after that?'

His dark eyes glittered. 'Don't you worry your pretty little head about the wheres and wherefores of tonight,' he said as he carried her into a bedroom that looked like a photo spread in a glossy magazine for what a bachelor's bedroom should be like. 'I like to be the boss in the bedroom as well as at work.'

Leah could see that already. But she didn't mind. She found his take-charge attitude exciting. Carl had never made love to her anywhere but in bed.

Leah realised now that her husband had been a lazy lover. And lacking in passion.

There again, he'd never really loved her, had he? She'd meant little more to him that one of the multi-million-dollar paintings he bought and displayed so proudly to everyone. She'd been a prized possession to show off. A status symbol. Joachim Bloom's daughter.

Jason didn't care that she was Joachim Bloom's daughter. He'd wanted her when he thought she was just a working girl.

They stood in the middle of the room. Their bodies were pressed tightly together. Leah wriggled her hips against Jason, making him gasp.

'Do it to me again, Jason,' she said, hardly recognising the husky voice that came out of her mouth. 'On that big bad bed of yours. The bath can wait. I can't.'

He laughed. '*I'm* the one supposed to be doing the seducing around here.'

'Then hurry up and seduce me again.'

'I thought I told you I like to be the boss.'

'I forgot.'

'I'll forgive you this once,' he said as he laid her carefully back across the black-and-white jungle print spread. Leah gasped with surprise when he pushed her long tight skirt upwards till it enveloped her upper half—and her head—in darkness.

Leah had never known anything so erotic. She could not see him. But she could feel him, as he pushed into her and then slid in and out, filling her, then leaving her feeling momentarily frustrated as he pulled back. His stroke was slow and strong, teasing her, pleasing her. That delicious tension began to build again, catching at her breath, making her muscles tighten around him.

She bit her bottom lip when he took hold of her hips and picked up his rhythm. She could hear him now as well as feel him. His breath was ragged, his fingertips quite brutal as they dug into her flesh. She'd be bruised in the morning, but she didn't care.

He was like some wild beast, holding her hard against him while he shuddered into her.

And then he was gone, leaving her lying there, with her dress still up over her face, her arms up-stretched, her legs apart, her body spent.

She heard water running, but still could not move. Finally, he came back to her and with gentle hands removed her dress. Not just from her face, but from her whole body.

She looked up to see that he was naked, too. Naked and smiling. When he stretched out beside her and started playing with her breasts, Leah realised that she wasn't as spent as she thought she was.

'I'm running us that spa bath,' he murmured, deserting her nipples to remove her ear-rings. 'Do you want to give your father a call tonight?' he asked as he dropped them one by one on his glass-topped bedside table. 'You could warn him you won't be back.'

'No, I...I don't think so. I'll call him in the morning.'

'He won't be worried, you know. This is what you said he wanted. You and me together.'

'I still can't believe you were his mystery guest. But he read some article about you in last Sunday's paper. It seemed to impress him. He showed it to me.'

'It didn't impress *you* though, did it? You weren't at all impressed when we met on Monday.'

'You've impressed me now that I've gotten to know you. Biblically speaking, that is.'

His hand went back to her breast, his expression speculative as he played with her nipple some more. 'Is this all you want me from me, Leah?' he asked when she gave a small moan of pleasure. 'You won't start wanting more, will you?'

Leah's heart twisted. She ached to throw at him that of course she would. She already did. But sex was all he was offering. So she said, 'That, and companionship. I've been very lonely since my divorce. I'm sure you can manage to deliver both, can't you?'

'No trouble. But I'll have to go condom shopping tomorrow. I do have a couple in my wallet, which I put there for emergencies. And possibly one or two in the bathroom somewhere. But with you, beautiful,' he said, tweaking her nipple again. 'I'm going to need some serious restocking.'

'I'll take that as a compliment,' she said with what she hoped was a sexy smile.

Leah knew full well that she was risking heartbreak by having an affair with Jason. But to give him up was out of the question. She simply could not resist the wild abandon that he evoked in her, and the sexual pleasure he gave her.

Already she was looking forward to that bath, to washing him all over, and being washed in return.

'You'd better check that bath,' she said. 'We don't want a flood.'

'Let's check it together,' he suggested, and scooped her up into his arms.

CHAPTER THIRTEEN

LEAH WOKE FIRST the next morning, surprised to find how natural it felt to lie next to Jason. She just rested there beside him for a minute or two, looking around the spacious bedroom and thinking how little she actually liked his apartment.

She'd seen enough of it last night to form an opinion.

It was huge, of course. Huge and modern, with lots of glass and black leather, along with acres of white tiles, stainless steel appliances and geometrically patterned rugs. The walls were all white, the artwork mostly black and white, the lighting recessed. There were no curtains anywhere, just darkly tinted windows and sliding glass doors, leading out on to grey stone terraces.

The interior decorator, whoever he or she was, obviously had no liking for colour. The place was cold and soulless.

Leah hated it.

But she loved the man who lived here.

Her eyes slid over to where he was still sprawled out on the other side of the massive bed, a black satin sheet tangled around the lower half of his magnificent body.

Leah liked the opportunity to look at his sleeping face, to trace his features with admiring eyes and try to work out what made him so attractive to her.

She could find no fault in his face. Everything was perfect. His high, wide forehead. His straight, but symmetrical eyebrows. His elegantly shaped nose. His squared chin. His lovely mouth.

Oh, yes, his mouth most of all, with its strongly sculptured upper lip and sexily full bottom lip. The perfect combination of masculinity and sensuality.

Leah didn't like to think it was just his handsomeness that drew her. But maybe it was. Because she'd been right when she'd told him last night that she only knew him biblically.

What did she really know about him other than what she'd read in that paper, plus the little he'd told her?

A lot more, her love for him piped up. You know a lot more!

Jason was a man quickly liked and respected by his employees. A man who hated taking advantage of a vulnerable woman. A man who was honest about what he wanted and didn't want.

And he was a man who'd once loved too much.

Leah had seen the pain in his eyes when he'd talked about his wife. She recognised that type of pain. She'd seen it in the mirror in her own eyes after her mother died. Then to a lesser degree, after Carl left her.

Loss could be a terrible thing when you cared. And Jason had cared.

Caring in a man was a good thing. It showed depth, and character.

Feeling better about loving him, Leah rose and tip-toed to the bathroom where she set about inspecting the damage in the vanity mirror.

There were faint fingerprint bruises on her hips and on her breasts. And one deeply purple love bite on her neck.

Leah touched it, surprised that it didn't hurt too much, but infinitely grateful that she had long hair, which could cover the evidence of her night of wild sex.

Not that she would bother to cover any of the bruises whilst she was here, in Jason's place. She rather liked the thought of his seeing what he'd done to her last night. Liked the thought of parading herself naked for him again today as well.

He'd insisted on her staying nude last night, not letting her cover up with a robe, forcing her to finally get over her squeamishness about her scars. After a while, she'd become quite shameless, and not at all self-conscious.

Pushing her hair back from her shoulders, she returned to the bedroom, and glanced back over at the bed.

Jason was still asleep.

The stainless steel digital clock on his glass-topped bedside table said it was ten past nine. Mrs B. was unlikely to have looked in her room as yet and discover she hadn't come home the night before. She would presume Leah was sleeping in late after the dinner party.

Leah would ring her father this morning, but a little later on.

Leah still felt irritated with him for doing what he'd done last night, inviting Jason to dinner, then letting her think his mystery guest was some rich old codger. He really should not interfere in other people's lives. He should be taught a lesson.

It would serve him right if she announced over the telephone this morning that she'd become Jason Pollack's mistress. Which was virtually what she now was.

Some time during the night, Jason had asked her not to resign, and to move into the penthouse with him. She'd refused on both counts. To work with him every day and sleep with him every night would be courting disaster. She'd survived Carl leaving her. She would not survive Jason leaving her.

At the same time she could not resist him totally. So she told him he could stay the night at her place when he wanted to, and vice versa. But she would not wrap her life solely around him. She would find herself another job and keep her own place. Because she knew that one day—and this was the part she didn't say to him—one day, he would grow tired of her as he had his previous girlfriend, and she would be cast adrift from his life.

The thought was horrible enough at it was. How much worse would the eventuality be if she worked and lived with the man, twenty-four seven?

Leah sighed, then wandered across to the wide, plate-glass window that faced east and was currently drenched in morning sunshine. She moved to press herself against the glass, soaking in its warmth, her arms lifting up in a languid stretch, flattening her breasts and tightening her belly.

It was a highly erotic stance. Not something she would ever have done before meeting Jason. But she revelled in it this morning, well aware that last night had changed her for ever. She was now a different creature. Much more sexually driven, her senses heightened, her desires expanded.

Common sense kept warning her against becoming too involved with a man who was never going to give what she now wanted: to be his wife and the mother of his children.

Common sense, however, didn't feel like this. It didn't send delicious shivers down her spine. Or make her body yearn and burn in a thousand exciting ways.

Neither did common sense ever make her forget, even for a moment, that she was basically still alone. During Jason's lovemaking she could pretend that everything was all right.

Even though it wasn't…

'My God, you're *her*!'

Leah whirled to the sound of Jason's voice, blinking madly to rid herself of the tears that had welled up in her eyes.

Jason was sitting up in bed, his expression both startled and excited. The black sheet was still over his lower half, for which she was grateful.

'Her who?' she asked, walking quickly back towards the bed. Some embarrassment had resurfaced at being discovered standing there like that.

'The girl in my dream.'

'What girl in what dream?' she asked as she dived under the sheet and pulled it up over her breasts.

'The dream I had just before I bought Beville Holdings. About this girl on a billboard advertising their shampoo. She was photographed from the rear, naked, with lovely long fair streaming down her bare back. She looked exactly like you looked a second ago...'

When he reached over to run his hands down her long fall of hair, his amazed expression abruptly changed to a frown. 'Good Lord, look at the state of your neck! Did I do that?'

'Do you see anyone else in this bed with me?'

'Why didn't you stop me?'

Leah laughed. 'Why don't I turn back the tides as well?'

'I can't believe I did that,' he murmured, his eyes back to amazed, his fingertips tracing the love bite.

'There's a few marks on my breasts and hips as well. But nothing quite like this one.'

'Will makeup hide them?' he asked unexpectedly.

'Possibly. But I'm not exactly going to walk round naked, except when I'm with you.'

'That depends.'

'Depends on what?'

'On whether I can talk you into becoming the face of Beville Holdings products.'

'What?'

'I've outlined a new advertising campaign based on that dream I had. I spoke to Harry about it yesterday and he said that its success would depend on my getting the right model.'

'Harry who?'

'Harry Wilde. He's an advertising genius and a friend of mine.'

'But I'm no model, Jason.'

'You're more beautiful than most.'

'But…but what about my scars?'

'No one will see them. I promise.'

'The photographer will.'

'You don't have to be really naked. You just have to look like you're naked from the back from the hips up. You can wear a low-slung sarong. And stick things over your breasts.'

'I don't know, Jason…'

'You'd be perfect, Leah. And you'd enjoy it.'

'I doubt it.'

'The pay would be good as well. Better than your current salary.'

'I don't really need my salary, Jason. I have this trust fund from my mother and—'

'Leah, you *like* earning your own money,' he broke in. 'Otherwise, why did you go and get a job in the first place?'

'I wanted to prove to myself that I could do it.'

'Which you have done. And I applaud you for it. Now give yourself a new challenge and do this.'

'You're very persuasive, aren't you?'

'That's what I've been trained to be.'

'You're far too used to getting your own way.'

'I haven't with you. You won't even move in with me.'

'You'll survive.'

'You loved him a lot, didn't you?'

The question threw Leah for a second. 'You don't usually marry someone you don't love,' came her careful reply.

'True.'

'This conversation has turned far too serious for me,' Leah said. 'I'm going to have a shower, then go into that dental-white kitchen of yours and make breakfast.'

'You don't like this place much, do you?' he said before she could escape the bed. 'Go on. Tell me the truth.'

'The truth? Okay. I think it's the coldest, most soulless apartment I've ever been in.'

He laughed a delighted laugh. 'I do, too.'

'Then why did you buy it?'

'Because it was convenient and a good investment. And because it matched its owner at the time,' he added, but without that haunted look she'd seen in his face before.

'Decisions made after someone dies are never good ones,' she told him. 'My father was going to sell the family home after Mum died. I dare say he might have bought something like this. He's all for good investments. I fought him tooth and nail and he didn't sell in the end. But I'm still a bit worried. It's not a good sign that he wants to sell the boat he named after Mum.'

'I could buy the boat for you, if you like.'

Leah glowered at him. 'You are not to buy me anything, Jason Pollack. Nothing expensive, anyway. Flowers and chocolates are fine. But no boats, or diamonds, or any of the other tell-tale gifts that rich men buy their beck-and-call girls.'

'You're not my beck-and-call girl,' he growled, pulling her over on top of him. 'Though I'd like you to be.'

'Would you just?'

'Damn right, I would,' he muttered, pushing her up into a sitting position, her knees on either side of his hips.

'I said I was going to have a shower,' she told him, trying not to give in to the urges he spurred in her. 'I have to ring home as well. As much as I'm still peeved with my father, I don't want to worry him.'

'Afterwards.'

'I…I'm not really in the mood for more sex right now, Jason.'

'Liar. I can *see* that you're lying. You can watch *me* come, if you'd prefer.'

Leah's head spun with his words. The idea excited her. She'd never done that. She'd always been too caught up in the act herself. How would it feel to remain fully in control whilst he lost it?

Taking a deeply gathering breath, Leah lifted herself up on to her knees, then reached down to take him in her hand, rubbing him till a tortured moan slipped from his mouth. Finally, she put him just inside her, then sank slowly downwards.

'You do realise,' she said when their bodies were together, 'that I'm not the only girl at Beville Holdings sleeping with her boss.'

Conversation, Leah hoped, would distract her from her own rapidly escalating excitement. Maybe she'd be able stay more detached if she chatted away to him.

'Hell, Leah, I'm not interested in talking about Trish and Jim right now.'

'I wasn't talking about Trish and Jim. I meant Shelley and Jim.'

His eyebrows lifted. 'So what else do you know that I don't know?'

'Management have wasted a lot of money lately.'

'You think I should sack the lot?'

'I think you should offer them incentives to leave.'

He smiled. 'You'd make me a good Girl Friday, you know. Say the word and I'll promote you.'

'I think you should settle for me being the face of Beville Holdings. I don't like the idea of sleeping with the boss.'

'I'll still be your boss.'

'No, you won't. As of next week, I'm signing myself up with a proper modelling agency. You'll have go through them if you want me.'

'I want you,' he said, his dark eyes gleaming as he grabbed her hips and began moving her up and down.

Yes, he did, Leah conceded with a rush of hot blood through her body. For now.

But not for ever.

'Lean forward,' he ordered her. 'Stretch your arms up over my head.'

'No. I'm supposed to be staying all cool while I just watch you.'

'Just do it, Leah.'

She did it, the position setting her breasts swinging towards his face, and his mouth. He licked the aching tips, then took one between his teeth.

The pain was delicious, but swiftly unbearable. She wrenched her breast out of his mouth, and straightened.

'You have to stop doing things like that,' she told him breathlessly.

'Why?'

'Because I might get to like it.'

'I hope so.'

'You have a wicked side to you, Jason Pollack.'

He laughed. 'And don't you just love it.'

She blushed. Not her first blush since she'd climbed into that taxi with him last night.

'And I love that about you, too,' he murmured, reaching up to stroke her pink cheeks before running his fingertips down over her breasts, down her taut belly into the damp golden curls that surrounded her sex. 'You haven't been like this with any other man, not even your precious Carl. *Have* you?' he demanded as he touched her there, where her nerve endings were gathered into an apex of exquisite sensitively.

'No,' she confessed shakily.

'Only with me,' he rasped. 'You *are* my beck-and-call girl, Leah. Make no mistake about that. But only because you want to be,' he said as his hand withdrew to take hold of her hips once more. 'You do want to be, don't you?' he said as he urged her on.

She didn't answer him. Just closed her eyes…

CHAPTER FOURTEEN

JOACHIM BLOOM HAD just finished breakfast when the phone rang. He guessed who it was before he answered it.

'It's me, Daddy,' Leah said with a touch of defiance in her voice.

'So I see,' he replied calmly. 'Am I to presume you stayed the night at Pollack's place?'

'Jason, Daddy. Call him Jason. And, yes, that's where I stayed. Did…er…Mrs B. say anything this morning when I didn't make it down for breakfast?'

'No. I told her you went out to a nightclub with a gentlemen friend late last night and wouldn't be back till later today.'

'That was presumptuous of you. What did she say?'

'I'm not quite sure. She mumbles a bit, does Mrs B. But it sounded something like, *it's about time*.'

'Oh…'

Joachim smiled. 'You sound piqued that we're not all shocked out of our skins, Leah.'

'I'm not shocked *you're* not shocked. After all, you

threw us together on purpose, didn't you? Though Lord knows why. That's what I'd like to know, Daddy. Why pick a man for me like Jason Pollack?'

Joachim knew it would sound ridiculous if he said, 'Your mother suggested him to me.'

'I liked the look of him in the paper,' he said instead. 'I like self-made men.'

'You implied to me that he'd married his first wife for his money.'

'Did I? I don't recall doing that. Maybe that was you, jumping to that conclusion. So, what do you think now that you know him better? Did he marry his first wife for her money?'

'No. He married her because he loved her. So much so that he never wants to fall in love again, or get married again.'

Joachim's dismay was sharp. It seemed he'd made a big mistake here.

Serve him right for listening to so-called messages from the afterlife. He'd never believed in the supernatural before. He suddenly felt very foolish for following that voice in his head. Of course it hadn't been Isabel talking to him, he reprimanded himself sternly. How could he ever have imagined it?

'I'm sorry, Leah. Are you very angry with me?'

'Not angry, Daddy. Just a bit annoyed. You really should learn to butt out of other people's lives. If and when I want another husband, *I* will find him. Do I make myself clear?'

'Absolutely.'

'Meanwhile, Jason and I do like each other. A lot. So don't be shocked if the tabloids start calling us an item. I suspect we're going to be seen out and about a bit together in the coming weeks. Oh, and another thing. I'm resigning my job at Beville Holdings on Monday and becoming a model.'

'A *model*! But…but…'

'Yes, I know. My scars. Obviously, I won't be becoming a swimwear model. But not to worry. I have my first contract in the bag. I'm to be the face of Beville Holdings products in a new advertising campaign they're launching in a few months.'

'You're joking.'

'Not at all. There has to some benefit to being the boss's mistress.'

'Mistress!'

'Mistress. Girlfriend. Whatever.'

Joachim finally heard it in his daughter's voice. The underlying pain. There could only be one reason for it. She'd fallen in love with Jason Pollack.

For a split second, Joachim felt devastated. Till that damned voice piped up in his head again, whispering that everything would be all right.

Against all logic, relief flooded his soul.

Have faith, my darling, the voice whispered to him.

It *was* Isabel's voice. He recognised it.

Joachim had to clear his throat to speak. 'That's good,' he said. 'Jason's a good man.'

'Daddy, have you been drinking?'

'Only coffee.'

'He just wants me for the sex. You do realise that, don't you?'

'Lots of relationships begin with just sex, daughter,' Joachim pointed out reasonably.

'He's still in love with his wife!'

'Possibly, he is. Love doesn't die just because of death. But she is dead, Leah, and you're very much alive. So is Jason.'

'Jason knows what he wants and doesn't want, Daddy. He's been very honest with me. Right from the start.'

'And when was the start, daughter?'

Leah sighed a weary sounding sigh. 'Friday night. After work.'

'I see.' Joachim didn't really see.

Have faith, Joachim.

'Just love him, Leah. There's no man on earth who could resist a girl like you loving him.'

'Oh, Daddy,' she suddenly sobbed on the other end of the line. 'I do so love him. It's nothing like I felt for Carl. I…I…'

'There, there, child,' he soothed. 'Everything will be fine. You'll see.'

'No, it won't,' she cried, then sniffed. 'I have to go. Jason will be out of the bathroom soon. I probably won't be back today. I'll call you later in the week,' she said, and hung up.

Leah lay face-down on the bed whilst she listened to the shower running and Jason whistling. He was happy and she was crying.

That was because he was getting what he wanted and she never would.

The time to get out of this relationship is now, Leah. Not in a few weeks, or a few months. Now, before it goes any further.

But she knew she didn't have the courage to do that. How could she possibly say, 'Sorry, Jason,' when he came out of that bathroom, 'but I've fallen in love with you and you're never going to love me back, so I've decided to call it a day.'

Impossible.

No, she'd smile and go along with what he wanted today. And every other day till he called it quits. That was her destiny now.

No, that's your choice, *her brain reminded her.*

Maybe. But does love ever really have a choice? And if it does, is that choice ever going to be the right one?

The bathroom door opened, and a dripping wet Jason emerged in a cloud of steam, a white towel slung low around his hips.

'I've been thinking,' he said, one hand lifting to fingercomb his hair back from his forehead.

'Yes?' Leah propped her chin up on her hands and did her best to look nonchalant.

'About your resigning...'

'What about my resigning,' she repeated warily. She hoped he wasn't going to try to talk her out of that again!

'I think it's a good idea. I could never keep my mind on the job with you around. I'd be wanting to find excuses to get you alone all the time. But you'll have to show up tomorrow. It'll take Bob a day or two to line up a temp.'

'Mandy could do the job. She fills in for me occasionally.'

'Are you sure?'

'Quite sure.'

'Best you still come in tomorrow.' He spun round and was about to walk back into the bathroom when he stopped and turned back again. 'Did you ring your father?'

'Yes.'

'I'll bet he wasn't at all shocked.'

'You're quite right, Jason,' she returned coolly. 'He wasn't.'

'See? You were worried for nothing.'

'I told him about my two new jobs.'

'*Two* new jobs?'

'Yes. Model and mistress.'

'For pity's sake, Leah.' Jason scowled. 'You are not my mistress. You'll have your father thinking I'm a worse cad than that creep you were married to. You're my girlfriend.'

'One in a long line.'

'That's not true,' he denied, his expression serious. 'Okay, so I had a lot of girlfriends in my younger days. But you are only the second girlfriend I've had since my wife died.'

And the first one I've really cared about, Jason could have added. But didn't.

Leah sat up abruptly. 'You're kidding me.'

'Not at all. I didn't date for four years after Karen's death. I just didn't want to. But about six months ago I met someone at a party, and I realised my celibate days were over.'

'And that was the girlfriend you broke up with recently?'

'Yes, Hilary. She was a nice enough woman, but she wanted marriage. I'd told her right from the start that I wouldn't marry again, so I felt I had no choice but to break it off. She was somewhat...upset. That's why I was worried when I met you. I didn't want to hurt anyone else. But you don't want to get married again, either, so everything's okay. Look, I still have to shave,' he added, rubbing his stubbly chin. 'You could pop in the shower while I'm doing that, if you like.'

'Oh, no, no, no,' Leah said, wagging an index finger at him. 'I'm not falling for that little trick. I'll wait till you're finished. I'd like to shower in peace, then get dressed and go home.'

'Wearing what, pray tell? Your panties are history and that little black number is not quite the thing for day wear.'

'Surely you have something in your wardrobe I can put on.'

'Not a thing,' he said blithely.

'Then you'll have to go out and buy me something.'

'You told me I wasn't to buy you anything except flowers and chocolates.'

'Oh, truly! You're being deliberately difficult. I have to go home eventually.'

'You'll just have to stay here till tonight, won't you? And then you can comfortably wear your black dress home in my car. Without panties, of course. But no one will know that.'

'*You* will.'

His grin was wicked. 'Yes, ma'am. I sure will.'

CHAPTER FIFTEEN

'YOU? AND *JASON*?'

Leah could not help smiling at Trish's surprise.
Clearly, she'd done a good job last week of not betraying how attractive she'd found their new boss.

'Yes,' she confirmed. 'Me and Jason.'

The two girls were having morning tea together in
the canteen, with Leah feeling she had to explain to
Trish what was behind her resignation.

'Oh, you lucky thing!' Trish exclaimed. 'I'll bet he's
fabulous in bed. No, you don't have to answer that. But
I can see by the look on your face that he is. So, is it
serious already? Is that why you're resigning?'

'Partly,' Leah said, and told Trish about Jason wanting her to be in his new advertising campaign.

'I wouldn't be able to keep on working here, Trish,
especially once it becomes known I'm going out with
the boss. You know what it'd be like. All the girls would
talk. So would the reps. There'd be gossip and jealousy
and accusations of favouritism.'

'Yeah. There was a bit of that going on when I was sleeping with Jim. Speaking of Jim, I think he's going to be asked to leave.'

'It wouldn't surprise me.'

'Bob said Jason was on to him.'

'Goodness, I forgot you went out with Bob on Friday night. How did that go?'

'Pretty good. It's not love at first sight, but he's a really nice man. We're going out again soon.'

'I'm glad, Trish. Jim was a total waste of your time for a girl who wants to get married and have children.'

'You're dead right. And let's face it, most of us girls do.'

'Yes,' Leah said with what was perhaps a too-wistful sigh.

Trish gave her a sharp look. 'Is there something wrong, Leah? You sounded…sad, just then.'

'No, no, I'm just tired.'

'Too much sex,' Trish said with a knowing little laugh.

'Could be.'

'Lucky you. That's how Jim got me in, you know. He's very good at it. Sex, that is. There again, he's certainly had enough practice,' she added tartly. 'Did you know he was having it off with Shelley as well?'

'Er…yes,' Leah admitted. 'I'm sorry, Trish. I didn't want to be the one to tell you.'

Trish sighed. 'Men like that should be castrated. You're lucky, finding someone like Jason.'

'He's not perfect, Trish.'

'How can you say that? He's utterly gorgeous and rich and nice and rich and utterly gorgeous! What's not perfect about him?' she asked with a frown.

'He doesn't want to get married again.'

'Oh. Oh, I see. Oh, that's too bad.'

'Yes.' Speaking the truth out loud had a very depressing effect on Leah.

'Maybe you should take your own advice then, Leah, and not waste your time on some man who isn't going to give you what *you* want.'

'I fully agree with you. But the problem is…I love him. A lot.'

'Maybe he'll change his mind. If anyone could make a man change his mind, it's you.'

Leah smiled. 'That's a lovely thing to say.'

'You're a lovely person.'

Leah knew she had to change the subject. Quickly.

'Do you think Mandy can do my job?'

'She's a bit young. Jason asked me that first thing this morning and I advised him to stay with a temp for a while. It won't do Mandy any harm to wait a bit.'

'Yes, I think that's wise.'

'You're sounding like you won't be staying much longer.'

'No, no, I won't be. Just a day or two.'

'We're going to miss you. *I'm* going to miss you.'

'We can still go out occasionally together.'

Trish's smile was wry. 'Not if you're going to be dating the boss. Being a billionaire's girlfriend sounds like a full-time after-hours job.'

Leah shook her head. 'It might not be a permanent job.'

Trish reached across the table to touch Leah gently on the wrist. 'You've fallen very hard for him, haven't you?'

Leah was to think about that expression for the rest of the day.

Fallen hard.

It sounded like she'd had an accident; that she'd already hurt herself. Which, in a way, she had.

For what good could come of entering a relationship that was doomed from the start? How was she going to survive it?

At four thirty, Leah tidied her desk and left the office. Jason had wanted her to go home to his place, but she'd insisted on returning to her own apartment at Gladesville on week nights. She'd compromised by suggesting she cook him dinner. Then, if he wanted to, he could stay the night.

He wanted to. Naturally.

On the way home, she stopped at the local shopping centre and picked up the ingredients for dinner. Then she dropped into the news agency and bought herself a diary. Not a large one. Something that she could carry with her and write in when the stress of pretending became too much, because that was what her life was going to be most of the time from now on.

Pretending.

But she would not pretend in her diary. There, she

would put down her real thoughts and feelings. She would say how much she loved Jason. She would express her hopes for the future, no matter how futile they were. She would give voice to her dreams. And her secret desires.

Seven o'clock saw her dressed casually in blue cotton slacks and a blue-and-white striped blouse. Her hair was up in a casual ponytail, her makeup and perfume freshened. A bottle of wine was chilling in the fridge and a Japanese chicken curry was simmering in her electric frypan.

She'd written a few lines in her diary earlier, bringing some release to her anxiety.

The doorbell rang right on time. Jason was, it seemed, a punctual man. Either that, or an eager one.

Leah experienced a mixture of excitement and fear as she went to answer the door. Tonight would set the tone for their relationship. Tonight she had to play the role she thought he wanted her to play.

Schooling her face into a coolly sophisticated smile, she opened the door.

'Come in, darling,' she said. 'Dinner's just about ready.'

CHAPTER SIXTEEN

LEAH RODE THE lift up to the penthouse floor of Jason's building, as she'd ridden it many times before. She had her own private keycard these days.

Six months had passed since she'd agreed to become Jason's girlfriend.

That was what Jason always introduced her as. His girlfriend.

Leah supposed it was a lot better than mistress. Though the tabloids did use that word occasionally.

They had become a rather high-profile couple, their photographs splashed across the gossip pages of magazines and newspapers, especially after she achieved fame in her own right as the face of the Sunshine range of products.

Jason's new advertising and marketing campaign had proved very successful. Beville Holdings was going from strength to strength, with new management and a new receptionist. Mandy. Leah was now a highly sought-after photographic model, a job she quite liked, but which she suspected would eventually run its course.

Her relationship with Jason seemed just as happy— on the surface. They did go out in public together a lot more, to restaurants and parties and other social functions that Jason was invited to. And she occasionally helped him entertain in his penthouse.

But Jason wasn't overly keen on the social side of being a billionaire. Often their weekends were quiet, allowing Leah to still visit the hospital on a Saturday, after which she would go home to visit her father, like in the old days. Jason would always join her there and they would stay overnight.

Mrs B. adored him. Her father liked him, too, despite his not offering to become his son-in-law. Jason was a very likable man.

Yes, everything seemed okay.

Lately, however, Leah would catch Jason looking at her sometimes with a slight frown in his eyes. Something was bothering him about her. She dared not ask him what the matter was, because she feared the answer.

Was he growing bored with her perhaps?

She'd tried terribly hard not to cling, sensing he'd hate that. And she never told him she loved him. Never ever. Not even when he was making love to her in that long, gentle way he did sometimes, and which totally overwhelmed her with emotion. The way he looked down at her as he rocked slowly in and out of her, often brought the words to her lips.

But she always bit them back. Always!

When the lift doors opened, Leah just stood there for a moment. She could hear voices coming from the depths of the open-plan apartment. She hadn't expected company tonight. Friday night they usually spent having dinner in the restaurant that occupied part of the floor below Jason's penthouse, followed by a spa bath, then bed.

Jason hadn't mentioned anything about having anyone over tonight when he'd called her around lunchtime. The thought of having to entertain some of Jason's hyped-up business colleagues did not appeal. Leah felt tired. Tired and dispirited. And worried.

With a weary sigh, she hooked her bag over her shoulder and stepped out of the lift.

Jason's stomach had tightened when he heard the purr of the lift.

It would be Leah, of course. Beautiful, intriguing, enigmatic Leah, coming to spend Friday night with him, as usual.

'That will be Leah now,' he said to Bob and Trish.

Trish beamed from where she was perched on the edge of a black leather armchair, sipping a celebratory glass of champagne. 'I haven't seen Leah in ages. Except on the telly, of course. And on those fabulous billboards.'

'Those billboards are really something, aren't they?' Bob remarked. 'Have you told Leah about us yet, Jase?'

Jason smiled at his obviously very happy PA. 'No. I thought we might surprise her.'

Bob had confided to Jason just after lunch at work that he'd popped the question to Trish the previous night, but hadn't as yet bought a ring. The proposal had been of the impulsive kind. So Jason had given him a hefty cash bonus as an engagement present and sent them both off ring shopping. When Bob had rung him around six to thank him, mentioning that they were on their way to a top city restaurant to celebrate, he'd immediately invited them up to the penthouse for a pre-dinner drink of champagne.

His first thought was to ring Leah, but he'd already rung her twice that day. Telephone calls to Leah were often uncomfortable experiences for Jason. Leah wasn't like other women, or any other girlfriend he'd ever had.

Even Karen—who was the most independent of women—had liked him to call her often. They'd talked for hours on the phone before they were married.

Leah, however, always cut him short on the phone, saying there was something she had to do, or somewhere she had to go. The only time he got to really talk to her alone was during their Friday night dinners. Even then, she had the knack of keeping their conversation to what had happened that day, never the past, or—heaven forbid—the future!

He glanced up and there she was, looking absolutely gorgeous in a forest-green woollen dress that hugged her body and gave his never-ending desire for her no peace at all. Her hair was up in that soft, sexy style he adored. A gold necklace—not one he'd ever bought her—adorned her lovely throat, matching earrings dangling from her small earlobes. Her perfume seemed to precede her into the room, a teasing tantalising scent that drove him insane.

'Trish!' she exclaimed, her beautiful but often too-serious face lighting up when she saw who his visitors were. 'And Bob! I'm so glad it's you and not some of Jason's old cronies.'

'I don't have old cronies,' he protested, and handed her a glass of champagne. 'I'm not your father.'

'You certainly aren't,' she said as she took it, dropping her handbag on an empty chair. 'What are we celebrating?'

Trish jumped up from her chair and wriggled her ring finger at Leah. 'This,' she said.

'Oh, my, you're engaged! How wonderful! And what a lovely ring.'

'The boss paid for most of it,' Bob said, and Leah swung round to smile at him. Yet she didn't really look happy.

Jason wished he could read what it was that made her eyes go like that. So dull and sad. Was she thinking of the time when her husband had given her a diamond ring? Damn and blast, would she ever get over that bastard?

'That was very generous of you, darling,' she said.

Jason winced inside. He hated it when she called him darling like that. It was so superficial sounding. So…meaningless.

He wasn't her darling. He would never be her darling.

What a dismaying thought.

Jason could not pin down the moment he realised he'd fallen in love with Leah. Perhaps it was the Friday night last month when she'd been running terribly late and he hadn't been able to get her on her mobile. A vicious storm had swept in from the west, bringing heavy rain and hail, along with lightning and thunder. He'd paced the rain-soaked terraces, staring out at the storm and worrying his guts out that she'd been one of the many people already involved in car accidents that night. He'd been on the verge of ringing all the hospitals when she'd finally arrived.

There *had* been an accident. In the harbour tunnel. She'd been caught right in the middle at the deepest part and her mobile simply wouldn't work.

Jason recalled feeling physically ill with relief, then being overcome with the need to hold her and make love to her. He'd dragged her down on to the nearest rug and ravaged her, right then and there. He hadn't even bothered to use a condom. Afterwards, when Leah said she'd have to get a morning-after pill, he hadn't wanted her to.

But he'd made no objections at the time.

He'd felt frustrated afterwards because he'd used sex to express his love instead of saying it. He *still* used sex to express his love.

But Leah didn't seem to want anything else from him!

Karen had told him that one day he'd fall in love again. He hadn't believed her at the time. But Karen had been a very wise woman. She knew time would heal his grief.

How much time did Leah need, Jason wondered, to heal her grief? How long could he bear loving her and not being loved back? It was becoming increasingly difficult, especially when he saw the way people in love acted together.

Bob and Trish could not stop touching each other, and looking at each other, their eyes full of love, their talk full of plans.

Leah didn't want to talk about the future at all. She just lived for the day. If he didn't know the good work she did at that hospital every week, he might have thought she'd become very selfish.

'We should toast the happy couple,' Jason proposed. 'To Bob and Trish.'

'And to love,' Trish added, clinking her glass against Bob's.

Jason saw Leah's reaction. Instantly negative.

It was another defining moment in Jason's life, the moment he decided that he could not go on with this relationship. Not the way it was.

Something had to give. He hoped that something would be Leah.

He's going to break up with me, Leah realised when their eyes met.

Her heart recoiled. So did her stomach.

'I'm sorry, everyone,' she said, and swiftly put her glass down. 'But I...I have to go to the bathroom.'

Leah fairly raced for the guest powder room, only just reaching it before her stomach heaved. It wasn't the first time that day. Or that week.

A pregnancy test this afternoon had confirmed her fear.

She was going to have Jason's baby.

Leah knew exactly when it had happened. The night of the storm. She should have gone to the doctor the very next morning. But she hadn't. She just couldn't.

And now here she was, having Jason's child. And he didn't want her any more.

'Are you all right, Leah?' Jason asked from the other idea of the door.

Leah leant a clammy cheek against the cubicle wall. 'Yes, I...er...must have eaten something that didn't agree with me. Sorry. I'll be out in a minute.'

'Bob and Trish have a booking for seven.'

'Tell them to go. Please. I might be longer here than a minute.'

'Will do.'

Leah stayed in the powder room for five more minutes, not emerging till she knew the coast was clear. The apartment was deathly quiet as she returned to the living room. Jason was standing at one of the largest of the plate-glass windows, his hands in his trousers pockets, his back to her. He could have been just standing there, watching the city lights, but Leah knew he wasn't. He was trying to find the right words to say to her.

Leah decided to help him out.

'It's all right, Jason,' she said tautly. 'You can just say it. I won't make a scene.'

He turned slowly, his handsome face more bleak than she'd even seen it. 'Say what, exactly?'

'That we're finished.'

'Is that what you want me to say, Leah?'

She could not stop the shudder from running down her spine. 'No!'

His expression startled her, because it carried surprise. 'You don't?'

Leah found her insides dissolving, along with the façade she'd carried all these months. 'Why on earth would I want you to say that?' she threw at him. 'I *love* you, Jason. I've loved you all this time.'

Jason could not believe how angry her declaration made him.

'*Love* me?' he threw back at her. 'You don't honestly expect me to believe that, do you? I know what it feels like when a woman loves me, and it isn't what I feel when I'm with you, madam. You don't really talk to me, even when we're together. All you want from me is what we share in bed.'

'That's because that's all you offered me!' she countered, startling him with *her* anger. 'If you think I've enjoyed this past six months with you, Jason, then you can think again. It's been hell, I tell you, pretending not to love you. If you don't believe me, then I've got something I think you should read.'

Read? 'What?'

'This.'

He watched in total confusion whilst she walked over and pulled a small black book from her handbag. He almost dropped it when she tossed it at him from a distance.

He stared at the cover. 'It's a diary.'

'Yes. *Mine*. I wrote in it whenever the pretence became too much for me.'

'But why in heaven's name would you think you had to pretend?' he asked.

She shook her head in a highly agitated fashion. 'And I thought you were an intelligent man. Because you told me right at the beginning that you couldn't possibly love me back, that's why!'

'Yes, I did, didn't I?' he murmured, his heart catching as he read the first entry. It was dated back in February.

I must remember never to tell Jason that I love him. He'll break up with me if I do. But I can tell you. I love him. I love him. I love him. Now I must go. He'll be here shortly for dinner. I can't wait.

Those last three words touched Jason the most. He flicked on through the pages, searching for last month's entries, knowing that she was sure to have written something about that night as well.

Yes! There it was.

Dreadfully late getting to Jason's place tonight. Traffic accident in the tunnel. At first I thought he was genuinely worried about me. That maybe he loved me. But that wasn't it. He just wanted sex, as usual. On the floor, no less. Without using protection. I wanted to cry afterwards. I almost did when he agreed with my suggestion that I go to the doctor for the morning-after pill. I don't want to go, but I guess I will. Dear God, it's cruel to love someone like this...

He looked up, his heart filled to overflowing with regret, and sadness. If only he'd known...

Slowly, however, the realisation of Leah's love sank in, and an unbelievable joy blossomed in Jason's chest.

'She really loves me, Karen,' he whispered.

Yes, my dearest, he thought he heard her reply.

Undoubtedly, it was only his imagination speaking to him.

But that didn't matter, because Jason knew Karen would be genuinely happy for him. A generous woman, Karen. A lovely, brave, generous woman.

'*What* did you say?' Leah asked, her eyes widening.

Jason walked slowly towards her. 'I said I love you, too.'

She blinked. 'You *do*?'

'I do,' he repeated.

'Then why on earth didn't you *say* so?'

'For the same reasons you didn't,' he explained, cupping her face and looking deep into her frustrated green eyes. 'I thought you didn't *want* me to love you. I thought you still loved your first husband.'

'But I don't. And I didn't say that I did. I just said people usually marry for love. But you, Jason, you definitely said you were still in love with your wife.'

'I do still love her. But that hasn't stopped me falling in love with you, Leah. Karen told me before she died that I would find someone else, someone special, someone more my age who would love me and give me children. Karen couldn't have children, you see. She'd had cancer of the cervix when she was younger.'

'Oh. But that's so sad. I didn't realise she'd had cancer before. The poor woman.'

'She was an amazing woman. And I did love her. But you are even more amazing, Leah, and I love you madly. Will you marry me and have my children?'

'Well…yes, of course I will. But…'

'But what?'

'Oh, dear. I hope you're not going to be cross with me.'

'Out with it, girl.'

'That night of the storm,' she blurted out.

'Yes, I just read that bit.'

'I…er…I didn't go to the doctor the next day.'

'And?'

'I took a pregnancy test today, and it was positive.'

Once Jason got his head around the fact that he was already a father, he could not contain his delight.

'Leah, that's fantastic!' he cried, hugging her to him. 'I couldn't be happier. A baby. Already.' He pulled back to hold her by the shoulders. 'We'll get married as soon as possible. And we'll go house hunting. I know how much you hate this place.'

'It's not so bad,' she said. 'I've gotten used to it. But not quite the place to raise children. You don't just want one baby, do you, Jason? I want at least two.'

'Have as many as you like.'

Tears filled Leah's eyes. 'I can't believe everything has turned out all right,' she said, still half-fearful of such happiness. 'I thought tonight was going to be the end.'

'Never. I was going to make you marry me, whether you loved me or not.'

Leah blinked back her tears. 'Really? *How?*'

'I have no idea. Bribery and corruption. No, probably persuasion and negotiation. That's what I'm best at. I would have worked out what you wanted more than me and given it to you in exchange for a ring on your finger. Which reminds me. First thing tomorrow we're going ring shopping. And I'm going to buy the biggest, flashiest, most expensive diamond ring in Sydney.'

Leah laughed. 'Has it been very hard on you, my telling you not to buy me anything over a hundred dollars?'

'Extremely. Now that I've been let off the hook, I'm going to go crazy, buying you things.'

'There is something which you could buy me. Two things, actually…'

'I'll get them for you tomorrow. Tell me.'

Leah smiled. Buying her mother's house would not be achieved in a day. But Leah was sure her father would sell it to them, along with the boat in the boathouse.

How wonderful it would be to raise her family there with Jason by her side as her husband. A real husband this time. A man she could depend on. A man who loved her as much as she loved him.

'It's going to cost you a lot of money,' she said teasingly, knowing her father would drive a hard bargain.

'Leah, I am a seriously rich man. There's nothing I can't buy.'

Except love, Jason realised. That was never for sale. Not true love.

'You're going to have to deal with a ruthless negotiator,' she warned him.

'I can be pretty ruthless myself. Look, just tell me who you're talking about and what it is you want.'

When Leah told him, Jason tried not to smile. Joachim had already expressed the wish on a recent visit to the penthouse that he'd love to live in a place just like it. Clearly, his future father-in-law was ready for a change.

'Piece of cake, my darling,' he said, his face breaking into a broad smile. 'Piece of cake.'

CHAPTER SEVENTEEN

JOACHIM KNELT DOWN to put the champagne-coloured roses in the vase built into Isabel's marble gravestone. She'd loved that colour of rose, ever since she'd had them in her wedding bouquet.

'Well, my darling,' he murmured. 'I did what you wanted and you were right. He was the man for our Leah.'

Joachim fell silent for a few moments, thinking of all times during their marriage that Isabel had cleverly got her point across, softly, subtly, without nagging. People often thought he wore the pants in their family. He would once have thought so, too.

But he wasn't so sure now. It wasn't till after Isabel had died that he realised how much he'd relied on her advice. And her very wise ways. She was an extremely intuitive woman. Especially about people.

Of course, being a very egotistical man, Joachim hadn't always agreed with Isabel.

'You never did like Carl, did you?' he went on softly.

'You said as much the day Leah married him, but I didn't listen to you. I listened to you this time, didn't I? They were married yesterday, at home. Their home, now. A quiet ceremony with Mrs B. doing the catering. She's staying on with them, by the way. Oh, and I bought Jason's penthouse. I needed to finally move on, Isabel. I hope you understand.'

Joachim smiled. 'I dare say you already know about the baby. And that it's going to be a boy. He and I are going to be great mates. We'll go sailing together, and camping, and fishing. Yes, Isabel, I happen to like camping and fishing. You don't know everything about me. I'll bet you never imagined I'd be talking to you like this. You always called me an old sceptic about God and heaven and the afterlife.'

Joachim stood up, stroking the grass from his trousers. 'Of course, I know you're probably not still actually *here*, my darling. But you're somewhere nearby, aren't you, still looking over me and Leah.'

Tears pricked at Joachim's eyes. Enough, he told himself, and blinked them away. Life went on.

'I must go, Isabel. I have lots to do. I have to buy a four-wheel drive, for one thing. And lots of fishing and camping gear. Yes, you're right again. I have no idea how to do either, but I can learn.'

As Joachim swung away, his attention was caught by the name on the headstone next to Isabel's.

POLLACK.

He hadn't noticed it before. He frowned as he stared down at the simple inscription.

'Karen Pollack,' he read aloud. 'Beloved wife of Jason Pollack. A lovely, brave, generous woman.'

Joachim stared at it for a very long time, then he smiled and walked slowly away.

THE SECRET BABY REVENGE

Emma
DARCY

Initially a French/English teacher, **Emma Darcy** changed careers to computer programming before the happy demands of marriage and motherhood. Very much a people person, and always interested in relationships, she finds the world of romance fiction a thrilling one and the challenge of creating her own cast of characters very addictive.

Don't miss Emma Darcy's new novel,
***Ruthless Billionaire, Forbidden Baby,* out in**
July 2009 from Mills & Boon® Modern™.

CHAPTER ONE

OPENING night at Sydney's new Havana Club and Joaquin Luis Sola stood at the extremely busy bar, waiting for the drinks he'd ordered and idly watching the talent on the dance floor swirl by. His friend, legal advisor, and highly eligible man about town, Tony Fisher, had promised all the *beautiful* people would be here, to see and be seen in the hotspot of the moment, and Quin could undoubtedly pick himself a partner for more than dancing.

Much waggling of eyebrows to underline the point, but for Quin, joining Tony's party was more an escape from a sense of restless boredom than a quest for casual sex. Having recently ended a less than satisfying relationship, Quin wasn't sure he wanted to complicate his life with another woman just yet. A one-night stand didn't appeal, either. He wasn't actually watching for targets of possible interest, just watching…

A colourful kaleidoscope of couples were swinging around the dance floor, doing the salsa. Latin American dancing was big on the social scene right now due to a number of popular television shows featuring competitions. The Havana Club was cleverly capitalising on this latest trend.

"Great way of meeting people," Tony had enthused. "Everyone putting themselves on display, strutting their stuff."

They were certainly doing that, Quin thought, somewhat bemused by the exuberant and very public plunge into fun and fantasy. Most of the people here had wildly embraced Latin dance fashion; the guys in fitted shirts with big cuffs, bootleg pants, much attention paid to their hairdos; the women very glamorous in slinky sheaths with side splits, skintight black pants with halter midriff tops, frilled skirts and strappy stilettos.

Being in this club was like being in an exotic and erotic foreign country. Quin could see its appeal—a quick fix escape from the pressures of today's fast and frantic society—a place where people could let their hair down, revel in uninhibited dress-ups, enjoy the primitive pleasure of moving to music, not to mention the sexual excitement…with the right partner.

A flashy couple caught his eye. The guy was all in white, his long black hair slicked back into a ponytail— very dramatic with his dark olive skin and hard featured handsome face. The woman partnering him was wearing a virtually backless black dress, its figure-hugging skirt ending in a ruffle edged in white. She also had long black hair, but it was a wild loose mass of curls falling to below her shoulder-blades, reminding Quin instantly of Nicole Ashton—not a memory he cared to dwell on.

"Your drinks, sir?"

Quin paid the bartender, cynically reflecting that the

price of cocktails in this club belonged to the fantasy realm, too, aimed at a clientele who never counted the cost. Strange how it didn't matter how wealthy he had become, the concept of value for money still counted in his mind. Not that it stopped him from doing or buying whatever he wanted. It was simply impossible to forget the lessons of poverty.

With the drinks firmly clutched in his hands, Quin turned to weave his way around the crowded dance floor to the tables Tony had claimed for his party, and found the woman with Nicole's hair twirling right in front of him.

She had a great body; lush breasts straining against a halter-necked bodice edged in white. The skirt was split up to midthigh, the ruffle following the opening up, diminishing to a white tie-belt around a hand-span waist. Her hips were female poetry and her long shapely legs flashed with sexy elegance.

The guy in white caught her and dipped her over his knee, her lovely lithe body arched, toes in their black stilettos pointed, head thrown back, hair sweeping the floor, stunning green eyes sparkling with pleasure, her whole beautiful face vividly lit by a laughing smile—a face that delivered such a jolt to Quin, the drinks he was carrying sloshed over the rims of the glasses.

It *was* Nicole!

The thump to his heart and the kick to his gut were instantaneous. Shock, he tried to reason, after he'd pulled himself back from shooting a blistering bolt of hatred at the guy in white and halted the rampant urge to tear Nicole away from him.

Quite simply hadn't expected to run into her like

this, hadn't expected their paths ever to cross again. She'd gone overseas after breaking up with him, taking herself completely out of his reach, yet here she was in this Sussex Street club, right under his nose. And attached to another guy.

Which also stood to reason, Quin savagely told himself. Why wouldn't she move on to other men? He'd moved on to other women, though never feeling the same intensity Nicole had drawn from him. In fact, he hadn't wanted to feel any deep emotional connection with anyone after *she* had walked out of his life. It was easier to function on the fast-moving business level without that kind of distraction.

And it was totally absurd to get in a twist over Nicole now. What was gone was gone. He wrenched his gaze away from the dance floor and guarded the drinks in his hands as he made his way back to those in Tony's party who were sitting out this number. He sat down next to Amber Piramo who'd requested the liquid refreshment, expecting him to pay and deliver, expecting her every whim to be indulged because she was the beautiful socialite daughter of old-wealth parents.

"Oh, thank you, my darling Quin," she gushed. "I am totally, totally dehydrated."

He wasn't her darling, and despite her obvious physical attractions, the overly flirtatious manner grated on him. He had to force a smile as he responded, "Sorry I was so long at the bar."

"No problem." She patted his thigh as she added, "It's been fun just watching the other dancers."

His leg muscles tensed, instinctively repelling the

touch. His jaw clenched, too. The only touch he wanted...but Nicole was with someone else now.

Amber withdrew the inviting hand and wrapped it around her glass. She drank too much, too fast, revealing a reckless disregard for the alcoholic content of the cocktail. Quin hoped she wasn't working up some courage to be more direct in coming onto him. While it might be an old-fashioned attitude these days, he still felt it was a man's prerogative to be the hunter.

His gaze instinctively targeted Nicole as the music stopped. Her ponytailed partner swept her to a table where another guy had just left a woman with wildly purple hair—definitely not a shrinking violet, wearing a black midriff top and skintight hot-pink pants. Intriguingly the three of them cosied up together, chatting and laughing—two women, one man between them, all very friendly.

Quin's view of them was blocked by Tony, comically miming wobbly legs and wiping his brow as he escorted his latest *amour,* Nina Salter-Smythe off the dance floor. "I need a fast and long injection of cold beer," he declared, leaving Nina at the table while he headed for the bar. She suggested a visit to the powder room to Amber and the two women went off together, leaving Quin free to watch Nicole without interruption.

He tried reminding himself this was a woman who had rejected him. He shouldn't be giving her a second thought, let alone a second look. It was an exercise in futility, in frustration.

Yet all his aggressive instincts were on fire. She'd been *his* woman and he wanted another chance with her.

If she wasn't actually married to the Latin lover who was flashing his eyes at both women indiscriminately, he had room to move.

And move he would.

His whole body was screaming at him to do it, mount an attack, get Nicole back into his life.

The moment Tony returned to the table, ready to play jovial host to the rest of his party friends, Quin was on his feet to intercept him before he sat down. "Spotted someone I want to meet," he explained. "Excuse me, won't you?"

"Wait a sec," came the quick protest. "How goes it with Amber? She's been eyeing you over."

"Non-event," Quin almost snapped, raising his hand to ward off any further comment as he swung to make a beeline for the woman who was *the only event* in his mind tonight.

CHAPTER TWO

NICOLE was having fun. She was glad she'd let Jade and Jules talk her into accompanying them here tonight. They had argued she should be armed with a firsthand report of the new Havana Club to pass onto her pupils, unaware that the dance school she was managing for her mother was in such dire debt that Nicole couldn't see a way out of it. She had accepted their invitation in a desperate need to push her worries aside for a while, to simply enjoy the zany company of her friends and not think about facing tomorrow until it came.

"Handsome hunk zeroing in on you, Nic." Jade rolled her big brown eyes expressively. "To your left. Nine o'clock."

Nicole laughed. "Score out of ten?"

"Ten plus."

She shook her head disbelievingly. Ever since Jade had returned from her extensive work experience with designers in Europe to set up business in Sydney, she had been trying to *fix* Nicole up with some guy, preaching one should keep involved with everything life had to offer, seeing Nicole's single status as unhealthy, even stunting her growth as a woman.

Jules leaned over and whispered in her ear, "Got to say Jade's spot-on. Mega macho bearing down on you. A star player."

Nicole winced at that phrase. Jules wouldn't know it—not his field—but it was the phrase used in banking circles to describe the top guns on the trading floor, and she'd once been intimately attached to *a star player*. Attached and burnt.

"Nicole…"

That voice…a convulsive little shiver instantly ran down her spine. Her skin went cold. Her stomach contracted as her head jerked around, reacting to the need to deny the recognition blasting her mind and thumping into her heart. Except the recognition was not a mad mistake.

"Quin…" His name fell from her lips before she could catch it back, and the awful part was the lingering sound of it seemed to carry a longing that was intensely embarrassing. She should have been expressing surprise.

It was certainly that.

He smiled, hitting her with the same megawatt attraction that had been her downfall seven years ago, his bullet grey eyes cutting straight through all lines of defence. The only thing that had changed about him were the silver threads shining through his thick thatch of black hair, giving a more mature authority to his strikingly handsome face—a face which had never lacked authority with its sharply chiselled features adding male strength and character to it. His tall, powerful physique shouted strength, as well, not to mention compelling sex appeal.

"Good to see you again, Nicole," he rolled out, the smooth deep timbre of his voice raising goose-bumps.

"What are you doing here?" The words burst abruptly from a surge of resentment at the way he could still affect her. He had dominated her life for two years—two years that had ultimately taught her she was nothing more than a sexual convenience to him.

His smile wasn't even slightly shaken. "I enjoy dancing...remember?"

She didn't want to remember *anything*. Though he had been a great dancer the few times it actually suited him to partner her at parties.

"Hi! I'm Jade Zilic." Typical Jade, too fascinated to wait for an introduction, hand thrust out in ready friendship. "And you are?"

"Joaquin Sola. Mostly called Quin." He took her hand, nodding a polite acknowledgment, looking enquiringly at Jules.

"My partner, Jules," Jade obliged, leaving Nicole exposed as partnerless tonight.

Jules thrust out his hand and it was promptly taken and shaken with vigour. "Pleased to meet you both," Quin said, warm pleasure positively emanating from him.

Field clear, Nicole bitterly interpreted, though second thoughts zipped into her mind. Quin could not be here womanless. A man like him didn't have to go anywhere alone and he wouldn't to a club. No doubt he had some banking clique with him, having a night on the town.

"I have one question for you," Jade shot at him, her eyes dancing wicked mischief.

"Yes?" he invited.

"Are you wearing *Nick's Knickers*?"

The charming smile definitely faltered at that point, his gaze swinging to Nicole, furrowed brow indicating fast reassessment of the situation. Did the somewhat bawdy question relate to knowledge of his being Nicole's former lover? Was he being cast as a bunny here? Someone to make fun of?

Nicole quite enjoyed seeing the brilliant Joaquin Sola lost for a moment. It made her feel slightly less vulnerable. Though when his thick black eyelashes lowered and a steamy look smoked through them at her, suggesting his thoughts had fastened on her knickers, she rushed out an explanation of the question.

"It's a new range of male underwear, designed and promoted by my friends here."

A deeper frown as his gaze sliced back to her friends. "*Business* partners?"

"Uh-huh. With very hot merchandise," Jules advised with a wide grin.

"Guaranteed to bring out the devil in a man," Jade backed up, then heaved a dramatic sigh of woe. "The advertising campaign can't be working as effectively as it should if Quin hasn't even caught onto the brand name."

"Don't judge by *his* ignorance," Nicole dryly commented. "Quin doesn't have the time nor the inclination to watch commercial television."

"Really?" Jade eyed him in arch disbelief, then trilled one of her coquettish laughs. "Well, can't say you look like a couch potato. More like an action man. Which is why you should be buying *Nick's Knickers*. A great turn-on, believe me. Jules tries them out on me to measure response."

"He...models them...for your approval?" Quin asked, pouncing on the chance to draw more information.

"Hey! I don't let him stop at modelling." Jade smooched up to her totally committed partner in every sense. "Do I, honey-bun?" she purred.

"Stokes the fire every time," Jules said with happy satisfaction.

It gave Quin satisfaction, too, having no doubt now that business was mixed with pleasure with this duo, confirming Nicole's availability for his own interest. "Nothing like personal endorsement," he said appreciatively. "Next time I'm shopping for underwear, I'll look for your range."

"No *wife* to choose it for you, Quin?" Nicole slid in coolly, trying to ward off the heat she knew he was going to turn on her.

"No. No wife," he quickly asserted.

"Perhaps I should have said partner," she drawled. "As I recall, you were commitment-shy."

"On the contrary, I'd say I had a history of excessive commitment." He effected an ironic grimace. "Unfortunately, not always choosing the right priority at the right time, much to my regret. I plan on correcting that error in judgment."

"Lucky for the woman you're with now," Nicole rolled back at him, burning over the smooth reference to regrets. Quin was a master at pressing the right buttons to get what he wanted and from the amount of forceful energy being directed at her, she had no doubt he was hunting her head for a new round of pillow-talk in the very near future.

He shrugged. "I'm not *with* any particular woman."

"You mean no one of any importance," she mocked, knowing the only people of importance to Joaquin Sola were those who served his ambition.

"Every person has value," he quickly slung at her, the clever grey eyes giving her a flatteringly high evaluation on the desirability scale.

"You're right," she agreed silkily, her own eyes sizzling with challenge as she added, "but to some people, money counts for a lot more than anyone's value."

Her eyes were locked onto his, watching his sharp intelligence go to work on the conflicts that had ruptured their relationship five years ago.

"Let's not pretend money doesn't count, Nicole. It adds a value to everyone. Like it or not, it's the way the world works," he asserted sardonically.

Too true. And the bottom was going to fall out of her world for the lack of it. A surge of hatred for all the moneymakers who cared for nothing else poured acid into her voice.

"How are you measuring your worth these days, Quin?" she mocked, goaded into striking directly at him. "Have you reached your target yet? How many million were you aiming for? Or was there no fixed number in your mind, just a cumulative amount that could never be enough?"

He cocked his head, weighing the load of bitterness he'd probably heard in her words. "What would you consider enough, Nicole?" he asked softly. "What would meet your needs?"

For a moment she was seduced by the thought that Quin might now have deep enough pockets to actually come to the rescue. But that would involve him in her life, and if she opened one door to him…no, she couldn't go there. Far more would be at stake than the financial ruin she and her mother were facing. Some wreckages one could recover from. Others lasted a lifetime.

She looked at him with arch scepticism and said, "*My* needs were never part of your equation."

"I'd like to make them so."

"Since when? Two minutes ago? The moment you decided to break in on my night out?"

"If the intention is sincere, the timing shouldn't be relevant."

She shook her head at this arrogant belief that her past experience with him and the years between then and now could simply be dismissed. "It's a bit late to be showing interest in me, Quin, and quite frankly, I have none in you," she stated bluntly.

"It shouldn't ever be too late to make some amends on past mistakes," he argued.

"Raking over dead ashes is hardly profitable," she mocked.

"Amazing how often a live ember is found."

He was just as aware as she was that the chemistry between them was still active. It had led her down a destructive path once and Nicole was determined it would not take her there again. "A spark of fool's gold, Quin," she strongly asserted.

"Not if it can be fanned into a flame. It's a cold life without fire, Nicole."

"I'm sure there are many warm hearths that would welcome you."

"One burnt more brightly than any other. I'd like to find my way back to it."

"Unfortunately I can't provide you with a magic door. You'll have to look elsewhere." She waved her hand in conclusive farewell. *"Hasta la vista."*

He nodded an acknowledgment of her dismissal, but there was no acceptance of defeat in his eyes as he answered, "Until we meet again." A whimsical little smile was directed at Jade and Jules. "A pleasure to make your acquaintance."

"And fascinating to make yours," Jade instantly replied, goggle-eyed over the encounter.

"Try *Nick's Knickers*," Jules advised. "Magic door every time."

Quin laughed, saluting them both as he moved off, no doubt warming himself with the satisfaction of knowing he'd made a winning impression on her friends.

Nicole gritted her teeth. One favourable comment about him from either Jade or Jules and she'd explode. The duel of words with Quin had left her pumped up— typical of any exchange between them. He'd got to her. He always had, putting an electric charge under her skin. No other man had ever come close to affecting her as Quin did, but that didn't mean he was good for her. No way! And something savage in her wanted him to taste defeat—taste it, know it, hate it as much as she had.

Both Jade and Jules were looking at her as though

they were seeing an entirely different woman to the Nicole they were familiar with, eyes avid with curiosity but mouths firmly buttoned until she opened up. Which she was not about to do. The door was shut on Joaquin Luis Sola.

"There's no going back," she stated flatly. "I don't live at that address anymore."

"The one you shared with him?" Jade quickly speculated.

"It wasn't a place of sharing. It was a place of possession. Always on his terms."

"Bad place," Jules muttered sympathetically.

Nicole nodded. "I live in a different space now."

"Maybe you've made your current space too tight," Jade posed seriously. "What if he no longer lives at that address, either? Time and timing—" she wriggled her fingers "—very tricky things. Shifting sands, different circumstances, revolving doors...how long ago was it when you and Quin were an item?"

Jade had not been in Australia then, but if Nicole pinpointed the time it would be like handing her friend a bone she would gnaw at with intolerable persistence. Jade was far too adept at putting two and two together.

"Doesn't matter," she said, shrugging as she stood up from the table. "Distance has not made the heart grow fonder so just let this one go. Okay? I'm off to the powder room."

"Seems a terrible waste," she heard Jade mutter in a disgruntled tone.

Nicole made good her escape, hoping the subject of Quin would not be revived when she returned. Even so, the fun had gone out of the evening. Just knowing he was here made her feel tense, her nerves prickling with the sense of a dangerous threat to the life she'd made without him.

She wished she could just walk away right now, but leaving the club would signal a vulnerability she didn't want to reveal, not to Jade and Jules, and certainly not to Quin Sola. If he was watching, if he came after her...no, she had to act as though she was totally impervious to his presence.

The powder room provided a safe refuge though she could only take a brief respite there if she was not to give the impression of hiding. The place was crowded—a queue for toilet cubicles and a crush of women along the vanity bench; washing hands, repairing make-up, restoring hairstyles. Nicole joined the queue and tried to block memories of Quin from crawling through her mind by eavesdropping on others' conversations. Ironically, not even here was she free of him.

"So how goes it with Quin Sola?"

The question came loud and clear through the babble of general chat, drawing Nicole's startled gaze to a pretty brunette in red who was looking archly at a tall beautiful blonde, definitely out of the same mould as Paris Hilton, dressed in a second skin blue mini-dress and practising a sexy pout in the mirror.

"Oh, I don't know that he's worth having," she drawled.

"Not worth having! The hottest trader in town? Everyone with any money is using his financial services company. The guy has made billions. And he's an eye-candy hunk, as well."

His company…*billions*…not the star player for an international bank anymore, Nicole realised. Somewhere along the past five years Quin must have moved to being his own man, no doubt accumulating far more personal wealth by working on *his* terms.

"Wow! Point me in his direction," someone eagerly requested, triggering a cheerful chorus of "Me, too," from other chance listeners.

The outburst was ignored.

"I really don't need his money, Nina, and going to bed with a cold fish does not appeal," the blonde said in a bored tone.

The brunette in red grinned. "You mean you made a move on him and he didn't bite."

Mistake, Nicole thought sardonically. Quin made the moves. He was programmed that way. The blonde shrugged as though she didn't care, although her ego had to be suffering some damage. She was wrong about Quin's coldness in bed but his decision-making was icily absolute, no melting around the edges when his mind was made up.

Until we meet again…

A convulsive shiver ran down Nicole's spine as the thought struck her that Quin might have been cold to the blonde because he'd already fixed his sights on herself. What if he didn't accept the rejection she'd just handed out? Five years ago she had fled to Europe to break all connection with him, but she couldn't do that now. She could only hope he would change his mind about pursuing another meeting, leave her alone.

The woman behind her nudged her towards the most

recently vacated toilet cubicle. Nicole hadn't even realised she now headed the queue. Nor had she noticed the two women who'd been talking about Quin make their exit from the powder room but they were gone. She hurried forward and closed herself into the small private space, wishing she could close out all the worries whirling around her mind.

From what she'd heard, Quin could easily afford to lend her the money needed to keep the dance school afloat. He might even do it if he got what he wanted from her. If it was only sex...

Nicole shocked herself with the treacherous desire that had prompted that thought. It was so stupid to want Quin for anything. He'd stripped her of self-esteem once. To even dally with an idea that would give him the power to do it again, was just plain crazy.

But she would be using him this time...using him to meet her needs. A vengeful streak in her whispered this was a justifiable course. After all, Quin put a money value on everything. Why shouldn't she?

A controlled situation could be set up—no intrusion on her real life. She wouldn't be hurt by confusing sex with love again. Not with Quin. In fact, there was a lot of savage appeal in turning the tables on him, only giving what she was prepared to give...on *her* terms!

The big question was...how much did Quin want her?

CHAPTER THREE

QUIN'S mind and body were firing on all cylinders, energised by the excitement of a challenging chase. He wasn't about to let Nicole escape him this time. However many obstacles she put in his path, he was determined on getting past them, breaking down her resistance and making her his woman again.

What he needed now was some information—where she was working, how her daily schedule ran. It would be easy enough then to set up another *chance* meeting so he could reinforce the mutual attraction she was trying to deny, work on it, build the sparks into a flame that would burn up her opposition to any future together.

He caught sight of Tony watching him make his way back to the party. Quin had learnt in his four years of professional and personal association with him, very little escaped Tony Fisher's notice. Whether it was taking care of legal matters or his keen observation of people, the man was invariably on the ball. He was short and rather stocky, but big with personality, aided by an infectious smile, wickedly merry brown eyes and a wild mop of chestnut curls framing his good-humoured face.

Having sidled around his boisterous guests, he caught Quin just before he joined them. "Trust you to pick out the expert in this crowd," he remarked, nodding in Nicole's direction.

For once, Quin wasn't tuned to Tony's wavelength. "Expert?" he queried.

"The dancing teacher," Tony supplied, raising his eyebrows in arch surprise. "You're slipping if you didn't find that much out about her."

Quin frowned. Tony wasn't making sense. Nicole had been in banking before going overseas. Armed with a top level business degree, she'd worked her way up to the key division of sales, making the most of big investors' money. One of the great things about their relationship had been her understanding of his work on the trading floor.

Though she could certainly dance like a professional—a natural at Latin American. Even so, Tony must have mistaken her for someone else. A woman with Nicole's brain for clever commerce had to be earning big bucks somewhere in the workplace and that would not be in a school for dancing.

"I think you've got it wrong here, Tony," he mocked his friend who prided himself on getting everything right.

One eyebrow lowered. The other was cocked higher. "Were you or were you not chatting up Nicole Ashton?"

Her name sent a shock wave up Quin's spine. Alert signals shot along his nervous system. He eyed his friend very sharply, seeking urgent entry into his mind. "What do you know about her?"

Tony's mouth formed a curious little smile. "Did she give you the flick?"

Quin tensed as he realised there was definitely some personal previous acquaintance here and he didn't like it. Tony would be unaware of his own past relationship with Nicole. It was before his time, so *the flick* question couldn't relate to that. Which meant it had to come from Tony's own experience with her.

"You have a good reason for asking that?" he said coldly, hating the thought of his friend having intimate knowledge of Nicole.

"Oh, just that I failed to get anywhere with her beyond the dancing lessons I paid for," he answered with a shrug. "That doesn't happen very often. I might not have the pulling power of your physical assets, but when I set out to charm a woman, I usually win her."

Quin knew that was true, which was why his gut had suddenly been in knots. "But you had no luck with Nicole Ashton," he pressed.

"Not one flirtatious spark from her," came the reassuring reply. "Always pleasant but her focus was fixed on feeling the dance, not feeling anything else. Not with me, anyway."

Relief coursed through Quin. His mind lifted out of a storm of black possessiveness and honed in on getting information. "When was this, Tony?"

"Two years ago. You know me, Quin. I hate not being ahead of the game, and Latin American dancing was becoming popular. I took a month of lessons from her to get all the moves under my belt."

"At a dancing school."

"Yes."

"Evening lessons?" He couldn't believe it was Nicole's day job.

Tony nodded. "Three times a week. Personal tuition, not a class. And all I ever found out about her was she helped run the school for her mother who owned it. Oh, and she'd won a lot of dancing competitions when she was a kid. Had photos and trophies on show to prove it. Like I said…an expert."

She'd never told him this. But then, he'd never told her about his childhood, either. He'd wanted her to accept him as he was at the time—no probing into the past—and having cut off the subject of family several times, insisting that their backgrounds were totally irrelevant to how they felt together, Nicole had given up on trying to change his attitude.

"Where is this school?" he asked, wondering if Nicole had actually gone into business with her mother.

"Burwood."

The suburb was reasonably close to the inner city where he lived and worked but far enough away for their paths to stay apart, given that Burwood was where she lived, as well as worked.

"So you didn't even get that far with her," Tony observed.

"I was just touching base, Tony, feeling for an opening."

"Any crack of encouragement?"

"None. But that was only the initial foray."

"From which you retreated in good order so you could take the fight to her again," Tony dryly deduced.

Quin smiled at his shrewd reading of the situation. "I do not accept that all is lost."

"Well, good luck, my friend. Nicole Ashton looks hot but she's one cool lady."

Not in bed, Quin thought.

"Ah, here's Nina and Amber back from the powder room," Tony announced, looking over Quin's shoulder and holding out an inviting arm for Nina Salter-Smythe— his current love interest—to be gathered in to his side.

Quin swung around to greet the two women's return, surreptitiously using the opportunity to glance back to where Nicole was seated, wanting to catch her looking at him, hoping for another chance to prove that her show of disinterest was not sustainable.

She wasn't there.

His heart thumped with the shock of finding her place vacant.

Had she left the club, intent on doing another runner before he could catch her back?

His gaze jerked to her friends who still occupied the table. Jade Zilic and her partner, Jules, had their heads together as though plotting something. Surely they would have accompanied Nicole out, at least to see her into a taxi, if she had gone.

Quin told himself it didn't matter, either way.

He had enough information to find her.

CHAPTER FOUR

WHEN Nicole emerged from the powder room, the dance floor was once again crowded, couples throwing themselves into the cha-cha with much energetic panache. This left an easy passage for her back to the table where Jade and Jules remained seated, watching the action.

"Got to say Quin Sola is a superb dancer," Jade immediately commented, pointing to where he was partnering the brunette in red from the powder room. "Did you teach him, Nicole?"

She shook her head. "It's natural to him. He once told me dancing is an expression of life in South America. He grew up with it."

"Where in South America?" Jules asked, his curiosity piqued.

"I don't know. He would never say."

"Ah! A mysterious past," Jade pounced, waggling her highly mobile eyebrows.

"Whatever…" Nicole waved dismissively. "He became an Australian citizen and left the past in the past. Now why don't you two go and dance? I'm happy to sit this one out."

She didn't want to talk about Quin.

She needed more time alone to think about him.

Jade and Jules obligingly left her to it.

Sexual memories bombarded her mind as she watched him dance, his strong, muscular legs snapping out the cha-cha rhythm, his taut cheeky butt almost mesmerising in its matching action. Quin *was* a great dancer. Better than Jules. Best on the dance floor, in fact. Best at everything.

Except actually caring about someone, Nicole savagely reminded herself. The trick with Quin was to take what he offered of himself, enjoy it, and not care back. She simply hadn't been capable of doing that when she'd been with him, caring too much about too many things and losing her own sense of self-worth because he hadn't responded in kind.

She shouldn't have measured herself by that.

The fault lay in Quin, not her.

Five years ago it had been a matter of survival to walk away from him and his lack of caring. Now she was facing a different issue of survival, based on the one commodity Quin apparently had in plenty. Since he put a money value on everything, she wondered how much he would give to warm himself at her hearth. Could she steel herself to shut out *everything else* and put the question to him?

If he said no…well, that was that, nothing lost, nothing gained.

If he said yes…since he'd more or less limited their previous relationship to the bedroom, it seemed logical he'd accept that same limitation again, so there should be no great risk in such an arrangement. In fact, satisfying the desire he was stirring up might do her a power of good. It was Quin who had caused the hole Jade perceived in Nicole's love life. A short, sharp dose of him might cure the long hangover from having been his possession.

Control was the key.

She had to hold it, not let Quin take it over.

Could she do it?

Could she?

The dance ended.

She watched him escort the brunette in red off the dance floor. Jade and Jules were noisily approaching their table. Bold, enterprising Jade. *She* wouldn't think twice about approaching Quin for help if she needed it from him. Striking deals were second nature to her. *Seize the day,* she'd say. *Make it yours.*

Nicole rose to her feet, standing firmly on her stiletto heels, moving forward with determined purpose. "I'm going to speak to Quin Sola," she informed her friends in passing.

Either he caught sight of her approach in some mirrored surface, or his personal antennae picked up her churning chemistry and swung him around to face her, negating any need to break into his social group. She halted a metre away, her mouth tilting into a wry little smile as she tossed at him, "I have a proposition for you, Quin."

He nodded towards the bar. "Let me buy you a drink."

The move would ensure some privacy from his companions, which certainly suited Nicole. It would also prolong this encounter which undoubtedly suited him since she'd cut him off earlier tonight. "Thank you. I'd like that," she replied, her ready agreement bringing a smile of satisfaction to his lips.

He led off without a backward glance at the people he'd been with, instantly making her the exclusive focus of his attention, shepherding her through the crowd without actually touching her—quite a masterful operation with people in front of them moving aside at the commanding wave of his hand or a look into the bullet grey eyes.

The force, Nicole thought. Quin had always had it—the power to draw or repel people at will. It was some form of energy he knew how to exert. Or maybe it was an innate thing in him, a kind of charisma he'd been born with. It made him special, out of the ordinary, and dangerous because it was all too easy to fall under his spell and then you belonged to him.

Even knowing this and being on guard against it, Nicole felt every nerve in her body quivering with excitement at being close to the source of this treacherous power. Locking horns with Quin on any ground was tantamount to playing with fire. But she had learnt lessons from being burnt. Nothing would induce her to let this man take over her life again. She'd go so far with him and no further.

They reached the bar and despite the crush of thirsty people, somehow space was made for them and a waiter was ready to take their order. "Two margaritas," Quin told him, not offering Nicole any choice, assuming command of the situation as he always had. But it was not going to be all his way this time, Nicole fiercely determined.

She recalled only too sharply that he'd bought them both margaritas on the very first evening they'd spent

together. If he thought he could stir some sentimental-
ity with the memory, he could think again. The cocktails were made. Quin handed over some notes and told
the waiter to keep the change. Nicole took her glass, not
waiting for it to be handed to her.

Quin picked up his and raised it in a toast. "To second
meetings. And second thoughts," he said whimsically, his
eyes warmly welcoming her apparent change of mind.

She baulked at entering into any flirtatious banter.
Nothing had to be won from Quin. He either went for
the deal or he didn't. "You asked me what would meet
my needs," she reminded him with sharp directness.

"I did," he agreed, adopting a more attentive expression. "Have you been concocting a list?"

She ignored that question. "You said you'd like to
make them your business."

"Within reason," he quickly amended, his eyes more
calculating now.

She sipped her margarita, needing to loosen up her
taut nerves, hoping a good slug of alcohol would do
it. Having worked up the courage to deliver the next
line, she plunged on. "You said money adds a value to
everyone."

He sipped his drink, silently weighing the thrust of
her statements before laying out his interpretation of
them. "Are you telling me you have a primary need for
money, and if I bring enough to the table, it will open
the magic door?"

"An urgent need," she corrected him. "So the
question is, Quin, how much are you willing to give to
get me back into your bed?"

"Give," he repeated, eyes narrowing. "We're not talking about a loan?"

"No." Her chin lifted belligerently, silently defying whatever he was thinking of her. It didn't matter. Only the chance of a positive outcome mattered. "We're talking about an outright gift. And it has to be available to me tomorrow," she spelled out unequivocally.

"And when will you be available to me, Nicole, assuming that I accept your proposition?"

Her heart was pounding at the possibility he would accept. She hadn't really believed it enough to work out how she would manage her side of the deal. What *was* possible for her, given her other commitments? She had to keep him away from her mother's home at Burwood.

"Where do you live now, Quin?"

"I have an apartment at Circular Quay."

Getting public transport to Circular Quay was not a problem—a twenty-minute train trip from Burwood. With a heavy sense of irony, she said, "I could warm the hearth of your home on two nights a week for…" What would be a reasonable offer for the money involved? There had to be a time limit.

"For as long as I want you," he pushed.

"No!" That would be handing control to him. "For three months," she quickly decided, not caring what he thought of it, intuitively knowing she couldn't risk more. Three months was as fair a bargain as she was prepared to offer.

"Twenty-six nights…" he said musingly, his eyes smoking with memories of sexual highs with her.

Panic galloped through Nicole. She hadn't done the

maths, just grabbed at a time limit. Could she sustain objectivity with Quin for that long, hold the line she had to hold?

It was impossible to recant now. Quin would instantly pick up on how vulnerable she felt about it. Besides, he himself might baulk when it came to the cost of those twenty-six nights with her. No doubt he could get a high class callgirl to satisfy his every desire for much less.

"How much money do you need, Nicole?" he asked, coming straight to the point.

Her own eyes issued a mocking challenge as she replied with the total figure of the debts to be paid. "Seven hundred and thirty-six thousand dollars and fifty-five cents." The numbers were deeply imprinted on her mind from having been so terribly plagued by them.

Quin digested them without so much as a flicker of an eyelid, maintaining a poker face as he checked on what she'd said before. "And you need it tomorrow."

"Yes."

"Or what will happen?"

She shook her head. "That's private. This is a take it or leave it proposition. You say yes or no."

"Spend tonight with me while I consider it."

"No! I'm not giving out freebies, Quin. I won't spend a night with you until you give me my value in money and it has to be given tomorrow."

"Your value…" he drawled derisively.

"You used those words," she fiercely reminded him, her stomach churning with the anticipation of imminent humiliation. "Yes or no," she repeated.

His eyes glittered with plans of his own as he reached out and took her glass from her, a glass that was empty although she couldn't recall having drunk all its contents. She saw that his was empty, too, as he placed both glasses on the bar. So this mad encounter was at an end, she thought, steeling herself to turn her back on it.

"I'll give you my answer after you dance this tango with me," he said with a relish that sent warning tingles down her spine.

Nicole was given no time to respond, no time to resist. Her hand was captured by his and strongly held as he pulled her after him, onto the dance floor. The band had only just started up again. No other couples had begun dancing. Quin swung her into the centre of the empty floor, then lifted her arms, arrogantly positioning the initial embrace for the traditional start of the tango.

Her body arched back in instinctive resistance as he assumed the dominant role, his strong legs forcing hers into the *salida,* the basic walking pattern, which Quin turned into a physical—*sexual*—stalking, igniting a volatile energy in Nicole that sizzled with the need to challenge him, fight him, beat him at his own game.

It was more than a matter of pride to match his perfectly executed figure-eights, his turns, twists and sweeps. Every chance she had she threw in some fancy embellishments to the hooks and kicks, challenging him to meet her creativity, beat it if he could. It goaded him to hurl her into a masterful drag, making her submit to a feet together slide, then swiftly engineering a *sandwich,* trapping her thigh against his, leaning into her, his arm circling her waist in possessive support as she arched back, his hand almost cupping the soft swell of her breast.

"Don't think you can take, Quin," she shot at him.

"Just checking the merchandise," he retorted.

Nicole's blood boiled at the crass term but there was no point in taking offence since it was in keeping with her proposition. Besides, it was best she knew Quin thought of her like that—a strong deterrent to any emotional attachment forming.

Merchandise...

She'd show him merchandise!

The intricate footwork and dark passion of their tango had drawn spectators who stood back, clapping them on, leaving them plenty of room to indulge themselves in the dramatic rhythm of the music. Nicole recklessly abandoned herself to the sexuality of the dance with a wild display of provocative wiggles and shakes until Quin claimed her again, sweeping her into a whirl of double-time steps, then re-establishing his dominance with a high lift and a body curl around him. Nicole hit back with a full contact downward slide which gave her undeniable evidence of his excitement.

"Nothing without the money, Quin," she reminded him, exulting in the hard bulge of his erection.

His eyes blazed raw desire at her. "Don't tell me you're not on fire, Nicole."

"You won't break my resolve," she taunted and maintained a haughty disdain throughout his heat-seeking manoeuvres for the rest of the dance.

They were breathing hard when the music ended, her breasts heaving against his chest, their bodies bent in the

traditional aggressive/resistant pose, her head, shoulders
and arms straining away from him, her long hair almost
sweeping the floor, his face hovering over hers. Although loud applause broke out around them, neither of
them acknowledged it. Quin wasn't yet ready to break
from the sizzling sexuality of this last embrace.

"Admit you want me!" he demanded.

"Prove that you value what I can give you," she
counter-demanded.

"Tomorrow morning, the money. Tomorrow night,
you come to me."

"Agreed."

His eyes glittered with animal savagery. "I'll have my
pound of flesh, Nicole."

But not my heart, she thought with the same depth
of ferocity. Quin Sola couldn't take it twice.

"Twenty-six nights," he reaffirmed.

"Payment in full," she promised.

"I'll hold you to it."

"I know."

"As long as you understand there is no escape clause."

"Understood."

"Right! So let's get down to necessary details."

He scooped her upright again and released her from
his embrace, retaining only her hand as he swung her
out beside him to perform an acknowledging bow to the
still applauding spectators. Their faces were a blur to
Nicole. She was gripped by a weird sense of shock that
the deal had actually been made. Quin was going to pay
off the ruinous debt and she was about to become his
sex slave for three months.

Being his sex slave was not something new, she sternly told herself, just a repetition of the past, but her legs started wobbling as they made their way back to the bar. Neither she nor Quin were inclined to head for their respective tables since there was still private business to be done. She hoped he understood that their negotiated intimacy should remain private, too.

"Another drink?" Quin asked.

"Just iced water," she replied.

He ordered two, probably feeling the same need to cool down. While they waited, a man came up and clapped Quin on the shoulder, claiming his attention and making Nicole's nerves even more jumpy.

"Got to say you've met your match, Quin," he rolled out with a grin, twinkling brown eyes spreading his good humour to both of them. "Great dancing! You should snag him for a partner if you're still doing dance competitions, Nicole."

Shock hit her hard, squeezing her heart and making her stomach contract in fear.

Tony Fisher!

She remembered giving him dancing lessons—something like two years ago—but she couldn't remember how she'd been working her situation at the time. Did he know about Zoe? Would he mention her to Quin? How closely were the two men connected?

"Tony…" she greeted him belatedly.

"Glad you remember me." He exuded happy warmth as he offered his hand.

She took it briefly. "Not many men have so much charm. I hope you're enjoying your own dancing."

"I am, indeed. As to charm…" He flicked a wry smile at Quin. "It seems my friend has considerably more."

Friend!

"Not so I've noticed," she said coolly. "But then, charm isn't a necessary component when doing business. The primary aim is to understand each other. Quin and I are trying to settle the details of an agreement, so if you'd be so kind as to…"

"Leave you alone together? Got it!" He raised a hand in a salute to both of them and moved away.

Quin handed her a long glass of iced water. "Very deft," he commented. "A pity you're wasting your talent for handling people in a dance school."

So he knew that much. "Believe me, it's not wasted there," she said dryly. When he made no other observation about her current life, Nicole's tension eased a little. "Let's tie this up quickly before we're interrupted again," she said briskly. "Are you carrying a business card with your e-mail address on it?"

"Yes." He put his drink down to get the card out of his wallet and give it to her. "Do you have yours in your handbag?"

"You won't need it. I'll e-mail you when I get home tonight, spelling out where the money has to be transferred. You can reply to sender, giving me your home address and what time you want me to arrive."

"That works," he agreed.

Nicole wanted to get away from him now, escape the tension of being this close. She had to spend twenty-six nights in his company but tonight wasn't one of them. "I want this deal kept private, Quin," she quickly stated.

His eyes mocked her concern. "I'm hardly likely to spread the fact that I have to buy sex from you."

A tide of scorching heat rushed up her neck and burnt her cheeks. "You didn't value it when I *gave* it to you," she fired back at him.

"I'll count the worth of every second this time."

"Do that!" Her chin lifted in defiant denial of any more seconds on the clock with him now. "In the meantime, please excuse me. My friends are probably wondering where I am."

"Oh, I don't think they're wondering, Nicole. Not after our tango. But I'll escort you back to their table to ensure they know you've been in good hands."

"I don't need to be escorted, thank you," she flashed at him as she turned to go.

"I wouldn't want your friends to think I'm not gentleman enough to give you that courtesy," came the insidiously determined voice behind her.

Nicole gritted her teeth and said no more, knowing there'd be no shaking him off until he performed his self-appointed role. Waste of breath to argue. In actual fact, Quin had always played the gentleman with women; opening doors, seeing them seated, extending protection whenever it was appropriate. It had once given Nicole the sense of being cherished, but his courtesies had nothing to do with cherishing. Quin simply followed standards he'd set for himself.

She sailed ahead, acutely aware of him trailing closely in her wake and inwardly stewing over how she was going to explain what she'd been doing with Quin to Jade and Jules. No doubt they had seen the tango performance, which certainly didn't gel with banishing the man from her life. There had been nothing cold about it, either.

Quin had caught up and was shoulder to shoulder with her when they arrived at the table. Both Jade and Jules had wide grins on their faces, probably thinking they'd been witnessing the rebirth of a passionate affair. Before Nicole could issue a polite dismissal to Quin, Jade surprised her by holding out a brilliant yellow butterfly, exquisitely fashioned from silk with silver glitter outlining its wings.

"For your tree," she rushed out. "I made it to brighten you up. Not that you probably need it now but I thought I'd give it to you before the two of you make off out of the club." Her eyes sparkled delight. "It can mark this reunion with Quin."

"It's beautiful, Jade. Thank you. But…"

"What tree?" Quin cut in before Nicole could deny the double departure Jade was obviously anticipating.

"The butterfly tree," Jules supplied. "It's a great fantasy décor piece. The branches are made of driftwood and…"

Nicole panicked, afraid he was about to mention Zoe. "It's a private thing, Jules," she warned, her eyes stabbing the point home. "And you're mistaken, Jade. Quin and I are not going off together. We were simply settling an old score between us." She quickly turned to Quin and held out her hand. "Thank you. We do have everything settled, don't we?"

He gripped hard, his eyes probing hers with nerve-tearing intensity. "Time will tell," he said, the sense of threat behind his words warning Nicole she had better deliver her side of the deal.

She nodded. "I won't keep you from your party any longer."

His mouth curled into a sardonic little smile. "Nor I from yours."

To her intense relief he said good night to Jade and Jules, taking his leave without another word. Which left her with the task of fending off their curiosity for the rest of the evening at the club. Fortunately they didn't want to stay late as they had an important business meeting in the morning. By one o'clock Nicole had been driven home and she was seated at her computer, ready to transmit the necessary figures for Quin to rescue her mother from losing everything.

Her fingers hesitated over the keyboard.

She stared at the e-mail address on the card he'd given her.

This was the point of no return.

Total bankruptcy or twenty-six nights with Quin.

Her chest felt very tight.

Don't think about it, she fiercely told herself.

Just do it.

CHAPTER FIVE

NICOLE tried to relax as the train carried her into the city centre for her rendezvous with Quin. The day had been loaded with stress—many phone-calls checking if the money had come through, confirming that all debts had been paid on time. Also, it had been impossible to avoid telling her mother how *the miracle* had come about since the two nights out a week had to be explained, especially since tonight was the first one. She needed her mother to look after Zoe.

The relief of having been saved from bankruptcy had quickly disintegrated into hand-wringing guilt over the deal Nicole had made with Quin Sola. "You would never have gone back to him but for me," her mother had wailed.

"It's only three months, Mum," Nicole had argued. "It won't kill me. In fact, it's much more acceptable than having to lose this home and the dancing school."

Which would have totally devastated her mother.

Nicole knew that her own qualifications, persistence and presentation would have eventually won a job somewhere in the finance world—a job with a big enough salary to support them. This would not have

been *the end* for her. But these losses, on top of the loss
of her beloved second husband, would have tipped her
mother into a deeper depression, possibly paralysing her
will to do anything. Perhaps now, some sense of responsibility for getting into this mess might pull her into
plotting some positive course for her future with the
dancing school.

The train arrived at Circular Quay and Nicole
promptly disembarked. Quin's e-mail had instructed
her to meet him at a restaurant called Pier Twenty-One,
situated on Benelong Point near the Opera House. She
glanced at her watch as she started the walk past the
ferry terminal. It was a few minutes short of eight
o'clock, the nominated time.

She walked fast, not wanting to be late. Quin had kept
his word. Keeping hers was essential. It was not only a
matter of integrity, but pride, as well. She would not give
Quin any cause to criticise her over the delivery of her
side of the deal. He had paid out a phenomenal amount
of money for his twenty-six nights.

Nevertheless, she had baulked at dressing up as
though for a dinner date. There was no romance in this
arrangement and she didn't want Quin to think there
could be in her mind. If he chose to spend his time with
her eating in a restaurant—fine!—she would eat with
him. No doubt they would eventually end up in bed
together, which was what tonight was really about.

She'd decided to wear jeans, flat walking sandals
and one of the filmy floral tops that were currently fashionable for teaming with jeans—day or night. She
would wear the same things when she left him

tomorrow morning. Her small overnight bag only held some toiletry articles and a change of underwear. As long as her mind was set on conducting this specifically limited affair on a completely practical basis, she should not get into an emotional tangle over it.

Quin's table had a front row view of the passing parade of people; commuters catching a ferry home, tourists taking in the sights of arguably the most spectacular harbour in the world, theatre-goers heading for their choice of entertainment; concert, ballet, play, opera. The outdoors dining section of the restaurant extended out beyond the great marble colonnade that sheltered the many boutiques, bars and restaurants along the way to the huge Opera House forecourt. It was a fine summer evening, a fantastic setting, but Quin's entire focus was fixed on watching for Nicole.

He had no doubt she would turn up at the appointed time and place, probably arriving at the quay early to ensure punctuality, and loitering somewhere nearby so as not to give him more of herself than she had to. Quin had no illusions about what had driven her to this deal—extreme duress over a financial situation, linked to a highly personal sense of payback for how he had conducted their previous relationship. It was the latter motivation that exercised his mind now. The money side of it was done.

He wanted sex with her and he would certainly have it, but his prime directive tonight was to challenge where she was coming from, sabotage her game-plan, make her play to his rules. She'd put a fire in his belly last night. The fight was on to get everything he wanted from Nicole Ashton and with twenty-six nights up his sleeve, Quin was confident of carrying out a siege that would eventually smash her defences and make her surrender all she was to him.

He'd had that once from her.

He wanted it again, free of the demons that had driven much of his life.

There she was!

Nothing hesitant about her approach.

She was striding out, unhampered by any tight sexy skirt or high heels. Her long legs were clad in blue denim and the flat sandals on her feet signalled casual comfort had priority over any female urge to excite desire in him. Clearly she didn't care what he thought or felt. It was unimportant to her. Her head was bent in private thought, a look of determined purpose on her face. She wasn't looking for him. She was simply making her way to the meeting place.

He noted the overnight bag she was carrying—only big enough to hold a few essentials—definitely no frills on Nicole's agenda tonight. Her long curly hair was loose, no tantalising pins to remove. The top she wore was more feminine than the unisex jeans, but not a *look at me* garment. Quin smiled to himself. If she thought her presentation would put him off the merchandise, she could think again.

As though she suddenly sensed his scrutiny, her head lifted, gaze swinging sharply towards where he sat, connecting with his, flashing a wry acknowledgment of *game on*. Her feet halted as she watched him rise from the table, ready to greet her. Quin felt his body zinging with anticipation. A strong blast of intuition told him she was eyeing the enemy before engaging with him. Retreat was not in the air. Let the battle begin, Quin thought, holding out an open hand to draw her in.

Nicole ignored the accelerated pounding of her heart and put on a determinedly cheerful face as she walked forward to greet the man who'd paid the price she'd put on herself. Since he would now expect value for it, an initial smile seemed the best way to get proceedings onto reasonably pleasant terms.

"Quin…" She took his hand, giving it a light squeeze. "Thank you for making the money available so quickly. It made today much less difficult than it could have been."

Just as well she had prepared that little speech because Quin's strong magnetism was zapping all the sensible thoughts out of her mind. The mere touch of his hand was shooting electric tingles up her arm. She'd put half a world between them to get away from the sexual hold he'd once had on her. Distance had not diminished the power of his attraction but she simply couldn't afford to fall victim to it this time. Somehow she had to keep whatever happened between them contained.

"I've built my business on being efficient and effective," he replied.

"Not to mention ruthless," she slung at him, the words tripping off her tongue, regardless of her earlier resolve not to revive old emotional wounds. Even worse, she withdrew her hand so quickly, her fingernails scraped along his.

His grey eyes glittered with sardonic amusement. "I

wondered how long it would take for the claws to come out."

"Sorry. I probably need a manicure."

"I was referring to your description of me."

Ruthless?

"Oh, come now," she chided. "You can't deny one of your greatest attributes—setting a goal and going after it with single-minded dedication."

"I'll concede that attitude has served me well, for the most part."

"Got the results you wanted," she pushed derisively.

"More often than not. I've even got you, Nicole. Which just goes to prove that a huge loss can be recovered—" he grinned provocatively as he added "—if one is ruthless enough."

She raised a mocking eyebrow. "Or prepared to sacrifice a great deal of money."

"But it's not a sacrifice. It's an investment in the future."

"A very short-term future."

"We'll see." He gestured to the chair opposite his at the table. "Please join me. I've ordered champagne to celebrate the beginning of a new chapter in our lives."

Not so new, she thought caustically, curbing her tongue as she settled on the chair. The adrenaline rush of crossing swords with Quin needed to be curbed, as well. It drew her into revealing how much he could still get under her skin and she didn't want to give him that satisfaction.

He signalled to a waiter to open the bottle of champagne which was sitting in an ice-bucket, conveniently placed on a portable stand beside their table. The waiter handed them menus and reeled off a list of chef's specials as he uncorked the bottle and filled their glasses.

"We'll both have a dozen oysters followed by the lobster in butter sauce with a side salad," Quin said, abrogating any choice Nicole might have made.

She didn't bother protesting, though once the waiter had left she dryly commented, "I might have wanted something else."

"You've got what you wanted, Nicole." He lifted his glass in a toast. "Here's to what I want."

She fiddled with her glass, watching him sip the champagne, his eyes challenging her to make some issue on how he was handling the situation. He knew she loved seafood and had invariably ordered it whenever they had dined out in the past. Lobster was terribly expensive, so in fact he was giving her treat. And knew it. But he was also claiming absolute dominance during her time with him.

"If you want your pound of flesh, Quin, why have me meet you in such a public place?" She gestured to the milling crowd of passers-by.

"They say the flesh is sweeter closer to the bone. I don't mind taking my time working down to it."

Peeling off layer and layer of protective skin, Nicole thought, a convulsive little shiver running down her spine. She couldn't let Quin get too close to her. He might tear her apart if she didn't remain on guard.

"Why not relax?" he invited with a teasing smile. "Obviously you are completely safe here amongst so many people. The night is young and I'm perfectly happy to revel in the exquisite pleasure of anticipation."

"Right!" She lifted her glass, determined on

blocking out the more intimate future for a while. "Here's to fine food…"

"Fine company," Quin slid in.

"And fine wine," she finished pointedly, sipping the champagne which was, indeed, very fine.

Nevertheless, it was impossible to relax with Quin sitting opposite her, watching her, silently revelling in his plans for tonight. Get his mind off them, she told herself. Ask him questions. Persist until he did talk about himself. He might even give her answers this time around.

"So how is the banking world these days?" she started.

He shrugged. "I run my own finance company now."

"Trading profitably?"

"That's what I do."

"Tell me about it," she invited.

"The money business is no different to when you were working in a bank, Nicole."

"But the transition from being employed to—"

"The work is the same," he cut her off. "I'd find it far more interesting to hear why you've chosen to teach dancing."

"You haven't changed a bit, have you?" she flared at him.

His eyes glittered with challenging speculation. "What do you want to change about me?"

Nicole quickly retreated from any personal element. "I'm not interested in changing you, Quin," she stated flatly. "I was merely commenting."

"On what?"

She shrugged. "You don't open up about yourself."

Suddenly seeing a line of attack, she added, "It makes me wonder what you're afraid of revealing."

"Fear doesn't enter into it," he answered.

"What does then?"

The waiter arrived with their first course. Nicole stared down at the oysters as he refilled their glasses before leaving the two of them alone again.

"This is just what you're like," she shot at Quin. "An oyster with an impenetrable shell."

"I'll let you eat me tonight," he said wickedly.

Sex! That's all it had ever been with Quin. He'd probably ordered the oysters because they were supposed to be an aphrodisiac. She picked up her fork and ate them, her mind skating around memories of Quin's body—his sexually aroused naked body—and how wildly they'd made love in the past. Except it hadn't been making love. It was just sex! Which was what she had to remember at all times with him.

"So why are you working at a dance school, Nicole?" he asked when the plates had been cleared away.

She looked directly into his penetrating grey eyes and defiantly answered, "Private reasons."

His mouth took on an ironic twist. "You know, money always leaves a trail. Mortgage on the school, mortgage on a house, big debt to a money-lender—all attached to one name, and that name is not yours. Who is Linda Ellis?"

The question tapped into a bank of resentment that had never been resolved. "You'd know if you'd ever accepted one of my invitations to meet my mother."

He ignored her reference to the old bone of contention between them. "Your mother. Why the different name?"

"A second marriage."

"Does she have a gambling problem?"

"No. What happened will not happen again."

"How can you be sure of that?"

"Because my stepfather is dead."

Her bald statement gave him pause for thought, a deep frown drawing his black eyebrows together. "*He* bled her of all that money?" he finally asked.

"No. The people who held out false hope bled her of all that money."

She heard the angry frustration in her voice, saw the sharp questions in his eyes and knew she might as well explain how the debts had mounted up, stop any further unwelcome speculation on the subject.

"Harry had liver cancer. My mother spent the last two years of his life taking him around the world to quacks and clinics that promised cures. She wouldn't give up. If there was any chance, any way—" Nicole sighed and gestured her own helplessness over the situation. "It didn't matter what it cost, she kept getting the money to do it. Harry was not going to die because they didn't have the money to save him."

"Blind faith," Quin muttered.

"She loved him," Nicole said defensively, ashamed of her own exasperation with her mother's belief in people who'd preyed on her desperation. It had been hard losing her father when she was fifteen, no doubt even harder for her mother. The thought of losing Harry, too, had probably been unbearable.

"The price of love," Quin mused with a quirky little smile. "The same price I've just paid for you, Nicole.

Maybe I should have negotiated for two years instead of taking only three months."

"Not at all. You've got prime time," she retorted mockingly. "Lust burns out much faster than love."

He laughed, adding a megawatt attraction to his handsome face. A warm flood of pleasure swept through Nicole, forcing her to acknowledge that no man before or since Quin Sola had done this to her, arousing such strong feelings she had to ride through them because there was no blocking them.

He leaned towards her, forearms on the table, his eyes dancing with a wicked inner joy. "I have missed you, Nicole," he purred. "Missed you very much."

"Not enough to drop everything and chase after me when I left you," she flipped at him as she leaned away, pressing against the back-rest of her chair, needing to put some steel in her spine, bringing out memories of the past to shield her from the weakening effect of his personal charisma.

His shoulders straightened, the twinkle in his eyes sharpening to a hard glitter. "Proving your power over me? I didn't have time for such games."

"You didn't have time for me."

"Not as much as you wanted, no," he retorted, his voice gathering a harsh intensity. "But more than I've given any other woman, before or since."

"Am I supposed to feel flattered by that?"

"Just stating a fact."

Nicole's cheeks were burning from the hot rush of aggression he'd stirred. She bit her lips, fiercely telling herself to retreat to a neutral place. This kind of exchange was not going to serve any good purpose. Though despite her attempt to regain a calmer composure, her hackles rose again when Quin smiled with wolfish satisfaction.

"You know what is worth every cent of my investment, Nicole?"

She shrugged, pretending disinterest.

"You're honour bound to stay with me—like it or not—for twenty-six nights. No running away from what we are together."

"What are we, Quin?" she asked with arch carelessness.

"I intend for us to be unstoppable."

"And I intend for us to be finally finished."

He grinned, not the least bit turned off by her claim.

He was still grinning as the waiter arrived, served their lobsters and refilled their glasses.

Quin lifted his champagne and said with a lilt of elation, "To a fine start and an even finer finish."

Nicole held her tongue.

But she did lift her glass derisively and drank to his toast. It meant nothing, she told herself. She wouldn't let it. The one thing she was certain about—Quin couldn't be trusted to commit himself to anything other than making money.

CHAPTER SIX

Now to the business end of the evening, Nicole thought, as they left the restaurant. The skin-prickling awareness of Quin walking beside her and the treacherous excitement he generated, made it extremely difficult to keep a level head and an objective attitude about what was going to happen when they reached his apartment.

"It's only a short stroll," he said amiably, showing no tension whatsoever over being with her.

Why would he?

He was in the box seat, directing the action.

It was okay to want sex with him, Nicole told herself. Take it, enjoy it, then leave it behind you when you go in the morning. Just don't believe it's anything else but physical chemistry driving a perfectly natural urge. After five long celibate years she was entitled—as a woman—to feel sexual pleasure again. Probably her highly personal knowledge of how Quin had given it in the past was stirring the desire.

"Look!" His hand curled around her arm to hold her still as he pointed to the shop window they were passing.

"At what?"

Her gaze swept around a display of Australian souvenirs. Being situated here, underneath the marble colonnade, the place was very much an upmarket boutique for tourists. A small group of Japanese were inside, stocking up on gifts to take home with them. There were many such shops around Circular Quay, catering for the same trade. This was an expensive one but beyond that...

"The blue butterfly," Quin enlightened her. "Come on. Let's go in and buy it for your tree."

Nicole's heart lurched—the shock of his knowledge only dissipating when she remembered he'd queried Jade's gift to her last night. Jules had explained it although she'd stopped him from saying too much. The butterfly tree was a special thing between her and Zoe.

A fierce wave of protest burst through her mind. She didn't want Quin associated with it in any way whatsoever. He didn't have the right to intrude upon it. He hadn't been part of it, never would be part of it. Yet before she could find suitable words to check his impulsive suggestion, his arm was around her waist, scooping her inside the boutique, and as always with Quin, a saleswoman instantly zeroed in on him.

"We want the blue butterfly," he said unequivocally.

"Ah yes, a beautiful piece." The woman smiled at him, then quickly moved to get it out of a glass showcase which contained a menagerie of Australian birds, fish and animals, some exquisitely fashioned in crystal, others delicately made of blown glass with colour swirling through them.

"It's a Ulysses, native to far north Queensland," the saleswoman prattled on. "You see them everywhere up around Cairns and the Daintree Rainforest. The natural colour of their wings is an iridescent electric blue, so you'll get the best effect if you can place this piece where sunlight shines through the delicate glass."

"We'll take it. Wrap it up," Quin instructed.

"Wait!" Nicole cried, frantically trying to come up with a reason to stop this purchase. "It looks terribly expensive. How much is it?"

The price stated was exorbitant. There was probably a huge mark-up on everything in the boutique because of its prime position near the Opera House.

"I can't accept this, Quin," she said firmly.

He looked incredulously at her. "After all you've accepted from me today?" He shook his head, took out his wallet, extracted a credit card and smiled at the saleswoman as he passed it to her. "Wrap it up. It's a perfect memento for a momentous evening."

There was no stopping him from making the purchase. Nicole recognised that. However, she could and would refuse to take the butterfly from him. She kept her arms rigidly at her sides when he tried to hand the boutique bag to her as they left the shop. "This isn't part of our deal," she insisted.

"I bet you haven't got one like it," he pressed temptingly.

"That's not the point."

"What is?"

She flashed a fiercely determined look at him. "I don't want a memento of tonight."

A ruthless gleam answered her. "I intend that you find it unforgettable anyway, Nicole."

Her hands clenched in a blind need to fight off the sense of very real danger to the life she'd made without him. "This will pass," she muttered in savage resolve.

"It didn't last time. Which is why we are here now." His eyes challenged her to deny it.

She couldn't. No-one else would have drawn her into bartering herself for money. It was because of who he was, what he was, and how unimportant he'd made her feel in the past when his obsession about amassing money had come ahead of everything else. But she was not about to admit that Quin was right. Feeding his ego was not on her agenda.

"We're here now because you represented a way out of a situation I didn't want," she stated flatly.

"Which, in turn, represented a way into a situation I did want," he slid back at her. "And both *wants* have their roots in the past...which definitely has not passed, Nicole."

Not for him. It had only been sex on his mind then and he had the hots for her again now. This was just a second round of the same. But it was different for her. She'd been wildly, blindly, heart-wrenchingly in love with him. That definitely had passed.

Not wanting this subject pursued, Nicole kept her mouth firmly shut. Quin waved her to turn under an archway which led into a lobby housing a massive spiral staircase and a bank of elevators—marble tiles on the floor, marble walls, huge chandelier hanging from a ceiling, two storeys high—the kind of place that screamed *exclusive to the very wealthy*.

"Here we are," he announced, using a key to operate one of the elevators.

The doors opened.

Quin ushered her into the softly carpeted compartment, stepped in after her, pressed a button marked P and closed out the rest of the world. P for penthouse, Nicole thought, panic skittering through her stomach as the elevator zoomed up to the private apartment where she would become Quin's penthouse playmate. Would it be more pain than pleasure? Had she been completely mad to enter into this contract?

Think of what had been achieved for her mother, she told herself, trying desperately to appear calm and composed as Quin guided her into a fabulous living room. Dominating it were floor to ceiling windows, giving a spectacular view of Sydney Harbour stretching from Bennelong Point right out to sea. Nicole automatically walked over to it, needing to face something other than Quin's material acquisitions, which had clearly meant more to him than she ever had.

The carpet underfoot was a soft teal colour. There were cream leather couches with lots of colourful scatter cushions, glass tables with creamy granite pedestals holding them up. Just props, Nicole thought in bitter dismissal. Status symbols. Expensive interior decoration did not make a home. Quin had never been interested in making a home.

It was a high view of the harbour. Although it was now dark outside, the foreshore with all its little coves was outlined by the lights of the houses crowding it. Boats riding at anchor could easily be seen, ferries carving through the water to their destinations. Nicole wondered if living up here made Quin feel he was on top of this city, king of his castle.

Did he know how empty his castle was, despite all his possessions, of which she was now one—but only a very temporary one.

Did he ever think this wasn't enough?

She shook her head over the foolish questions.

They sprang from her own emotions, not his, and she was not—*not*—going to get emotionally involved with Quin Sola again!

Quin stood by the broad serving bench of the open plan kitchen, watching Nicole take in the multimillion dollar view. He made no move to join her, though he sensed she was armour-plating herself against the inevitable intimacy of the bedroom. Her shoulders were rigidly squared. Her stillness seemed to form a self-protective cloak. She would give what she had to give but nothing more.

Under normal circumstances, women coming here for the first time showed some curiosity or interest in his personal living quarters; checking out the furnishings, fossicking through his kitchen, making admiring comments. Nicole's stiff back shut it all out and her silence affirmed her lack of caring. She no more wanted to be part of his life than she wanted him to be part of hers. The adamant rebuff of the butterfly gift underlined her determination to stay detached where it really counted—in her mind and heart.

He felt his own jaw tighten with determination as he looked down at the chic boutique bag he was still

carrying. Nicole had used the tissue-wrapped blue butterfly nestled inside as a weapon against him, telling
him very sharply he didn't belong in her world and she
would not let him put even one small step into it. Nevertheless, her strongly negative reaction to the gift told
him he could use it as a weapon, too, hitting at what obviously had some personal meaning to her.

"Would you like some coffee, Nicole?"

"Yes, please," she answered without turning her head.

"You used to like cappuccino. My coffee machine
can make it if that's still your preference."

"Yes. Thank you."

A tight flat voice and still no glance around.

It increased Quin's determination to crack the wall
she was putting up between them. He made her coffee,
opened a small box of Belgium chocolates, set both of
them down on the low table which serviced the sofa
closest to where she was standing. At the slight clatter
of china on the glass surface of the table—or maybe it
was the strong scent of the steaming hot coffee—she did
turn, finally acknowledging his efforts to please her
with a dry little smile.

"Chocolates, too," she said as though mocking any
attempt to sweeten her up.

"Since you're so entranced with the view," he
drawled, mocking her right back. "I'll leave you to enjoy
it while I slip into something more comfortable. Excuse
me, won't you?"

The startled look on her face gave him immense satisfaction. He grinned to himself as he headed down the
hall to his bedroom. It wasn't *his* comfort on his mind.

The aim was to keep tipping Nicole out of any comfort zone she thought she had, and there was nothing more effective to gain ground than a surprise attack.

Nicole frowned in confusion as Quin disappeared down a hall.

Slip into something more comfortable?

That was a woman's line—a woman intent on seducing a man.

What was Quin playing at?

Champagne, oysters, an expensive gift, chocolates…were these things meant to melt some expected resistance to him? It made no sense. He didn't have to play a seductive game to get her into bed. She was his for the taking. That was the deal and she wasn't about to welsh on it.

He was probably getting his gear off to save the inconvenience of undressing later on. Quin had always been perfectly comfortable in his skin. And why not? He had a flawless male physique. Her stomach fluttered at the thought of seeing him naked again.

She moved to the sofa and sat down, sipping the hot creamy cappuccino in the hope of calming her nerves. She didn't touch the chocolates. Taking any of them might suggest she was enjoying herself, thereby giving Quin the satisfaction of thinking he *was* seducing her.

This was not a love affair.

She wouldn't let Quin draw her into thinking it could be.

He was playing a game with her. She couldn't imagine him ever having paid money for sex before. No doubt he wanted to turn it into a conquest so his male ego would triumph over the means to the end he desired.

The coffee cup was empty and still he had not returned to the living room. Was he deliberately holding her in waiting, demonstrating who was now master of this situation?

Stop thinking of him, Nicole silently screamed at herself. He was winning by dominating her thoughts!

She rose from the sofa and returned to gazing at the view. Let him find her where he'd left her, ignoring the penthouse proof of his success at making money. Determinedly blanking her mind to everything else, she stood by the window, staring out.

But her instincts picked up Quin's presence the moment he re-entered the living room. There was no sound of footsteps. He didn't speak. She felt the atmosphere change as though some elemental force made it vibrate with a sudden flow of dynamic energy. She knew he was there, watching her, willing her to turn around and acknowledge him. Her whole body felt the tug of his silent command and she had to steel herself to deny it.

Let him come to her. She was here in his apartment for the night. That was the letter of the agreement between them. What he wanted to make of it was up to him.

He came. Her heart drummed his approach as though it sensed every footstep bringing him closer and closer to her. Then his hands were on her hips, sliding up underneath her top, unclipping her bra, reaching around to push the lace cups from her breasts, freeing them for his touch, his fingers lightly kneading the soft fullness, his thumbs fanning her nipples to a responsive tautness.

Nicole found herself holding her breath, her whole being consumed with the desire to feel. It had been so long…so very long…and Quin knew how to touch, how to excite, how to build a pool of pleasure that turned her insides to warm liquid. She finally released her breath and quickly sucked in more air as he lifted her top up over her head, removing the bra with it.

"Stay still," he commanded, his fingers raking through her hair, parting it, lifting the long tresses from her back and pushing them over either shoulder to flow down over her breasts.

She stayed still, but could not prevent a convulsive little shiver as he kissed the bared nape of her neck, his mouth hot and seductively sensual. His fingertips feathered down the curve of her spine, drew tantalising circles on her rib-cage, moved slowly upwards until they reached the fall of her hair which he gently rubbed over her sensitised breasts.

"I always did love the feel of you, Nicole," he murmured.

Don't use the word, *love,* to me, she thought fiercely. Arouse me sexually all you like, but love is something you know nothing about.

His hands glided down to the waistband of her jeans. He pulled the stud apart, opened the zipper. Her stomach contracted under the warmth of his palms spreading over it as his fingers targeted the heat he'd already generated between her thighs. He knew how to touch there, too, softly, softly caressing the folds apart, using her own moistness to tease her clitoris, building an excitement that she knew would drive her beyond all control.

Her breathing quickened, little gasps escaping her lips even as she mentally fought to remain still as though nothing was really happening. She wanted Quin to think her body was simply responding naturally to nothing but expert stimulation. He, as a person, didn't count. She stared unseeingly into the darkness of the night sky, telling herself she was just experiencing and taking pleasure in *touch*.

"Let's get these clothes off," he said gruffly, removing the intimate contact to hook his thumbs over the waistbands of her panties and jeans. Both garments were swiftly pushed down her legs. He lifted one of her feet, then the other, stripping them of the sandals as he also freed her of clothes.

Nicole didn't resist any of Quin's actions. Submitting to them actually kept him at a distance. She was being undressed by someone she couldn't see, being ministered to by someone she couldn't see. Now she was completely naked, yet in a strange, detached way she didn't feel vulnerable. She had a sense of liberation from all the responsibilities she had carried for so long. Right at this moment she existed only as a woman, revelling in the re-awakening of her sexuality.

His hands grazed her inner thighs as he straightened up behind her. They cupped the rounded voluptuousness of her bottom, then parted the soft cheeks enough for him to press the hard thick shaft of his erection along the cleft. Then his arms were around her waist, drawing her whole body back against his, making her acutely aware of his nakedness.

It was both strange and familiar—strange because she

hadn't been with a man like this since Quin—familiar because it *was* Quin and her body recognised every inch of him. And she could not stop a wildly primitive wave of exultation in the recognition. Her man…her mate…

Except he wasn't.

Quin Sola belonged only to himself.

"What are you seeing out there?" he asked.

"Nothing," she answered, her voice sounding oddly rough, as though it was being resurrected from a long period of disuse.

"Then let me show you something to see."

He dropped his embrace, took her hand, and led her across the living room and down the hall he had entered earlier. He stopped at a door, opened it, and took her into a large bedroom. Nicole barely noticed the bed. Beyond it was another wall of glass but her gaze was not drawn to yet another view of Sydney Harbour. It was instantly captivated by what was set up in front of the middle window.

The glass butterfly had been placed on a pedestal and spotlighted by a lamp shining up behind it and turning the wings into a stunning fluorescent blue.

CHAPTER SEVEN

No DOUBT about it, Quin thought triumphantly. As a tactic to crack Nicole's wall of indifference to him, placing the blue butterfly centre stage and spotlighting it was an act of pure genius. Gone was the submissive sex slave. She spun to face him in full frontal attack, her green eyes shooting furious sparks, outrage pumping through her, shoulders back, breasts lifting, and if her taut nipples had been pistols, there would probably be blood on the floor right now.

"What do you think you're playing at?"

Definitely a *kill* note in her voice.

"It's a beautiful piece," he stated calmly. "It should be displayed like that. Why are you upset by it?"

"You did it deliberately."

Violent accusation.

"Yes, I did," Quin agreed. "I wanted to get the best effect."

"Since when have you been interested in doing home decoration?"

Blistering scorn.

He smiled. "You inspired me to start tonight."

"Why?"

"Because it means something to you."

"No, it doesn't!" she denied heatedly, her hands clenching, her need to fight the point making Quin all the more certain he'd hit on a highly vulnerable area in her current life.

"Then it shouldn't be upsetting you, Nicole. My aim was to give you pleasure."

"Pleasure!"

The fury in her eyes whirled into confusion, followed by flickers of fear at having reacted too strongly, consequently revealing there was far more to the issue of the butterfly than she wanted him to know.

"Pleasure beyond what we share in bed," he said silkily, moving in to claim what she owed him, taking her in his embrace, ignoring the stiff resistance of her body as he pressed his to it. "It's something beautiful for you to look at tonight. And when you wake in the morning."

Her hands were still clenched at her sides. Her eyes burned with an angry hatred. There was nothing cool and detached about her now. Why she should hate him, he didn't know, but hate was infinitely better than indifference. Quin sensed she was steaming inside, wanting to lash out at him, and he exulted in having stirred so much volatile emotion. He didn't want a passive Nicole in bed. He wanted the passionate Nicole who'd left an indelible imprint on his memory.

"Bed," she bit out, pouring a mountain of venom into the word. "Right! Let's get to it!"

He laughed at her boiling impatience to get it over

and done with. "Not so fast, Nicole. We haven't even kissed yet."

"Not a good idea, Quin," she flashed back at him. "I might bite your tongue out."

"I think I'll risk it anyhow."

"Whores don't kiss."

"You're no whore, Nicole. The money is totally irrelevant to what pulses between us."

"That's your ego talking, Quin. I wouldn't be here but for the money."

"Okay. Then give me my money's worth." He whipped a hand up to cup her chin, holding her face so she couldn't turn it away. "Use your tongue for something other than talking."

She opened her mouth to speak again and he swooped on it, his own passions aroused by her refusal to acknowledge the powerful chemistry between them. He kissed her hard, determined on crashing through any resistance.

There was a non-responsive moment of shock.

Then her tongue was tangling with his in a fierce duel for possession, no holding back, no sharp teeth trying to beat him into retreat. She assaulted his mouth with as much pumped up passion as he assaulted hers, and the excitement of it was so intense, Quin's entire body was seized with the need to drive it further.

Her arms had wound around his neck, hands thrust aggressively into his hair to enforce *her* kiss. It was easy to lower his hold on her, using the leverage of her lushly cushioned bottom to lift her up enough for him to stride to the bed and move them both onto it. Her legs sprawled apart invitingly as he came down on top of her.

An exhilarating rush of adrenaline surged through him at the obvious proof that she wanted him as urgently as he wanted her.

Swiftly positioning himself, feeling her moist heat, knowing she was ready, her flesh quivering, craving what he craved, Quin was on the point of plunging forward when she suddenly slammed her hands against his shoulders and cried, "No! No! Wait!"

"What for?" he snapped, every taut nerve and muscle protesting the delay, his mind angrily whirling over the thought of her playing some sadistic, teasing game with him.

"You have to use protection, Quin," she said forcefully, her breasts heaving against his chest, her knees up, feet planted to give her pushing strength if she had to use it.

"You've got some infectious problem?" His voice was harsh with frustration. Apart from which, he didn't believe that a woman as fastidious as Nicole would have taken any health risk with sex.

"How do I know *you* haven't got one?" she retaliated. "Don't tell me you've been celibate for the past five years."

"No, but I'm not stupid, Nicole."

"I want you to use a condom," she pressed aggressively.

"That's not as pleasurable for you or me."

"Tough!" Her eyes savagely mocked his argument. "Me getting pregnant is not part of our deal."

"Pregnant? You're worried about getting pregnant?"

"It happens," she said fiercely.

He frowned over the sharpness of her concern. It seemed unreasonable, given the effectiveness of modern means of contraception.

Perhaps realising it needed some credible explanation, she blurted out, "I'm not on the pill, Quin. By insisting on having me with you tonight, you didn't give me time to get myself safely protected."

His mind swiftly processed what she was saying. "So you haven't been sexually active for some time… months…years?"

Five years? he wondered, recalling her crack about the possible length of his celibacy.

"That's none of your business." Again her eyes were savagely mocking as she added, "The point is, you don't want a child out of this any more than I do. Such a responsibility would interfere far too much with your life. Though, of course, you could just turn your back on it, leaving me to deal with the consequences of our… *pleasure.*"

Was that a bitter tone in her voice?

Quin forgot about the enforced pause to their current pleasure, his mind totally engaged with Nicole's response to him on other levels. "I've never shirked responsibility," he stated, ironically conscious of the family debt he'd carried and eventually paid out. "Nor did I turn my back on you, Nicole. It was you who walked away."

"After you shut about a million doors in my face," she said derisively. "Only the bedroom door was always open. But let's not go down that road, Quin. We're dealing with now and I don't want any mementoes— butterflies or babies—of this time together. I brought a packet of condoms in case you didn't have a ready supply. It's in my bag."

The raging desire was gone. The act of getting up and doing the whole condom thing was a passion killer anyway, Quin told himself, moving to lie beside Nicole. The whole night stretched ahead of them. There was no need for any haste in satisfying the hunger for a deeply sexual connection with her. Other intimacies also had appeal.

"Shall I get the packet?" she asked, turning towards him and propping herself up on her elbow.

"Sure! Might as well be prepared for when I get another erection," he drawled sardonically.

She glanced down and winced at the limp evidence of doused arousal. "Sorry, Quin. I should have spoken before. I didn't deliberately hold back on it."

He cocked a challenging eyebrow. "Caught up in other things?"

Her lips compressed. No admission that she'd wanted *him*. But she had. No doubt about that in Quin's mind. The triumphant knowledge of it simmered in his eyes as he said, "I put your bag in the ensuite bathroom." He waved to a door beyond the bedside table closest to where he lay. "It's through there."

It meant she had to clamber over him or get up on her side and round the bed, passing directly by the blue butterfly which he'd cunningly displayed with the only light switched on in the room. He watched her as she took the latter action. Her naked body was briefly silhouetted against the spotlight as she headed for the bathroom, her gaze rigidly fixed on the door, not so much as a glance at the butterfly.

Her lovely full breasts seemed heavier, not quite as

perky as he remembered. A more mature figure five years down the track, he thought, but certainly no less sexy. To his mind, her body was still the most beautifully feminine he'd ever seen; curves where there should be curves, flowing in perfect harmony, her bones softly fleshed, long shapely legs.

He was glad she wasn't inhibited about it, feeling no need to cover up in front of him. Which would have been absurd anyway, given they'd been lovers. Nevertheless, it conceded a familiarity she might have wanted to reject in these current circumstances with hostility a strong thread in her attitude towards him.

Quin brooded over the hostility while she was out of sight in the bathroom. He didn't really understand it. When they'd first met at the bank where they'd been employed, the sexual chemistry between them had been instant and compelling. They'd both been swept away by it. There'd been no courtship. One dinner date followed by blazing passion. It had taken enormous discipline for him not to become obsessed with her, not to lose sight of the goal he'd set himself.

Despite the cost to the financial momentum he'd been building, he'd moved out of his mother's home and rented an apartment so he and Nicole could be together as much as possible. Nicole had been happy with the arrangement. The sexual excitement had been intense and they were also highly compatible out of bed, with her understanding the pressures of trading and his being able to converse knowingly about her work in sales.

She was the only woman he'd ever lived with, the only one he'd ever wanted to live with. Being with her had always been an enormous buzz. It still was. But in the end she hadn't been satisfied with what they had.

He couldn't remember when she'd started agitating about meeting each other's families. He hadn't wanted to go there. It meant getting more tied up with Nicole than he already was and he didn't want to think about future relationships when he hadn't yet discharged the burden of the past. One thing at a time. He'd been adamant about simply continuing to share what they did—just the two of them—which didn't have anything to do with their families.

He had sensed an emotional withdrawal from her—a coldness stemming, he'd thought, from not getting her own way. He hadn't fallen in with her design for their lives, whatever that was—marriage, babies, setting up a family home. Nevertheless, she had seemed to accept that he wasn't about to change his mind—remaining with him for two years before deciding to break off their relationship and go overseas.

He recalled her bitter claim that making money had been more important to him than she was. To Quin's mind, the two things should not have been in conflict. Both had been important to him. But she had gone, deliberately putting so much distance between them, it wrote off any second chance with her, and since that was her choice…why did she now hate him?

Had she wanted him—expected him—to drop everything and chase after her?

He'd missed her. He'd missed her one hell of a lot. But he'd had a job to do, a vow to fulfil, and he'd driven himself to carry it through and have done with it. He was free now. His mother was back home in Argentina, welcomed into her family circle again. She'd wanted him to stay, too, but the life there had no appeal to him. Australia had become his home country.

Having returned to Sydney and established his own business, he had been feeling the need for someone to share his life with. He'd tried several attractive women, all of them falling short of satisfying him in one area or another. He hadn't been consciously comparing them to Nicole, yet the moment he'd seen her again, he knew she was the one he had to have.

She emerged from the bathroom, coming straight to his side of the bed and handing him the packet of condoms. "You might as well get one out ready," she said, her green eyes glittering determined purpose as she moved to sit astride him, intent on arousing his flesh with her own.

"I did mention there was no hurry, Nicole," he reminded her, though he proceeded to extract the contraceptive device, wanting it ready when he chose to use it. "I'm happy just to talk for a while."

"Then talk away," she answered carelessly, moving her lower body over his in tantalising provocation.

She looked magnificent sitting there on top of him, her breasts swaying to the voluptuous roll of her hips, her long curly hair a cloud of sensual promise, shimmering against the backdrop of the spotlighted blue butterfly.

Had she positioned herself like this so it was behind her, out of her line of sight? "I'm glad you want to make love to me," he said as a goad to revealing her thoughts.

She flicked him a veiled look, her thick lashes almost

hiding—but not quite—the hot daggers behind them. "I might just be satisfying myself."

"Then I'm glad to be of service to you."

She raked her nails lightly down his chest, not scratching but possibly delivering a warning that the claws could be unsheathed if he pushed her too far.

Quin rather relished flirting with danger. "How long has it been since you were with a man, Nicole?" he asked, wanting his curiosity satisfied on that point. If there'd been no other since she'd left him...

"Obviously I've been occupied by other things," she tossed out as though he should have realised that from the situation she had already laid out to him.

"Even as far back as two years ago?"

It stilled her for a moment. But she was quick at making the connection. "Your friend, Tony Fisher, is not as irresistible as he might think he is."

"Most women find Tony very attractive."

"Guess it's a matter of personal taste." Her eyes flashed derisively as she bent forward to kiss one of his nipples, swirling her tongue around it and sucking on it as though revelling in its taste.

If it was meant to be a powerful distraction from any further conversation, it certainly hit its mark. The sheer physical excitement of it tested his control to its limits. Only the thought that she was winning gave him the will power to remain still and keep his brain working, though he didn't realise his breath was trapped in his chest until she lifted her mouth away. He quickly exhaled and gulped in more air as her head moved towards his other nipple.

"Did you find satisfaction in London?" he shot out,

trying to pinpoint how she'd spent the years of her absence overseas.

She ignored the question, delivering the same sweet torment again, driving the desire to subject *her* to it until her whole body ached for the release he could give her, until she was begging for it. He had twenty-five more nights for talking. It could wait. This couldn't. Not even for one more second.

He grabbed her waist, hurled her onto her back, rolled to pin her down under his weight. She tore at his hair as he swooped on her breasts. She kneaded his shoulders when he pushed himself down to wrap his mouth around more intimate places. Her body bucked, writhed and finally she did beg.

For a moment he hesitated over donning the condom.

If Nicole did get pregnant and had his child, she'd be tied to him for life.

But that wouldn't be a free choice.

He wanted her to want him in her life.

And he didn't want to be stopped now.

So the protective sheath had to be used.

She climaxed as he drove his triumphant possession of her as deeply as he could go, but that wasn't enough for Quin. He was consumed with the burning desire to feel her coming again and again, rolling from one ecstatic peak to the next. He wanted to drive the memory of any other lover she'd had right out of her mind so she remembered only him. He used every bit of sexual expertise he knew to keep her body tuned to his, responding instinctively, blissfully, lustfully, lovingly, long into the night.

As she had in the past.
Oh, yes, he wanted that back.
And more!

CHAPTER EIGHT

IT WAS the twelfth night coming up. Almost halfway through the deal, Nicole told herself, trying to quell the growing sense that she would never really be free of Joaquin Luis Sola. He was like a drug. The more she had of him, the more she wanted him. Just like before. And labelling what they had together, *just sex,* did not lessen the impact of it. Walking away from him a second time was not going to be any easier than the first.

She stared at the reflection of her eyes in the bath-room mirror. They literally glittered with excitement, all because she could tell him tonight they didn't have to use condoms anymore. She'd now been taking the pill long enough for it to be effective. They didn't have to think about protection, didn't have to stop, didn't have to blunt the feeling of absolutely natural intimacy.

She couldn't even pretend her skin was tingling from the brisk towelling she'd given it after her shower. Her whole body was anticipating his touch. And here she was blow-drying her freshly shampooed hair so it would look good for him, feel good to him, silky and sensual and…

"Nicole…" Her mother called out, knocking on the

bathroom door to gain her attention. "You're wanted on the 'phone."

"Coming…" She quickly switched off the hair drier, laid it on the vanity bench, then grabbed her bathrobe and wrapped it around the nakedness she hadn't bothered to cover before, secretly revelling in a sense of wanton expectation. She opened the door to find her mother still loitering in the hall, watching for her to emerge. "Who is it?" Nicole asked, wondering why she appeared anxious.

Linda Ellis looked at the happy glow emanating from her daughter and felt her own heart tighten with concern. That same aura of happiness had been totally blighted by the man Nicole had picked up with again. If that happened a second time, it would be completely her fault for not ever having stopped to count the cost of trying to save Harry. A futile sacrifice in the end. And this sacrifice by Nicole could also end in wretched grief.

"It's him," she said flatly.

"You mean Quin?" Nicole asked, the sparkle in her eyes disappearing under a sudden cloud of worry.

Linda nodded.

Frowning heavily, Nicole hurried down the hall to the kitchen where the house telephone resided. Linda trailed after her, disturbed by this direct contact with the man who had never wanted to meet her, never wanted anything to do with Nicole's family. She propped herself in the kitchen doorway, needing to eavesdrop on the call, needing to know where all this might be leading

* * *

Nicole snatched up the telephone receiver which had been left waiting for her on the kitchen bench. Her heart was racing, her stomach fluttering. "How did you get this number?" she demanded, the fear of Quin encroaching on her real life shooting through her mind.

"I looked it up in the telephone book," he answered matter-of-factly.

"It's in my mother's name," she snapped back.

"The same name, Linda Ellis, attached to the debts I paid off, including the mortgage on a house in Burwood," he drawled.

Nicole paused to take a deep, calming breath and to get her wits in order. Of course Quin had enough information to find her. The question was...why bother? He never had before.

"Calling me at home is not in our deal," she stated pointedly.

"I am calling out of consideration for you, Nicole. I didn't think you'd like coming to my apartment tonight and not finding me there."

Not there tonight? The sexual excitement she had been trying to contain all day took a dive into disappointment. Anger at herself stirred. She was letting Quin get to her far too much. A determination to halt that process put a coolness in her voice.

"Thank you for letting me know you're forfeiting the twelfth night of our deal in favour of something else."

"I have no intention of forfeiting any night," he whipped back.

"You just have, Quin."

"I'll be home tomorrow. A mere postponement."

"We made the arrangement—Fridays and Mondays. I'm not available to you on any other nights."

"Be reasonable, Nicole." His voice was very terse now. "I'm in Melbourne. A business meeting ran over and—"

"And, as always, making money comes ahead of being with me," she cut in bitingly. "That's fine, Quin. Your choice. But don't expect me to accommodate your choice."

She could hear him exhale a long breath of exasperation at her refusal to oblige him. Nicole felt pleased with herself for not giving in to him. *Score one for me,* she thought, remembering how she'd done whatever was needed to fit around his work in the past.

However, her moment of grim satisfaction was abruptly ended by Zoe rushing in from the living room, calling, "Mummy! Mummy! Come and see what's on television."

Nicole swung around from the kitchen bench, caught sight of her mother in the doorway and shot her a wildly pleading look.

Zoe was swiftly scooped up in her grandmother's arms. "I'll come and look," she was assured and carried back into the living room.

"But I want…"

"Shh…"

The door was shut behind them, keeping them both out of earshot.

Nicole was gripped by shock, the childish voice of her daughter still ringing in her ears as she fearfully wondered if Quin had heard it. The suspended beating of her heart broke into an erratic pounding when he spoke again.

"Mummy?" The puzzled query was followed by a sharper question. "Whose child was that, Nicole?"

Her mind wrenched itself out of its distressed daze and flew to desperate defence stations. "The daughter of one of my friends. They dropped by to—" she deliberately huffed over the lie before adding "—but that's none of your business, Quin. Thank you for calling to warn me tonight is off. Is Friday night a firm date or can I expect another cancellation?"

He huffed. Or rather a long heated breath hissed through his teeth. "You'll be seeing me," he said curtly, and ended the connection.

Nicole fumbled the receiver back onto its holder and sagged against the bench. That was too close a call. The relief of having come up with a swift explanation for Zoe's presence still had her trembling inside.

It hadn't occurred to her that Quin might contact her at home. He never had in the past. But then they'd been living together and working for the same bank. When she'd visited her mother, he had viewed it as time out from their relationship and didn't intrude on it.

This was a different situation and she could hardly criticise Quin for giving her a courtesy call. She should have been more prepared for possible glitches in their arrangement. Although he had her e-mail address, e-mailing was not an immediate means of communication unless one was sitting at the computer all the time. And she would not have logged on before leaving this evening.

Shame wormed through her as she thought of how fixated her mind had been on having sex with Quin. He was starting to dominate her life again and she had to protect herself from that. Fourteen more nights…what if she didn't want to end it?

Nicole shook her head angrily. That was crazy thinking. Right now she was caught up in indulging her sexuality. Quin was good for that but not for anything else. If she didn't keep everything in perspective she'd be in bad trouble. And right now Zoe needed her attention.

She quickly entered the living room to find her daughter sitting on Nanna's lap, placidly watching "The World Around Us" program on television—no apparent upset at having been ignored by her mother. Nicole paused for a moment, taking in the two people who did occupy the central core of her life.

They personified love, not lust. Without her mother's ready support, Nicole knew she could not have managed the period of Zoe's illness nearly as well. Then for Harry to have been hit by cancer… Nicole could not begrudge the extreme lengths her mother had gone to in search of a cure. It had been done out of love. And it had to be very hard to lose two husbands. Losing out on Quin's love had devastated her five years ago.

We three are the survivors, Nicole thought, *three generations of the one small family.*

In the past few weeks her mother had pulled herself together and was back managing the dance school. The grey had been dyed out of her short curly brown hair and her trim dancer's body and still pretty face belied her fifty-five years. Occasionally Nicole glimpsed a haunted look in the generally warm hazel eyes, but at least the depression that had followed Harry's death had lifted.

As for Zoe, she was always a delight—a wonderfully

healthy delight—and to Nicole's mind, the most beautiful little girl in the world with her large smoky grey eyes and the amazingly thick, glossy, black hair which Zoe wanted to grow long so it could be braided. Nicole was smiling over this ambitious aim as she walked over to the three-seater sofa facing the television screen.

"You missed it, Mummy," Zoe informed her, heaving a disappointed sigh.

"I'm sorry, darling. I was busy on the 'phone and couldn't cut off the person calling me." She sat down beside her daughter, smiling encouragingly. "Tell me what you saw."

Her little face lit up with awe. "It was a butterfly farm."

"An enclosure, like an aviary," Nanna supplied.

"And there were lots and lots of big pretty flowers for the butterflies to land on."

"Tropical flowers," Nanna chimed in. "Most of them hibiscus."

"It was near the rainforest at Kranda. Could we go there, Mummy?"

"Kuranda," Nanna corrected. "Up above Cairns in Far North Queensland."

Nicole shook her head. "That's too far away, Zoe. It was lucky you saw it on TV."

Zoe heaved a sigh but didn't argue. She knew only too well that some things could be done and some things couldn't. "They were all blue, the butterflies. The man called them—" she frowned, trying to recall the word "—Issies."

"Ulysses," Nicole recollected with painful irony. The glass one Quin had bought was still prominently displayed in his bedroom—a tormenting reminder of what he didn't know, what he wouldn't want to know.

Zoe cocked her head appealingly. "If we can't go and see them, could you make one for my tree, Mummy? We haven't got a blue one. Not all blue like the Ulysses."

Nicole inwardly winced, knowing it would be forever connected to her nights with Quin. "Butterflies mark special occasions, Zoe. You'll have to wait for one," she said, hoping her daughter might forget about the blue Ulysses. "Now I must go finish drying my hair before I tuck you into bed for the night. Okay?"

"Okay, Mummy."

Nicole caught a frown from her mother, worry in the hazel eyes. "Are you…going out?" she asked warily.

"No. I just want to finish doing my hair or it will end up frizzy," Nicole rattled off carelessly, hoping to dismiss anything her mother had overheard from the kitchen doorway.

However, after she'd put Zoe to bed and read her a story, she found her mother pacing around the living room in an agitated state, the television switched off. "What's wrong, Mum? You're missing your favourite crime show."

"I don't like this, Nicole," was shot back at her. "On the 'phone to that man, you sounded so bitter…vengeful." She wrung her hands. "It's wrong, wrong. I shouldn't have let you do this."

"You didn't let me, Mum. I did it on my own. *My* choice," Nicole insisted quietly.

"It's not good for you."

"Oh, I don't know. In a weird kind of way it is."

"How?"

Nicole managed a wry smile. "I doubt there's a man alive who's as good as Quin in bed. It's not exactly a hardship to spend twenty-six nights with him."

"Do you still love him?"

"No."

"I don't believe you can have really good sex without loving your partner," her mother argued heatedly.

Nicole tried to shrug off the point. "Well, Quin and I still have a strong physical connection. It's okay, Mum. Don't worry about it."

"No, it's more than that. You're getting hurt by him again. I heard it in your voice. You can't change people, Nicole. They are what they are. And paying them back for not living up to what you want of them…"

"It's not about what I want," Nicole cut in fiercely. "Quin and I have a deal. A deal is a deal. No changes. That was all I was insisting upon, Mum. Now please… leave it alone. I do not wish to spend any more of my time on Quin than what he's paid for."

But, of course she did. He was on her mind more often than not. Her mother respected her wishes enough to drop the subject for the time being but her silence didn't stop Nicole from thinking about him, nor brooding over what her mother had said.

When they both retired for the night, Nicole lay awake and very acutely alone in her own bed, hashing over what she did feel about Quin Sola. The bottom line was she did wish he would change and her bitterness stemmed from having her wishes thwarted. Her mother was right. Being vengeful did not bring about some magical transformation. On the other hand, it did satisfy a dark sense of justice to belittle his role in her life, as he had belittled hers when she'd desperately needed something else from him.

There was no good answer to any of this, she finally decided, and set her mind to counting sheep in the hope it would send her to sleep. It must have succeeded because she was jerked awake by the loud and persistent ringing of the doorbell.

She looked at her bedside clock: 23:17. Was the house on fire or something? She sniffed but didn't smell any smoke. Nevertheless, there had to be an emergency to account for such determination to arouse the people in the house. She tumbled out of bed and met her mother in the hall heading for the front door. She stopped as she heard Zoe calling out, alarmed by the bell which was still being rung aggressively.

Not for one second did it occur to Nicole that Quin Sola might be at the door, that a determination not to forfeit one night with her had caused him to cut his business meeting short, catch a plane from Melbourne to Sydney and come to this house in Burwood to collect her before midnight!

CHAPTER NINE

HAVING jettisoned his plans and travelled hard for the past few hours to get here, Quin was not a happy man to find the house in darkness. It was an old but solid red brick Federation-style home with a neat front lawn and garden—typical of the whole street—yet with no light on anywhere, its old-fashioned respectability felt forbidding. Definitely unwelcoming.

And this was the house he'd saved for her!

So what had Nicole done, having thrown down her challenge about his priorities? Gone out with her mother for the night? Taken herself off to a bed that didn't have him in it? She certainly hadn't been waiting around to see if he'd turn up. Which made Quin fighting mad. She wanted the deal kept to the letter, then let her keep it, too. Tonight she had to be available to him!

The worst of it was he'd thought she'd been softening towards him, actively wanting to spend time together, enjoying their nights. He'd believed he'd been making headway towards drawing her into the same close relationship they'd had before. Tonight it had struck him forcibly that he now had more than enough money to do anything he wanted, and what he wanted most was Nicole Ashton. It didn't matter if he lost a lucrative client. It did matter if he lost Nicole again.

If she needed a demonstration of how important she was to him, fine…but it wasn't fine to have his demonstration shown up as totally irrelevant to her. A fierce resentment put a savage twist to his ringing of the doorbell, which was an old-style metal mechanism, not a modern button, and much more satisfying to operate— snapping it back and forth, back and forth. However, the loud clanging seemed to echo through an empty house, which drove his frustration higher.

If Nicole had gone out, he'd camp on this porch until she returned and insist she make up the time he'd been kept waiting. His gaze skated around, looking for a chair. No chair. But in the far corner…a doll's pram? Must have been overlooked and left behind by the friend who had the little girl.

His hand was still working the bell when light suddenly shone through the glass panels of the door. So someone was at home! He kept the loud ringing going to encourage a fast response to it. The blurred image of a woman appeared behind the stained glass. The door rattled as it was hastily unlocked. Quin dropped his hand to his side and composed himself to confront Nicole with his refusal to forfeit.

The door opened.

The woman facing him was not Nicole.

She had short hair and was middle-aged. Her dressing-gown had not been properly adjusted and her hair was mussed—clear indications that she'd been disturbed from sleep. Her initial expression of confused alarm changed to sharp annoyance as he simply stared at her, coming to the realisation that this had to be Nicole's mother, Linda Ellis.

"Who are you? What's the problem?" she rapped out.

He looked her straight in the eye and said, "My name is Quin Sola and I have business with your daughter, Mrs Ellis."

"You!" It was a gasp of shock. In the next instant her whole body was recoiling from him as though he was the worst possible news.

Quin frowned over the reaction. Although they'd never met, Linda Ellis certainly knew his name and obviously it didn't conjure up good feelings. Which raised the question…what had Nicole been telling her about him? Didn't being rescued from financial ruin give her mother cause enough to be more welcoming towards her benefactor?

"Is Nicole here?" he asked, deciding quite a few things needed to be confronted and settled in this household.

Linda Ellis didn't answer.

She didn't have to answer.

Over her shoulder he caught sight of Nicole stepping into the hall from a room at the back of it. She carried a child, a little girl whose head was snuggled into the curve of her neck and shoulder. Both of them were wrapped in hurriedly donned dressing-gowns.

"What is it, Mum?"

The words had tripped off Nicole's tongue before she saw him. When her mother stepped back to reveal his presence and recognition hit, her forward momentum along the hall came to a dead halt, shock radiating from her frozen stillness.

The little girl lifted her head and looked directly at Quin, wanting to find a reason for the sudden stop, the silence. She had short black hair, cut in a bob. Her large and thickly lashed eyes were surprisingly light—a smoky grey—and Quin thought there was something familiar about her face, but...

"Do you know this man, Mummy?" the child asked.

Mummy!

Quin's gaze jerked to Nicole's. Anguish in her eyes now, not shock. A flood of heat turned her cheeks scarlet. Her throat moved convulsively, swallowing hard, needing words to emerge from it but not finding them easy to form. Her chin lifted, signalling defiant pride before she finally spoke.

"He's just someone passing by, Zoe." This relegation to insignificant status in her life was accompanied by a glare that rejected any other possibility in the future. "Please excuse me while I put my daughter back to bed."

The child looked curiously at him over her mother's shoulder as Nicole wheeled and headed back down the hall. There was something about the little girl's eyes, her face...the odd familiarity niggled past the stunning fact of her existence in Nicole's life. His mind almost burst with the intuitive leap that speared through it.

My child!

Certainty gripped him as he judged the little girl to be about four years old. Mother and daughter disappeared from view, re-entering the room from which they had emerged. He switched his attention to Linda Ellis, his eyes boring into hers for the truth.

"She's mine, isn't she? *My* child!"

Her hand lifted to her throat as though instinctively moving to choke off any admission. She shook her head in frightened agitation. To Quin's mind there was no reason for fear unless the connection was true and the plan was to keep him in ignorance. *As they had for the past five years!*

He brushed past Nicole's mother and charged down the hall, the need to have his certainty absolutely confirmed pumping through him. The door to the bedroom had been left slightly ajar. He pushed it open.

The overhead light was still on and Quin was momentarily distracted by the startling vision of the butterfly tree, set in front of a bay window, its long, twisted, greyish white driftwood branches loaded with dozens of beautiful butterflies in all sizes and colours. A wonderful decoration for a little girl's room, he thought, wrenching his gaze away from its fascination to target the mother and child who'd just flipped his life into another dimension.

Nicole was by the bed, bent over in the act of removing the little girl's dressing-gown, blocking him off from her daughter—*their* daughter. The urge to stake a claim here and now was far too strong for Quin to deny.

"Your mother is mistaken, Zoe," he said.

Nicole straightened up and whipped around, shooting him a killer look for intruding on what she considered her territory.

Not just hers any more, he silently resolved, strolling forward, his gaze fastened on the child who was so clearly flesh of his flesh, blood of his blood. *She* was not frightened of him, not his daughter. She stood her ground, looking gravely at him, waiting to hear what the mistake was, and Quin was flooded by a tumultuous mix of emotions—wonder, pride, tenderness, a fierce need to protect, the desire to hold her close, hug her tight.

But he was a stranger to her and restraint was called for until she accepted him for who he was. He squatted down to speak to her at eye level. "I'm not just someone passing by," he explained. "I've been away for a long time. All your life so far. But I aim to stay around for the rest of it."

"Quin!" The grated protest from Nicole drew Zoe's attention to her.

"That's my name," he quickly said, offering a smile that promised he was harmless. It persuaded their daughter into looking directly at him again. "My full name is Joaquin Luis Sola, but most people, like your mother, call me Quin for short. I'm very, very glad to meet you, Zoe."

He offered his hand.

She glanced up at her mother for instruction but none was forthcoming. Quin could feel Nicole staring at him—huge tension emanating from her—but he kept his concentration focused on Zoe, willing her to respond to him.

Her gaze dropped to his hand. After a long, breathless moment, she tentatively offered hers. Quin couldn't help grinning in happy triumph as he took it. Her sweetly curved mouth—Nicole's mouth—returned a shy smile.

"Hello," he said encouragingly, loving the soft warmth of her little hand in his.

"Hello," she returned, her eyes locked onto his, wanting to know more of him.

And the words simply spilled out of Quin.

"I'm your daddy."

CHAPTER TEN

NICOLE'S mind was jammed with so many conflicting thoughts it was impossible to produce any sensible response to Quin's declaration. She listened dumbly as Zoe started her own childish interrogation, trying to understand where Quin was coming from, why he was here now.

"My daddy?" she queried wonderingly.

"Yes," Quin confirmed, admitting no doubt whatsoever. "Look for yourself," he invited. "We have the same eyes, the same hair, the same nose. I'm your father."

Silence while she studied the face in front of her. Then she looked up at Nicole for assurance. "Is it true, Mummy?"

Nicole's head ached from the terrible mental traffic racing through it. Her heart was squeezed by so many painful emotions, it struggled to keep beating. Her mouth was hopelessly dry. "Yes," she croaked out, realising it would be futile to deny it.

Zoe returned her gaze to the father who had been missing all her life and with artless innocence asked,

"Where have you been, Daddy? Why have you come now in the middle of the night?"

Quin didn't even pause to think. He came straight out with, "I've been lost in another world to yours, Zoe. And I've only just found my way here. I couldn't wait until tomorrow to see you. I hope you don't mind."

Magnetic charm was pouring out of him.

And Nicole hated him for it.

Winning over their daughter when he hadn't paid a moment's pain for her wasn't fair. Nowhere near fair.

"Will you be here tomorrow?" Zoe asked.

"That depends on whether your mother will let me stay," he answered.

"Mummy?" A look of appeal from Zoe.

"We mustn't count on it," she warned her daughter before shooting a fuming look at Quin. "Your father might have to go back to his other world."

"Do you have to, Daddy?" Zoe asked directly.

"Not if I can help it, but your mother and I need to talk about how we can be together. If I'm not here tomorrow, I promise I'll be back very soon. Okay?"

He smiled at her.

She smiled back, believing him. "Okay."

"Back to sleep now," Nicole commanded, unable to bear any more togetherness between Quin and her daughter. She lifted Zoe into bed and tucked her up tightly, wanting to shield her precious child from the man who could make a terrible mess of their lives.

"Good night, darling," she murmured, pressing a fervent kiss on her forehead—a kiss of love that spanned years, not a few minutes.

"'Night, Mummy. Is my Daddy going to kiss me goodnight, too?"

"Yes, he is," Quin asserted before Nicole could reply, and she had to stand back and let him do it, fighting a mountain of fierce resentment at his assumption of a role he hadn't earned.

She closed her ears to the all too intimate murmurs between them and walked to the door, impatient to usher Quin out, get him away from her daughter.

He came promptly enough not to stir her anger any higher, glancing at the butterfly tree before he passed out of the room. She switched off the light, closed the door, and led off to the kitchen which was far enough away from Zoe for a private conversation to be held without any risk of disturbing her.

The smell of newly made hot chocolate—a comfort drink—indicated that her mother was still up, anxiously waiting to be cued about what to do next. She burst into fearful speech the moment Nicole entered the kitchen.

"I didn't tell him, Nicole. He guessed."

"It's not your fault, Mum. It's mine for not agreeing to a postponement. He came to claim his night." Acutely aware of the man just behind her, she turned to shoot him a derisive look. "Right, Quin?"

"Right!" he agreed ironically.

"But it is my fault!" her mother cried, looking hopelessly wretched about the situation. "If I hadn't got so deeply in debt, you would never have gone to him, never..."

"Wrong, Mrs. Ellis," Quin cut in strongly, moving up to stand beside Nicole. "The moment I saw Nicole again, I was determined to get her back in my life one way or another. Your debt was simply a means to the end I wanted."

The ruthless purpose in his voice sent a convulsive shiver down Nicole's spine. Would he now *use* Zoe to keep her sexually tied to him?

Her mother looked distractedly at Quin, not understanding the strict parameters attached to his idea of a relationship. "Why? It's not fair!" she cried. "You didn't want my daughter enough to marry her when it counted."

"At the time, I didn't know how much it counted, Mrs. Ellis," he replied in a tone of quiet gravity.

Didn't *want* to know, Nicole thought.

"You carry no blame for anything to do with me and Zoe, Mum," she quickly asserted. "You've been wonderfully supportive all along. So please don't fret over this. It's up to me to sort it out with Quin. If you'll just leave us alone…"

Her mother heaved a ragged sigh, rubbed her forehead in agitation, then picked up her mug of hot chocolate and moved to leave the kitchen, looking totally dispirited.

Quin spoke. "This probably won't mean much to you, Mrs Ellis, but I'm sorry I wasn't here for Nicole and Zoe, and I thank you very sincerely for supporting them throughout my absence."

She stopped beside him, looked sharply into his eyes, shook her head as though the situation was completely beyond her, then walked off without another word, heading for her bedroom.

Nicole moved briskly to the refrigerator, intending to

get out the milk to make a hot comfort drink for herself *and* gain some fighting distance from Quin. When her mother's bedroom door closed loudly enough to punctuate their privacy in the kitchen she turned on him, spitting mad.

"Sorry? You aren't sorry about one damned thing, Quin! Nothing was ever going to stop you from doing what you wanted. Not back then. And not now, either. You just don't care how *what you want* affects other people."

He was still just inside the kitchen, his immobility radiating the air of a powerful animal, watching and waiting for the moment to move into attack. "I would have made adjustments if you'd told me you were pregnant, Nicole," he stated unequivocally, his eyes burning that truth into hers.

She glared her own truth straight back at him. "You didn't make any for me, Quin."

"I did, actually." His mouth twisted with irony. "It cost me quite a bit to set up an apartment so we could live together."

"Money!" she retorted with blistering scorn.

"Money that wouldn't have been spent, but for you."

"Because you *wanted* me."

"And I would have wanted our daughter, too," he returned as quick as a whip.

"Well, I chose for us not to be your possessions, Quin," she flashed back at him. "That was all I was to you, and all our daughter would have been, too. Possessions you had to pay for."

In a fury of resentment she jerked the refrigerator door open, removed the bottle of milk, slammed the door shut, turned to the sink, got a mug from the overhead cupboard and started spooning in chocolate powder from the tin her mother had left on the bench. Her hands were shaking.

"I'm sorry I made you feel that."

She gritted her teeth. No way would she let the soft tone of his apology get to her. Empty words. All too easy to say when the past was the distant past. She willed her hands to be steady for pouring the milk over the chocolate powder.

"I thought we were two single adults, making careers for ourselves, and lucky enough to have something good and mutual going," he added ruefully, then had the hide to say, "I was as much your possession as you were mine, Nicole."

She swung around to shoot him down. "Only when we shared a bed! Out of it you had your own agenda, which possessed you far more strongly than I ever did." Her eyes stabbed any possible protest from him. "Don't deny it, Quin. I lived with how it was for you. And how it was for me. I know."

His face visibly tightened at the hit.

He said nothing.

She turned back to shove the mug into the microwave and set the timer. The seconds on the digital clock started ticking down. It was a terribly slow countdown compared to the galloping beat of her heart, but she watched it obsessively, willing time away because she wasn't ready to face what Quin's knowledge of Zoe might mean to their lives.

"If you don't want me in your life, Nicole," he said

slowly, quietly, "why did you risk coming to me that night in The Havana Club?"

"To make you pay," she blurted out.

"Pay for what? I never did anything to you that you didn't want."

"It was what you didn't do," she muttered fiercely, then braced herself to swing around and directly argue her case. "I used the sex, which was all you wanted me for, to pay for this roof over our heads, to pay for the dance school to keep going so it could support us. So you've done your paternal duty, Quin. You don't have to put yourself out to be *a father* to Zoe. We can manage just fine without you."

The timer on the microwave beeped.

Quin's gaze was locked on hers and she could feel him gearing up to use every atom of power he had to fight the position she'd just taken. It had better not be just pride driving him, she thought savagely. Zoe would be expecting more than that from her new *daddy*.

"I guess I deserve that," he said, finally acknowledging he had put limitations on their relationship in the past.

Unaccountably a rush of tears blurred her eyes. Rather than let him see them, she swiftly turned to the microwave oven, taking out the mug of steaming hot chocolate and nursing it in her trembling hands.

"But the punishment for my crimes of omission stops here, Nicole." The ruthless determination in his voice battered her frayed defences. "I didn't come tonight to claim what you owe me. I came to prove that being with you was more important than anything else. To show that I didn't want to miss any minute that you would grant me." Then more softly, "To make it different for you this time."

She shook her head, desperately trying to ignore the painful strike at her heart. "I don't believe you've changed, Quin."

"The circumstances have changed."

A bubble of hysteria burst through her brain with the recognition of how drastically they had changed. "Yes, you've found out you have a daughter. And you've put your foot into fatherhood before thinking of what that might mean to a little girl who doesn't know any better than to believe you."

"I won't give her any reason not to believe me," he blasted back without a moment's hesitation.

Anger spurted through her, stiffening her spine and putting a stop to her shakiness. She banged the mug down on the sink and spun to face him, flinging out a mocking gesture as she cried, "Oh sure! Daddy will be on hand whenever Zoe wants him, not just when Daddy finds it convenient to him."

He cut straight through her blistering sarcasm to the heart of the issue. "She wants me on hand tomorrow. Are you prepared to let that happen, Nicole, or isn't it convenient for you?"

The challenge blazing from his eyes allowed her no room to protest the arrangement. If she didn't concede, she was the one keeping *Daddy* away. "It will have to be the morning then," she said belligerently, knowing it would take time off his precious money-making. "Zoe comes with me to the dance school in the afternoon and we stay there until quite late."

"Expect me at seven o'clock tomorrow morning. I presume our daughter is awake by then." He gave her a curt nod and turned towards the hall.

"You're not staying to take your pound of flesh tonight?" she hurled after him, stunned by his decision to leave her now and to return first thing in the morning for Zoe.

He paused in the kitchen doorway and subjected her to a long searing look. "I only ever took what you gave, Nicole," he said quietly. "Perhaps you could start remembering that."

She stared at the empty space he left, listening to him walking down the hall, letting himself out of the house, closing the front door behind him. Everything inside her was aching with a sense of emptiness.

Quin didn't want her tonight.

But she still wanted him.

And it hurt—it really hurt—that he'd spurned the deal they had made.

She was not in control of anything anymore.

Had she ever been in control with Quin or had she simply been deceiving herself, using the deal as an excuse for taking what only he had ever given her?

Now, with their daughter known to him…was everything going to change?

Nicole pushed herself to walk down the hall and lock the front door. Tomorrow morning she would have to unlock it again and let Quin walk into Zoe's life.

He'd better not break her daughter's heart.

She could never forgive him that.

Never!

CHAPTER ELEVEN

QUIN arrived at the Burwood house ahead of time. The early morning traffic had not been as heavy as he had anticipated and he'd been lucky in getting green lights most of the way out of the city centre. Having parked his Audi at the kerb of the suburban street, he remained in the driver's seat, waiting out the minutes before seven o'clock.

Being early would not endear him to Nicole. Given her bitter view of how he'd conducted himself with her in the past, Quin wasn't sure anything was going to endear him to Nicole. Even so, no way would he give up the battle to win her over to his presence in her life, especially now with their daughter in the picture.

Zoe...

Four years he'd missed. And the pregnancy. All because the timing had been wrong for taking his relationship with Nicole beyond immediate needs. He hadn't meant to belittle her place in his life, and he understood why she had felt no deep commitment coming from him, but having his child without his knowledge...that was so big a hit at the kind of man he was, Quin was still trying to come to terms with it.

First and foremost he was a man of honour.

He would have stood by Nicole.

But clearly she hadn't wanted him to, preferring to be on her own, to raise their child without him at her side.

That had to change. He would make it change. The big question was…how best to do it?

He checked his watch. Almost seven o'clock. He picked up the bag containing the blue butterfly from the passenger seat, alighted from the car, locked it and headed for the house, determined on making a positive impact on his daughter's life. Hopefully that might influence Nicole into viewing him with less hostility.

The front door opened just as he reached the porch. Nicole quickly stepped outside, pulling the door closed behind her—an action which instantly signalled her reluctance to let him into the house. Quin halted, observing her keenly as he waited for her to state what this move meant.

Her lovely green eyes were dull with fatigue. Not much sleep, if any, Quin thought. Her long curly hair had been brushed and her general appearance—T-shirt, jeans, sandals—was neat and tidy, but her face was nude of make-up and her skin looked pale and drawn, the strain of having to confront him this morning all too visible.

She stared too long without saying a word and he knew she was seeing him as belonging to a different world in his grey business suit. He sensed it represented pain to her and she didn't want to be anywhere near it again. The problem was they had obviously been at different places in their lives five years ago and she had nursed expectations of him which he hadn't met.

"I'm not in that place anymore, Nicole," he said impulsively, hoping to ease her stress. "I do have to go to work today. I have a business to run, just as you have a dance school to run with your mother. But I no longer have a pressing need to make as much money as I can in as little time as possible. I now have a different perspective on what I want in my life."

She shook her head, a tired disbelief in her eyes. "I realise Zoe came as a shock to you, Quin. You reacted to it without thinking through how much a commitment fatherhood would be." Her mouth moved stiffly into a wry grimace as she amended her words. "Should be."

"I don't have to think it through, Nicole. We're not talking about a proposition here. Zoe is a reality."

"She doesn't have to be," came the swift, anxious rejoinder. "I could explain last night away as a dream. She's not awake yet. You could leave and let me handle all the parenting."

"No!" Steel shot down his backbone. Every muscle tensed in fighting mode. "I won't be wiped out of my daughter's life."

"That's ego talking, Quin, not love." Her eyes searched his in frantic concern. "I don't think you know what love is, and it's not fair to tug on a little girl's heart, then leave it empty of what she'll want from you." Her hands lifted in urgent appeal. "Please...take the time to think about it. At least, leave the decision until I come to you on Friday night."

"Waiting won't make any difference to my decision. You agreed to my coming here this morning, Nicole. I'm not going away."

"I wasn't thinking straight last night."

"Well, I was. And I'm thinking straight this morning, too." He checked his watch. "It's past seven and while you're not delighted to see me, I think my daughter will be, so can we stop this futile argument now and keep to the agreement?"

She looked at him with an angry mixture of fear and frustration. "You don't care, do you? It has to be your way or no way."

"Was your way so good, Nicole?" he countered. "Keeping Zoe to yourself? Not caring if she might want her father?"

Hot colour raced into her pale cheeks. "You weren't good for *me,* Quin. Why would I believe…"

"Yes, I was," he cut in vehemently. "I *was* good for you or you wouldn't have lived with me for so long. I just wouldn't dance to your strings and I'm not going to dance to them now, either."

He took a step closer to her, his whole body emanating the aggression she had triggered. "Let me into the house, Nicole. We do this peaceably or you'll be facing a court order for visitation rights. You want our daughter dragged into that kind of conflict?"

She shrank back against the door, confused and frightened by the threat, not having imagined he would feel so strongly about claiming his child. But he did. The need to forge a bond with his daughter was raging through him, fuelled by the sense of having been arbitrarily deleted from being a factor in her life for the past four years. On the other hand, if he alienated Nicole too far, he wouldn't get all he wanted.

He tempered the tumult of feeling, forcing himself to speak calmly. "Let's move on from the past, Nicole. We have a future to build for Zoe and cooperation is a better foundation than conflict. Okay?"

Her hand fluttered to her throat as though it was too constricted to allow speech. Her eyes filled with a helpless vulnerability, as though he'd stripped her of defences and she didn't know which way to turn.

"It will be okay. I promise you," Quin pressed earnestly.

She scooped in a deep breath, released it in a shuddering sigh, then stepped back, pushing the door wide open to let him enter. "That's the first really important promise you've made to me, Quin," she said shakily. "I hope it will be kept."

He stopped beside her, lifting a hand to gently cup her face and tilt it towards his, wanting her to look and see the burning sincerity in his eyes. "Let's seal it with a kiss, Nicole."

He didn't wait for a verbal consent. It was enough that she kept looking at him, making no attempt to twist out of his light grasp. The need to connect with her, as well as their daughter, surged through Quin, dictating a kiss of persuasion, not possession. It was important to soothe her concerns, make her feel that he truly, deeply, cared, and the strong sexual desire she'd always stirred in him was not the one and only reason for them to come together.

For a few moments she was completely passive, letting him kiss her but not engaging in it herself. Then her inner tension collapsed and her lips moved in a tentative response, as though curious to taste what he was offering, unsure where he was going with it. Quin didn't push for more. Gaining acceptance and making it stick had to be his primary goal this morning.

He withdrew slowly, softly brushing his lips against hers as he murmured, "A new beginning. For the three of us."

"You'd better make the most of this time with Zoe," she said huskily. "You know the way to her bedroom."

It was a dismissal but not a hostile one.

Satisfied that he had made some breakthrough, albeit a small one, Quin moved on down the hall and quietly opened the door to their daughter's bedroom, quite happy just to look at her if she was still asleep.

He hated having missed four years of her life, deprived of seeing her grow into the child she was now. He should have been familiar with her face and every expression of it. As it was, he was acutely conscious of the need to memorise it so he could call it to mind whenever he wanted.

Zoe was not asleep. She was lying on her side, gazing at the butterfly tree. Early morning sunshine was pouring through the bay window, lighting up the multi-coloured wings, creating a magical sight. A child's wonderland, he thought, giving him a quick appreciation of how loving a mother Nicole had to be. How many women would put their time into such a project?

Then Zoe caught sight of him and scrambled to sit up, a look of pure amazement breaking into a smile of absolute delight. "You came again!"

The tension he had carried into this room instantly slipped away. Deep pleasure in the artless welcome from his daughter warmed his own smile. "And I brought you a present."

He handed her the boutique bag and sat on the bed beside her, happy to watch her surprise, her eager anticipation as she removed the tissue-wrapped glass butterfly, her look of awe when the gift was revealed.

"A Ulysses!" she cried. "How did you know I wanted this one, Daddy?"

"I didn't know." He was amazed she knew the name of the butterfly. "I just noticed last night that you didn't have one on your tree."

"I saw them on TV and I asked Mummy could I have one and she said I had to wait for a special occasion."

"Well, this is a very special occasion," Quin assured her.

"Yes, it is!" Zoe clapped her hands with glee. "My first day with my daddy!"

Something curled around Quin's heart and squeezed it tight.

How many first days had there been?

The day she was born...he didn't even know her birthday!

Her first word...

Her first step...

"Do all the butterflies on your tree mark special occasions, Zoe?" he asked, working hard at keeping his tone light and interested, belying the clawing sense of loss at having been eliminated from every significant signpost in her life.

"Mmm..." She cocked her head, considering her answer. "Most of them I got when I was sick. That was when Mummy started the tree."

Quin frowned over this information. "Were you very sick?"

"Very, very, very sick," she replied, nodding gravely. "I had to be in the hospital 'cause I got…" She hesitated, frowning over the name given to her malady. "Mingitis," came the triumphant recollection.

A chill ran down Quin's spine. "Do you mean…meningitis, Zoe?"

"Yes. That's it!" She looked pleased with his knowledge and repeated the word with careful precision. "Men-in-gitis."

Horror struck hard. Zoe could have died. It was probably a miracle she had survived the deadly illness. He might never have known this beautiful child had ever existed. *His* child…lost before he had found her.

"I'm sorry I wasn't there to make you feel better," he said, heaving a sigh to ease the ache in his chest.

"You were in your other world?"

"Yes." He was intensely grateful for her simple acceptance of what he'd said last night. "I didn't know what was happening to you. I wish I had known."

"That's all right, Daddy. You couldn't help it."

He would certainly help it from now on, Quin fiercely resolved.

"I was too sick to get out of bed when I was in the hospital," Zoe went on. "Mummy said I was like a little caterpillar in a cocoon and I had to wait there until I was strong enough to be a butterfly, free to dance in the open air and feel beautiful."

"You *are* beautiful."

Her eyes shone with happiness. He wanted to pick her

up and hug her tight but caution insisted not yet. It might be too soon for her to feel comfortable with it. He was still virtually a stranger to her, despite their blood relationship.

"Let's find a place for the Ulysses on the tree," she cried excitedly, throwing off the bedcovers and jumping onto the floor. With the glass butterfly being carefully carried in her little hands, she was halfway to the bay window when she stopped, glancing back at him.

Quin hadn't moved. He was entranced by everything about his daughter; the cute girly way she walked, the soft roundness of her arms and legs, the smooth perfection of her young skin, the black bob of thick hair somewhat awry from a night in bed.

He was smiling and she flashed him a quick smile in response before saying, "I've got to get Mummy. She sticks the butterflies on the tree with glue tac."

"Right!" he approved.

"And I have to go to the bathroom," she confessed shyly.

"We all need to do that when we first get up in the morning," he assured her.

Relieved by his understanding, she rushed back and handed him her gift. "You mind the Ulysses until I come back." Her big grey eyes flashed an eloquent appeal. "Don't go away."

"I'll stay right here."

"That's good, Daddy."

Another quick smile and she was off, pelting out of the bedroom to do what had to be done in double-quick time.

He heard her calling out to Mummy and Nanna, her high childish voice bubbling with excitement. Quin had to concede that both women had given his daughter a loving home and brought her up to be a wonderfully natural child. Even the trauma of a serious illness had not left a shadow on her life.

He probably hadn't been missed at all.

Nobody missed what they hadn't ever known.

Nicole was worried about his intrusion, worried about its effect on Zoe. She didn't trust him to follow through on this initial impact. Quin realised that only time would prove her wrong, but how long was it going to take? He had already lost too much time he could never get back.

He looked down at the blue butterfly Zoe had placed in his hands as a surety against his departing before she returned. At least his daughter trusted in his word. Quin vowed she'd never have reason not to trust it. While it might be impossible to shield her from pain in her life, he would try his utmost not to be the cause of it.

And one thing Nicole could not deny—he had given his daughter pleasure this morning. Every opportunity he had, he would continue to do so. What he needed to do was set up as many opportunities as possible.

Zoe came racing back into the room, Nicole following her reluctantly despite the excited urging. "Come and see, Mummy. It's made of glass. Show her, Daddy."

Nicole flashed him a hard, resentful look.

Quin stood up, holding out the gift to his daughter. "You show her, Zoe. It's yours."

She took it carefully and turned to her mother who hadn't wanted him to buy it, who'd refused to take it from him. He now understood Nicole's intensely negative attitude towards it. Butterflies were too intimately connected to the life of her daughter—a life he hadn't shared and wasn't intended to ever share.

"I think it will be too heavy for glue tac to hold it on the tree, Zoe," she said with a seriously concerned look on her face. "You wouldn't want it to fall off and break."

Quin felt himself tensing up.

Okay, he hadn't been a part of the tree but he'd been given no choice in Nicole's decision to keep him ignorant of his daughter's existence. Given the chance, he would have been here for Zoe, looking after her as best he could. To deny him a place at this point in time was being deliberately obstructive to any new beginning. If she couldn't give this much…

"But, Mummy, we have to put it on," Zoe insisted. "It's my first butterfly from Daddy. Could we tie it to a branch?"

Out of the mouths of babes, Quin thought, looking at Nicole to see how she would fight the challenge from their daughter.

"That would spoil the look of it, Zoe. It's too beautiful to put string around it. Why don't we just put it on the windowsill and pretend it's fluttered down to rest there?"

Zoe swung around to face the bay window and study the position. After a few moments she walked over and carefully placed the Ulysses on the sill, then stood back to gauge the effect. She slowly shook her head. "It's not the same as being on the tree, Mummy. It looks lonely down there."

The outcast, Quin thought grimly.

"Well, maybe your father will buy more in the future

to keep it company," Nicole answered, her eyes glittering a fierce challenge at him.

"This won't be a one time thing, Zoe," he quickly assured her, also notifying Nicole he was not about to go missing in the future. "But if you want the Ulysses on the tree, I'll buy a silver chain to tie it on and make it shine even more beautifully. How about that?"

Her little face lit up with delight. "Oh, that would make it very special, Daddy!"

"Right!" He didn't care how much Nicole might resent it. In fact, seizing opportunity rather than waiting for it seemed a very good idea. "I'll bring the chain with me on Saturday morning and if it's okay with your mother, we could spend the whole day together."

"Mummy?" Zoe cried expectantly.

Nicole forced a smile for her daughter. "Okay. Now I think you should get dressed and go and have the breakfast Nanna is preparing for you."

"Can Daddy have breakfast with me?" she asked eagerly.

"No, your father has to go to work. That's why he's wearing a suit. It was very good of him to come this morning especially to see you. Have you thanked him for his gift?"

"Oh, no, I haven't!" Zoe looked at him, appalled at having forgotten to do so.

Seizing opportunity again, Quin smiled encouragingly and held out his arms to her. "How about a hug and a kiss?"

She flew at him in happy relief. Quin lifted her up against his shoulder and her little arms wound around his neck as she planted a big wet kiss on his cheek. "Thank you, Daddy. I love my Ulysses."

It was said with such fervour, Quin felt his heart turn over. It was all he could do to control his embrace and not squeeze her too tightly. This beautiful child was his and he didn't want to let her out of his possession. Then he caught sight of the pained look in Nicole's eyes and knew that pushing this visit any further would be counter-productive to holding the ground he'd already taken.

"I'm glad it's very special for you, Zoe," he murmured, his voice husky with pleasure. "I'll come again on Saturday."

"Don't get lost in your other world again, will you, Daddy?"

"No. Now that I've found you, there's no chance of that happening."

"Good!"

She grinned happily at him and he grinned right back as he set her down on her feet. "Better do what Mummy says. Bye for now, Zoe."

"You won't forget the silver chain?"

"I'll go shopping for it at lunchtime today. You work out where you'd like to hang the Ulysses on the tree, and we'll do it first thing on Saturday morning."

She sighed her contentment.

"Be a good girl for Mummy," he said in parting.

"I will. Bye, Daddy."

Nicole accompanied him out of the bedroom in tight-lipped silence, shutting the door behind them. As they walked down the hall, Quin asked, "Do you have any photo albums of Zoe's life so far?"

"Yes," came the curt, uninviting answer.

"I'd like to see them," he pressed.

"I'll bring them with me on Friday night."

Not letting them out of her possession.

"Thank you. And thank you for Zoe, too, Nicole. She's a wonderful child."

"Yes, she is."

It was said so vehemently, he could hear the unspoken words—*And you'd better not change that, Quin Sola!*

They stepped out on the front porch and Nicole halted by the front door. "Don't start spoiling her with what your money can buy, Quin," she warned.

He nodded. Money was the big issue between them. Quin realised they could not truly make a new beginning until he'd addressed Nicole's perception of him.

"We'll have a lot to talk about on Friday night," he said, locking eyes with her. "Whatever you feel I did or didn't do in the time we lived together, you've paid me back with a vengeance, Nicole, withholding my child from me all these years."

She flinched at the hit, then lifted her chin defiantly. "It was for the best."

"We'll never know, will we? Just don't forget the photo albums. That would be inflicting serious injury on top of insult."

He left her with those words.

There was a lot to be organised and achieved before Friday night.

CHAPTER TWELVE

NICOLE had not heard from Quin since Tuesday morning, not by telephone nor by e-mail. She arrived at his apartment at eight o'clock on Friday evening, not knowing what to expect from him, trying not to expect anything but the usual sex-fest that characterised their nights together.

This was the thirteenth night, and while she wasn't superstitious, Nicole could not shake an ominous feeling about it. The deal was still on but the limits of the situation had changed with Quin's knowledge of Zoe and his determination to be a father to their daughter.

A new beginning...but a new beginning to what?

Was Quin capable of making the future different to the past?

She was carrying a much larger bag than usual, having brought the photo albums he'd requested and her grip on its handles was so tight, her nails were digging into her palm as she waited for the door to open. It hurt to let Quin into the years that had belonged to her and Zoe. She felt she was giving up too much too soon. If he didn't keep his promise...

The door opened.

Her heart skittered nervously as she came face-to-face with Quin again. He beamed her a welcoming smile which she couldn't return. The turbulence in her mind and stomach overrode any normal civility.

"Come on in," he said warmly. "There's someone here I want you to meet."

Shock completely paralysed any movement forward. She couldn't believe he would bring a third party into a night of personal and private revelations. Or weren't the photos of Zoe's life important to him—just a curiosity which could be satisfied any time at all?

Her mouth finally returned to working order. Enough to say, "I don't think so, Quin." Glaring steely determination, she added, "Our deal doesn't involve anyone else."

He sucked in a deep breath. The bullet-grey eyes seared hers with their own determination and the welcoming air changed to ruthless purpose. "It's my mother, Nicole. Come all the way from Argentina to meet you and her grand-daughter."

His mother!

Whom she had never been invited to meet in the past!

Nicole's mind reeled over this totally unexpected move from Quin. What did he mean to gain by it? How was she supposed to respond?

"Argentina?" she repeated dazedly.

"That's where her family lives. My mother returned there three years ago to be with them. It's her home country."

"Yours, too?" Nicole croaked, desperately trying to slot this new information into her very limited knowledge of Quin's background.

A careless shrug accompanied his reply. "Not any-more. I've made my home here. Please…my mother is tired from the fourteen-hour flight from Buenos Aires, but she wants so much to meet you…"

He stepped back, beckoning Nicole into his pent-house. Her feet moved, pulled by a curiosity that demanded satisfaction. As Quin ushered her past the open kitchen area, she saw a woman rising to her feet from one of the leather sofas near the view of the har-bour—a tall, handsome woman, whose strong-boned face was etched with fatigue, her heavy-lidded, dark eyes looking almost bruised by the shadows around them.

Her only make-up appeared to be a plum-red lipstick, and her iron-grey hair was pulled back into a neat bun. Despite this austerity, or because of it, she exuded a rather intimidating dignity, probably enhanced by the stylish black suit she wore and the jet earrings and necklace, all of which made Nicole feel overwhelmingly underdressed for this meeting in her jeans and peasant blouse.

Her feet faltered, coming to a halt as the thought struck that she was probably viewed as a loose woman by Quin's mother—living with her son, having his child out of wedlock, not even telling him about the pregnancy so they couldn't be properly married as *good girls* undoubtedly would in Argentina. A tide of hot embarrassment raced up her neck and burnt her cheeks even as she feverishly reasoned this was all Quin's fault, not hers. She'd done what *he'd* wanted until it had become too…too *wrong!*

Quin pried the carry-bag from her grip, passing it to his other hand as he took hold of her elbow to draw her forward. "Nicole, this is my mother, Evita Gallardo."

"Not…not Sola?" Nicole babbled in bewilderment.

"When I returned home, I resumed my maiden name," Quin's mother explained, wincing apologetically at her son as she added, "There was too much shame attached to the name of Sola."

"Shame?" Nicole repeated, feeling utterly confused.

Quin's mother had moved to meet her and was now holding out both hands in what seemed like appeal…or was it in greeting? Nicole quickly offered her own and they were taken and pressed, the dark eyes of Evita Gallardo suddenly transmitting an anxious concern.

"It is a long story," she said. "And I have come because I owe it to you. I hope you will understand."

Understand what? Nicole almost blurted out, but conscious of already sounding like a parrot, she constrained herself to nodding. Then realising she hadn't even greeted the woman, she hastily said, "I'm very pleased to meet you, Mrs.…um… Miss…? Gallardo."

"Please…call me Evita. We are already family. You have borne me a grand-daughter," came the soft reasoning.

"Right," Nicole agreed, relieved to see no hint of criticism in the dark eyes. There seemed to be more a wish—a need?—for acceptance.

Because of Zoe!

The answer was so obvious, Nicole berated herself for getting uptight about her own impact on Quin's mother. Regardless of how she was viewed, Evita Gallardo would undoubtedly be very guarded against offending the legal custodian of her grand-child. This meeting had to be about establishing amenable contact, opening a gateway into Zoe's life. Which meant Quin had to be very seriously intent on being a constant part of their daughter's future.

"I brought some albums with photos of Zoe," she said, impulsively offering to Evita Gallardo what she had begrudged giving to Quin. Somehow it was different—woman to woman with the shared knowledge of how it was to have a child. "Perhaps you would like to look through them."

"I would like it very much." She squeezed Nicole's hands in fervent gratitude, then released one to wave her own towards the sofa she'd left. "Please come and sit with me."

"Coffee, Nicole?" Quin asked, distracting her momentarily from his mother.

His eyes glimmered with satisfaction, giving Nicole the instant impression this scenario was going exactly as he had planned. Ruthless in going after what he wanted, she thought, but what end did he have in mind? He'd caught her by surprise with this introduction to his mother, and Nicole could feel any control over what would happen next slipping right out of her hands. She saw no alternative but to ride this evening through as best she could. "Yes, please," she answered.

At least having coffee when she first arrived was normal routine. After their first night together she had declined any further dinner invitations, preferring to eat the evening meal with her mother and Zoe before she left home. Besides which, dining out with Quin had seemed too much like dating and she'd wanted to keep the deal a deal with a finish line, not slide back into a relationship with him.

As she accompanied his mother to the sofa, Nicole reflected that it was now impossible to avoid an ongoing relationship, given Quin's stated commitment to being far more than a nominal father to Zoe. Involving his mother was definite proof of how serious he was about it.

Though his mother would undoubtedly return to her home in Argentina and visits from her would probably be few and far between, so her presence here tonight didn't really prove anything.

Nicole sternly cautioned herself against taking mental leaps into a future that might not materialise. She sat down with Evita Gallardo, very conscious that she should take only one step at a time in this murky situation. Assume nothing. Trust nothing. Just go with the flow tonight.

Quin placed her carry-bag on the coffee table in front of them. "Wait for me before you start with the albums," he said. "I don't want to miss anything."

His eyes seared hers with the message he'd missed far too much already and Nicole inwardly bridled at the implied accusation of having shut him out from where he should have been. If he'd given *her* any sense of commitment during their two-year relationship, she wouldn't have chosen to be a single parent.

"Of course, we will wait," his mother answered a touch anxiously, as though pleasing her son was of paramount importance.

Quin headed off to the kitchen to make coffee and Nicole turned to Evita Gallardo, wanting the background information that Quin had always denied her. "You said the name of Sola carried too much shame. Would you explain that to me, Evita?"

She sighed heavily, giving Nicole the distinct impression that it took a huge effort to reveal a history, which was obviously a source of personal pain and embarrassment. The dark eyes held sadness and deep regrets as she began to speak.

"My husband, Luis Sola, was a very handsome, very charming, very clever man. I was…under his spell…for many years, believing he was everything he portrayed himself to be. But he used our marriage to gain access to people of wealth he would not have met otherwise, and he defrauded them, as well as members of my family, of a great deal of money. One day, everything seemed normal, and the next he was gone, leaving me and our son to face the scandal of his treachery."

"That must have been very difficult," Nicole murmured sympathetically.

Evita shook her head and heaved another sigh. "I could not bear it. And it was particularly bad for Joaquin, who had to carry the stigma of his father's crimes at school. He was only thirteen and suddenly he was ostracised from everything. Even my family shunned him. Because he looked so very much like Luis, he was most unfairly cast as a bad seed who would also bring shame upon us all."

"But you didn't believe that," Nicole said encouragingly, caught up in the story and wanting to hear more.

"I know my son. He is a Gallardo through and through." There was a flash of pride in the pained eyes. "It was better for him that we accept exile in Australia than to stay in Buenos Aires where he would never be trusted. So we came here and Joaquin vowed he would prove them all wrong."

"How?"

"By making restitution, returning all the stolen money."

This was the driving force behind his single-minded ambition to make as much money as he could, Nicole realised, stunned by how little she had known about the man she had loved.

"Once we were settled here, he worked very hard. Studied hard," his mother went on. "He won a special scholarship to a university and got a business degree, then moved straight into a bank to learn how to make money from money."

"Which he proceeded to do with extraordinary success. The star player," Nicole commented wryly.

Evita nodded, then eyed her ruefully. "When he met you and left the house my father had provided for us to be with you, it meant his feeling for you was very strong. It worried me that it would pull him away from fulfilling what I had dreamt about—returning to Buenos Aires with great pride in my son and what he had achieved."

She lifted her hands in an appeal for forgiveness as she added, "I would not meet you. I would not give you any status in Joaquin's life. I would not let him even speak of you to me. So it is because of my selfishness…"

"You don't have to go that far, *Madre*," Quin interrupted as he carried the cappuccino over to where they sat. "I wasn't about to let anything prevent me from achieving what I'd resolved to do." He set the coffee cup down on the table and looked straight at Nicole. "I thought I could have my cake and eat it, too, but in doing so, I lost far more than I'd bargained for."

Zoe, he meant.

The restitution mission had won out over any commitment to the relationship they'd shared, no matter how strongly he had felt about her. Though she guessed the deep-seated trauma of what had happened when he was thirteen was not something that could be easily set aside, especially when he had the end-goal in his sights.

"I presume you did win respectability back in Buenos Aires since your mother now lives there," she remarked.

"Yes. All the debts were paid with interest three years ago," he answered almost cynically, no pride at all in his achievement.

His mother promptly supplied the pride. "It was such an honourable deed, my family finally embraced him as one of their own."

"Why didn't you stay?" Nicole asked, curious to know why he'd turned his back on the status of hero.

His eyes flashed mockingly. "My name is Joaquin Luis Sola. I am still my father's son, and that means nothing in Australia."

"A clean slate," Nicole interpreted.

"Not so clean." His gaze dropped to the carry-bag. "Could we look at the photo albums now?"

His mother's words—*an honourable deed*—kept playing through Nicole's mind as she removed the albums from the bag and stacked them on the table in the right order. Was his *not so clean slate* centred on Zoe now? Was it a matter of honour for him to be a good father to his daughter?

Honour wasn't love.

And neither was lust.

She would have to be very, very careful not to colour

Quin's current moves with feelings he didn't have. That could lead to big mistakes, and it wasn't just herself who would end up paying for them. She didn't want Zoe's innocent acceptance of Quin as her father to result in a long string of hurtful disappointments. Though how she could prevent that now, she didn't know.

He sat down beside her as she rested the oldest album on her lap, ready to turn to the first baby photograph of Zoe. It meant she was sandwiched between her daughter's father and grandmother on the long leather sofa, and the sense of inevitable involvement with both of them weighed heavily on her mind and heart, making her feel tremulous inside.

She couldn't stop her hand from shaking a little as she opened the album and her voice turned husky from a sudden welling of emotion. "This is Zoe on the day she was born."

She looked so tiny in the hospital baby trolley, all bundled up with only her face showing—a rather red face framed by a surprisingly thick mass of spiky black hair. Her eyes were shut and the crescents of long thick eyelashes were also stunningly black.

"Oh! She looks just like Joaquin when he was born!" Evita marvelled, clasping her hands over her heart as though all her prayers had been answered.

"No, *Madre*." Quin's arm reached out, a finger gently touching the baby's full lower lip in the photograph. "This perfectly shaped mouth comes directly from Nicole. And Zoe is very much a little girl, not a boy."

A mouth he knew all too intimately, Nicole thought, feeling his strongly muscled thigh pressing against hers and cravenly wishing there was more than hot sex driving the desire that constantly simmered between them. It hurt that there wasn't, even more now than it had in the past as she continued to show the baby photographs of their daughter whom she now had to share with him.

After that first correction to his mother, he sat in silence, intently viewing the progression of Zoe's infancy to the toddler stage. It was Evita who peppered Nicole with questions and made increasingly infatuated comments about her beautiful grand-daughter. Quin just looked, and Nicole grew more and more conscious of tension emanating him, a turbulent tension that swirled with all he restrained himself from saying. She could feel him thinking, *I missed out on this, and this, and this*…and the bitter vengefulness that had driven many of her thoughts and actions started sliding into guilt.

Had she been terribly wrong to keep Zoe from him?

His silence continued through the second album and almost to end of the third. It wasn't until Nicole turned a page to reveal a much thinner Zoe standing beside the newly constructed butterfly tree, that he made a sound— a low gravelly rumble in his throat. Then…

"This must be after she was struck down with meningitis."

"Meningitis!" Evita cried in horror.

Shock rolled through Nicole. She had not told Quin of Zoe's illness so how did he know? Her head jerked around to look at him and she caught a poignant look of pain and anger in his eyes before he bent forward to answer his mother.

"Fortunately Zoe recovered with no long-term ill

effects from it, *Madre*. And Nicole came up with the brilliant idea of creating a butterfly tree to help her look forward to being completely well again. Which she is. Delightfully so," he added gruffly.

Zoe must have told him when he gave her the Ulysses butterfly. He was glossing over the terrible worry of that time to soothe his mother's concerns, but Nicole was deeply disturbed by the reaction he was now covering up. Did he really care so much? Had she been selfishly unfair in depriving him of his child?

As she proceeded to leaf through the fourth and last album where the photographs demonstrated beyond doubt that their daughter was, indeed, a normal healthy little girl, her mind kept zipping to the fact that Quin would have been free of the long hangover from his father's crimes when Zoe contracted meningitis. But even after he'd returned from Argentina, he had obviously continued to pursue the accumulation of wealth, so he wouldn't have had much time to give to a sick child, anyway.

It was all very well for him to think he might have acted differently. Nicole told herself he had a lot to prove before she'd be convinced his priorities had been reshuffled. Though he had walked away from a business client so as not to lose his time with her. Then visiting Zoe on Tuesday morning...

"Oh! She's learning ballet!" Evita exclaimed in delight.

It was the last photograph in the album—Zoe in her pink dancing costume with a many layered tulle tutu, striking a typical pose with arms arched above her head, one foot planted firmly on the floor and the other pointed.

"She's into all forms of dance," Nicole answered.

"My mother has a dance school and I teach there. Zoe has been attending children's classes most of her life. Not because I put her into them. She just loves dancing."

"Do you think she would dance for me while I'm here?" Evita asked hopefully.

"Let's not leap too far ahead, *Madre,*" Quin swiftly interposed as Nicole closed the album, her mind whirling around his mother's request and not finding a ready reply.

It seemed stupid to feel fearful, yet she had only met Evita Gallardo tonight and she'd had no time to think about introducing another grandmother to Zoe. The sense of being trapped into acknowledging a relationship instead of having a choice about it raised a wave of panic. First, Quin. Now his mother in quick succession. It seemed as though the special bond she had with her daughter was being threatened.

"I did not mean to presume," Evita said, anxiety in her voice and in the hand that reached out and pressed Nicole's. "I am very tired, and seeing the photographs…" She sighed, patting Nicole's hand reassuringly. "I will retire to my room now and leave you with Joaquin to decide on what is appropriate."

Quin stood as his mother rose from the sofa and quickly moved to take her arm. "Is there anything you need, *Madre?*" he asked caringly.

"No." She leaned against him for a moment, then squared her shoulders and nodded to Nicole. "Good night, my dear. I am sorry our meeting was so long delayed."

Nicole returned the nod, unable to bring herself to say anything beyond a courteous, "Good night."

"Stay, Joaquin," his mother commanded. "I can make my own way to my room."

"If you're sure…"

"Yes." She kissed his cheek and walked off alone.

"I'm going to drive Nicole home now. I won't be gone long. An hour at most," he assured her.

Was that *it* for tonight?

Nicole sat in stunned disbelief, watching Quin watch his mother move to the hall leading to the bedrooms.

Then it hit her.

No sex on Monday night.

No sex tonight.

The deal had become irrelevant.

Everything now centred on Zoe.

CHAPTER THIRTEEN

NICOLE didn't notice the class or the comfort of Quin's Audi as he drove it through the city to link up with Parramatta Road which would take them directly to Burwood. She was far too acutely aware of the man sitting beside her and the burning issues that lay between them. They hadn't spoken since leaving his apartment and the silence tore at her nerves.

Having worked some moisture into her dry mouth she asked, "How long will your mother be staying?"

"Until the wedding," came the matter-of-fact reply.

She looked sharply at him. "What wedding?"

Quin flicked her a glittering glance that mocked the question. "The wedding that should have taken place five years ago," he drawled, returning his attention to the road ahead.

She gritted her teeth, barely containing a fierce wave of resentment at his assumption. When she could bring herself to speak again with some semblance of control, the words were grated out with biting emphasis. "We lived together for two years, Quin. Marriage was not on your agenda. I didn't want and still don't want a shotgun wedding because of an accidental pregnancy."

"It *was* accidental then?"

"I certainly didn't plan it," she threw at him, shocked that he could think otherwise.

"You were supposed to be taking a highly effective birth control pill," he reminded her.

"My doctor explained it can lose its effect if one has a bad stomach upset. You might recall the food poisoning I got from a party we attended," she answered curtly, then shot him a puzzled look. "Why on earth would you think I'd deliberately get pregnant?"

He shook his head. "I'm trying to understand why you didn't tell me. Zoe is part of me, too, Nicole. Why couldn't you share her with me? I've missed so much..."

"Why couldn't you share with me what your mother told me tonight?" she shot back at him, refusing to let guilt worm through her consciousness.

"It had nothing to do with you," he answered, instantly justifying the decisions she'd made five years ago.

"You're right!" she snapped. "I was only ever on the edge of your life, not at the heart of it. I couldn't live like that with you any more. And I didn't want it for Zoe, either."

"You were at the heart of pleasure for me, Nicole," he said quietly. "The other was pain."

"Well let me tell you, Quin, love is about sharing both pain and pleasure, and you'd better start learning that if you intend to be a good father to Zoe."

Her voice shook with the strong emotions that had been coursing through her all evening, and she tried valiantly to clamp down on them, not wanting to reveal how much she wanted his love, how much she had always wanted it. His focus on their daughter was actually making her feel jealous of Zoe, and that couldn't lead anywhere good.

They stopped at a red traffic light and Quin turned to her, a deadly serious expression on his face, his eyes intensely concentrated on hers, making her heart thump in the helpless hope she was important to him—deeply, irrevocably important to him. Not just for the pleasure of the sexual intimacy they could so easily achieve. Not because she was the mother of his child. She needed to be the woman he loved above all others, the one he truly would share his life with. All of it. Not some piece he selected to give, excluding her from other parts.

"What you heard from my mother tonight…it wasn't only my life story, Nicole," he said earnestly. "It was hers, too. A very private, painful story that drove her into exile from her home country. She didn't want it told to anyone here. And that wasn't ever going to end until I ended it, as I did when I paid back the money. I'm free of it now, free to take on other responsibilities and give them the attention they should have."

Responsibilities…was that how he thought of marriage and fatherhood? She didn't want it to be a point of honour for him to marry her—a responsibility he had take on and carry for the rest of his life.

"I understand you felt…sidelined…when we were together before," he went on. "I can't go back and change that, but I promise you it will be different this time."

"What? No sex?" she scoffed, the crass challenge

spilling out of her own thwarted desire for him, heating her whole body with an instant wave of shame.

For several seconds the air in the car was charged with steaming frustrations—his and hers. Then a car-horn behind them honked its driver's frustration. The red traffic light had turned green. Quin switched his attention back to the road, put his foot on the accelerator and the Audi responded with a swift surge of speed.

"As much sex as you like," he growled, once they were travelling smoothly again.

Nicole couldn't stop herself from sniping, "Really? I thought that had been sidelined since you met your daughter."

"There've been other things to consider," came the terse reply.

"Like planning a wedding without bothering to get my consent?"

"Like trying to clear up the past so we can build a future on mutual trust."

"We need more than trust to build a future."

"I thought great sex was a given, but if you need that reinforced…"

"I wasn't talking about sex."

"Yes, you were." His eyes smoked anger at her. "If that's the only thing I'm good for, as far as you're concerned, I'll make it so good you can't live without it."

He deftly manoeuvred the Audi across traffic lanes as he spoke and suddenly took a left hand turn, startling Nicole into asking, "What are you doing?"

"Going to a hotel where we'll be assured of absolute privacy."

Her heart catapulted around her chest. She hadn't been talking about sex. Love had been on her mind. Trust and love. Yet she couldn't deny the adrenaline rush at the exciting thought of going to bed with Quin, having him to herself again, drowning out the confusion and conflicts of the past few days with sheer, mind-blasting physical chemistry.

Though it wouldn't solve anything, she told herself, and surrendering to this move without a protest would probably make Quin think he had the power to push her into whatever he wanted. "You told your mother you were taking me home and would soon be back," she rattled out.

It made no impact on him. He turned the car into Elizabeth Street, heading towards Circular Quay instead of out of the city centre. "My mother has my cell-phone number," he stated reasonably. "I doubt she'll worry about where I am but she can always call me to find out."

There was no answer to that.

"And *your* mother won't be expecting you home to-night," he added, shooting her a derisive look. "Right?"

He was referring to the deal.

It was the thirteenth night—a night for which he'd paid an exorbitant amount of money and she had to deliver what had been promised. No argument. The weird part was she had wanted the deal back in place, resenting his involvement with their daughter and the intrusion of his mother, yet now that Quin was obliging her...why was she feeling so at odds with it?

Because too much else was involved now.

And as much as she wanted to, she couldn't just

forget how far he seemed determined to push himself into her life.

They turned into the entrance driveway of a very grand hotel facing Hyde Park. As soon as the Audi halted, a doorman and a parking attendant offered their services. With the car taken care of, they were ushered into a palatial lobby and Quin wasted no time in securing a suite. Within a few minutes, they were in a plush elevator, zooming up to their designated floor.

"Amazing what having lots of money can accomplish," Nicole remarked cynically, thinking of the speed with which Quin's requirements had been met.

"Yes, it wiped out my mother's disgrace, your mother's debts, got you back into bed with me…"

The harshly cynical retort jerked her gaze up to his. Soul-searing anger looked back at her. It stirred all the fermenting emotions that had been plaguing her since he had found out about Zoe.

"You're trying to take more than your pound of flesh, Quin."

"I have a right to more than you agreed to give me."

"You want to be a father to our daughter…fine! But that doesn't mean I have to be your wife."

The elevator doors opened. Quin grasped her arm, steering her out of the compartment, along a corridor, halting briefly to unlock and open the door to their suite, then pulling her inside and kicking the door shut behind them. The fierce turbulence emanating from him was all too evident when he swung her into his embrace for a close face to face confrontation. Stormy-grey eyes raged at her brittle defences.

"Why not? Why not be my wife? You want this as much as I do."

His mouth crashed down on hers, igniting all the pent-up lust that should have been simple and straightforward and easily satisfied with Quin making himself sexually available for this thirteenth night. Nicole responded to his savage plundering with a passionate abandonment of every other concern, but she could not stop her heart yearning for more than a physical union.

Her arms wound around his neck, holding him with a wanton possessiveness. Her body plastered itself to his, seeking its heat, its strength, wanting its rampant need to envelop her, seep into her, fill her with the sense that only she could be his life mate. Her breasts were crushed against his chest, her stomach furrowed by the hard roll of his erection, her thighs quivering under the muscular power pressing against them. A wild chant was running through her mind—*love me, love me, love me…*

He rained kisses on her face, her hair, her neck, her shoulders, and she gloried in the feeling that his mouth was branding her as his. His hands slid down and clutched her bottom, pressing her closer and she ground herself against him in a delirium of desire. He lifted her off her feet, keeping her pinned to him as he strode across the room. They landed on a bed, his body covering hers, their hands tearing at each other's clothes in a frenzied need to be rid of all barriers between them.

At last they were naked, panting from the wild haste to come together. Quin took her hands and slammed them above her head, assuming a domination she would not allow him to have. As he hovered over her, his face

close to hers, his eyes blazing an arrogantly male ownership, she lifted her legs and locked them around his
hips, her own eyes hotly defying him to deny the possession was mutual.

"Tell me it's never been like this with anyone else,"
he demanded, his voice a harsh rasp, as though scraped
from feelings he didn't want to acknowledge, but they
were bursting through him and couldn't be contained.

"You tell me the same thing," she fiercely challenged.

"There's been no other woman in my life who could
match you in any respect," he conceded.

"Well, you top the list, too," she retorted, jealously
wondering how many women that amounted to. "So far,"
she added to stop him thinking he had it made with her
and nothing more was required of him in the longer term.

"Are you expecting to do better?" he growled.

"Maybe the best is yet to come," she answered,
goading him to take their relationship to deeper levels.

"You're right," he said unexpectedly, a wolfish grin
breaking out on his darkly handsome face. "We haven't
got there yet. Just let me get a condom out ready."

"You don't have to use one tonight."

"Then the best—" his lips brushed over hers in tan-
talisingly seductive play as he murmured "—can certainly be achieved."

And he kissed her so erotically, her mind spun with
sensual excitement and every nerve in her body zinged
with anticipation of the intense pleasure Quin would undoubtedly deliver. Which he did. Pure physical bliss.
Her entire being hummed with delicious exultation as
he drove her through climax after climax. Somehow it

was like an ecstatic celebration of being a woman, feeling every part of her femininity being loved, adored, savoured, and she revelled in every moment of it.

And she knew in her heart of hearts, that she would only ever respond to Quin like this. She didn't understand why it was so, but in some deeply primitive way she belonged with him. Maybe it was wrong to expect him to think and feel as she did. He was a man with a strong hunter's instinct, a man who would always go after what he wanted, letting nothing distract him from his prime target.

Could she blame him for being what he was?

Hadn't that always been an integral part of his attraction?

She let herself love him with her hands, her mouth, her legs—a sweet voluptuous loving as she moved in rhythm to the swift, concentrated drive towards his own climax, luxuriating in the fine tension of his body, knowing he was totally focused on reaching this final intimate union with her and nothing else mattered but the moment of spilling himself inside her, the hot fusion that made them one.

She lifted her body in an arch of uninhibited giving as his release came, her inner muscles convulsing in pleasure around him, and her arms tightened their embrace as he collapsed on top of her, hugging the sweet intimacy for as long as she could. Good, better, best...they were meaningless words. It was heaven being with Quin like this. Always had been.

He rolled onto his back, carrying her with him so they still lay entangled. She loved lying on top of him, feeling the rise and fall of his chest as his breathing gradually slowed to normal. He played with the long tresses of her hair, stroked her back, every caress delightfully sensual, and she couldn't imagine ever wanting to make love with anyone else.

But sex was only one part of marriage.

It hadn't been enough to keep her happy with Quin in the past. Would he really share more of himself with her this time around?

The memory of something her friend, Jade Zilic, had said on that fateful night at the Havana Club slid into her mind. It was in answer to her own comment about her previous relationship with Quin—*I don't live at that address anymore.*

Maybe he doesn't, either, Jade had remarked, going on to say that time and timing were very tricky things… shifting sands, different circumstances, revolving doors.

What had driven Quin back then was over, no longer holding any power to influence his behaviour or decisions. Maybe he could really focus on being a decent husband and father. In which case, shouldn't marriage with him be given a chance? The sands had shifted. And Quin had opened the door to fatherhood and walked right in, committing himself to being Zoe's daddy in a very real sense.

The big question was…how far could she trust his commitment?

"Did you buy the silver chain for the Ulysses butterfly?" she asked, testing if he'd remembered his promise to Zoe.

The fingers feathering down her spine stopped their

caress and pressed into her skin. "Yes, I did," he answered emphatically. "I'll bring it with me tomorrow."

So he wasn't about to disappoint their daughter.

But that didn't necessarily mean he would keep the promises made at a wedding ceremony. Zoe was his flesh and blood. Nicole wasn't. And Quin had never said he loved her.

The fingers dug in. "What about my mother, Nicole? She would love to meet Zoe."

She sighed and he lightened his touch, not pressuring for a quick reply. It wasn't easy to decide what to do about his mother. Everything felt so rushed. Yet the woman had flown all the way from Argentina to make amends for her rejection in the past. Though that might only have been because she wanted access to her grand-daughter.

Flesh and blood again.

But to get to it, Nicole Ashton could not be ignored any more. Zoe was her flesh and blood, too.

So it came down to sharing a child who not only belonged to herself and her own mother, but to Quin and his mother, too. *Everything* between herself and Quin came down to sharing and not sharing, she thought with bitter irony.

It had to be conceded that he had taken forceful steps this week to redress their previous situation, and tonight's revelations did explain a lot. They didn't make her feel any better but at least she could understand where he'd been coming from, which made acceptance of his presence in her life a little easier. And if she accepted him, she probably had to accept his mother, too.

Having come to a decision, she took a deep breath

and cautiously lowered her hard-held barriers. "Not tomorrow, Quin. Zoe is expecting to have the day with you. I'll need to speak to my mother about it but perhaps we could all have lunch together on Sunday."

His tense stillness was instantly broken. An audible intake of air expanded his chest, then whooshed out as he heaved himself up and rolled Nicole onto her back. Propped on his elbow, he grinned down at her, pleasure and triumph sparkling in his eyes.

"Don't think that means we're going to talk about a wedding," she shot at him, refusing to be manoeuvred all his way.

His grin diminished into a wry little smile. "Thank you, Nicole. To my mind, there has been more than enough punishment for crimes committed. I'm glad you agree."

Punishment…she frowned over the term. Had she been punishing Quin for not loving her by keeping any knowledge of his child from him? Not consciously, though she certainly had to admit to many vengeful thoughts since meeting him again at the Havana Club.

He lifted a hand and gently smoothed the creases from her forehead. "Don't worry," he murmured in his rich velvet voice. "It will be all right. I promise you."

It was an impossible promise, Nicole thought, but she didn't want to think any more because Quin was kissing her again and stressing over the future could wait until tomorrow. Nothing was going to change between now and then.

He made it easy to pretend there was caring in his kisses, tenderness in the sensuality of his caresses.

Maybe if she pretended enough, she could bring herself to believe he loved her.

And it wasn't just great sex.

CHAPTER FOURTEEN

THIS was his woman, Quin thought, holding Nicole close and revelling in the pleasure of their naked intimacy. It seemed absurd to him that she wouldn't simply accept that he was her man. The sex wouldn't be so good—so great—if they weren't in tune, instinctively meeting each other's needs, responding to whatever was wanted. Why was she resisting the idea of marrying him?

Surely she understood that nothing now stood in his way of giving a firm commitment to a future together. It would be best for Zoe to have her parents married and all three of them living under the same roof. Travelling back and forth for visits was an inefficient use of time.

Quin told himself to curb his impatience. Nicole was a very intelligent person. And reasonable. She was allowing his mother to meet Zoe. That was a big step, given that she had been shut out of his mother's life in the past. It was probably enough at this point to have planted the seed of a wedding, start her thinking about it, not push too hard. The sense of so much time lost was eating at him, but maybe his best play now was a waiting game, gradually wearing down Nicole's resistance to his plan.

She heaved a sigh, the warm spread of her breath across his chest making his skin tingle. His hand automatically began gliding down her spine, seeking more sensory pleasure. He loved every feminine curve of her body, loved the voluptuous softness of her bottom.

"You should go back to your mother, Quin. It must be hours since we left her. The hotel can call a taxi to take me home."

Unwelcome words.

He wanted to immerse himself in feeling.

"It's our night together," he said.

She hitched herself up to address him face to face. "*You* brought your mother into it. People are usually out of kilter with their sleep patterns after a long flight. If she's restless…"

"She can look after herself, Nicole."

Her expression of concern hardened to glittering mockery. "What? She's served your purpose so you don't have to give her any more attention? Still working on that basis, Quin?"

He frowned at the harsh criticism. "My mother understands how important you are to me. She understands I'll be spending as much time with you as I can."

"Of course." Her tone was bitterly ironic. "Your needs come first. They always have."

Before he could counteract the allegation she rolled away from him, off the bed and onto her feet, defiantly declaring, "I'm getting dressed and going home."

"We have a deal," he reminded her, more in frustration than with the intent of keeping her to it.

She had already bent to pick up her clothes from the floor. Very slowly she straightened up, standing with her chin lifted high, meeting his gaze with a look of fierce scorn. "How remiss of me! What with your visit to my daughter tomorrow, and your mother's visit to come on Sunday, I quite forgot I was your paid whore. Perhaps we should revise the arrangements for these family visits."

"No!"

Her arms folded belligerently. "You expect to get everything your own way, Quin?"

He'd struck the wrong note with her and the danger of losing the ground he'd made forced him into a fast re-appraisal of the situation. He propped himself on his side and grimaced apologetically, gesturing an appeal for a stay of judgement as he conceded, "Okay, I guess I'm being selfish, not wanting to let you go. The truth is… I never will have enough of you Nicole, so I'm greedy for whatever you'll give me."

"You're getting more of my time than we bargained for," she stated tersely, not softening one bit.

"I know. And I'm grateful for your generosity."

She looked away from him, thinking her own private thoughts. The tension emanating from her put Quin on edge. Should he get up and hold her, cut the distance she was putting between them? Or give her room to move whatever way *she* wanted?

He waited.

She shook her head, chiding herself as she muttered, "I agreed to stay the night. Twenty-six nights." Her gaze met his derisively. "This is the thirteenth. You still have another thirteen, Quin. I shouldn't have let myself get distracted by other considerations."

The number, thirteen, had never sounded so ominous to him. He had to change what she was trying to put back into place right now. It was suddenly very clear that not even great sex would get him what he wanted with Nicole. He quickly rose from the bed and gently grasped her upper arms to hold her still and concentrate her attention on what he had to say. Her eyes locked onto his, challenging the kind of man he was. He spoke quietly, injecting each word with intensely serious purpose.

"I don't want you as my whore, Nicole. I want you as my wife."

Instant recoil in her expression. No pause to consider. "I guess that would be very convenient for you, Quin, but I don't feel like serving your convenience for the rest of my life," she stated flatly, then nailed her point of view by adding, "I'd like you to see things my way, too."

Red Alert signals went off in Quin's brain.

He instantly moved into damage control.

"You're right. We'll get dressed and go. Which I hope will prove I do care about how you feel." He tried an appealing smile. "Give me time, Nicole. I've been so fixated on forcing my way back into your life, fighting for every minute I get with you, I haven't had the chance yet to show we could have a good future together."

She searched his eyes as though she wanted to believe him but couldn't quite bring herself to do so. "You were free to come looking for me after you finished your business in Argentina three years ago. It took an accidental meeting for you to decide you wanted me again."

"I thought I'd lost you. Seeing you again made me determined to change that."

"I don't want how it was before," she cried.

"It won't be. I swear to you it won't be."

She looked uncertain, fearful.

"Give me time, Nicole," he pressed.

Her eyes closed, as though she couldn't bear to look at him any more. "Well, tomorrow is another day," she said on a deep sigh. "Let's get going."

Knowing he would win nothing by holding onto her any longer, Quin released her arms and they set about dressing in the clothes they had discarded earlier. A sharp sense of disappointment made him wonder if he was fighting a battle that couldn't be won. Her response had not been hopeful. Not even particularly interested.

The silence in the room felt oppressive. It triggered the memory of other silences just before she left him five years ago. They meant an inner withdrawal from him, a retreat to a personal space he couldn't touch, let alone share. He wanted to break into it, reach out to her, drag her back to him, but he realised force was not going to get him where he wanted to be.

For thirteen nights he'd ruled on what he and Nicole did or did not do together. She had been compliant, keeping to the deal, but here they were at the halfway mark, and Quin doubted any progress had been made towards his end goal—keeping her as his life partner.

He called down to reception and ordered his car to be brought up from the parking lot. As he was putting the telephone down, Nicole broke her silence. "Please ask for a taxi to be called, too."

She was brushing her hair, not looking at him.

"I'll drive you home," Quin said decisively.

"That's not necessary."

"It's the middle of the night," he argued. "I'll see you safely home, Nicole."

"What if I don't want you to?"

"Then you'll just have to suffer it because I'm not going to see you off in a taxi as though you were my whore," Quin retorted in exasperation with her determination to stay independent.

No reply to that.

She put her hairbrush back in her handbag and headed for the door. As Quin escorted her out of the hotel room to an elevator, the sobering thought hit him that he was going to fail if he didn't change what was wrong for her.

Their relationship had always been handled *his way*.

Somehow he had to turn that around.

But not on the point of driving her home.

"What time suits you for me to come tomorrow?" he asked as they rode the elevator down to the lobby.

Her head was lowered, the long silky curtain of her hair almost hiding her face. She didn't look up to answer him. "Zoe will be worn-out with excitement if you don't come in the morning," she said dryly. "Nine o'clock would probably be best. Ten at the latest."

"You can tell her I'll be there at nine."

"Don't forget the silver chain."

"I won't."

She nodded, not so much as glancing at him.

Quin could feel his jaw tightening, his hands clenching. He had to battle the instinct to fight. There was no physical conflict between him and Nicole. It was mental, emotional, and laying out his side of the past tonight was not enough to remove the hurt of being consigned to a secondary role in his life. She might very well be thinking that their daughter now had first place. He hadn't brought up marriage before meeting Zoe.

Bad timing.

It had always been bad timing with Nicole.

He needed to make a new plan to win her over.

His car was waiting at the entrance to the hotel lobby. The doorman ushered them over to it and opened the passenger side for Nicole to get in. She stepped forward quickly, lowering herself onto the seat and fastening her safety belt, keeping her head averted from Quin.

Tomorrow is another day, he told himself, reining in his frustration with the current situation as the doorman closed Nicole into the car and he rounded the bonnet to take the driver's seat. He started the engine, but before accelerating away from the hotel he shot a glance at Nicole, wanting to catch her looking at him. She wasn't. Her thick lashes were lowered but they couldn't quite catch the tears that were trickling through them, making shiny wet tracks down her cheeks.

Shock ripped through Quin.

In all the time he'd known her he'd never seen her in tears, and the certain knowledge that he must have caused them appalled him.

What had he said to give her grief?

What had he done?

His mind was in absolute tumult as he automatically manoeuvred the Audi back onto the route to Burwood. It was impossible to shake the image of Nicole sitting miserably alone, sad and defeated by forces that were beyond her control—forces that made her feel terribly vulnerable—no way out because he was Zoe's father.

There was no use arguing he didn't want to hurt her. He had in the past. A promise that it would be different this time probably sounded like empty words to her. Why should she believe it, given her past experience with him when he'd concentrated solely on his needs?

Words were useless.

Taking her to bed with him was useless, too. That was the same as before.

The thirteenth night…

He had to change what was happening on their nights together, show Nicole it was different. He could arrange a dinner party, invite not just his friends but hers, too, like the couple he'd met at the Havana Club, Jade and Jules Zilic. Involving other people might get Nicole to relax more in his company, and drawing her into his social circle would prove he wanted her by his side for more than just sex—his woman—*his wife!*

He heard a siren wailing and immediately checked his speedometer, aware that he hadn't done so and they'd been on Parramatta Road for some time without much traffic to slow them down. It was all right. He wasn't driving above the speed limit. He hadn't drunk any alcohol, either. Maybe the siren came from an ambulance on its way to an emergency.

If that were the case, he might have to pull over into another traffic lane. The rear-vision mirror didn't show any vehicle with flashing lights yet the siren was definitely louder now, probably coming from a nearby street. He thought of Zoe, seriously ill with meningitis. Had she been rushed to hospital by ambulance in the middle of the night? He should have been at her side. At Nicole's side, as well.

It didn't occur to him to stop at the next intersection. The lights were green. There were cars in front of him, cars behind him. He was thinking of the daughter he hadn't known about, the years he'd lost, the years ahead of him and how he wanted to spend them.

He didn't see the car that hurtled straight past the red lights, speeding straight across the intersection towards him until it was too late to take evasive action. There was a split second when he knew it was going to crash into the Audi. Then the impact came and he lost consciousness.

CHAPTER FIFTEEN

PAIN.

Nicole struggled against sickening waves of it, a sense of urgency driving her to keep on fighting them, make it through. There was something she had to remember but her head was swimming in a whirlpool and it couldn't reach the important thing that hovered on the edge. She felt wetness on her face. Panic clutched her heart. Was she drowning?

Her eyes flew open and were hit by a swarm of dots.

Not water.

"Ah! You're awake," someone said.

The dots gradually grouped themselves into an image—a woman, dipping a cloth into a bowl on a tray.

"I'm just cleaning up your scalp wound which bled a lot," the woman said, gently applying a damp cloth to Nicole's head. "Going to need quite a few stitches. We'll have to shave the hair around it, I'm afraid. But it will just be a strip. You've got so much hair, you'll have no problem covering it over."

Scalp wound...

She tried to speak, to ask what had happened, but

all she could produce was a croak. Her throat was horribly dry.

"Want a piece of ice to suck?" the woman asked. Without waiting for an answer, she grabbed a paper cup from the tray and popped a small piece of ice into Nicole's mouth. "Better not drink a lot of water right now. You'll be going up for X-rays soon."

She must be in a hospital. And apparently there was uncertainty about the extent of her injuries if she had to have X-rays. The pain in her head made her wonder if she had a skull fracture.

Having worked some moisture off the piece of ice, Nicole managed to ask, "How…why…?"

"You've been in a car accident, dear," she was calmly informed.

A car accident meant she'd been in a car. Travelling where? For what reason?

She tried to concentrate her mind, clear the thick fog. Gradually memories seeped through—the argument in the hotel, Quin insisting on driving her home, the anguish of wanting to believe they could have a good future together, the conflict of how he had made her feel in the past still churning through her. She remembered sitting in the car, silently fighting the tears welling from the torment in her heart, but she could find no memory at all of the car crashing—where it happened, why it happened, *what had happened to Quin.*

Alarm crashed around her head, making it feel like a bomb about to explode. Quin would be here with her if he could be. He'd feel responsible. No way would he leave her side until he was assured she was all right.

Her hand automatically lifted and clutched the arm
of the nurse who was lifting the wet cloth to her head
again. She needed her attention. Her full attention. The
action startled the woman into looking directly at her.

"Quin…was he hurt, too?"

"Who, dear?"

"Quin Sola. He was with me. The driver of the car."

The nurse shook her head. "I don't know. He's not
in this ward."

"What ward? Where am I?"

"The emergency ward at St. Vincent's Hospital. It's
in Darlinghurst near the inner city."

"What time is it?"

The nurse checked her watch. "Almost two-thirty in
the morning."

They'd left the hotel at about midnight. Not so very
long ago. Nicole's chest felt so tight, she had difficulty
finding enough breath to speak. "Quin would have
stayed with me if he wasn't hurt. They would have
brought him here, too, wouldn't they?" she demanded,
her mind instinctively shying away from the dreadful
possibility he might be dead.

"I'm sorry. I know nothing about him."

"Can't you find out for me?"

"A doctor will see you shortly," the nurse answered
evasively. "You can ask him about your friend." And
having resolved the matter to her satisfaction, she
calmly removed Nicole's clasp on her arm, laid her
hand back on the bed, patted it reassuringly, and went
back to dabbing away at the scalp wound.

Full-blown panic swirled through Nicole, making her

headache much worse. Her whole body ached. Finally she burst out, "He's not my friend. He's the father of my daughter. And…and we're getting married."

That made her almost next of kin. She had a right to know what had happened to him. *What was happening.* He couldn't have been killed. Not Quin. He was the ultimate fighter. A winner, not a loser.

She clutched the nurse's arm again, her fingers digging in with the ferocity of feeling racing through her. "Stop that right now!"

Frowning, the nurse started to chide, "You mustn't…"

"I need to know about Quin. Go and call the admissions desk. Ask about him."

"I'm not supposed to…"

"I'll fight you until you do," Nicole threatened, totally uncaring of hospital protocol. "His name is Joaquin Sola. Have you got that?"

"Yes."

Nicole released her arm. The nurse set down the cloth on the mobile tray and hurried away. The effort of fighting for action had exhausted Nicole. Her head spun sickeningly. She closed her eyes and grimly held back a wave of nausea. How long she lay there, waiting for news, determined to remain conscious, she didn't know.

She kept willing Quin to be alive. For all she had railed against his intrusion on the life she'd made without him, and the terrible turmoil he'd given her over how good a father he'd be to Zoe, she couldn't bear the thought of never seeing him again, never being with him again. In her heart, she desperately wanted the chance for a different relationship to grow between them. He'd promised it would. A new beginning…

"Miss Ashton?"

A male voice.

She opened her eyes.

The nurse was back, accompanied by a man who obviously had more authority. "I'm Dr. Jefferson," he said. "Your fiancé is in surgery. He has broken ribs, one of which punctured his lung. I can assure you he's in good hands."

In surgery.

Fear sucked the breath out of her lungs.

Her father had died in surgery.

Which was why her mother had frantically sought other ways of ridding Harry of his liver cancer.

You can't die, Quin, she thought fiercely. *I won't have you die on me.*

"Now we have to get you up to X-rays, Miss Ashton," the doctor carried on. "It appears you're only suffering from concussion and deep bruising but we have to check. Do we have your co-operation?"

"Yes. Thank you."

She clung to the thought that Quin was in good hands while she was X-rayed and had her head-wound stitched up. He was very fit and healthy. Most people did live through surgery. Quin would surely recover. It was just a matter of time.

As soon as she could, she'd tell him they could start planning to get married. The plain truth was she didn't want to live her life without him again. Pain or pleasure…she no longer cared…as long as they were making a future together as best they could. For Zoe. And for each other.

She gratefully accepted the sedation the doctor ordered. She needed the pain to go away, needed the gnawing treadmill of worries and resolutions to stop for a while, needed to blot out the waiting time before she could go and see Quin for herself. The last hazy thought drifting through her mind was…

Tomorrow will be a new day.

No looking back…only looking forward.

CHAPTER SIXTEEN

QUIN could hear his mother talking to him in Spanish. She was telling him about the games she'd played with Zoe, what an imaginative child she was, how sweet and caring and clever. It struck Quin there was something wrong with this scenario and he struggled to work out what it was. His mind seemed to have acquired layers of cotton wool. He concentrated on peeling them away. His mother continued to rave on about her beautiful grand-daughter.

But you've only seen photos of her, Quin suddenly thought, and the jab of that memory opened the door to other memories. The car accident. Nicole unconscious, bleeding from her head. His eyes flew open. He was in hospital, tubes attached to him, his mother sitting by his bed.

"Madre!" he croaked. His vocal chords felt as though they were rusty from disuse.

Before he could manage to say more, his mother leapt up from her chair in shock and alarm. "You are awake! *Gracias Dios!*" she cried as though it were a miracle, clasping her hands together in prayer. "I beg you, Joaquin, do not move. I must fetch a doctor."

She was already turning to do so when he got out the most important word. "Nicole…"

It halted her only momentarily. "Nicole is fine," she threw back at him in an agitated rush. "They only kept her here two nights to watch over her concussion and ensure there was no infection in the head wound. She has been home for days. Now please lie still while I get the doctor."

For days?

Relief at being assured of Nicole's well-being mixed with confusion over what had happened to him. How long had he been out of it? The tubes suggested they had been feeding him intravenously. He was attached to some kind of monitors, as well. He wriggled his toes to check that he still had mobility. His chest was sore. He had a hazy memory of being prepared for surgery.

But everything was okay. Nicole had not been badly hurt and he was alive, though not exactly kicking at the moment. His mother returned with a doctor and he was subjected to a series of medical checks, as well as a host of questions testing his memory and cognitive ability. Apparently he'd been in a comatose state since the surgery—broken ribs, punctured lung—but he was mending very nicely due to the absolute rest of not being conscious for the past five days.

Orderlies came in and cranked up the back third of the hospital bed so he could sit up with comfort and support. In moving, Quin caught sight of the blue Ulysses butterfly on top of the bedside cabinet. Seeing it caused a severe jolt to his heart. What did it mean? He hadn't forgotten the silver chain. Being injured through no fault of his own didn't deserve rejection.

He reached out to it. "How did this get here?"

"Zoe insisted on bringing it to make you feel better," his mother answered with an indulgent smile.

The surge of fighting adrenalin eased.

"Your daughter and fiancée have been regular visitors," the doctor remarked.

Fiancée?

Another thump to his heart.

"Oh!" His mother cried, clasping her hands again. "I have to call Nicole. I promised I would if you woke up."

"Then do it, *Madre,*" Quin urged, wanting very much to ascertain if Nicole had changed her mind about not marrying him. It was highly encouraging news that she had come to visit him in hospital, bringing Zoe with her, too! Or had she simply been obliging Zoe's wish to see her Daddy since he'd been in no condition to visit her. She might have simply called herself his fiancée to get easy access to him. Quin couldn't quite bring himself to believe she'd had a complete change of heart since Friday night.

The doctor told the orderlies to bring Quin a light meal, then took his leave, satisfied that his patient had come out of his coma with no ill effects.

His mother returned in a flurry of excitement. "I couldn't get onto Nicole. I forgot about evening classes at the dance school. But I spoke to Linda and she'll let Nicole know. I expect she'll come and visit you tomorrow morning, Joaquin."

Would she? Now that he was out of the woods?

"Is it evening?" he asked, the artificially lit room making it impossible to tell.

"Yes, dear, and Nicole won't get home until ten-thirty. Too late to visit tonight."

"You've met her mother, as well as Zoe?"

"Oh, yes. The police informed us separately of the accident—how they'd been chasing a car thief and he ran the red lights, ploughing straight into your car. We both rushed here to the hospital and introduced our-selves to each other in the waiting room. I must say Linda has been very kind, giving me her company and welcoming me into her home to visit Zoe."

"Did Nicole welcome you, too?"

She hesitated, possibly hearing the doubt in his voice. "She did not object, Joaquin," came the cautious reply. "Nicole has been very quiet. Mostly we've met in passing. We have taken turns to sit with you, trying to talk you out of the coma."

But he had not woken to Nicole's voice.

Had she talked to him?

If so, what had she said?

He looked at the blue butterfly—his gift returned to him.

Or was it at the heart of a circle linking Nicole and Zoe and himself for the rest of their lives?

He wouldn't know until Nicole came to see him…if she did.

Nicole stood outside the private room Quin had been moved to this morning and took several deep breaths, trying to calm the host of fluttering butterflies that had invaded her stomach. Evita Gallardo had assured her Quin was fine, completely himself again, and his first concern on waking from the coma had been to ask about her. So that had to mean he cared about her, didn't it? Cared deeply?

Or maybe he'd just remembered the accident and wanted to know if she'd survived it. After all, there was Zoe to consider. She was the mother of his child and it wouldn't be good for their daughter to be motherless.

Not good to be fatherless, either.

Zoe talked of little else but *her daddy*, her innocent little heart completely captivated by Quin. She'd been dancing around the house all morning unable to contain her joy and excitement at hearing he was better, sure in her own mind that the Ulysses butterfly had worked its magic on him.

Nicole knew she'd kept her own heart tightly guarded from the moment Quin had appeared in her life again, determined on hauling her back into his. She'd kept reminding herself of how it had been before, refusing to believe it could be any different this time around.

People didn't change.

But circumstances did.

Quin was now ready for the commitment of marriage and fatherhood. It was what she had once wanted from him. And the past few days of dreadful uncertainty had made her face the fact there was only ever going to be one man for her and he was lying behind this door, alive and well enough to make a future with her.

She didn't have to lay her heart open to him.

She just had to go in and say she'd decided to marry him.

Quin would take it from there.

All that would be required of her was to keep saying, *yes*, give him his own way and let it happen, ignore any pain and take the pleasure.

Her heart was pounding.

She took another deep breath and opened the door.

Waiting for Nicole to come had sharpened all Quin's senses. The click of the door opening was like a clash of cymbals in his ears. He felt his heart kick into overdrive as she stepped into his room, the instant impact of her unique beauty hitting him straight in the eye—a vision of such intense pleasure, all the magic moments she had ever given him streamed through his mind.

In one way it was like the very first time he'd seen her in the bank where they had both been employed seven years ago—the stunning sensuality of her long dark curly hair, swishing silkily around her lovely face; the thickly lashed green eyes, lit with a sharp intelligence that invariably challenged the man he was; the perfectly curved full-lipped mouth that promised so much sensual passion; the marvellous femininity of her entire body calling to everything male in him.

His woman...

He'd known it then. He knew it now. He'd let her go five years ago but he'd never succeeded in blocking her out of his memory, never succeeded in supplanting her with another woman, never felt so brilliantly alive with anyone else. He wanted her. He needed her. He had to have her.

A flush brightened her cheeks. Was he discomforting her with his staring? Did she feel the strength of the desire pouring from him? "Hi!" he said, trying to sound normal, flashing a warm smile to welcome her into his life again.

"Hi!" she echoed, returning a curiously shy little smile as though she felt awkward with the situation. "I'm glad you're back with us, Quin," she added, her eyes eloquently expressing relief at his recovery.

With us. Not *with me.*

But she hadn't wished him dead, hadn't wished him completely out of her life. And she wasn't wearing jeans today, either. In place of her usual uniform for carrying out her deal with him, she wore a clingy green top outlining her lovely full breasts and a swinging frilled skirt in green and orange and brown—strappy orange sandals on her feet. Did this mean she felt differently about their relationship?

"I'm glad to see you looking so...so well," he replied, his mind quickly skipping any words she might not want to hear from him. It was important not to make her feel pressured, he remembered, but he couldn't stop himself from asking, "Please...will you sit with me for a while, Nicole?"

"I want to talk to you," she said with an air of resolution, moving forward to take the chair beside his bed.

Perfume wafted into his nostrils. Quin breathed in the wonderfully exotic scent—the sweet smell of hope. Surely no woman wore perfume for a man she wasn't interested in, but he warned himself not to assume too much. Casting around for a safe topic, he smiled whimsically and said, "The blue butterfly has been keeping me company. Please thank Zoe for it."

The green eyes met his directly. "I promised to bring her in to visit you this afternoon, so you can thank her yourself, Quin. She'd like that. I needed to speak to you first, get things straight between us."

Tension streaked through him. His mind pulsed with the certainty she was about to recant the title of his fiancée. Everything within him moved to battle-readiness and it took an enormous effort of will to remain still and silent and simply wait for her to lay out her position.

Her lashes swept down. She took a deep breath, clearly gathering herself to speak. Then her gaze lifted and locked onto his and the windows to her soul reflected a desperate need to make everything right.

"I was wrong to be so mean-hearted towards you, Quin," she rushed out. "Using your…your desire for me to make you pay debts that had nothing to do with you."

"I hurt you with my obsessive pursuit of the money my father took," he said quietly. "Do you think I don't understand that, Nicole?"

"You had good reason to do what you did," she argued.

"I sacrificed *us* to a boyhood trauma."

"Your mother held you to it, Quin."

"No it was me, too. My pride. Worth too little in the end," he said with a rueful grimace. "I don't know if you can forgive me that, Nicole…"

"Yes, I can. I will," she asserted emphatically, then

hesitated, her expression flicking to eloquent appeal. "If you can forgive me for keeping Zoe to myself."

"My fault for not sharing with you."

"No. What I did was wrong. It was mean and nasty and vengeful. And I'm sorry…sorry…" She shook her head fretfully. "You gave your mother back her life. You gave *my* mother back her life. And all I've done is bitterly condemn you for not…not…" Tears welled and she quickly veiled them, looking down at her lap where her hands held each other tightly. Keeping her courage screwed to the sticking point?

"Not giving what we had together enough value," he finished for her. "I should have, Nicole," he added gravely. "I didn't realise until after it was gone how much I should have valued it. I've been trying to show you…"

"I don't want to talk about that," she choked out, then took another deep breath and lifted her chin, wet eyes defiantly open to meet his. "It was a different time and place, Quin. This is now. You said on Friday night that you wanted me to be your wife."

His lungs stopped working. His chest hurt. His heart drummed in his ears. He worked hard at forcing up enough breath to say, "I do," desperately hoping this confirmation wouldn't draw another rejection.

"Okay. I've decided to marry you. Zoe should have her father on hand and I—" she swallowed hard "—I want to be with you, too."

Relief surged through him, easing the pain caused by tension. Elation danced through his mind. He smiled. "We belong together, Nicole."

"Yes," she agreed.

But there was no answering smile, no joy in her eyes.

"Nothing like a crisis to bring people together," he said ironically.

"Yes," she agreed, echoing his irony.

At least it wasn't loaded with bitterness, Quin thought, though he was acutely aware that she wasn't professing any love for him. Maybe that was forever lost. He was sensing only a recognition and an acceptance that they had a strong enough personal connection to make a marriage work, given that their daughter's best interests should be considered.

A heavy weight settled on his heart. He'd done this to Nicole, failing to meet her emotional needs in the past, draining her of the love she had given him. Forgiveness for his failure didn't guarantee restoration of what they'd once had together. It just meant moving on, leaving the bad emotional baggage behind, and her love for Zoe was probably a prime mover in her decision to marry him.

"What happened to the photo albums?" he asked, suddenly recalling they'd been in the car—precious mementoes of Zoe's life so far.

"They weren't damaged," Nicole quickly assured him. "They were recovered by the police and handed over to my mother."

"Well, thank God they weren't lost," he muttered, closing his eyes as a sickening wave of weakness rolled through him. The coma might have been good for healing after surgery but the days of immobility had sapped his body of its normal strength, letting him know it when he least expected it, telling him now that the energy spent on this meeting with Nicole came at a cost.

Everything did. His determination to restore family honour had cost him Nicole's love, cost him four years of his daughter's life. Getting Nicole to connect with him again had cost him a lot of money. Not that he cared about that. He just wished he could have worked it all differently.

"Quin?"

He heard the quavery note of anxiety in her voice and savagely told himself that some measure of caring was still there and he could build on it. He felt her hand clutch his, enfolding it in warm softness, gently pressing. She didn't want to walk away from him. Not this time.

"Are you all right? Should I call a doctor?"

"No. Just feeling a bit faint. It passes."

"Maybe I should leave you to rest."

Her hand started releasing his. He grabbed it, holding onto her. She was his woman. She had to know it.

"I'll be back this afternoon with Zoe," she assured him.

He opened his eyes, shooting her a look of blazing need that was totally beyond his will to control. "Kiss me, Nicole. That will make me feel better."

It startled her, fear and uncertainty flicking across her face. He tugged her hand, pulling her towards him. She rose from the chair, stood beside the bed, her eyes worriedly searching his. "Are you sure, Quin?"

"Yes."

She bent and grazed her lips gently over his, her free hand resting on the pillow beside his head. Quin closed his eyes again, breathing in her scent, savouring the taste of her, wishing he could hold her close, ruefully accepting it would be unwise, given his present condition.

His tongue flicked out to tease her into kissing him more deeply. She responded, making a slow, sensual and very intimate assault on his mouth. Pleasure flowed through him. He was sure there was an edge of passion in the feelings she transmitted, her own need and want tightly restrained, yet tugging at her to re-affirm the decision she'd made to marry him, be with him for the rest of her life.

When she drew back, her face was flushed, her eyes glinting with worry again. "You're sure this is all right?"

"Yes. Thank you."

It was all right.

He felt the love was still there, set at a distance but still there.

One way or another, he'd close that distance.

Nicole wasn't going away.

She had agreed to marry him.

CHAPTER SEVENTEEN

HER wedding day—the day when she said the really big *yes* to Quin. The reality of it was all around her in this penthouse suite at the Intercontinental Hotel—her mother, Zoe and the bridesmaids all dressed ready to go to the ceremony. In another thirty minutes, a stretch limousine would be taking them to the venue. Three o'clock, Quin had said, and time was ticking away. Yet Nicole couldn't quite shake the feeling she was in a dream.

"What kind of wedding would you like?" Quin had asked.

"I don't know," she had answered truthfully. "What do you want?"

"Something beautiful, truly memorable…"

"Why don't you plan it, Quin?"

He'd frowned. "It's the bride's special day. I want you to be happy with it."

"Then make it special for me."

The challenge had tripped off her tongue, spurred by wanting to have some measure of how special the occasion was for him. Let him have his way. All his way.

It might reveal quite a bit about how much *she* meant to him, too.

As Nicole sat still while the beautician moved around her, putting the last finishes to her bridal make-up, she couldn't help thinking that if one put a money value on this wedding and that was the measure of how special it was to Quin, then it was spectacularly special. On the other hand, she wasn't sure if he was putting on a show for her or for other people.

Her side of the guest list was relatively small. She had a few friends amongst the mothers of little girls at the dance school, and two of those were her bridesmaids, along with Jade. Her mother's friends in the world of dance were not exactly numerous, either. Quin's side not only carried a lot of people from the Sydney social set and important business clients, but quite a large contingent from Argentina—the Gallardo family and their close friends.

Not that it mattered, she told herself.

They were getting married.

That was the only really important thing.

"I've never seen you look so beautiful, Nicole," Jade remarked, a note of awe in her voice.

Amazing what cosmetics in skilled hands can do, she thought, smiling at her friend. "You, too. I really like that burnt copper shade of red for your hair."

Jade laughed. "Couldn't leave it purple. Since I'm chief bridesmaid, it might have distracted from the bride."

"Thanks for everything you've done, Jade. You and Jules. The dresses you designed and made are wonderful."

"Well, we did have instructions from Zoe and Quin,"

she said archly. "Got to say that guy has moved to a great address, Nic. Wherever he was in the past, what you have now is a man who's totally committed to giving his woman a wonderful wedding. Namely you."

Yes, he had moved, Nicole silently agreed. Certainly since he'd come out of hospital two months ago, he'd won over her mother with his kindness and consideration, bonded deeply with their daughter, and had set about introducing her to his friends, taking her out to dinners and shows, not concentrating their entire relationship on sex, which was still great, but no longer the only thing they shared.

"You do love him, don't you?" Jade asked softly.

"Yes," she answered unequivocally, looking down at the magnificent emerald and diamond engagement ring Quin had given her. *For better or for worse,* she thought, *as long as we both shall live.*

Zoe came dancing into the bedroom. "Is it time for your dress now, Mummy?" she asked excitedly.

"Yes," the beautician answered, satisfied with the result of her artistry.

"I love *your* dress, Zoe," Nicole said, thinking how well the deep blue suited her dark colouring.

She twirled to show it off. "It's the same blue as the Ulysses butterfly. I told Daddy that was what I wanted. And then we decided the bridesmaids should be like the Australian sky, light blue in the morning, bright blue in the middle of the day, and dark blue after sunset. Wasn't that a good idea, Mummy?"

"A lovely idea, Zoe," she agreed, and it had been transmitted by Jade and Jules into beautiful floor-length georgette gowns with the three shades of blue graduating down from the light colour for the strapless bodice to the deeper shades in the skirt.

"And Daddy had these butterfly clips in my hair made specially for me," Zoe declared proudly.

"They look very pretty."

As did the blue silk butterflies adorning the hair of the bridesmaids. Quin's idea, Jade had told her, to mark a very special day.

Her mother, dressed in a very elegant deep violet outfit to blend with the bridal party, made a brisk entrance. "It's twenty to three, Nicole. We're not going to be late, are we?" she asked anxiously.

"No, Mum. I'm all ready bar for the wedding gown, and as you can see, the dresser is taking it out of its plastic wrapping now."

The wedding planner Quin had hired, had staff running everywhere, ensuring everything was perfectly done; the hairdresser, the beautician, the dresser, the florist. Nothing was overlooked and each step of the preparation was on schedule.

The gown was unzipped and held out for Nicole to step into. She stood up and discarded the wrap-around she'd worn through most of the afternoon.

"Wow!" Zoe cried, her eyes popping at the sexy underwear.

Nicole gave a nervous laugh, hoping Quin would appreciate her own personal contribution to their wedding later tonight.

"Is that bride stuff, too, Mummy?"

"It sure is!" Jade answered, laughing at Zoe's innocent remark. "I just hope you're going to love the dress, Nic."

She'd never seen it. She'd been fitted for it with the underlining for the bodice, not once with the dress itself. A froth of white georgette was pooled on the floor. There seemed like many layers of it. Nicole stepped into the space at the centre of it, careful not to snag her high heels in the fabric. She fitted her arms through shoe-string shoulder straps as the gown was pulled up her body. Then the dresser zipped it into place and Nicole stared at her reflection in the cheval mirror placed ready for her to see herself.

The bodice was tightly fitted from her breasts to her hips and intricately and beautifully beaded with tiny crystals creating the shape of a butterfly. There was a centre split in the front skirt to just above knee high for easy walking up any stairs, which might have been difficult with so many floating layers of georgette. At the back, the skirt fell gracefully into a train, making it very bridal.

Her mother heaved a happy sigh. "You look wonderful, Nicole."

"Spectacular!" Jade said with satisfaction. "Are you happy with it?"

"Yes. It's…it's stunning!" Nicole said dazedly. "Thank you so much."

"The concept came from Quin. Jules and I simply translated it as best we could."

Quin had gone to so much personal trouble to get everything right for her. Right in a very meaningful sense. Surely no man tried to please a woman so much if he didn't love her, but he'd never said the words. He would today, in the wedding ceremony. Would he mean them, or would he just be repeating the traditional marriage vows?

"Now your flowers," the dresser said, handing Nicole the three red roses she was to carry as her bouquet.

Not hot-house buds. These roses were in full bloom and strongly scented. As was the one that had been positioned in her hair, just above her left ear. Jade had told her Quin didn't want a bridal veil to be worn—nothing to hide her hair, just a red rose to enhance its natural beauty.

Red roses for love.

Please let it be true, she thought, her heart yearning for a fairy-tale ending to all she had been through with Quin.

The bridesmaids' bouquets were handed out, posies of roses in every colour. "Because butterflies like lots of pretty colours, Mummy," Zoe informed her.

Nicole's nerves were fluttering as they were all led down to the waiting limousines which would take them to the wedding venue—still a closely guarded secret.

It was another stunning surprise when they were driven only a short distance—to the Sydney Opera House!—and escorted up to the northern Concert Hall foyer which featured the fantastic arch of windows overlooking the harbour. Rows and rows of white-sheathed chairs had been placed on red carpet—all of them filled with wedding guests. White pedestals held spectacular arrangements of red roses. The whole scene was fantastic.

But Quin was no fantasy. He broke away from the standing line of groomsmen at the front, and looking heart-wrenchingly handsome in his formal black dinner suit and snow-white dress shirt, he strode confidently down the make-shift aisle to claim her, his megawatt smile shining, telling her he was brilliantly alive.

"Happy?" he asked, his grey eyes smoking warmly with pleasure in her.

"Yes." She returned his smile, openly expressing her pleasure in him. "Very happy."

"Good! Today I'm trying to make up for all the romance I didn't give you, Nicole."

Romance...was that love?

"You truly are a star player, Quin. In this, as well as everything else," she said, feeling overwhelmed by all he done to make their wedding special for her—beautiful and very memorable.

"You count most of all," he murmured huskily, taking her arm and linking it around his.

Those words kept fizzing in Nicole's mind like a cocktail of joy as Quin walked her down the aisle to the marriage celebrant. Her mother and Zoe had already gone ahead to take their chairs in the front row. Her bridesmaids brought up the end of the little procession and lined up beside her as she and Quin halted beside his groomsmen.

The ceremony was short, but very emotional for Nicole. Both Tony Fisher, Quin's best man, and Jade delivered moving readings about love and marriage. Someone with a beautiful voice sang "All The Way." When Quin spoke his vows, his voice vibrated with deep feeling, bringing tears to her eyes. She only just managed to blink them away as they signed the marriage certificate, composing herself to meet the well-wishers who crowded around them afterwards.

The fabulous surprises weren't over.

They kept coming.

After leaving the Opera House, they boarded a luxurious catamaran and cruised the harbour. Wedding photographs were taken with the background of the great coat hanger bridge and a glorious sunset. French champagne flowed, gourmet canapés were served, and the guests partied happily, many wanting their photographs taken with the bride and groom.

Quin's elderly but still very distinguished-looking grandfather, Juan Gallardo, welcomed Nicole into *the family,* congratulated his grandson on acquiring such a beautiful wife, and remarked that he could understand why Quin had decided to make Sydney his home. Even Buenos Aires could not outshine such a splendid city. And, of course, since the woman of his heart was Australian…yes, he understood…but Joaquin must bring Nicole to Argentina for a visit sometime in the near future.

Quin's mother had a lovely time, busily showing off Zoe to all her Gallardo relatives. "My grand-daughter…" she kept saying proudly.

Nicole was pleased to see her own mother mingling happily with her old associates from dancing competitions, no doubt catching up on all the professional gossip and swapping stories about especially talented dance pupils coming up. It was good to know she was really getting back to normal, interested in business and people again. Even better, that she seemed to have picked up an admirer who was dancing attendance on her.

There was nothing Nicole could do about the empty nest syndrome. She and Zoe would be moving in with

Quin after the honeymoon and her mother would be alone in the Burwood house. At least running the dance school should keep her occupied most of the time and they'd meet there several days a week. They weren't dropping out of her life.

The catamaran docked at Mosman, almost directly across the water from the Opera House and they were transported to another mystery location—the landmark Taronga Centre at the Taronga Zoo, once again overlooking Sydney Harbour.

The reception room was decked out in traditional white linen with red roses on all the tables. They feasted on Sydney rock oysters, Tasmanian salmon and chocolate coated strawberries with King Island cream, and were entertained by a live band backing a great singer. A three-tier wedding cake—a decorator's wonderful work of art—waited to be cut. Before that happened, however, came the speeches.

Tony Fisher stood up and soon had the guests laughing with his charm and wit, finally declaring that only his good friend, Quin, could have danced the elusive and lovely Nicole off her feet and into wedlock. He called for a toast to the bride and groom, which was heartily raised and drunk.

Quin rose from his chair.

Nicole held her breath, her heart hammering her chest. He'd made their wedding day unbelievably special—the ultimate peak of romance. Would he top it now with what she most wanted to hear?

"Earlier this evening my grandfather, Juan Gallardo—" he gestured to the table where the old man sat "—rightly recognised Nicole as the woman of my heart." He turned and smiled at her, and her own heart stopped its wild pounding and flooded with pleasure. She even started breathing again as he resumed his speech to the guests.

"When I first met Nicole seven years ago, what instantly flashed through my mind was…this is my woman. Fortunately the desire for us to be together was mutual and she did become my woman. She filled that role, giving me her love for two years, but I made the huge mistake of not really appreciating how big a gift that was. I didn't share my heart with her and I made her feel as though she was no more than a possession which I picked up and put down at my convenience. So I lost her…"

The sadness and regret in his voice was poignant and the dead silence in the room respected his feelings. Nicole was stunned that he was revealing so much and found herself flushing at his use of the bitter accusations she had thrown at him.

"I not only lost my woman, but I also lost the child she bore me—our beautiful daughter, Zoe—who has known from her mother all the love I didn't value enough."

Her stomach contracted at the acknowledgment that she had loved him. Did he know she still did?

"Five years passed before our paths crossed again, more than long enough for me to know how empty all my achievements were without her at my side. I would have done anything to win her back and this was where Fate smiled kindly on me. Nicole needed help and I could give it. Which earned me time with her. Time enough to demonstrate I would not repeat the mistakes of the past."

He was humbling himself in front of all these people, humbling himself to atone for the hurt he'd inflicted. Nicole would not have asked it of him. Yet she was totally captivated by the deeply personal confession.

"I learnt the importance of sharing. I learnt that open communication is the cornerstone for trust and under-standing. I learnt that the gift of love is infinitely precious and must always be nurtured and cherished, never neglected."

He paused, then fervently added, "I hope I can carry these lessons into the future that Nicole has granted me in becoming my wife today. I certainly aim to because I don't want her to ever doubt how very much I do love her and will always love her."

There it was! He'd said it! And there wasn't a skerrick of doubt in her mind about it as he turned to her once more, smiling his love, shining it straight into her eyes, her soul.

"Nicole is more than the woman of my heart. She is the Queen of my heart," he stated emphatically, then held out his hand to her. "Will you do me the honour of dancing with me, my love?"

An incandescent happiness was bursting through her. "Yes," spilled joyfully from her lips as she took his hand and rose from her chair, wanting to be taken into his embrace, feel him close to her, pour out her own love for him.

All the guests stood up from their tables, wildly ap-plauding them as Quin led her onto the small dance floor. The band began playing the sentimental ever-green tune of *Moon River*—and she and Quin were together again—truly, deeply together—as they waltzed around the floor in perfect unison, every step a harmony of the heart.

They were not aware of being watched by all the guests wearing benevolent smiles, some of them wiping emotional tears from their eyes. They were only aware of each other—the strong sexual chemistry they'd always had, now enhanced by the magical feeling of so much more bonding them for the rest of their lives.

"I love you, too, Quin," she whispered, her eyes openly avowing what she had kept hidden in her heart, frightened of having it crushed again.

The fear was gone.

Quin had demolished it.

"Thank you for such a perfect day," she added, loving him all the more for giving it to her.

"*You* make it so," he murmured.

"I'll treasure it in my memory for as long as I live."

"We'll build a treasure house of beautiful memories, Nicole."

She smiled. "Like our very own butterfly tree."

He smiled back. "Yes. Our very own."

They danced on to the music of love in their hearts, knowing they would *always* dance together because the love would last forever.

THE ROYAL HOUSE OF KAREDES

Two crowns, two islands, one legacy

Volume One
BILLIONAIRE PRINCE,
PREGNANT MISTRESS
by Sandra Marton

Wanted for her body – and her baby!

Aspiring New York jewellery designer Maria Santo has come to Aristo to win a royal commission.

Cold, calculating and ruthless, Prince Xander Karedes beds Maria, thinking she's only sleeping with him to save her business.

So when Xander discovers Maria's pregnant, he assumes it's on purpose. What will it take for this billionaire prince to realise he's falling in love with his pregnant mistress…?

Available 17th April 2009

www.millsandboon.co.uk

M&B

MILLS & BOON®
MODERN™

...International affairs, seduction and passion guaranteed

8 brand-new titles each month

Available on the first Friday of every month
from WHSmith, ASDA, Tesco
and all good bookshops
www.millsandboon.co.uk

GEN/01/RTL11

MILLS & BOON®
MODERN™
Heat

If you like Mills & Boon Modern you'll love Modern Heat!

Strong, sexy alpha heroes, sizzling storylines and exotic locations from around the world – what more could you want!

2 brand-new titles each month

Available on the first Friday of every month
from WHSmith, ASDA, Tesco
and all good bookshops
www.millsandboon.co.uk

GEN/06/RTL11